Elizabeth Falconer lives  spends part of the year
Wings of the Morning
first three novels, *The Golden Year*, *The Love of
Women* and *The Counter-Tenor's Daughter* are
also published by Black Swan.

Also by Elizabeth Falconer

THE GOLDEN YEAR
THE LOVE OF WOMEN
THE COUNTER-TENOR'S DAUGHTER

and published by Black Swan

WINGS OF
THE MORNING

Elizabeth Falconer

BLACK SWAN

WINGS OF THE MORNING
A BLACK SWAN BOOK : 0 552 99755 2

First publication in Great Britain

PRINTING HISTORY
Black Swan edition published 1998

Set in 11pt Melior by Kestrel Data, Exeter, Devon.

Black Swan Books are published by Transworld Publishers Ltd,
61–63 Uxbridge Road, London W5 5SA,
in Australia by Transworld Publishers (Australia) Pty Ltd,
15–25 Helles Avenue, Moorebank, NSW 2170
and in New Zealand by Transworld Publishers (NZ) Ltd,
3 William Pickering Drive, Albany, Auckland.

Printed, reproduced and bound in Great Britain by
Cox & Wyman Ltd, Reading, Berks.

To Edward

*If I take the wings of the morning, and
dwell in the uttermost parts of the sea;
Even there shall thy hand lead me, and
thy right hand shall hold me.*

Psalm 139:9

Chapter One

Phoebe McGrath stood in the slow-moving queue at the supermarket, willing herself to remain calm. Nervously, she glanced at her watch: ten past three. Panicking slightly at the swift passage of time, she decided to make a detour and pick up the children from school now, rather than take the shopping home and go out again to collect them. After that, Gwen, thank God, would cope with everything, while she had a wash and changed before the long drive to Gloucester to meet Christian's train. She passed through the checkout, paid the enormous bill, and pushed her trolley towards her estate car, almost breaking into a run in an attempt to make up for lost time.

Alexander and Chloe stood together at the school gate, looking glum, the last children to be collected. The teacher on duty looked meaningfully at her watch and gave Phoebe a reproving stare as the children scrambled into the back of the Volvo. Feebly, Phoebe felt obliged to give her an appeasing smile as she drove away. The smile was not returned.

'Why can't you *try* to get here on time, Mum?' Chloe spoke in a high, querulous whine. 'Miss Trubshawe doesn't like it, you know.'

'It makes *her* late getting home, too,' said Alexander. 'She knows it isn't *our* fault,' he added, smugly. 'She said it wasn't, didn't she, Chloe?'

'Yes, she did.'

'Oh, well,' said Phoebe. 'I'm very sorry. There was a long queue at the checkout.' She felt like adding: I wish *my* working day ended at half past three, with three months' paid holiday, but refrained from such an indiscretion. I may not have a proper full-time job, she thought, but it sure as hell feels like it sometimes. She drove home in silence through the lanes, in an atmosphere heavy with disapproval.

Abbot's Court, a medieval hall house, enlarged and altered over the centuries, was invisible from the road and lay hidden among trees on the steep slope of a heavily wooded valley. It was approached by a narrow, winding track. At the entrance to this track a rusty farm gate hung off its broken hinges, permanently open, and a faded sign said 'Private – keep out'. There was no other mark of identification, which was exactly how Christian liked it, though Phoebe herself thought it rather unfriendly. She turned into the track, and the car climbed up through the winding dark tunnel of overgrown yews, finally emerging into the sunlight of the long, gravelled courtyard that divided the main house from the long stone building, part barn, part stable, now used mainly as a garage.

Phoebe stopped the car, and undid her safety belt. 'Be a dear, Alex, and see if Gwen's in the kitchen, would you?' Silently, still disapproving, Alexander got out of the car, picked up his school-bag, and headed towards the kitchen door, scuffing the toes of his shoes as he went, knowing that it would annoy his mother.

Phoebe got out of the car, opened Chloe's door and watched as she struggled to undo the catch of her belt. 'Shall I do it for you, darling?'

'I can do it.' Chloe was scarlet with determination, but the buckle defeated her and finally she allowed her mother to help her. Though small for her eight years, and frail, with the fine fair hair and blue eyes of her father and brother, she was by far the more dominant of the two children. Alexander, very tall and well built, looked much older than his age, nearly thirteen, and did not seem on the whole destined to be a leader of men. Where his younger sister led, he followed, and from time to time Phoebe worried about how Chloe would react when Alexander went away to boarding school, leaving her alone at home. She lifted the tailgate of the car and began to unload the shopping bags and the long polystyrene box containing an elaborately decorated dinner-party salmon. Chloe took hold of a bulging bag and staggered towards the kitchen door, just as it opened and Gwen appeared, smiling and businesslike in her blue apron, with a scarf tied round her crisp curly grey hair.

'There you are, Gwen,' said Phoebe. 'Thank heavens.' They took the shopping to the kitchen and dumped everything on the long tiled worktop. Nervously, Phoebe unfastened the fish-box, praying that the festive salmon had not been damaged during the journey home. Thankfully, all was well. Gwen fetched the long white fish platter, and together they transferred the salmon, perfectly intact and glistening with aspic, onto its dish.

'In the fridge, do you think?'

'Yes, or the jelly will melt, won't it?' Gwen made room on one of the shelves and slid the salmon inside. 'I'll take it out half an hour before you need it,' she said. 'That way, it should be perfect.'

'Great,' said Phoebe, relieved to let Gwen take over. She looked at the kitchen clock. In an hour she must go to the station. She examined her filthy fingernails, black from her long morning's work in the vegetable garden, and sighed.

Gwen laughed. 'Go on,' she said, giving Phoebe a little push. 'I'll deal with everything, and Jill will be here soon to help. You go and get tidy, dear.'

'What about the table?'

11

'Done.'

'And the wine?'

'Cooling. I chose a white Rully, OK?'

'Fine. What about champagne? Chris likes it, pre-dinner.'

'In the fridge. Two bottles.'

'Brilliant. I couldn't cope without you, Gwen; I really couldn't.'

'I expect you could if you had to. Go on, get a move on, or you'll be late for the train. And call the children to come and have their tea, will you? They're in the garden, very likely.'

Phoebe left the dark, friendly, stone-flagged kitchen and went out into the courtyard. She paused for a moment, listening, but could hear nothing except the twittering of hedge sparrows in the thicket of clematis that clothed the ancient stone walls of the house, and the crooning of the fantailed pigeons lined up along the ridge of the barn in front of her. She turned left and walked quickly towards the high, clipped yew hedge that grew like a solid dark-green wall, connecting the two buildings. It was pierced by a clipped, round-topped arch that led into the formal gardens below the south-facing aspect of the house, and she passed through it, calling the children's names as she went. The lawn was newly mown and sweet-smelling, soft under her boots. She turned and looked back at the house, its walls golden, its leaded windows like diamonds in the sunlight, the stone tiles of the high medieval roof green with moss. Over the wide archway leading into the main entrance to the house was carved the date, 1307. Attached to the house was a square tower, containing four rooms, one on top of another. A parapet enclosed the tower's stone-tiled roof, embellished at each corner by carved stone gargoyles, from whose gaping jaws issued long pipes for the disposal of rainwater. Inside the parapet the roof rose to a central, finial-topped point, surmounted by a gilded weathercock. It was a magical house and Phoebe had lived there since her marriage, scarcely ever leaving the place. Christian had seen the house advertised for sale just after they became engaged, and had taken her to see it. In spite of its rundown condition and the daunting prospect of restoring both house and garden, Phoebe had fallen in love with the place on the spot. She still loved it dearly, almost passionately, and could not imagine living anywhere else. The concept of spending her entire life in the sometimes exhausting task of maintaining such a house and its exquisite grounds seemed to her to be both rewarding and incredibly fortunate. She turned away from the house and walked down the slope of the long lawn towards the line of beeches that separated the garden from the meadow beyond. A small stile, slippery with mould, was built into the low wooden fence that kept the cattle in their proper place. As well as their modest herd of Jersey cows, two New Forest ponies occupied the field and Phoebe could see the children feeding them; Alexander holding the bucket, Chloe patting their silky, quivering flanks and talking to them as they crunched their way through their nuts. 'Children!' she shouted. 'Tea!'

Their heads turned towards her. 'OK! Coming!'

Phoebe hurried back to the house, through the arched entrance and into the hall, cool and dim, its stone walls limewashed a soft terracotta, faded and powdery, its cold flagged floors bare and uneven. She turned right under another arch into the small library, then right again into the minute glass-walled internal court which gave access to the tower. This place was the home of many tender plants, grouped around a large lead statue of the Blessed Virgin, a gift from Christian's mother, Flavia. Phoebe ran swiftly up the spiral stair to the second-floor bedroom she shared with her husband. The room was small and low-ceilinged, though well lit by the mullioned windows

13

in three of its walls. The ceiling was beautiful, a masterpiece of ribbed and decorated seventeenth-century plasterwork, as crisp and fresh as a wedding cake, the patterns thrown into sharp relief by the light from the low windows. Against the fourth wall stood their tall, elaborately carved Renaissance four-poster bed, backed by a vast russet-coloured Mortlake tapestry, which hung in folds from the rings of a long, stout, ebonized pole. The bed occupied the major part of the room, leaving no space for wardrobes or chests, so they had turned the room below into a bathroom which also served as a dressing room, with built-in cupboards to house their clothes, bedlinen and towels. This arrangement was a little awkward, especially in winter, but Phoebe and Christian loved the privacy their rooms in the tower gave them, and were happy to be at a small distance from their children, Gwen and their occasional guests.

Phoebe went to the bathroom, kicked off her boots, pulled off her jeans and sweater, and washed quickly, scrubbing her mud-blackened nails. She put on black tights, an ankle-length plaid skirt and a green lambs-wool sweater. The sweater seemed a snugger fit than the last time she had worn it, and she sighed, promising herself to start dieting seriously, tomorrow. She brushed her straight, mousy, shoulder-length hair, regretting that she had been unable to find the time to wash it. Opening her lacquered jewel-box, she took out her single strand of pearls, a wedding present from Chris, and fastened it round her neck, then took her diamond and ruby engagement ring from its velvet-lined box and put it on her finger. She slipped her feet into black patent loafers, peered into the mirror, dabbed a little gloss on her lips and a little scent on her wrists. Then she ran downstairs and went through the hall to the dining room, where the formally laid table glimmered with silver and glass, the soft pale honey colour of tallow candles and the simply folded perfection of Irish linen napkins. She cast an appreciative eye over the table, straightened a fork and proceeded to the kitchen in search of her bag and the keys to the car. They were lying on the long pine table, next to two empty milk glasses. Gwen stood at the sink, scraping new potatoes. A large bunch of apple mint thrust into a jug of water filled the air with its scent. Phoebe picked up her bag. 'I'll be off then, Gwen,' she said. 'Have the children gone out again?'

'Don't worry, I'll round them up presently, and Jill can supervise their baths. They'll have had their supper and be in bed before you get back from the station, I promise. Go on, off you go, or you'll be late for the train.'

As she drove slowly down the drive, and along the single-track lane towards the road to Gloucester, Phoebe reflected on her great good fortune in having Gwen by her side. She had been with the McGrath family for thirty-five years, since Christian's birth. She had been twenty-five at the time, two years older than Chris's mother, Flavia. It had been her second job and, being a Scot herself, she had found herself in employment that suited her perfectly. Flavia's second child, Emma, had not arrived until Christian was ten, and already away at school, but the question of Gwen's usefulness being at an end had never arisen, and she had proved herself to be a woman of many capabilities, whether there was a child in the house to care for, or not. As for Phoebe, Gwen had quickly become more of a mother-figure to her than an employee. Phoebe's own mother had died when she was seven and her father had remarried a year later. Since her own marriage, she scarcely saw her family, and they made little attempt to keep in touch with her. They lived in a big ugly house in Edgbaston and had three strapping sons in their early twenties. They exchanged cards at Christmas and birthdays, and that about summed it up. It was from

Gwen that Phoebe received the warmth and love so cruelly taken from her on her mother's death. How lucky I am, she thought. I have a good, successful husband and two lovely children, as well as the most beautiful house in England, probably. And Gwen. I am a fortunate and happy woman, even if I'm fat, and not terribly clever or well organized. She turned into the main road, and drove towards Gloucester.

Flavia McGrath sat quietly in a pew at the back of the empty church, her well-worn Missal and rosary in her hands, patiently waiting on the off-chance that Fr Gordon would come into St Botolph's and find her there. She did not like to call on him at the house he shared with two other fathers, and in any case detected a certain cynicism, even hostility, in the eye of his housekeeper. Mrs Burroughs was a formidable woman in her late forties, used to over-enthusiastic parishioners, and made it her business to protect 'her' fathers at every step of the way. When Flavia telephoned to speak to Fr Gordon, it was Mrs Burroughs who invariably answered the phone, always responding to Flavia's request with the familiar words: 'One moment, please. I'll just see if he's in.' Occasionally, Fr Gordon did in fact come to the phone; more often, Mrs Burroughs, after a short pause, would say, 'Sorry, Mrs McGrath, he's just popped out. Can I take a message?' Now, rather than run the risk of the usual stonewalling, Flavia lay in wait for him in the church, intending to invite him to lunch. She had been reading a fascinating article on the subject of the Immaculate Conception and its relevance to the modern world and longed to discuss it with her priest.

Flavia was not exactly in love with Fr Gordon, though he was a very well-set-up young man with pale red hair, and aquiline though rather freckled features. He looked like the kind of man one expected to see reading the television news, though not wearing his

16

cassock, of course. She glanced round the church, gloomy without the lights on and all the statues wrapped in their purple cloths for Lent. She stared at the niche on her left, where the statue of Our Lady stood. Behind the purple cloth, Flavia could see quite clearly, in her mind's eye, the pale-blue cloak over the long white robe, the pretty pink and white face with the golden halo, the left arm cradling the equally pretty child. Flavia was quite aware that this piece of Catholic imagery was far from being a work of art, was in fact mass-produced, tawdry and, to some people, meretricious. To Flavia, however, it was beautiful, a continual source of strength and comfort, and had been from her convent childhood. Quite often, when the statue was in its normal, uncovered state, she would sit and stare at the Virgin's sweet face until her own eyes went out of focus. It was then that the Virgin sometimes smiled at Flavia, her painted lips parting to show white teeth, like tiny pearls. No, Flavia was not exactly in love with Fr Gordon, but she was utterly in love with the idea of the religious life. As a child in the convent, she had spent many hours on her knees, praying for a vocation, longing to be a nun. Her two older brothers were priests, one in an African mission school, the other in a poor parish in Huddersfield. Her younger sister Alice had become a nun in an enclosed order in Spain. So many vocations in one family had brought joy and great credit to Flavia's family, and it was to her a matter of huge regret, even shame, that she had failed to follow her siblings into the religious life. Instead, and quite violently and inexplicably, she had fallen in love with Ludovic McGrath. He had been the first and only man to show any interest in her, although she had been quite a pretty girl, blue-eyed and fair, and fond of dancing.

After the protracted and extremely painful birth of their son Christian, a year after her marriage, Flavia had fallen equally violently out of love with Ludovic, the cause not only of all her anguish, but also her regrets concerning the religious life. She had transferred all her affection to her little son, determined that he, at least, should have the fulfilment and joy of an unblemished upbringing and ultimately, she prayed, a true vocation. But Christian had eluded her. At eight years old, his father had insisted that he go away to a boarding prep school, and thence to Ampleforth. At these establishments, to his father's great relief, he resisted all forms of indoctrination and, after university, joined a merchant bank, where his progress had been rapid and very profitable. Since his marriage to the Protestant Phoebe, and their departure to their damp and underheated house in the Forest of Dean, Flavia rarely saw him, but took comfort in the knowledge that his children had been baptized into the Catholic faith. Flavia prayed for them all, night and morning. She also prayed for the conversion of Phoebe, of course.

After Christian had departed to boarding school, and effectively from Flavia's sphere of influence, she had fallen into a deep and lasting depression. To her surprise and disappointment, she could find little comfort in her church. The priest at St Botolph's at that time had been old and weary, and had little time for self-pitying, rather well-off women with little to occupy them. She had tried a bit of sermon-tasting, doing the rounds of the more fashionable Roman Catholic churches in London, but without finding the consolation she sought. She therefore tried another approach to anaesthetizing her unhappiness; she began to drink. She did this quite openly, just one more gin at lunchtime, and two or three extra glasses of wine at night. Ludovic did not appear to notice her occasional lapses of speech, or unsteady gait, but Gwen did, and one day, finding Flavia still in bed at three o'clock in the afternoon, and unable to lift her head from the pillow, she came straight to the point. 'There's nothing wrong with you, my girl. You've got a hangover, that's all.'

'I feel ghastly, Gwen.'

'Of course you do. It's your own stupid fault. You drink too much.'

'I'm sure I don't.'

'I'm sure you do!'

After hot tea, a glass of hot lemon and some paracetamol, Flavia had recovered sufficiently to sit up and try to tell Gwen how lonely and sad she was without Christian.

'And what about your poor husband? How do you think he feels?'

'Without Christian?'

'No, of course not. I mean with you carrying on as if there was a death in the family. The boy's not dead; he's simply growing up. What you need is another baby.'

Flavia looked startled, and glanced briefly at Gwen, her blue eyes apprehensive. 'I couldn't do that; it's not possible.'

'Whyever not? You're only thirty-one, aren't you?'

'It's not a question of age.'

'Well, what is it, then?'

'*You* know.' Flavia looked embarrassed, twisting the edge of the sheet in her fingers.

'No, I *don't* know.'

'Ludovic and me. We don't do it.'

'What, not at all?'

'No.'

'Since when?'

'Since Christian was born. It was so awful, I couldn't bear the thought of any more babies.'

'Going to bed with your husband doesn't necessarily lead to pregnancy, for heaven's sake.'

Flavia gazed at her hands, resting on the crumpled sheet. 'That sort of thing is not an option for me, Gwen. You know that. I'm a Catholic, birth control is a sin.'

Gwen had stared at her for a long moment, then patted her hand and stood up, removing Flavia's tray. 'You must decide for yourself, of course, but I still think another baby is what you need. Think about it, anyway.'

So Flavia had thought about it and had even gone to see a well-known gynaecologist, who had assured her that it was perfectly possible for her to have a virtually painless confinement. Much encouraged by this news, she had cut down on her drinking, paid more attention to her appearance, and had little difficulty in persuading her astonished husband that his presence in her bed would once more be welcome. Two years later, Emma had been born, and Ludovic was exiled to his own room once again.

Flavia's love for the baby Emma had been intense, even though she had proved to be an ugly little thing, olive-skinned, with dark hair and grey eyes and straight black brows, quite unlike her angelic-looking brother. She grew skinny and tall like her father, whom she closely resembled. Not wishing the same educational fate to overtake her second child, Flavia had been extremely careful not to let Ludovic observe how devotedly she set about preparing Emma for the religious life. As it happened, she was aided in this endeavour by Ludovic himself, who was much less frequently at home, his work taking him abroad for much of the time. Subtly, slowly, step by step, Flavia was able to carry out her mission. Morning and evening prayers were said daily, the little girl kneeling on the prie-dieu in Flavia's room. She accompanied her mother to Mass every Sunday and on Wednesday evenings as well. When the time came to go to school, Flavia enrolled her in the nearby convent. Each day they walked there together, utilizing the time to learn by heart the Acts of Faith, Hope, Charity and Contrition, the Devotions of the Blessed Virgin and the Saints, and the Devotion for the Conversion of

England. Emma's favourite was the Litany of the Most Holy Name of Jesus and she would repeat it after her mother, in a fast cheerful gabble, keeping to the rhythm of their footsteps as they walked along the Camden pavements to and from the convent.

Jesus, King of Patriarchs,
Have mercy on us.
Jesus, Master of Apostles,
Have mercy on us.
Jesus, teacher of Evangelists,
Have mercy on us.
Jesus, strength of Martyrs,
Have mercy on us.
Jesus, light of Confessors,
Have mercy on us.
Jesus, purity of Virgins,
Have mercy on us . . .

'Every time you recite this litany right through, Emma,' said Flavia, as they arrived at the convent steps, 'you get three hundred days' indulgence, isn't that nice?'

'What's indulgence?'

'It means God won't punish you for your sins. Of course, you do have to be sorry for them.'

'Oh.' Emma turned her grey eyes on her mother, frowning. 'I try not to do sins. I really do try to be good.'

Flavia laughed. 'Of course you do, darling. I know that. You are good, very good, most of the time.'

Emma looked relieved.

'Of course, you have Our Blessed Lady by your side, so it's easy to be good.' Flavia bent and kissed her daughter. 'Off you go, darling. You mustn't be late, must you?'

Emma mounted the steps to the studded oak door. At the top she turned, her hand on the twisted black metal handle. 'It's not always easy,' she said.

'What isn't?'

'Being good isn't.'

21

Emma was popular with the nuns, and quite soon began to be thought of as a girl with distinct possibilities. However, the Mother Superior was adamant that no pressure of any kind be put on her, despite Flavia's frequent references to the traditions of her own family, and hints as to the probable dowry that Emma would bring to any order she might wish to enter.

Emma herself, though well aware of her mother's wishes for her, was grateful for the tact and serenity of the nuns, and at eighteen, without consulting Flavia, she spoke to her father about her future. 'Father, do you think I could go to Florence for a year? Learn Italian, and maybe study the history of art? Giotto, that kind of thing?'

Ludovic looked at his daughter, so pale, serious and dark; secretive, like himself. He smiled at her kindly. 'Is that really what you'd like to do, Emma?'

'Yes, it is.' She took from her pocket a folded piece of newsprint. 'Look, I found this in the educational section, in *The Times*. It's an ad for a combined art and language course in Florence. It sounds great, just what I'd love to do.'

Ludovic took the piece of paper from her and read it carefully through. 'Have you spoken to your mother about this, darling?'

'No, not yet.'

'Well, if I were you I wouldn't mention it for the moment. I'll send for the particulars; find out about suitable accommodation and so on, and then we'll see.' He smiled at her again. 'We'll keep it a secret, shall we?'

'Is that OK?'

'Certainly it is.'

'Won't Mother be angry?'

'Probably. That's why I don't think we should tell her unless and until it's a *fait accompli*.'

'That sounds rather awful, but you're right, it would be better.' Emma laughed, and gave her father a quick, shy kiss, but couldn't help wondering how many indulgences she would need to offset this flagrant piece of devious behaviour. It did not occur to her to consider the state of her father's soul, or *his* chances of redemption.

So, after a brief and terrible struggle with her mother, Emma had departed for Florence and, after a week in bed, Flavia had been forced to console herself with her priests, her good works, and a skilfully managed renewed relationship with alcohol.

Now, sitting alone in the darkening church, Flavia slid onto her knees, closed her eyes and, holding her rosary close to her lips, said the Prayers for the Night, and the Prayers for Souls in Purgatory. She kissed her rosary, and got stiffly to her feet. Then, her knees cracking like pistol shots, she genuflected in the general direction of the shrouded Crucifixion, and then, more personally, to the hidden statue of Our Lady. She made her way out of St Botolph's, disappointed that Fr Gordon had failed her yet again, and chilled by her long vigil in the church. She hurried home, thinking with some eagerness of the first drink of the evening. As she unlocked her front door, she remembered that it was Friday. She had completely forgotten that Ludovic was coming home for the weekend.

In the kitchen, Flavia poured herself a stiff brandy and drank it quickly, standing by the sink. Then she looked in the freezer to see what she could find for Ludovic's supper. She chose prawn cocktail and vegetarian lasagne and put the packets into the microwave oven to defrost. She arranged the prawns in two glass bowls and put them back into the fridge, to keep cool. She decanted the lasagne into an ovenproof dish to make it look home-made, and put it, with two dinner plates, into a low oven. She would heat it properly when Ludovic arrived. She poured herself another drink, and thought about laying the table. She went into the dining room, overlooking the street, its windows hung with net curtains to foil the prying eyes of passers-by. Since it was Lent, she had turned off the heating, so the rarely used room was rather cold; very cold, in fact. We can eat in the kitchen, she thought, it'll be warmer there, with the oven on.

Flavia closed the door and went upstairs to her bedroom, carrying her drink with her. She looked at her bedside clock: seven-thirty. She wondered whether there was time for a bath. Her knees were stiff and painful; the hot water would ease them, perhaps. Ludovic would probably arrive from Brussels at about a quarter to nine; there would be time for a bath if she hurried. She sat down on the Victorian armchair, her mother's old chair, and took a swallow of her brandy. She eased off her shoes, flexing her toes gratefully, and let her eyes wander round the room that was her special place, her sanctuary. It was in this room that she had been born and would probably die, and here that she had given birth to both her children. She looked at their photographs, in large silver frames on her night-table. Christian, her first-born, blond and smiling, with Phoebe and their children, and Emma, the joy of her life, in her novice's habit, at the Abbaye de La Falaise. Flavia had gone to Britanny to attend the Clothing ceremony, when Emma had made her first vows and received her first habit, together with the white veil of the novice nun. She had been at the abbey for three years, first as a postulant and now as a novice, entering immediately after her long years at the painting school in Florence. Flavia rarely saw her, but wrote to her regularly, giving her news of the family and of St Botolph's. Gazing at Emma's picture with envy, Flavia thought that she looked almost beautiful as a nun, which was strange, for she had been quite plain as a girl.

Though her bed was large and comfortable, a Victorian brass affair, Flavia had gone to some lengths to make the room as bare as possible. The walls were papered with cream lining paper, and the two wall-hung oak shelves were filled with her library of religious books. Flavia had in her possession other literary works, notably Henry Miller's *Tropic of Cancer*. These books she had found in Christian's bedroom, and after examining their contents she had confiscated them, on the grounds that such an action was necessary for the good of her son's soul. A subsequent thorough examination of *Tropic of Cancer* had both astonished and appalled her, and the book was now secreted under her mattress, and furtively re-read from time to time. Above the bed was a large ebony crucifix, with an ivory figure of Christ. A plaster statue of Our Lady stood on the night-table, beside the photo of Emma.

Flavia raised her glass to her lips and found that it was empty. She got up from her chair and went down to the kitchen for a refill. As she descended the stairs, the clock in the hall struck eight, and she abandoned the idea of a bath. She decided against another brandy, and opened a bottle of red wine, knowing that Ludovic would expect wine with his meal. She looked at the label: Château Lacoste. Flavia poured some into a glass and took a swig. She was not hugely impressed; it tasted rather inky, she thought. Still, it must be all right; Ludovic had bought it, he knew about these things, after all. She ate a cheese biscuit, then took another sip of the wine. It tasted rather better, quite nice in fact. She emptied the glass and refilled it.

She put knives and forks on the small plastic-topped table, and teaspoons for the prawn cocktail. She got a packet of margarine from the fridge and, cutting a slice, put it on a saucer, and laid that on the table too, with a butter knife. The butter knife had a thistle on the end of the handle, and had been a present from Gwen. Darling Gwen, I do wish she was still with me, she thought, with a pang of self-pity and loneliness. Still, it was a real act of self-denial on my part to let her go, and lovely for Christian's babies to have her. She's a good woman, even if she's not a Catholic, poor deluded soul.

Flavia topped up her glass again, and put the bottle on the table. She was surprised to see that a third of it was already gone. Perhaps she should open another bottle? She went into the hall to fetch one from the cupboard under the stairs, and heard the unmistakable sound of a taxi drawing up outside the front steps and, after a brief pause, her husband's key in the Yale lock. The door opened, and Ludovic entered the hall. Tall, with smooth well-cut grey hair and grey eyes, he was still very handsome in a forbidding way. Four years older than Flavia, he carried his sixty-two years with grace and distinction. He had an air of quiet authority, and a cool, secret quality about him. He wore a grey flannel suit, English, naturally, and carried over his arm a black trenchcoat. This luxurious waterproof came, in fact, from Saint Laurent, though Flavia paid scant attention to such niceties, and would have been morally outraged if she had known its price. She hesitated for a second, then advanced towards him slightly unsteadily, an insincere smile on her lips. 'Hello, darling,' she said brightly, holding up her face to receive his kiss.

'My God, Flavia, it's cold in here!' He pecked her proffered cheek, then stepped smartly back, overwhelmed by the shattering odour of her breath. 'What's wrong? Has the heating broken down?'

Flavia shot him a reproving glance. 'It's Lent, Ludovic, or had you forgotten?'

'I'm afraid so, yes.'

She pursed her lips, looking pained. 'We'll eat in the kitchen if you don't mind. It's quite warm in there.'

'I'll just go up and have a wash.' He hung up his coat, taking a mobile phone from a pocket, picked up his briefcase and went upstairs.

Flavia got the extra bottle of wine from the cupboard and returned to the kitchen. She took the warm plates

26

from the oven, and turned up the heat, putting a foil-wrapped loaf under the lasagne. Ten minutes later, Ludovic came down. He had taken off his jacket and was wearing a thick black wool sweater.

'Pour the wine, will you, darling?' Flavia took the glass dishes of prawn cocktail from the fridge and put them on the table. Ludovic poured wine into the glasses and sat down on the hard kitchen chair opposite his wife. He was surprised to see the prawn cocktail, thought about making a small joke about Lent, decided against it, spread the inadequate paper napkin over his knees and picked up his teaspoon. The fish tasted of nothing, except possibly wet cotton-wool, but he ate it anyway. He looked at Flavia, consuming her food with evident enjoyment, and forebore to make a comment.

'It makes a nice treat, doesn't it?' She got up to change the plates. 'After all, you're at home so seldom nowadays, aren't you?'

Ludovic looked at her as she bent down to remove the hot dish from the oven, but could detect no hint of reproof in her face as she turned and placed the lasagne on a mat in the centre of the table. 'That smells very nice,' he said. 'Did you make it?'

'M'm.' Flavia smiled at him as she served the food, her faded blue eyes bright with alcohol, a slight sweat on her downy upper lip. With detached pity, Ludovic observed the puffy eyelids, the bags under his wife's eyes, and the folds of wrinkled skin on her copper-coloured neck, quite different from her carefully made-up pink and white face. He took a forkful of the lasagne. 'Excellent,' he said, then put down his fork and refilled their glasses.

In spite of her protests, Ludovic stacked the dishwasher, while she made coffee. Real coffee, he was thankful to observe. They went into the sitting room to drink it, and he sat in one of the wide, overstuffed armchairs of his mother-in-law's three-piece suite to watch *News at Ten*. Flavia sat down at her small writing desk and continued a letter to Emma, begun some days before.

At half past ten, Ludovic got up and switched off the television. 'Oh, sorry,' he said. 'Were you watching?'

'No, no. I hardly ever do.'

'Well, it's been a pretty hard week, I think I'll go to bed.'

'Good idea, you must be tired. Good night, darling. Sleep well.'

'Good night.' At the door, he turned back. 'By the way, I have to be off tomorrow. Duty calls, I'm afraid.'

'Oh, dear, what a shame.' She lifted her eyes to his, then returned to her letter.

Ludovic went quickly upstairs to his room, piled his pillows into a comfortable heap, kicked off his shoes and lay down on the bed. Then he picked up his phone and dialled a Paris number.

'*Oui?*'

'Hello, my love. It's me.'

'Ludo! Where are you?'

'In bloody London, where else?'

'Oh. Yes, of course.'

'I'll come tomorrow. I'll be with you by six.'

'Wonderful! Is that all right, darling? Shouldn't you stay till Sunday, really?'

'Absolutely not. The house is freezing, the food is revolting, the whole thing is a dreary nightmare, as usual. I'm coming home.'

'Well, fine. If you're sure.'

'I'm sure.'

'I love you, Ludo.'

'And I love you, Claudia.'

Claudia Renaud replaced the telephone in its cradle, turned up the volume of her CD player, and lay down again on her cushions, lifting her long, thick, newly washed and still damp hair away from her neck so that it fell in a wavy auburn curtain over the end of the low sofa. She smiled, happy that Ludo had telephoned, and that his duty visit to his wife was to be cut short. She closed her eyes, letting the music of Scarlatti's B minor sonata flow over her, and began to plan tomorrow's shopping.

Claudia lived in a small house, or, more accurately, two small houses separated by a paved courtyard, hidden in a narrow *impasse* just off rue Mouffetard. She lived with Ludovic in the main house, formerly a cabinet-maker's workshop, and across the tiny garden lived their daughter, Allegra, now twenty-one years old and reading natural history at the university. Like her mother, she was tall, ivory-skinned, with the same Pre-Raphaelite red hair, but her eyes were a luminous grey, those of her father. Ludovic and Claudia had lived in this quiet, secluded place for twenty-two years, since their first meeting at a late-night supper party given by friends after a performance of *Pelléas et Mélisande* at the opera. They had been seated together at the restaurant, and shyly, feeling at a disadvantage because of her comparative youth, she had waited for him to speak first. She had been twenty-four at the time, just out of the *conservatoire*, and he a man of forty, dynamic, handsome in a hawkish way, making his mark in the world of European politics, so she had been briefed by her hostess.

'What do you do?' he had asked, turned towards her, his elbow on the table, giving her his full attention.

'I am a musician,' she had replied. 'A cellist.'

'Are you a soloist? Should I have heard of you?'

'Absolutely not. I play in an orchestra, and teach a little.' She had looked at him then, her slender arms crossed, her hazel eyes direct. 'I am rather talented, in fact, but I lack ambition. The idea of travelling the world, living out of a suitcase, performing the same repertoire over and over again, has little appeal for me.'

'What a mature decision to make, so soon.'

'Are you patronizing me, by any chance, Mr McGrath?'

'Certainly not, I mean it. But with such beautiful hair as yours, I'm surprised you haven't been inundated with offers.'

Claudia had laughed then, and relaxed visibly. 'Well, I have had a few, and it was probably more on account of the hair than the playing, if the truth were known. Maybe I should get it cut?'

'Please don't, ever.'

Claudia had laughed again, thinking that he had a pretty smooth technique, for an older man. 'And you, what do you do?' she asked.

'I am a superior civil servant,' he replied.

'Why superior?'

'Well, I do it in Brussels.'

'Is that good?'

'It will be, eventually.'

'Oh.' She could not think of anything to say, and applied herself to her excellent *soufflé aux champignons*, for she was hungry.

'Are you married?'

Surprised by the sudden question, Claudia had raised her napkin to her mouth and stared at Ludovic. 'No, I am not. Are you?'

'Yes, I am.'

The feeling of disappointment, almost pain, was a shock. She felt her heart sink. This is ridiculous, she thought, her hunger quite forgotten.

'Will you have lunch with me tomorrow, at La Coupole?'

Not being a young woman much inclined to dissembling or coyness, Claudia had lifted her eyes to his, happiness flowing through her. 'Yes, I will,' she said; 'I'd love to.' She had picked up her fork again, suddenly ravenous.

Life with Ludovic had been exciting, stimulating and fun. At first, like most lovers, they did not think about the future, but snatched every moment to be together. At that time, Claudia had rented an attic in a rather rundown small hotel in place Dauphine, where she was able to practise her cello and give lessons in the afternoons, two or three times a week. She never knew when Ludo would arrive, often without telephoning. He would take her out to dinner, they walked under the bridges of the Seine, they went to the theatre or a concert, if she was not engaged to play herself. They saw all the new exhibitions together; and at night, and sometimes in the afternoons, they made love on the hard, narrow hospital bed in her attic. For both of them, this proved an illuminating experience, which grew even more rewarding as time passed, until neither could imagine the possibility of life without the other. Then, in spite of their efforts to avoid such a contingency, Claudia became pregnant.

'Do you mind?' she asked anxiously. 'Do you want me to abort it?'

'Do *you* want that?'

'I don't know. I need to know how *you* feel. After all, you are already married, no?'

'Yes, I am. My wife is a Roman Catholic. As far as she is concerned, there is no question of divorce.'

'Well, I am a Catholic also. That's to say, I was brought up in the faith, though I no longer subscribe to it.'

'It's the same for me. For Flavia, it is different, utterly.'

'Yes, I can see that.'

'Claudia, there's something else I must tell you.' Ludovic had sat down beside her and taken her hand in his. She had stared at him then, really alarmed for the first time, fearful of what he was about to say. 'I should have told you at the beginning. I have two children already, a boy of thirteen and a little girl of three.'

'What are their names?' she had asked, stupidly, for something to say, not really wishing to know.

'Christian and Emma.'

'Why such a long gap between them?'

Quietly, Ludovic explained the circumstances of his sexual relationship with his wife.

'So you have not slept with her, except to make the children?'

'You've got it.'

Claudia put her arms round Ludovic's neck, half-laughing, half-crying, and kissed him. Then she looked at him, her hazel eyes still wet with tears, soft beneath the untidy mass of red hair. 'So now, our baby will be only four years younger than Emma?'

Ludovic held her tightly, and a huge happiness had filled his heart. 'What about marriage, illegitimacy, all that? Don't you mind?'

'Not at all. Do you?'

'No, I don't.'

Immediately, they had started house-hunting, and had eventually found the disused workshop with its large-paned windows giving on to a tiny courtyard, three minutes' walk from rue Mouffetard. Since Flavia owned the Camden house outright, Ludo was not involved in heavy mortgage repayments, so felt perfectly able to undertake the purchase and refurbishment of his and Claudia's home. He did not tell Flavia about his new involvement, or the coming child, but neither he nor Claudia made the slightest attempt to conceal their relationship, and whether anyone had taken the trouble to inform his wife of the situation, he neither knew nor cared. He continued to pay the usual allowances to Flavia, as well as the school fees of the children, but this was not a matter of great concern since he was increasingly well paid as time went on, and Claudia continued to work in the orchestra and give lessons in her beautiful and unusual home.

In due time, Allegra had been born and her childhood in Paris had been happily ordinary. The little girl had often played with her friends in the nearby Jardin des Plantes, and this magical botanical garden, full of old trees, charming statues, and tall glasshouses housing gigantic tropical plants, was the motivation behind Allegra's later decision to study natural history. As well as the gardens, the small *ménagerie* in the Jardin des Plantes was a constant source of joy to the little girl. Ludovic took her there often, making bad-taste jokes about the greedy Parisians eating the animals one by one during the Siege of Paris in 1870. 'Jugged kangaroo, Allegra, imagine!' he would say, and receive an angry kick on the shins for his pains. To this day, he only had to look at her and say 'Kangaroo' for her to rush at him, grey eyes flashing, fists clenched, and beat him up while he collapsed on the sofa, helpless with laughter.

As an eighteenth birthday present for his daughter, Ludo had restored the funny little building across the courtyard, used to store bicycles and general junk, so that Allegra could have her own private apartment, with her own newly built front door, giving directly on to the alleyway leading to rue Mouffetard, thus making her comings and goings entirely her own affair.

Ludovic, as Claudia was well aware, was a very private and rather secretive man. Never having told his wife of his long liaison with Claudia, neither had he spoken of it to Christian or Emma. Equally, Claudia herself had never felt any need to discuss Ludo's previous life with her own child, and, in view of the fact that Allegra bore Ludovic's name, the little girl had rather naturally assumed that her parents were married. There was nothing unusual in Claudia's retaining her maiden name and, rightly or wrongly, Allegra was still quite unaware of the true state of affairs. From time to time, Claudia worried about this, realizing that sometime she and Ludo really should discuss how best to tell their daughter the circumstances of their life together, but somehow the appropriate moment never seemed to arrive.

The music came to an end, and Claudia opened her eyes and looked around her. After more than twenty years, her spacious airy sitting room still had an atmosphere of nonconformism, as though they still hadn't decided on a style for it. The large high windows were uncurtained, so that the little garden seemed part of the room, especially at night, when it was lit by star-shaped Moroccan tin lanterns, hanging in the ancient and grotesquely distorted mulberry tree that shaded and cooled the entire enclave in summer. One wall of the room was filled with shelves, which groaned under the weight of hundreds of books and magazines, as well as musical scores and a curious assortment of objects, bought impulsively at sales, and at the Sunday flea markets so beloved of Claudia. Among these treasures was, predictably, a large marble bust of Brahms, but there were other things, equally loved. An enormous model eye, made of glass and originally used for the instruction of medical students, was wedged between a stack of fat, crumbling, leather-bound books and a battered verdigris Medici urn. From this graceful pot trailed a spider plant, frequently near to death from drought, and requiring a recuperative spell in the garden. The floor, in a herringbone pattern of grey-painted elm blocks, was bare. Claudia disliked carpets, or even rugs, considering that they wrecked the acoustic qualities so characteristic of the room, and so important for her work. On the floor were more books, stacked in untidy piles beneath an eighteenth-century oval table. The table top was a single piece of mahogany and rested on a pediment, painted pale grey and edged with a gilded leafy pattern, as were the legs. It was on this table that Claudia worked, for she had recently begun to compose, and where they sometimes ate. At such times, it was necessary to push to one side the clutter of books and papers, the bowls of plaster fruit, skulls, fir cones and the grinning blackamoor's head, adorned with a paste tiara, that occupied the space. The table was surrounded by metal garden chairs, painted grey; and two rather valuable Louis XV armchairs, still in their original though tattered up-holstery of pale-blue silk, stood near to the long Recamier sofa. This, too, was blue, but had an old grey and rose striped silk curtain thrown over it, with a soft pile of cushions made from its twin.

Against the wall facing the windows, an ordinary black Bechstein piano stood in front of a tall eighteenth-century glass-fronted cabinet, filled with a collection of English Leeds pottery, pierced baskets and bowls, the pale ivory of their glaze opalescent against the deep brown-red of the cabinet's painted interior. On a shelf by itself stood a large tureen in the shape of a green cabbage, with a fat pink snail forming the handle of its lid, and once a year, in October, when the pumpkins were in season in the street-market in rue Mouffetard, Claudia made *soupe au potiron* and they used the beautiful tureen to serve it in.

Beside the cabinet stood Claudia's cello, resting on its stand, covered with a Spanish shawl to protect it from dust. The white walls of the room were rela-tively pristine, the only pictures a small collection of botanical prints, but a large baroque gilded mirror hung on the wall behind the sofa, reflecting the book-shelves opposite. There was no overhead lighting in the room, but several heavy ormolu table lamps, with rough natural linen-covered shades, cast golden circles of light onto both the ceiling above and the surfaces beneath them. Over the years, Claudia had collected many candlesticks, most of them second-hand silver, and four large carved wooden altar candelabra. Two of these had been rescued from a skip, but the other two had been bought, rather guiltily, from a flea market. Candlelight was Claudia's passion, and often she would light all her candles at the same time, turning off the lamps. The multiple reflections of their leaping flames in the glass windowpanes, the doors of the china cabinet and the big mirror filled her with a kind of ecstasy, and when she felt lonely, as she sometimes did during Ludo's necessary absences, she always lit her candles, sending up prayers for his safety and swift return, in spite of her declared agnosticism.

On either side of the china cabinet, doors led on one side to the bedroom and bathroom, on the other to the kitchen. The bedroom was white, spacious and lined with even more books and *objets trouvés*. Allegra's former bedroom, now empty, was on the first floor. A low-ceilinged, simple attic space, reached by means of an iron staircase in the courtyard, it now served as a spare room, and a place to store the magpie overflow of Claudia's possessions. Often, when her cleaning lady complained about the difficulty of dusting all these things, Claudia would smile and agree with her. 'I know. We could never move house, could we?'

The next morning, Claudia got up early, made herself some coffee, and, taking a large shopping basket from its hook in the kitchen, left her house and walked down the alleyway to rue Mouffetard, where the street-market was already in full swing. All along the steep and narrow street, with its little church at the bottom of the hill, the stallholders were doing their usual brisk trade, and there she found everything she needed to celebrate Ludo's homecoming. She bought a loin of young lamb, already studded with garlic and rosemary, a kilo of early potatoes from Provence, and a bag of baby spinach leaves to make a salad. For the starter, she bought a pot of Ludo's favourite jellied eels, and a bunch of watercress. She chose some small *crotins de brebis*, some peaches from Italy, and bought two fresh, crisp baguettes from the *boulangerie*. Coffee and wine she already had at home, so her last port of call was the flower stall, where she bought an armful of white lilac.

All day long, the spring sunshine had filled the courtyard with unseasonal warmth, and Claudia was in the garden, barefoot, her hair screwed into a knot on top of her head, watering her pots, when Ludo came through the French windows onto the terrace, filled with the sensual smell of warm earth after rain. He put his arms round her waist and kissed the back of her bare neck, then removed the tortoiseshell comb from her hair, so that it fell in a coppery shower over her shoulders. Laughing, she dropped the hose and turned in his arms to receive his kiss.

'God, I've missed you,' he said softly.

'And I you, my love.'

She turned off the hose, and they went into the house together, closing the door behind them.

Chapter Two

Although there were signs of early spring and the sun shone in a blue sky, a cold wind blew off the Atlantic, so that the nuns at the Abbaye de La Falaise were glad that they had not yet exchanged their winter habits for the long blue cotton garments they wore for work in summer.

'If you really want to know,' said Sister Miriam, sloshing a bucket of water over the hen-house floor, 'the thing I miss most of all is sex. Real sex, I mean, not just sex in the head.'

Emma, vigorously trying to remove the hen muck with a heavy yard-broom, did her best to look uninterested in this electrifying confidence, though in fact she was longing to hear more. She knew that Miriam was testing her in some way, as she often did, when her Irish sense of humour got the better of her.

'Don't you want to hear about it?'

'Not particularly,' said Emma, untruthfully, and banged the head of the brush against the hen-house wall, so that a foetid shower of brown drops fell on the bunched-up black skirt of Miriam's habit. 'Oh, sorry!' she exclaimed, meaning it.

'Doesn't matter, it'll dry,' said Miriam cheerfully. She looked at Emma, her green eyes sparkling in her freckled face, framed in the starched white wimple. 'Doing it yourself isn't enough, after a while, is it?'

'Really, Miriam!' Emma said severely, and shot her a reproving glance. 'How sordid,' she added, primly.

Miriam laughed, not at all put out by Emma's disapproval. 'It's a good job it's not my day for confessing my sins, isn't it? Or yours for reporting the sins of others?'

'I hate that.' Emma spoke quietly, her eyes cast down, and brushed the brown slurry towards the hen-house door.

Miriam turned off the hose, and hung the bucket on its hook. 'What do *you* miss, Emma? Tell me, I won't tease you, I promise.'

'I miss my work.'

'But we work all the time; the farm, the kitchen, the vegetables, the guest house. We never stop, except when we're in chapel, or the refectory, or asleep.'

'That's not what I mean. I *expected* that, when I was a postulant. I was glad to do it; I understood that it was a form of spiritual testing, if you like. But when I became a novice, I rather hoped I'd be allowed to do what I've been trained to do, and what I thought was my vocation.'

'The painting thing?'

'Yes, of course. I didn't spend three years in Italy mastering the technique, just to have it thrown away so dismissively.'

'Do you think it has been, really?'

'Yes, I do. Or at any rate, I'm beginning to. If I'm not allowed to do it soon, I'll forget everything I've learned. Three years is a long time to wait.'

'Have you spoken to Mother Abbess about it?'

'No.'

'Why don't you?'

'I wouldn't dare.'

'She can't eat you, Emma.'

'She could throw me out, though.'

'Perhaps that's what you really want?'

'No, I don't think so.'

The bell rang for Sext, and immediately they put away their tools, and went to the wash-house. They took off their aprons, unpinned their skirts, replaced their gumboots with sandals, and washed their hands carefully under the cold tap, rolling down their sleeves afterwards.

After Sext in the abbey church, the whole community filed into the refectory for lunch. The nuns ate in silence, while one of their number read a passage from the texts of the saints. A generous bowl of excellent vegetable soup was followed by cauliflower cheese, beautifully prepared with a well-flavoured sauce. At each place was a large hunk of bread, of the four-grain variety, and a carafe of water from the abbey spring. Every single thing eaten there had been grown by themselves, with the exception of tea, coffee and salt. They milled their own flour from their own wheat, made butter and cheese from their own cows, and used their own honey for sweetening. They ate no meat, except the occasional old hen, past laying, and considered a real luxury. Any surplus produce was sold locally.

Emma ate hungrily, and then sat listening to the reading, with downcast eyes, while her neighbours continued to eat their meal, skilfully transferring their food from plate to mouth without making a sound. As they had been instructed to do, Emma carefully collected together the remaining crumbs of her bread with her fingers, and formed them into the shape of a cross in front of her empty plate. This was an exercise intended to prevent their attention wandering from the reading. In Emma's case, the exact opposite applied; her entire mind was focused on forming a perfect cross with her crumbs.

When lunch was finished, grace was said by the Abbess, followed by an act of thanksgiving in the church. After this, the sisters either had a rest in their cells, or, in fine weather, sat in the shade of the cloisters, reading. As they had been up since three-thirty in the morning for Prime, followed by Lauds and the conventual morning Mass, this hour of rest was welcome and necessary, especially for the older nuns, who greatly outnumbered the postulants and novices.

After the hour of rest and silence, a bell summoned the nuns once more to work. Emma went to the kitchens with another novice, Sister Marie-Luc, to do their stint with the washing-up, not only that of the community refectory, but the guest-house dining room as well. As she stood at the stone sink, up to her elbows in greasy water, for they were not permitted to use modern detergents, Emma did her utmost to offer up the task in hand, to try her best to make it a joyful, gladly offered sacrifice, but failed miserably in the attempt. She worked with pursed lips, and a barely concealed disgust, putting each imperfectly cleaned glass, bowl or plate on the draining board with an audible click. Sister Marie-Luc, drying the dishes at her side, glanced at her nervously from time to time, not daring to speak for fear of incurring her scorn or, worse, her insulting silence.

After the washing-up was finished and everything put away, they laid the tables for the guests' tea. In her mind's eye Emma saw the fresh piles of washing-up that would follow, as night follows day, and, for a moment, the crazy idea of barring the door to prevent the guests entering the dining room crossed her mind. Then, the kitchen-duty sisters brought in the plates of scones and jam, the tea urn was filled, the large jugs of milk were set down, followed by the cheerful arrival of the guests, hungry after a day's sightseeing in the fresh air. Emma suppressed her negative thoughts, and walked calmly and kindly among the visitors, fetching a high chair for a small child, pouring tea, wiping up spills.

After Vespers at six o'clock, the nuns had their own supper, a simple cold meal of cheese and bread, requiring few plates. Then they walked in the garden, or in the cloister, either alone or in pairs. Sometimes, a senior nun would read aloud in the cloister, while the Abbess sat opposite her, listening, joined by a group of the older, professed nuns. For the novices, like Emma and Miriam, the precious free time took the form of exercise, idle chatter and laughter. It was their only means of ridding themselves of the tensions of the day. For Emma, at any rate, this proved a better way of regaining some kind of balance, and acceptance of the status quo, than the endless submissive and self-abnegating prayers prescribed by their mentors. Although they had been warned not to spend so much time together, Miriam and Emma walked in the apple orchard, enjoying the fresh air, and the sweet soft grass beneath their sandals.

'Tell you what, Em. I'd love a glass of cider, wouldn't you?'

'Or better still, a slug of Calvados.' Emma laughed. 'That'd set the cat among the pigeons, wouldn't it?'

Compline, the last service of the day, was at eight o'clock, and by nine they were all in their cells, and mostly fast asleep, to snatch every moment of rest they could before the bell for Matins rang at three-thirty the next morning.

For Emma, her time in Italy had exceeded her wildest expectations. She had arrived at the end of September, ready to start her course in October. Her father, who knew Florence well, had arranged for her to stay with old friends near Fiesole, who received groups of girls as paying guests in their country house, the students travelling into Florence each day by bus. Immediately, she felt welcome in the Italian household, and was ravished by the surrounding countryside. It had been an Indian summer, the weather was still warm and balmy, and on most evenings the family and their guests dined on the loggia, looking down across the fields and little rounded hills, vineyards and dusty roads studded with clumps of fat, dark cypresses, to the twinkling lights of Florence. Hanging out of her bedroom window, which overlooked the lane below the high rear wall of the villa, Emma watched with astonishment and delight the large square white cattle making their way home in the evening, their bells clanking sonorously as they passed. She breathed the scented Tuscan air and felt her soul expand, like a butterfly unfolding its wings, still damp and crumpled from their long sojourn in the chrysalis.

The Italian lessons took place every morning, from nine-thirty to one-thirty. The students were then free to lunch as they wished, in Emma's case a sandwich or a slice of pizza bought at a stall or a bar. In the afternoons, various tutors took groups of students to look at particular treasures of the city, and though these visits were interesting, they were also extremely tiring. Quite soon Emma felt that she had seen too many buildings, inspected too many statues and baptistry doors, and walked for too many miles along stone alleyways and across tiled or marble floors. One afternoon she joined a group going to visit San Marco, and saw for the first time the frescoes of Fra Angelico. She listened attentively as their guide informed them that Cosimo di Medici had, in 1434, procured for the Dominicans the ruined convent of San Marco. Fra Angelico had been commissioned to decorate each individual monk's cell with a fresco, depicting an episode from the life of Christ. As the intention of these paintings was not primarily to instruct, but rather to encourage an atmosphere of peaceful contemplation to the occupant of the cell, the artist had carried out the commission with a restraint and lack of ornamentation unusual at the time. As she gazed at each astonishingly simple yet potent painting, Emma felt as though her eyes and her mind had been peeled. She realized at once that these works had nothing to do with the tawdry plaster images of her upbringing, and nothing to do with her convent, smelling of boiled sprouts and Mansion polish, incense and Nescafé.

On her way out, she bought postcards and a booklet on Fra Angelico, and that night, in her halting Italian, she told her hosts about the visit, and how glorious she had found the frescoes. After dinner, they took her to their library and showed her old books of reproductions of all the great fresco masters in Italy. 'We must take you to Arezzo,' they said, 'and Sansepolcro and Urbino.' Signor Petacci, in particular, was delighted that the daughter of his old friend should show such a keen interest in the glories of Italian art, and it was he who took Emma on a tour of the shrines where the marvellous frescoes of Piero della Francesca were to be found.

They left Fiesole at seven in the morning, carrying with them a picnic lunch. They were to drive first to Arezzo, a distance of some seventy-five miles, then on to Sansepolcro. There they would lunch, then drive another sixty miles to Urbino, where they were to spend the night with friends of the Petacci, returning to Fiesole the following day.

They took the *autostrada* to Arezzo, arriving at Chiesa di San Francesco just before nine on a fine October morning. There was already a crowd in the church, mainly touring parties of retired Germans, it seemed, and they made their way to the apse with some difficulty. The extensively damaged frescoes, high up on the walls above the choir, were in the process of being restored and were partially covered. Nevertheless, quite large sections of the brilliantly restored paintings could be seen by means of electric lights, though these had the disconcerting tendency to switch themselves off after a certain time, necessitating reactivation by feeding coins into a meter. In spite of this disturbing element, Signor Petacci explained to

Emma the artist's theme, *The Legend of the True Cross*. She listened carefully, noting with pleasure the soft colours of the pigments Piero had used, the gentle blues, ochres and rose-pinks, and the extraordinarily modern appearance of the faces of the characters depicted. She felt that they could have walked in off the piazza that very morning, and could probably be seen, sitting at a café table having a drink, that very evening.

They came out of the crowded church into the fresh air, and went in search of a coffee and a *panino*, which they consumed standing at the bar of a café. Signor Petacci explained that it cost more to sit at a table, and three times as much to sit on the terrace. Refreshed by the coffee, they drove slowly out of the city and took the road to Sansepolcro, some thirty-five miles further on. 'There's a wonderful Piero at Monterchi,' he said. 'That's a little village on a minor road, but we'll see it on the way home tomorrow, otherwise we might be too late to see *The Flagellation* at Urbino.' Emma, already beginning to feel slightly confused, looked up Urbino in her guidebook, to jog her memory.

They arrived in Sansepolcro and parked close to the Palazzo Communale. Signor Petacci bought the entrance tickets, and they walked through the rooms of the palace, glancing at the many works displayed there, until they reached their objective, *The Resurrection*. Against a landscape of leafless trees and dark hills dotted with scrub, barely lit by a viridian-green dawn sky, the strong stern figure of Christ, wearing a pink shroud around his naked body, climbs out of the tomb, blood dripping from his hands and feet, as well as from the wound in his side. He is carrying a large banner in his right hand. In the foreground, his four Roman guards are sleeping, and Christ stares out over their slumbering bodies, with pain-filled, angry eyes. Emma, riveted by the power of that gaze, understood what he must have gone through, both physically and mentally, in the days leading up to the crucifixion and during the barbaric execution itself.

'The man with his neck resting on the edge of the tomb is supposed to be a self-portrait of Piero,' said Signor Petacci.

'Really?' Emma looked at the soldier. 'He looks terribly ordinary, doesn't he?'

'People so often are, my dear.'

They found a quiet little square with a few shady trees, where they ate their picnic: bread, salami, olives, tomatoes and some soft cheeses wrapped in vine leaves. They had a short rest, Signor Petacci dozing under his hat, while Emma gazed around her, admiring the peaceful piazza with its fountain and trees, basking in the sunshine. Then her host woke up, and they continued their journey to Urbino, driving away from Tuscany and into Umbria, along a winding road that climbed higher and higher into a completely different landscape, wild and rugged, a far cry from the seductive hills of Fiesole. They drove through the mountains towards the Marches, across a great plain that seemed endless and rather hostile, so that Urbino, when they finally reached this beautiful and perfectly preserved hill town, was all the more remarkable and rewarding. They parked the car and made their way to the Palazzo Ducale, dominating the heights of Urbino. The palace, built by the Duke Federico di Montefeltro, was astonishing, with wide marble staircases, cool impressive rooms and a tranquil courtyard. In the ducal apartments they found *The Flagellation*, Piero's enigmatic masterpiece.

'How *small* it is!' Emma exclaimed at once.

'It's quite probable that it was commissioned to hang in a private apartment, like this, rather than a public place like a church.'

Emma stood silently, awed by the brilliance of the composition, astonished that the distant figure of Christ and the men engaged in whipping Him seemed almost to play a secondary role. In the foreground, to the right of the painting, stood three large figures apparently engaged in serious conversation, and completely disregarding the fate of the pale man tied to a marble pillar behind them. A golden-haired youth in a long raspberry-pink tunic stood barefoot, one hand on his hip, his blue eyes gazing straight ahead in a face of composed sweetness. On either side of him, two middle-aged men, both in formal Renaissance robes and boots, one bald and one in a large black felt hat, stared at each other in a strangely disturbing manner.

'What can they be doing?' asked Emma. 'They look awfully sinister, don't you think?'

'There have been many interpretations, but I don't think anyone really knows. It's enough, really, that it's such a wonderful picture, isn't it?'

'Yes, of course it is.' She glanced at him, then back at the picture. 'I wonder who the young man is?'

'Very probably Oddantonio di Montefeltro, who was murdered in mysterious circumstances in 1444. It's frequently suggested that the picture was commissioned by the duke as a memorial portrait. But there have been many theories over the centuries, you can imagine.'

They remained silently in front of the painting for some time, thinking their own thoughts. Then they made their way back down the marble staircase, through the peaceful courtyard and out into the street. For a moment, with the image of the incredible little painting still vividly before her mind's eye, Emma could not remember where they were. Urbino, of course, she said to herself. They walked around the town for a while, up and down steep alleyways. Signor Petacci showed Emma the house where Raphael was born, then they returned to the car and drove to the home of the family with whom they were to spend the night. They proved to be delightful, typically Italian and welcoming, and Emma found herself increasingly confident in their language, even attempting a brief appreciative description of the marvels she had seen that day.

'The best is yet to come,' said Signor Petacci. 'Tomorrow we go to Monterchi.'

'Ah!' Signora Capestrani's eyes shone. 'The *Madonna del Parto*, what a treasure!' She turned to Signor Petacci. 'Did you know that she has been removed from the chapel, for restoration? She's in the old primary school at the moment.'

The next morning they left Urbino soon after breakfast and drove back across the forbidding, monotonous plain and through the tortuous mountain passes to Sansepolcro. Soon afterwards they turned into the country road that took them to Monterchi.

Signor Petacci pointed out the tiny chapel, apparently standing in a field, that had originally sheltered the *Madonna*, then they drove into the village and found the old primary school and its sublime inhabitant. Flanked by two robust-looking winged angels, holding back the heavy folds of a brown velvet, gold-encrusted canopy, the tall powerful *Madonna del Parto* stands, one hand on her hip, the other half-covering the open front-fastening of her long blue gown. She is so far advanced in pregnancy that she can no longer fasten the buttons over her enormously distended stomach, and her white undershift is plainly revealed. The protective gesture of her right hand appears to be not so much one of an understandable modesty, but rather a confident acknowledgement of the Child within.

Looking at that calm young face, pink-cheeked, the heavy eyelids looking slightly downwards, the gentle mouth soft and serious, Emma suddenly experienced an extraordinary sensation in the pit of her stomach, followed by a wave of nausea. A loud noise like a diesel engine filled her ears, the ground seemed to tilt towards her, and she would have fallen if Signor Petacci had not caught her. He sat her down and thrust her head between her knees, and in a few minutes she recovered and sat up. 'Goodness,' she said, laughing shakily. 'That's the first time I've ever done that!'

Signor Petacci shook his head, looking worried. 'Empty stomach, I expect. You need your lunch, my girl.'

'I expect that's it.' She stood up, and took a long last look at her *Madonna*, hovering on the brink of her moment of truth, and knew that hunger was not the cause of her faintness.

Two days later, she returned to the convent of San Marco to look again at the Fra Angelico frescoes in the monks' cells. Long and hard she studied each ascetic image and was filled with elation. Her mind was made up; she knew exactly how she wished to spend the rest of her life.

Towards the end of her course, Emma began to make enquiries, and with the help of Signor Petacci soon found exactly the diploma course she had in mind. She wrote to her father for his approval and financial support for three further years in Florence, both of which he gladly gave. When everything had been arranged, Emma wrote, slightly guiltily, to her mother, telling her of her plans. In order to turn away Flavia's possible disapproval, she described at some length her aspiration to be a painter of sacred frescoes. Flavia's response was ecstatic; she could not imagine a more glorious way of bringing joy to the hearts and minds of the faithful, or even bringing about the conversion of the unbeliever. She expressed her profound regret that her own talents had not led her in such a noble direction, but had withered away, stifled by the confines of married life.

The course, though fascinating and deeply rewarding, was physically arduous, and at the end of each day Emma felt exhausted and emotionally drained, so intensely did she apply herself to the work. She continued to board with the Petacci family, who treated her like a daughter. They endeavoured both to protect Emma, and equally to introduce her to young people they considered socially acceptable. In spite of their enthusiastic efforts on her behalf, Emma's career as a debutante was a spectacular flop. In the first place, she found the local young Italian males of good family too smartly dressed for her taste, too well groomed and overpoweringly scented, and extraordinarily rapacious in their behaviour towards the female sex, especially the English. Their strongly held conviction appeared to be that all English girls were entirely unable to resist their overheated advances, and lost little time in making this perfectly clear. Affronted by this offensive attitude, Emma was not slow to disabuse them. To add insult to injury, she rapidly learned how to defuse their ardour by launching into long accounts of the intricacies of laying an *intonaco* or making a *sinopia*, and took malicious pleasure in observing their eyes glaze over with boredom, before they excused themselves and made a sharp exit. At the end of three months of such fruitless socializing, the local talent drifted away, and the Petacci family were unable to lure any more young men in Emma's direction, to her profound relief.

Her days at the painting school were a constant joy and inspiration to her, and as the months and then the years passed she fell into a routine of work, eating and sleeping that seemed to suit her temperament exactly. When she thought about it, which was not often, Emma felt little regret at the lack of male companionship, much less the idea of love and marriage becoming a possible part of her life. Her own parents' marriage seemed to her to be a cold affair, a polite charade of barely concealed indifference, even hostility. Presumably her father's successful career gave his existence meaning and the satisfaction of achievement, but her mother's daily life appeared to Emma to be an exercise in absolute futility. The very last thing she wished for herself was the boredom and humiliation of such a destiny, and her dearest wish was to continue exactly as she was, doing the work she loved more than anything else.

The course came to an end, Emma got her diploma, and had to consider her next move. At the age of twenty-two she was intact, so to speak, both physically and mentally. Apart from the odd bottom-pinching episode on Italian public transport and a couple of swiftly avoided embraces from the Petacci young men, Emma's sexual experience remained completely non-existent. Sometimes, gazing out of her window at Fiesole on warm spring evenings, she wondered a little uneasily if she was missing out in some way, or whether, perhaps, she was actually frigid, that there would never be a place for a man in her life. Certainly, she had yet to meet one who raised the slightest response in herself. Slowly, little by little, the idea of becoming a postulant nun grew in her mind. She saw herself very clearly, her sleeves rolled up, wrapped in a stout apron, making a *sinopia* on a freshly laid *intonaco* of plaster, and the thought filled her with confidence and happiness. What a privilege to do such work, all alone, cut off from the necessity of subscribing to the social interaction unavoidable in the lives of most people. How wonderful to live in a beautiful, sparsely furnished building with only a small bare space to call your own. How appealing to escape from the hassle of having to think about shopping and cooking, and all the other humdrum tasks that occupy most people's lives, she told herself decisively.

Emma returned to London, to her mother's house. Before discussing her ideas with either of her parents, she went back to her old convent and asked the advice of the Mother Superior. She explained to her old mentor what she had been learning to do in Italy, and what it was she now had in mind. 'Do you think that it is completely out of the question that a vocation could be expressed in such a way? Making religious images?'

'Certainly it could, my dear. Many nuns bring exceptional gifts and aptitudes to the religious life. One nun I know is a bookbinder, and makes exquisite illuminated books in beautiful leather bindings. Some compose new music for chants, as well as playing various instruments. Others are computer literate and specialize in that kind of thing, completely beyond me, I'm sorry to say. Some nuns are wonderful cooks and bakers, and some work miracles with needles and sewing machines and take care of all the linen and the making of habits. In the Cistercian abbey the talents are many and varied. Everyone contributes to the weight of prayer that is our prime function, but some nuns are able to offer particular specialities that enrich the life of the whole community, and sometimes earn much-needed revenue, into the bargain.'

'So you think I might be able to enter with the idea of doing such work as mine?'

'How convinced are you that you have a vocation at all, Emma?'

'Well, the general idea appeals to me very much, and I can't think of anything else I'd *rather* do. But I couldn't put my hand on my heart and say for sure that I don't have doubts. I did have a strange experience a few years ago; I wondered then if it could be a sign, but I don't really know if it was, or not.'

The Mother Superior smiled. 'Well, at least you're honest enough to admit that you have doubts. As a matter of fact, most of us have at the beginning.' She looked at the young woman across the familiar dark-oak desk that Emma remembered from her childhood. 'I think you should discuss it very carefully with your parents, and your priest. Then, if you still want to put your hopes of a vocation to the test, I could propose you as a postulant at the Abbaye de La Falaise in Britanny. Such a step would in no way commit you to the life. It would be in the nature of a probationary period, for both the postulant and the order.'

'And how long would that stage last?'

'Usually, about a year. Of course, I doubt if you would be allowed to exercise your special talents during that time. Postulants are expected to do all the general duties of the house; it is a question of hard work and long hours. It is the best way of finding out whether the life would suit you.'

'I see. And after that?'

'If you feel ready to continue, you become a novice. You take your first vows, and receive your first habit.'

'And the final vows?'

'They are the binding, life vows. It depends very much on the individual, but they are taken anything from four to six years later. Very often, of course, they are not taken at all.'

'I see. So, if I ask to be admitted as a postulant, I am not committed in any way?'

'That's exactly right. Neither side is committed at all.'

'Thank you, Mother,' said Emma. 'You've made it all very clear to me. I'll talk to my parents and Fr Gordon, and then come back to you, if I may?'

So, after long discussion with both her parents and Fr Gordon, and in spite of the strongly worded doubts of Ludovic, who expressed his regret that she had had so little experience of the real world before taking such a step, Emma entered the Abbaye de La Falaise as a postulant. A year later, she took her first vows, confident that after the willingly offered drudgery of the probationary year, it would not be long before her hopes and dreams would be fulfilled.

Now, unable to sleep, Emma lay on her hard bed, reflecting bitterly on the realities of her two years as a novice nun. Far from being singled out from the other nuns, and given the opportunity to practise her skills, every modest approach on the subject from herself had been met with a cold and negative response from the Abbess, who seemed to think such a request somehow frivolous. It never occurred to Emma that the fact that she had a strong pair of arms, ideal for heavy work in the fields, and could also drive a tractor might have something to do with the old woman's reluctance to release her from the daily agricultural labour so vital to the maintenance of the community.

Disappointed, and deeply depressed on a daily basis at her own inability to accept the position in the convent hierarchy forced upon her, Emma nevertheless did her best to hold on to the belief that if she persevered, enduring the mortification of mind and body she had suffered for so long, somehow the Lord's intentions for her would be made clear to her superiors and she would eventually be freed, to fulfil her potential as a religious artist. Only then, she knew, would she be able to make a meaningful contribution to the life of the community, and find the personal spiritual ecstasy that had appeared to be such a possibility on that day at Monterchi, when the *Madonna del Parto* had seemed to speak to her in such a spectacular manner. She stared miserably at the crucifix on the bare stone wall at the foot of her narrow bed, and wondered what else she had to do, what more was expected of her, to enable her to break out of the trap of boredom and frustration in which she found herself.

She got out of bed, folding back the single coarse brown blanket, and took off her cotton shift. She stood against the rough wall of her cell, and deliberately scraped her back against it, until she was sitting on the cold stone floor, her jaw clenched, tears of anguish falling silently down her face. Getting to her knees, she prostrated herself on the floor, her arms outstretched. Shivering with cold, she prayed for mercy, for forgiveness and salvation. Then she got up, and put a hand behind her back to see whether it was still bleeding; it was, quite badly. Still naked, she got back into bed, and lay face down on top of the blanket, in order not to stain the undersheet with her blood. She listened to the wistful song of a bird in the orchard, far below her small square open window. How beautiful, she thought, perhaps it's an early nightingale. Presently, she fell asleep, and dreamed of mixing her pigments with egg tempera, on a glass plate, and applying them to a freshly laid *intonaco* of fine sand and lime. Against the delicately drawn leaves of a tree, she painted a soft brown nightingale, perched on a slender branch, his haunting nocturne pouring from his joyfully open throat.

Christian McGrath felt bored, and at a loose end. He wished that it was Friday and his day for going down to Abbot's Court, especially as the weather was so pleasant. London was beginning to be quite hot and humid, and he knew that in the West Country it would be several degrees cooler and much fresher. In a couple of days he would be there, and maybe he could take Alex sailing on the river. In the meantime he felt irritated that his dinner engagement had been cancelled at the last minute. The excuse had sounded rather lame. Those bloody Parkinsons, he thought, it'll be one of their matrimonial crises, no doubt. Why the hell don't they learn to make the best of things, like we all have to; go with the flow, grin and bear it? Surely they could put on some sort of show, for the sake of the kids, at the very least? Moodily, he stared out of the windows of his rooms, at the quiet, empty street below, peaceful in the early evening. Goddamnit, this is a pain, he said to himself. I'll go and see Ma and kill two birds with one stone; get her off my conscience, and cadge some supper off her.

He took a cab to Camden Town, and stood for a moment looking at the narrow little Georgian house in which he had been born and spent his early childhood.

I must say, he thought, I'm glad Phoebe and I decided not to live in the city; it's really no place to bring up children. It's incredible that this place would fetch about the same as Abbot's Court. Just as well, I presume the old girl will leave it to me when she pops her clogs, now that Emma's out of the picture. That's always assuming Dad goes first. Unless, of course, I could persuade her to hand it over to me now, to avoid death duties. Good idea; I'll choose my moment, and put it to her tactfully.

As things turned out, that was not the moment. He had forgotten to bring his latchkey, so he stuck his hand through the letterbox, trying to locate the string on which he knew Flavia kept her spare key, but was unable to find it. He knocked and then rang, and when Flavia finally came to the door, in response to his repeated assaults on the bell, it soon became clear that she was somewhat the worse for drink. He could hear her behind the door, and saw the letterbox opening and closing as she tried to peer through it. Christian knelt on the step and met her suspicious gaze through the letterbox. 'Open the door, Ma! It's me, Christian!'

'Oh, darling! Wait a moment!'

A passer-by looked at him as he knelt on the step, and laughed. 'Lost yer key, mate?'

Christian ignored him and got hastily to his feet, as the door opened. Pushing Flavia aside impatiently, he entered the house and slammed the door behind him. 'Ma, you're drunk, as usual. What am I going to do with you? Where's Dad? I thought he was going to spend some time in London, for a bloody change?'

'Oh,' said Flavia, with a tinkling laugh, wavering down the hall towards the kitchen, 'he did come, but he could only stay a night; he had to rush off again. Poor thing, he's such a very busy man, isn't he?' She looked up at Christian, her blue eyes roguish, her greying blond hair untidy, her sagging cheeks pink.

'I've got a visitor, darling,' she whispered. 'Do come and meet him!'

Christian followed his mother into the kitchen. There, sitting at the plastic-topped table, a glass of whisky in front of him, together with an impressive assortment of cocktail nibbles on little dishes, sat Fr Gordon, looking acutely embarrassed.

Jesus, thought Christian, taking the priest's damp proffered hand and accepting a glass of whisky, this is all I bloody need; a session with one of Ma's creepy little clerics.

Chapter Three

Phoebe knelt on the damp grass beneath the tall, clipped yew hedge that enclosed her special secret garden, planting Regale lily bulbs. She expected them to flower, white, fruity-smelling and magnificent, in the late summer, spectacular against the green-black hedge. The small garden, barely four metres square, was laid to lawn with an armillary sundial on a stone column in the centre. It was a very private place for Phoebe, calm and comforting. In the spring the grass was carpeted with snowdrops, and in early summer Iceberg roses, lax and floppy, pure white and exquisitely scented, flowered extravagantly in each of the four corners. After the summer glory of the lilies had passed and the little place was bare once more, a green space with only the soft blue verdigris of the armillary to relieve its severity, Phoebe still visited it from time to time, when she felt more than usually stressed. Now, as she tenderly buried each precious bulb in its dark, well-manured bed, she pondered her marriage and wondered whether Chris was unfaithful to her. She suspected that he found her dull, rather slow-witted and socially inept. Nonetheless, she was quite aware that he valued her capacity to look after their house and garden so well, and was inordinately proud of Abbot's Court. He was always enchanted to show the place off to visitors, though he rarely acknowledged publicly his wife's enormous contribution to its maintenance.

For Phoebe herself, the ownership and care of the property was an end in itself; she had no need, or indeed desire, for an audience to applaud her efforts. She did not find it at all pleasurable to have the place inspected, even by friends, and she stubbornly resisted all Christian's efforts to induce her to allow her garden to be opened to the public. Every time she drove past one of those yellow posters saying 'Garden Open Today' she shuddered, vowing never to give way to her husband's wishes on the subject, however persistent he might be. Phoebe sighed, and sat back on her heels, inspecting the neatly raked soft black earth close to the hedge, and the tiny pink shoots of the lily bulbs just above the surface. Darling things, she thought, and smiled, marvelling that such a wizened, distorted, dead-looking corm would be able to produce such a stunningly beautiful flower in the space of a few short months. She looked at her watch: five-forty. She wondered whether there was still time to finish planting the last couple of metres, or whether she should really go and round up the children for their supper, and check whether Alexander had any prep still to do. Just another ten minutes, she thought, and moved to her right, dragging the trug of bulbs with her. She had just thrust her trowel into the earth once more, when she heard Gwen's voice, high, urgent, calling her name. 'Phoebe! Phoebe! Where are you?'

Good heavens! thought Phoebe. Whatever's up? She got to her feet, calling, 'I'm here, Gwen; what's the matter?' She stepped through the arch in the yew hedge onto the main lawn, and saw Gwen running towards her, her face flushed, distraught. Phoebe began to run and they met in the middle of the grass.

'There's been an accident,' Gwen gasped, holding her side. 'It's Chloe. She's unconscious.'

'Where?'

'In the road; a motorbike.'

'Where's Alexander?'

'In the kitchen.'

Phoebe felt unnaturally calm. 'I'll go to her,' she said firmly. 'You phone the ambulance, Gwen, please.'

'Right,' said Gwen.

Phoebe ran across the grass and under the entrance arch, crossed the gravel courtyard, then hurled herself down the winding drive through the trees to the lane below. At the gate, she looked from side to side but could see nothing, then, her heart pounding, she opted to go to the right, up the hill. She had made the right choice, for as she ran as fast as she could round the next bend, she saw the motorbike lying on its side and a young man in black leathers sitting on the grassy bank, holding the still body of Chloe in his arms. As she reached his side, Phoebe noticed with detachment that tears were running down his face. She knelt beside him and he gently transferred the unconscious child to her arms. Chloe felt incredibly limp, almost weightless, as Phoebe cradled her, desperately trying to assess the damage. Her clothes were bloodstained, torn and dirty, and, in the crook of her own arm, Phoebe could feel the warmth of the blood which flowed from the matted hair at the base of Chloe's skull, and was soaking into her own sleeve. The little girl's eyes were closed, her small face unbelievably pale.

'What happened?' asked Phoebe, her voice seeming to come from a great distance.

'There was nothing I could do.' The young man's voice was thick with tears. 'She just leapt down the bank in front of me; I couldn't stop in time. I wasn't going fast, it's such a twisty narrow lane. She just went right over the bike and into that tree on the other side. I think she hit her head on that big root, poor little girl.' He began to weep again, harsh racking sobs.

'Don't cry,' said Phoebe. 'I'm sure you're not to blame.' He did not seem to hear her words, or, if he did, could find no comfort in them. They sat there for what seemed like an eternity, then the urgent wail of the ambulance sounded far off, then drew nearer and nearer, until the vehicle drew to a stop close to them, and two paramedics jumped out and ran towards them. One of them put a hand on Chloe's neck, then put his ear to her chest. He looked at Phoebe. 'When did the accident happen?'

'Just now.'

'How long ago? Ten minutes? Half an hour?'

'About twenty minutes,' said the young man.

The paramedic put a brace round Chloe's neck, and strapped her carefully to a stretcher. 'We must get her to the hospital as fast as possible, to have any chance at all.' He turned to Phoebe. 'Are you the mother?'

'Yes.'

'Do you want to come with her?'

'Yes, of course.'

As they drove away, Phoebe looked through the rear window and saw that the young man had sat down again on the grassy bank. He had taken off his helmet and his forehead rested on his leather-clad knees. He had a shaven head.

At the hospital they took Chloe away and told Phoebe to wait. She asked the receptionist whether she could use the telephone to call home.

'Yes, of course. Help yourself.'

Gwen answered the phone at once.

'They've taken her to be scanned, I think,' said Phoebe. 'I've got to wait.'

'Is she all right?' Gwen sounded anxious.

'I don't know. I've got to wait. She's unconscious still.' Gwen said nothing. 'Have you phoned Christian?' Phoebe went on, in the same flat, calm voice.

'Yes, he's on his way. He'll go straight to the hospital from the station; he thought that would be best.'

'Yes, that seems sensible,' said Phoebe. 'How's Alexander?' she added, almost as an afterthought.

Gwen hesitated, unwilling to add to Phoebe's burden. 'He's very upset, of course. I phoned the police, and they came out to question him about the accident, but he seemed unwilling to talk to them. They'll come again tomorrow, when you're here. Poor boy, I think he's blaming himself.'

There was a pause. 'Well. I'd better get off this phone, Gwen. I'll wait here till Christian turns up.'

'Yes, that's probably best. Goodbye, dear.'

'Goodbye.' Phoebe hung up.

She sat down on a bench and waited. At a little after half past seven, a tall man wearing pale-blue overalls that looked as though they were made of J-cloths, with a matching cap covering his hair, came down the corridor and spoke to the receptionist, who nodded in Phoebe's direction. Phoebe stood up, her legs like jelly, her stomach in turmoil, as the man in blue approached.

'Mrs McGrath?'

'Yes.'

'Come with me, will you, please?'

He took her elbow and led her to a small side-room. There he told her that Chloe had not regained consciousness. The impact with the tree had broken her neck. She was, in fact, dead. Stunned, unable to grasp the full implications of the surgeon's terrible words, Phoebe stared at him blankly. 'Is there nothing you can do?' she stammered at last. 'Put her on a life-support machine, that sort of thing?'

'It was too late, I'm afraid. Even if we had managed to resuscitate her, after such a long time without oxygen, she would have been seriously brain-damaged.'

'I'd rather have her brain-damaged than dead,' said Phoebe stubbornly, refusing to believe that there was no hope, nothing to be done.

'I'm very sorry indeed,' said the surgeon. 'I have children myself; I know how you must be feeling.'

'No you don't,' said Phoebe rudely. 'They're not dead, are they?'

'Is anyone coming to be with you?'

'Yes. My husband is on his way here. I'll wait till he comes.'

The surgeon hesitated, then spoke gently. 'Would you like to see your little girl, Mrs McGrath?'

'Yes, I would.'

Chloe lay on a high bed, surrounded by a formidable number of machines, none of which appeared to be in use. A sheet was pulled right up to her small pointed chin, and her fair hair was spread damply on the pillow. She looks as if she's just sleeping, Phoebe thought, my poor little baby. She bent and kissed Chloe's forehead. It was as cold as ice, and felt hard, like stone. Shocked, Phoebe recoiled from the unexpectedly reptilian touch of her child's skin against her lips, and in that moment she understood that there was no hope, that Chloe was dead. She turned to the surgeon, her dark eyes full of despair in her round soft face. He put his arms round her. 'I'm so sorry,' he said again.

The door opened, and a nurse in a dark-blue uniform appeared. 'I'll take care of Mrs McGrath,' she said. She led Phoebe to another room, gave her a cup of tea and talked to her quite kindly for what seemed like hours. Phoebe did not cry, or say very much. She waited for Christian to come. When he arrived, it felt like the middle of the night; in fact, it was only half past nine. 'Hello,' said Phoebe. 'Have you seen her?'

Christian's face was grim, but his fair skin was flushed and his blue eyes unnaturally bright, like those of a child on the brink of tears. Phoebe stood up and Christian put his arms around her and held her tight. 'Yes,' he said. 'I've seen her. Poor little girl.'

Phoebe held on to him, her eyes closed. 'Have you seen the doctors? Do we have to inform the coroner, or anything?' She took deep breaths, struggling not to lose control. 'Have you got a car? Can we go home now?'

'I've seen them. They'll take care of everything.'

'Can we take Chloe home with us?'

'No, not now. But after the formalities, the undertakers will bring her to Abbot's Court, if that's what you want?' Christian sounded extremely strained, his voice shook a little.

'Is that what you'd like, darling?' asked Phoebe, gently.

'Well, we have got the oratory, haven't we? It's still got a licence to celebrate Mass; it would be so much more friendly to have the funeral there, wouldn't it? And Mother would like it, of course.'

'I suppose so.' Phoebe did not feel that she had an opinion on the most suitable place for a funeral. It seemed to her to be entirely irrelevant. After all, it could not matter to Chloe, could it? She would not be there. 'Whatever you feel is right, darling,' she added, her heart like lead. 'Let's go home.'

The hired car and driver were waiting in the car park, and they drove home through the darkening lanes. As soon as she saw them, Gwen knew that Chloe was dead. She said nothing, but led the way to the kitchen, where she had some soup on the stove. Alexander was sitting at the table, and he looked up as they came in. 'It's all my fault, Mum,' he said. 'I was chasing her through the woods. It wasn't the biker's fault, it was mine.'

'She's dead,' said Phoebe, staring at him, and a sharp stab of pain shot through her, so that she sat down heavily on a chair, bent double.

'Dead? What do you mean, *dead*?' Alexander got to his feet, scraping the floor with his chair. He looked wildly from one of his parents to the other.

'She's dead,' repeated Phoebe. Her voice rose in a shrill wail. 'You've killed her! My poor little Chloe, you've killed her!' She began to cry, a horrible deep wrenching sound.

Christian, horrified, took a step towards his son, but

Alexander turned on his heel and rushed from the room, banging the door behind him.

'I'll go after him,' said Gwen.

'No, leave him for a bit.' Christian knelt beside Phoebe, his arms around her heaving body. He looked at Gwen with frightened eyes. 'Call the doctor, Gwen,' he said. 'I'll talk to Alex later.'

Flavia had gone to bed when the telephone rang. She was not actually in bed, but saying her prayers for the night, kneeling at her prie-dieu. Startled, she opened her eyes and looked at her watch: ten to eleven. Who could be ringing at such a late hour? She got to her feet and went to the far side of her bed, where the extension phone sat on a night-table, beside the lamp and her stack of books. She picked it up. 'Hello?'

'Ma? It's me, Christian.'

'Hello, darling. Is anything the matter?'

'Yes, I'm afraid it is.' In a low, halting voice, quite unlike his usual brisk tone, he told his mother what had happened. 'Alexander and Chloe were playing a game in the woods. Alex was chasing her and she ran down the slope and into the road, right in the path of a motorbike.'

'How terrible, Christian. I'm so sorry.'

'Poor Alex. He blames himself for chasing her.'

'Yes, he would, poor boy. I shall pray for God's forgiveness for him,' said Flavia. 'Did she suffer, the little one?'

'No, they don't think she could have felt anything at all after the impact.'

'God is merciful, darling.'

Christian sighed, sounding exhausted. 'Ma, I was wondering, could you phone Dad, and Emma and everyone? I'll talk to Phoebe's father, I expect he'll want to come to the funeral.'

'When *is* the funeral, darling?'

'I thought Thursday if we can arrange it. Here, in the

oratory, then the RC cemetery. I suppose it would be nice if one of your brothers could say the Mass?'

'What a lovely idea,' said Flavia.

'Well, I'd better get on now, Ma, and talk to Phoebe's family. I'll call you tomorrow, OK?'

'Yes, of course, and I'll telephone your father in Brussels. How is poor Phoebe?'

'Not good.'

'That's very understandable. I shall pray for her, of course.'

'Thanks. Goodbye for the moment, Ma.'

'Goodbye, darling.' Flavia hung up, and sat on the edge of her bed, staring at the phone. A vision of the delicate little girl, so fair-skinned and blonde, with such intensely blue eyes, rose before her and gentle tears filled her eyes. But how wonderful, she thought, what a divine intervention to die so young and in a state of such perfect grace. She does not need my tears, or my prayers to help her; she will have gone straight to heaven, the darling child. Nevertheless, she got up and lit one of the many votive candles that stood in readiness before the statue of Our Lady, and repeated some of the prayers for the dead. Then she picked up the phone again and dialled Ludovic's number in Brussels. She got his answering service and left a message asking him to ring her urgently, first thing in the morning. She decided to delay telephoning Emma, and her brother in Huddersfield, until the morning. In the meantime, she would write to her sister Alice, in Spain, and her brother Anselm in Zaire, asking them to pray for Chloe, since they were unlikely to be able to attend the funeral at such short notice. After she had written the letters, and stamped them ready for posting, Flavia went downstairs to make herself a cup of tea. She felt wide awake, and curiously elated, as if the necessity of making calls and writing letters had released a latent energy in her. She was not conscious of the fact, but she felt quite excited at the thought of the Requiem Mass in the oratory at Abbot's Court. What a fortunate circumstance that they have such a place, she thought, so private and beautiful; and how lucky that we can keep it in the family, no need for any outsiders at all, no intrusions of any kind. She poured a drop of brandy into her tea and began to plan the flowers.

Chloe's small white coffin was brought to Abbot's Court and installed on a trestle in the oratory. Phoebe, heavily sedated, was still lying in bed in the tower, alternately weeping and sleeping, with Christian in constant attendance at her side. Gwen, assisted by Jim from the village, swept and dusted the rarely used oratory, and polished the oak benches. She went out into the garden and picked all the white flowering things she could find, wild plum blossom, some narcissi and a few long strands of clematis *montana* in bud. She found two tall glass jars and made identical sprawling arrangements, 'tangles' Phoebe called them, one for each side of the foot of the coffin. The little white box on its trestle looked sad and lonely in that pale stone space, harshly lit by its lancet windows, and Gwen went upstairs to Phoebe's linen closet. There, she found what she was looking for, a cream linen tablecloth with a deep heavy lace border, brought back from Cyprus after Phoebe's honeymoon. She took it down to the oratory and draped it carefully over the coffin, so that it fell in soft folds to the stone floor. She straightened the cloth, smoothing out the creases with her hands. Uncertain of the proper ritual, she wondered about candles. The small flame in its red glass lamp burned, as usual, before the tabernacle, but that was all. I'd better wait and ask Christian, she said to herself. A little self-consciously, because she was Wee Free herself, Gwen made the sign of the cross for Chloe and said a short private prayer for the repose of the little girl's soul. Then she left the oratory, closing the door behind her in case the dogs should go in, and went upstairs to prepare the bedrooms for the visiting relatives. Mrs McGrath and her brother Fr Benedict were expected this afternoon; Mr McGrath and Emma later this evening. It seemed that the other grandfather, Phoebe's father, was not coming. He was abroad on business, but was sending a wreath.

Alexander had observed the arrival of the coffin. He had concealed himself in the upper floor of the barn, among the pigeon droppings and smelly feathers, crouching uncomfortably, his knees under his chin, in the stone embrasure of the narrow window over-looking the courtyard far below. Miserably, he had observed the comings and goings of the morning. First came the postman in his little red van, a nice burly young man in trainers, a friend of Alexander's. He got out of the van and glanced nervously round the courtyard, as if the idea of meeting someone from that stricken household appalled him. Then he opened the grey-painted door to the cupboard set in the stone wall to the left of the kitchen door and hastily stuffed the mail into it. He gave another rapid glance round, jumped back into his van, did a U-turn and drove off, his tyres skidding slightly on the gravel. Poor bloke, thought Alexander, he can't wait to get away. He's not the only one, I wish I could get away, far away, try to forget; pretend it never happened.

The police had been quite nice really, quite sym-pathetic. They had not been angry or seemed to blame him for the accident. 'It was an accident,' they had said, several times. 'These things happen; it was no-one's fault.' They had come twice to talk to him; once before Mum came back from the hospital, and once after. The chief inspector was a nice man, quite old, with silver hair like Grandpa.

'Tell me, Alexander, in your own words, exactly what happened. Take your time.'

'Um, we were playing a game, Chloe and me.'

'What kind of game? How do you play it?'

'Well, one of us is "it", that was Chloe, and the other one, that was me, shuts his eyes and counts to fifteen. Then he can open them again and if he can see the "it" person he shouts "Gotcher" and then he can chase and catch the "it" person.'

'Is that all?'

'Well, it's quite fun really, because the "it" person can run from tree to tree while the other one is counting, and hide behind them, so it's quite hard to know where the "it" person has got to, if you see what I mean?'

'Yes, I see. So then what happened?'

'Well, Chloe had got quite far away from me. She's very thin, you see, so she can hide behind quite young trees very easily. Then suddenly I saw her red skirt sticking out and I shouted "Gotcher" and began to run after her, but she ran away fast through the trees, down the slope towards the lane. I did call out to her to stop, but she only laughed and kept on running, and disappeared into the bushes. I couldn't see her then.'

'Then what happened, Alexander?' asked the chief inspector gently.

'I heard a horrible noise of tyres skidding, down in the lane.'

'Then?'

'Then I ran down the bank to the lane.'

'What did you find there?'

'I found the biker sitting on the other side of the lane holding Chloe. The man was crying. Chloe was all bloody and dirty; she looked to be knocked out. Her eyes were shut.'

'What did you do then?'

'I said, "I'll go and get someone to help," and the biker said, "Thanks," and I ran as fast as I could to Gwen and told her.'

'That's Miss Nicolson?'

'Yes, that's right.'

'Thank you, Alexander. You've been very helpful indeed.'

'It wasn't the biker's fault,' Alexander had said insistently, as if he thought it important that they understoood, 'it was mine. If I hadn't chased her, it wouldn't have happened.'

'It was no-one's *fault* at all,' repeated the chief inspector firmly. 'It was simply a tragic accident. Unfortunately, these things do happen.'

'Yes,' agreed Alexander, but he had sounded unconvinced. He had taken the two policemen to the woods and shown them how Chloe had flitted from tree to tree, and how she had then broken cover and run away down the steep slope towards the lane. Then the chief inspector had gone up to the tower with Dad to talk to Mum, and Alexander had climbed the ladder to the upper floor of the barn and had watched from his window until the police car drove away. It had not had its siren going, but the flashing blue light had been on.

After the postman came the milkman, and Alexander watched as Gwen came to the kitchen door and spoke to him. He got two more bottles of milk and a large carton of yoghurt from the van and gave them to Gwen, then they stood for a moment, talking quietly. Alexander could not hear their voices, but he saw Gwen shake her head several times. The milkman got back into his van and drove off, and Gwen went back into the house.

The stable clock gave a rusty-sounding wheeze and struck twelve as the long black shiny car with glass sides came slowly out of the darkness of the wooded drive, and stopped in the middle of the courtyard, immediately below Alexander's hiding place. Four men in black got out of the car, as Gwen emerged from the kitchen. She spoke to the men, and pointed towards the arch in the high yew hedge. Alexander guessed that she must be telling them to bring Chloe in through the front entrance, rather than go through the kitchen. He watched as they lifted the tailgate of the car, slid Chloe's white coffin out, then, carrying it on their shoulders, disappeared under the arch, followed by Gwen. In his mind's eye he could see the little procession going through the garden, across the lawn, under the arched entrance next to the tower, carrying Chloe down the long echoing hall and into the oratory. He was surprised that it needed four men to carry such a small box. They seemed to be a long time inside the house, and he wondered what they could be doing. Had they opened the lid to see whether Chloe had got shoggled about on the way there? Or maybe they had little wedges to stop the bodies sliding about? What if she wasn't dead at all, only in a coma? She might wake up and knock on the lid to be let out and no-one would hear her, how horrible that would be. The hair on Alexander's scalp prickled and he shuddered involuntarily. His head ached, he had a stiff neck and his chest felt tight. He wished that he could cry, like Mum, but he could not, though his eyes felt swollen and painful with unshed tears. Even at night, in bed, he couldn't cry, though he tried very hard to do so, even banging his nose several times with his clenched fist to induce the tears, without success.

At last the four men came out of the kitchen door, and Gwen shook hands with one of them. They got back into the black car, and the driver did a neat three-point turn, then drove away quite fast, disappearing into the trees. Gwen stood at the door for a moment, looking vaguely round the courtyard and up at the barn. Alexander drew back and flattened himself against the stone embrasure. He heard Gwen's voice as she called his name, though not very loudly or urgently. He stayed silently where he was. The next time he looked, she had gone in again and closed the door.

*   *   *

Flavia arrived at Abbot's Court in the middle of the afternoon. She had been driven down by her brother, Fr Benedict, in his old Morris Traveller, accompanied by her other brother, Fr Anselm, fortuitously on leave from his African mission and staying with Benedict in Huddersfield. The air inside the vehicle was heavy with the scent of the pots of tuberose and jasmine, stacked in the rear of the car and intended for the decoration of the oratory.

Gwen came out of the house to greet them. She and Flavia embraced solemnly, and Gwen shook the hands of the two priests. She was surprised to see Fr Anselm, but said nothing, merely allocating him a room in her mind, and allocating for herself the time to make up the bed for him.

'Poor souls,' said Flavia, in a sepulchral voice, 'what a terrible tragedy. How are they bearing it, Gwen?'

'I'm afraid Phoebe is quite devastated. She's been sedated by the doctor, so she sleeps for quite a lot of the time. It's best, really.' The two priests nodded, making sympathetic murmurs.

'She *will* be able to attend the funeral, one presumes?' Flavia's tone was suddenly quite sharp. 'She must be at her own child's Requiem Mass, it goes without saying.'

'I expect she will be, Mrs McGrath,' said Gwen quietly. She took them into the house and showed them to their rooms.

'Where's Christian?' asked Flavia. 'And the boy? Where is he?'

'Phoebe is deeply asleep just now, so they've taken the dogs for a walk. Christian hasn't been out for days, he needed some air, poor man.'

'I see.'

Gwen went downstairs and prepared a tray of tea for the visitors. She took it to the drawing room and put it on the coffee table in front of the small fire she had made for the sake of cheerfulness, since it was a chilly, grey day. She poured a cup of tea and went up to Phoebe's room to see if she was awake. She knocked on the door and went in. Phoebe was lying on her back, her eyes open, staring at the pretty plaster ceiling above her head. As Gwen approached with the tea, she turned her head and smiled faintly, and her hand moved slightly as it lay on the coverlet.

'I've brought you some tea, dear.'

'Thanks, I'd love some.' Phoebe tried to raise herself on her elbow.

'Hang on, I'll plump up the pillows.' Gwen put the tea on the night-table, and stacked the pillows.

Phoebe leaned back against them gratefully, and taking the cup from Gwen she drank the cooling tea in one go. 'What's happening?' she asked, not sounding as if she really wanted to know. 'I thought I heard voices.'

'You did. It's Mrs McGrath and her two brothers. They arrived about half an hour ago.'

'*Both* her brothers? The two old priests?'

'I'm afraid so,' said Gwen. 'In fact, if you're OK for a bit, I must go and make up Father Anselm's bed.'

'Oh, Gwen, I'm so sorry. I've left everything to you, haven't I? I must get up, and try and pull myself together.'

'You stay where you are, at least until Christian gets back. He won't be long now, I'm sure.'

'Well, perhaps I will. I don't feel much like coping with her just yet. Don't let her come up, Gwen, please.'

'Don't worry, I'll tell her you're still sleeping.' Gwen took Phoebe's cup and went to the door.

'Gwen?'

'Mm?' Gwen paused, her fingers on the doorknob.

'Did they bring Chloe home?'

'Yes, dear, they did; this morning. She's in the

oratory. I went out and got some blossom and stuff from the garden, and made a pair of tangles for her; nothing fancy, just like the ones you do.'

'Thank you.' Phoebe's face looked blotchy, and Gwen looked at her anxiously, in case she should break down again. 'It's all right, Gwen. I can't cry any more. I don't think I've got any tears left. You go and cope with them, I'll be OK now.' She was wrong.

Christian and Alexander had walked across three fields to the river, and were now on their way back. The two yellow labradors, fat elderly Winnie and her daughter Nell, walked sedately at Christian's heels. Usually, Alexander threw sticks for them, but today he did not, and the dogs seemed to understand that he was not feeling like it. Christian felt uneasy. Alexander had said very little during their walk, and had made no mention of either Chloe or Phoebe. He was polite, but rather distant and detached, and kept his eyes on the ground as they walked. I must talk to him, said Christian to himself, otherwise I won't get another chance to have him on his own. Ma and the old black beetle will have arrived by now, and then Dad and Emma will come. He cleared his throat nervously. 'Alex?'

'Yes, Dad?'

'You remember when I brought your mother back from the hospital?'

'Yes, I remember.'

'You remember what she said?'

'You mean about me killing Chloe?'

'She didn't mean it, old chap. You do understand that, don't you?'

Briefly, Alexander looked up at his father, then turned his eyes to the ground again. He said nothing.

'It was just a stupid hysterical reaction. She had to blame someone for the accident. She didn't mean it, of

74

course. I don't suppose she even knows that she said it. It's all a ghastly blur now.'

'Yes, I expect so,' said Alexander. She did mean it though, he thought, and she was right; it was my fault. I kept saying so.

'Well, good,' said Christian, 'as long as we understand each other. Women can be tricky sometimes. Often say things they don't really mean, you know.'

'Yes.'

'OK, then? No problems?'

'No.'

They crossed the last field and made their way through the cows, over the stile and into the garden. They went into the house, and Christian turned into the library, intending to go through the glass court and up to the tower. He hesitated, and turned back to his son. 'Would you like to come up and say hello to Mum, old chap? I'm sure she'd like to see you.'

'No, it's OK, Dad. I'll take the dogs to the kitchen.'

'OK,' said Christian. 'Perhaps that's best.'

Alexander carried on down the hall to the dining room, and saw with some surprise that the table was laid for a formal dinner. He went through to the kitchen, where he found Gwen, rolling pastry. 'Have they come?' he asked.

'Yes, they have.'

'Where are they?'

'They're in the oratory, I think. Your grandmother is doing the flowers.'

'I thought *you* did them, didn't you, Gwen, this morning? I saw you in the garden, picking them.'

'Well, I expect she knows best. There's some tea in the pot, if you want some.'

'I'd rather have a Coke, thanks.'

'In the larder, behind the beer.'

*   *   *

Flavia was in her element, transforming the oratory into a floral celebration of a child's brief life. She had moved Gwen's rather amateurish arrangements to less prominent positions on either side of the altar, and had surrounded the coffin with banks of her own tuberose and jasmine, supplemented with long arabesques of ivy obtained from the woods by Fr Benedict, on Flavia's instructions. She had brought with her several boxes of expensive tallow candles, proper holy ones. She had asked Gwen for a dozen jam-jars, into which she stuck candles and dispersed them through her flower arrangements. Gwen, on request, had also produced four tall silver candlesticks, and these Flavia disposed upon the altar, two on each side. She walked to the other end of the oratory and surveyed her handiwork. That's better, she thought, that's really lovely now, not so bare. She wished that Christian had put a few statues in the place. It really was awfully spartan in atmosphere, almost Protestant.

Fr Anselm and Fr Benedict came into the oratory together, looking purposeful.

'Hello,' said Flavia. 'Are you going to say prayers for the little one?'

'Well, we thought perhaps the Litany for the Dead might be appropriate?'

'Indeed,' said Flavia, and took her place in the front pew, kneeling before the coffin.

Alexander drank his Coke and ate a biscuit, then went out to the garden again, followed by the dogs. He got a bucket of horse nuts from the tack room and went down to the paddock to feed the ponies. When they had finished eating he took the bucket back to the tack room and hung it on its hook. He looked at his watch: ten to six. I wonder when Grandpa will get here, he thought; I do wish he'd come. He did not really like his grandmother very much, and was glad that she rarely came to Abbot's Court. In the first place, she was forever banging on about church, and in the second place, she smelt nasty, like rotten eggs. Grandpa was different. He was fun, and kind, and he listened to you. Best of all in Alexander's eyes, he was extremely cool, not given to forcing his opinions on you. In Alexander's short experience of life, very few grown-ups were like that.

He crossed the yard and went to the head of the drive to see whether he could hear the car coming. He could not, so he walked right round the back of the house until he came to the deep lancet windows of the oratory, now shimmering with unaccustomed light from within. Inside, he could hear droning voices and guessed that the old priests must be doing their thing already. Poor old Chloe, he thought, how boring. Bloody interfering old farts, why can't they leave her alone? He walked back the way he had come, ran across the gravelled courtyard and up the ladder to his hiding place. There he jammed himself into his window, silently cursing his grandmother and her daft old brothers under his breath.

Just as dusk was beginning to fall, Alexander heard the sound of a car and saw two beams of light flash across the yard. The car stopped and his Aunt Em got out, followed by his grandfather. He got stiffly down from his lookout and stumbled across the loft floor, down the ladder and out into the courtyard. As he ran, Ludovic turned to meet him and Alexander hurled himself into his arms, gasping for breath.

'Hello, young Alex, where did you spring from?'

'In the barn, waiting for you.'

Ludovic and Emma retrieved their bags from the back of the car, and Alexander took Emma's bag and led the way through the yew hedge to the garden entrance; he thought Gwen would prefer that.

'Are you all alone, Alexander?' asked Emma. 'Where is everyone?'

'Well, Gwen's cooking supper. Mum's in bed. Dad's

with her, and the others are hard at it, doing the heavy stuff with Chloe in the oratory.' Alexander cast a nervous eye at Emma's habit. 'Sorry, Aunt Em, I didn't mean . . .'

'Don't give it a thought,' she said, and smiled at him. 'I know exactly what you mean.'

Chapter Four

The next day, after lunch, Phoebe got out of bed, took a shower and dressed herself carefully in her grey London suit. The Requiem Mass was to take place at four o'clock in the oratory, and afterwards the undertakers would transfer the coffin to the cemetery for the interment. Everything had been organized, and Christian, with Gwen's help, was looking after the family visitors, so that all Phoebe was expected to do was attend the rites with as much dignity as she could manage. She had hoped that after that she would be able to retire once more to the sanctuary of her tower, but Christian had made it plain that he expected her to stay down for the dinner that he and Gwen had arranged. 'It would be very rude of you not to, when they have come so far to be with us,' he had said; 'it would hurt their feelings, and mine.' And what of *my* feelings? Phoebe said to herself, staring at her round white face reflected in the mirror, what of them? She expected that such a self-pitying thought would provoke a fresh bout of weeping, but it did not. In fact, she felt little actual physical pain at present, just a numb despair and hopelessness.

At twenty to four, Gwen appeared with a cup of tea. 'Do you mind if I sit down for a moment, Phoebe?'

'No, of course not!' Guiltily, Phoebe glanced at Gwen, who looked exhausted, and somehow diminished. Isolated in her own private grief, she had not given her a single thought. Now, she got up and, putting her arm round Gwen's shoulders, led her to the little armchair by a window, and sat down herself on the wide stone window seat. 'Poor Gwen, you must be dog-tired. I'm so sorry, I shouldn't have left it all to you; it was awful of me.'

'It's not that. I don't mind that at all. I'm thankful to have so much to do, really.'

'Yes, I can understand that.' Phoebe took a sip of her tea, and waited.

'I expect it's me being over-sensitive,' said Gwen. She hesitated, frowning. 'I really shouldn't bother you with it, especially at a time like this.'

'What's the matter? Tell me, Gwen, please.'

'It's nothing. I'm being stupid.'

'Tell me.'

Gwen sighed. 'It's the flowers. Mrs McGrath has taken mine away and replaced them with all the hot-house stuff she brought with her, and loads of candles.' She looked at Phoebe, sadly. 'I expect they're really very nice, it's just that I did what I thought you'd rather have.'

'Where are yours?'

'At the back, beside the altar.'

'Well, I can't really change them now, but I shall only look at yours, Gwen, I promise.'

Gwen got up and took the cup from Phoebe. 'I shouldn't have told you; it was silly of me. It's not that important.'

'It is to me, and to Chloe,' said Phoebe. She got up, put her arms round Gwen, and kissed her. 'I'm glad you warned me, anyway.' She looked at her watch. 'You go on down now, and I'll follow you in a couple of minutes.'

At the door, Gwen bumped into Christian, coming to take Phoebe down.

'Ready, darling?' he said to Phoebe.

'Yes, I'm ready.'

Christian and Phoebe sat close together on the front bench, and Alexander sat on his father's other side. He wore his Sunday suit, and stared straight ahead, his face expressionless. Behind them were Flavia, Ludovic and Emma. The scent of tuberose and jasmine was overpowering at such close quarters, and even reached Gwen, sitting alone near the door.

The service was long, and to Phoebe as a non-Catholic, largely incomprehensible. The two old priests in their splendid vestments celebrated the Mass with the fluency and grace of long practice, and Fr Benedict swung his censer with supple movements of his wrist, adding the powerful smell of incense to the already potent atmosphere in the little oratory. If this goes on much longer, thought Phoebe numbly, I shall pass out. Alexander took his handkerchief from his pocket, intending to stifle the sneeze he felt coming on. It was a clean handkerchief, unused, and as he unfolded it, he looked down and saw that it was one of Chloe's, with a picture of a spaniel's head embroidered on the corner. His throat closed, and a strangled half-sob, half-laugh emerged, an obscenity in that holy place. He did his best to control himself, but could not, and began to giggle hysterically, his hand over his mouth. In agony, he looked up at his father, but Christian stared straight ahead, ignoring him. Alexander felt a touch on his shoulder. He looked round, his hand still clapped desperately over his mouth, and saw his grandfather making a sideways movement of his head. Alexander stumbled to the end of the bench, Ludovic put a firm hand on his shoulder and they walked quickly out of the oratory together. In the garden, Alexander's unseemly laughter abruptly turned to tears. It was the first time since Chloe's death that he had been able to cry, and he leaned against his grandfather on the damp wooden seat and wept as though his heart would break. Chloe's hanky was soon sodden with tears, and Ludovic handed over his own clean one, and waited for the storm to pass. At last the weeping ceased, to be followed by shuddering sighs and an attack of hiccups.

'It was the dog that did it,' said Alexander, wanly.

'What on earth are you talking about?'

Alexander took Chloe's wet hanky from his pocket and showed his grandfather the picture of the spaniel on the corner. Ludovic examined it carefully. 'I can quite see that in the circumstances, that dog would undermine anyone's composure. If it had happened to me, I would have laughed, too.'

'So would Chloe,' said Alexander, hugely relieved at Ludovic's reaction. 'She was always giggling in church. Like in Jacob waxed ill and was sick.'

'Is that funny?'

'Well, if the priest turns over two pages by mistake and says "And the lot fell on Esau", then it *is* funny, isn't it?'

'It is,' said Ludovic, smiling. 'Very funny.' He stood up. 'I expect it's nearly time to go to the cemetery. Would you rather stay here, or do you want to come?'

'Are *you* going?'

'Yes, of course.'

'Can I be with you?'

'Yes, but strictly no giggling, OK?'

'OK.'

At the cemetery, Alexander stood close to his grandfather and watched, dry-eyed, as the small white coffin of his sister was slowly lowered into the grave. He did not feel in the least like laughing.

It was nearly seven o'clock when the family returned to Abbot's Court, and Gwen went at once to the kitchen, to put on the potatoes, already peeled and waiting in their pan. She added salt and a sprig of mint, and covered the pan with its lid. Only then did she take off her coat and her black felt hat, and hang them on the back of the kitchen door. She went to the larder and got the heavy iron casserole of chicken and vegetables, already cooked, and put it in the slow oven to reheat. She had relaid the dining-room table immediately after lunch, so that all that remained to be done was to make a salad, and put out bread and some cheese. What about wine? she thought. I'd better ask Christian. She guessed that they would all be having a drink in the drawing room, and went through the dining room to the hall. The drawing room door was half-open; she could see that the lamps were lit, and heard the murmur of voices. She put her head round the door and saw Christian dispensing drinks at the long table behind the chintz-covered sofa. The others stood about, as if at a cocktail party, chatting politely. Alexander went round the room, offering a dish of potato crisps. Phoebe, pale but composed, sat alone on the sofa.

Gwen went to the table and touched Christian's elbow. 'I was wondering about wine for dinner,' she said.

'What are we eating?'

'Chicken casserole.'

'I don't know. Nothing special. A light red, I should think; a Côtes du Rhône, perhaps. Anything you like, Gwen. You choose, OK?'

'Right,' said Gwen.

'What time will we eat?'

'Half an hour, if you like.'

'Thank God,' said Christian. 'I'm starving.' He looked at Gwen, his blue eyes tired. 'Thank you for everything, Gwen. What a tower of strength you are.'

At a quarter to eight the family stood behind their places at the dining-room table and Fr Anselm said grace. They took their seats and Gwen brought in the food on a trolley. Phoebe sat at one end of the table, with Fr Anselm on her left and Ludovic on her right.

Christian was at the other end, with Flavia on his right and Fr Benedict on his left. Emma and Alexander faced each other across the middle of the table. Gwen began to serve the food. Emma got up and passed the plates, and Christian poured the wine. Gwen departed with her trolley and they began to eat, in a self-conscious silence at first, then with a more normal level of conversation. Phoebe, with an attempt at politeness, turned to Fr Anselm. 'It was so good of you and your brother to come down,' she said. 'We are so grateful.'

'It was a privilege to be of assistance,' he replied. 'It was a lucky chance that I happened to be on leave from Zaire.'

Thankfully, Phoebe grasped the conversational opening. 'Tell me about your work in Africa,' she said. 'It must be fascinating.'

The elderly monk needed no further encouragement to embark on a lively account of his mission to what he always referred to as 'the dark continent'. On Phoebe's other side, Ludovic covertly studied his daughter-in-law as she feigned deep interest in the old man's rambling tale. He wondered what anguished emotions were concealed behind her smooth, rather bland face and downcast eyes. Poor young woman, he thought, and took a sip of Christian's excellent Côtes du Rhône. He became aware of his wife's voice at the other end of the table, high-pitched and gushing. Anxiously, he glanced in her direction as she eagerly clutched Christian's hand in hers. 'But my darling *boy*!' she insisted. 'You mustn't look on it as a *tragedy*! For the little one it has to be the ultimate glory!'

'Mother, how can you say that?' Christian sharply withdrew his hand from his mother's grip.

'Because it's *true*! Darling little Chloe died in a state of perfect grace. Don't you realize how miraculous that is? She will have gone straight to heaven, with none of the heavy baggage of sin that nearly everyone carries with them. This should be a time of rejoicing and joy; you should be *happy* for her.'

God forgive her, bloody woman, thought Ludovic. I should have tried to stop her diving into the whisky bottle before dinner. He turned towards Phoebe, praying that she had not heard Flavia, but realizing at once that she had, only too clearly. Ashen-faced, Phoebe pushed back her chair and stalked from the room, her hand over her mouth.

Before anyone else could collect their wits, Emma put down her napkin and stood up. 'I'll go to her,' she said firmly, and left the room. She found Phoebe, eventually, in the vegetable garden, pulling out nettles with her bare hands. She was kneeling on the muddy ground, her skirt and tights ruined, and tore at the weeds hysterically, gasps of pain and despair engulfing her. Emma knelt down on the gravel path beside her, and waited. At last, Phoebe stopped crying and sat back on her heels, staring at her blistered, throbbing hands.

'I'll find a dock leaf,' said Emma. 'That'll soothe the sting.'

'Don't bother; it doesn't matter.' Phoebe stared at Emma, her eyes red and bloodshot. 'I hate your bloody mother, she's a cow. I wish *she* had been killed, and not my poor little Chloe.'

'I don't blame you, Phoebe. It was an inappropriate and insensitive thing to say. She is a foolish woman.'

'I hate your cruel God, too. What kind of a monster is He, that lets innocent children get killed, and allows good, kind people to die of cancer, in agony, like my mother?'

'I know,' said Emma gently. 'It is often extremely difficult to understand the purpose behind the paradox. It's a question of faith, at the end of the day, an unshakeable belief that everything has meaning.'

'Meaning? *Paradox*?' Phoebe's voice shook with fury. 'What a load of utter crap, Emma! Look around you!

Are you blind? Don't you see that practically every frightful thing that's happening in the world is down to religious intolerance? Ireland? Genocide in Bosnia? The Jews and the Arabs killing each other? It's everywhere, isn't it? Why doesn't your wonderful God stop it all happening? Can you tell me that?'

'No, I'm afraid I can't.'

'Of course you can't,' said Phoebe triumphantly, 'because if you're honest, you know that this supreme being doesn't really exist, don't you?'

'It's not always easy to have faith in the possibility of His existence, Phoebe. I do know that.'

'You bloody Catholics are all the same. You're brainwashed into the mumbo-jumbo of sins and penances, practically from the cradle, aren't you? Be good or the man with the big stick will get you, that's the great cry, isn't it? You're beaten into submission all through your childhood by the fear of God, and going to hell, aren't you?'

'Well,' said Emma, 'not exactly.'

'Oh, come on! What about all that confession, and saying fifty thousand Hail Marys will make it OK, and you're absolved, and in a state of grace. Then you can go out and do the sin all over again if you feel like it. When it comes to the crunch, you're a bunch of hypocrites, Emma.'

'Why do you think that?'

'Well, look at your own father, for instance.'

'What about him?'

'Well, how can he be a good Catholic and all that, and a respectable married man, when all the time he's got a mistress in Paris, and an illegitimate child?'

'Whatever gave you that idea?'

'Don't you know about it, Em?' Phoebe spoke quietly, the anger suddenly gone from her voice.

'No, I don't.'

'Oh.' Phoebe hesitated, feeling herself to be on dangerous ground, and anxious not to offend her sister-in-law. 'It was stupid of me to mention it; I didn't realize it was a secret. Chris told me about it; I think a friend of his in the Paris office knew all about it and told him. Chris thought it a bit of a laugh.' She looked up at Emma, her eyes red, and smiled wanly. 'Sorry if it's a shock, Em.'

'Don't worry about it.' Emma made a huge effort to set aside her consternation at Phoebe's disclosure, intending to think about it later, and perhaps speak to her father, if the opportunity arose. She took Phoebe's hands in hers, and bathed them with her handkerchief dipped in cold water from the watering can standing on the path, close by.

'I'm sorry, Emma.' Two exhausted tears rolled down Phoebe's dirty face. 'I shouldn't have said all that to you. It was rude and hysterical of me. Your faith is your own business, not mine.'

'It's what we're here for, isn't it?' Emma smiled at her sister-in-law. 'You are hurt and angry; you need someone to blame. It's OK to blame God, through me. I am happy to take it, if it helps.'

'Now you're making me feel guilty.'

'Don't be,' said Emma. 'Come on, it's time you went back to bed, you've had a dreadful day. I'll get Gwen to bring you some hot milk.'

They walked slowly back to the house together, and up to the tower. Gently, Emma helped Phoebe to undress and get into bed. Then she fetched a flannel from the bathroom and wiped her face and hands.

'Poor little Chloe,' said Phoebe wearily. 'She must be so cold and lonely in that beastly cemetery, all by herself.'

'She's not there, Phoebe, I'm sure of that.'

'I wish I could believe you, Em.'

'I'll get your milk, darling. Then I'll sit with you till Christian comes up.' Emma went to the door and opened it. She looked back at Phoebe, but she had closed her eyes and turned her face away.

*   *   *

Emma woke before dawn, from force of habit. She knelt beside her bed and said the first office of the day. She thought it very likely that her two uncles would presently be celebrating Mass in the oratory, and decided not to join them, but to go for a walk instead. She washed and dressed, turning her back to the mirror in the pretty and comfortable guest room allocated to her. The mattress of the bed was so soft that it had caused her to sleep badly and to wake with a headache and a stiff neck. In the bathroom, the thick white towels, as well as the scented soap and bath essence, had filled her with embarrassment, and a sharp dismay at her pleasurable response to them. The warm carpet under her bare feet, too, had felt sensuous and comforting. She was mortified at her capacity to enjoy such things, when the house was so full of grief at the death of a little girl. Perhaps Phoebe is right, she thought, and we *are* just a bunch of hypocrites. Perhaps it *is* all just a question of dogma, for me, and I have become anaesthetized and no longer capable of real human feeling?

Silently, she closed her door and went down the stone stairway to the hall, then to the garden door. Finding it unlocked, she went out onto the dew-drenched lawn, and walked slowly towards the gap in the trees that framed the pasture, where the cows lay in a group, half-hidden in early mist. Her heavy skirts dragged across the wet grass, and the grey worsted stockings inside her leather sandals soon became saturated. When she reached the stile, she stopped and looked back at the house. There were no signs of life, no early lights in the windows; the old grey building was as silent and submerged in its woodlands as the Sleeping Beauty's castle, and as sublime. Emma hitched up her skirts, climbed over the stile and sat down on the wooden rail of the fence. She straightened her back and inhaled the cool morning air, listening to the chirping of the birds as they woke, one by one, until the woods echoed with their noisy clamorous greeting to the day. Presently, a huge red sun appeared over the trees to the left of the meadow, and the cows lumbered to their feet, as if responding to a signal, and began to browse. In the still moist air, Emma could hear quite distinctly the ripping of torn grass and the sound of the cows' rhythmic munching.

'Hello, Emma. You're up early.'

Emma turned her head and saw her father standing beside her, his hand on the fence. She smiled at him, glad of his grave, calm presence, but nervous at the prospect of raising the questions Phoebe had so bluntly sown in her mind. 'It's not especially early for me, Dad. I'm usually up at three.'

'Of course.' He leaned on the rail, and looked at her affectionately, so sombre in her habit, but still recognizably his daughter Emma underneath. 'Getting up early is a good trick, if you have the knack of it, and the willpower,' he said. 'It's the best part of the day, isn't it?'

'It is, but not always in January!' Emma laughed. 'The flesh is pretty unwilling then, I can tell you.'

'I have to confess that in my case the spirit would be remarkably unwilling, too.' He smiled. 'I've always found it quite difficult to drag myself out of bed in the morning.'

Emma looked gravely at him. It's now or never, she thought, and took a deep breath. 'Dad?' she said.

'Mm?'

'When I was with Phoebe last night, she was quite hysterical, poor thing, and she said rather a lot of things that she'll probably regret this morning.'

'That doesn't altogether surprise me.'

'She said something pretty shattering about you, Dad.'

'Oh?'

Emma hesitated, staring at the muddy ground below.

'She said you had a mistress in Paris, and an illegitimate child. It's nonsense, isn't it?'

In the silence that followed, Emma thought for a moment that she might be sick. Then she turned her head towards her father and their eyes met. Ludovic hesitated for a second, then smiled faintly. 'No, it's not nonsense, Emma, except that "mistress" is not a term I would apply to Claudia, who earns her own living. Neither do I consider our daughter to be illegitimate. She bears my name and yours. She is your half-sister.'

Emma looked down at her folded hands, doing her best to adjust to this entirely new image of her father as the lover of a woman not his wife, and worse, procreator of a little girl born out of wedlock. At last she turned towards him, shyly. 'I'm sorry, Dad, I didn't mean to be offensive. Tell me about it, please.'

'I will. Come on, let's go for a walk.'

Emma climbed down from the fence and they walked across the lawn and through the yew hedge to the courtyard, then past the house and into the woods, overhanging the lane where Chloe had met her death. Quietly, they walked through the trees, taking care to avoid treading on fallen, rotten branches as they went.

'Poor little girl,' said Ludovic. 'What a tragic waste of a young life, almost before it had properly begun. Poor Phoebe, I do feel terribly sorry for her. Her heart is breaking, one can tell. Just as mine would be, if anything were to happen to you, or young Alexander, or Allegra.'

'Allegra?'

'My second daughter, Emma. She is four years younger than you.'

Emma stared at her father, really shocked. 'It didn't take you long to betray my mother, did it?'

'Let's sit down, my love. There are things I must tell you, that's if it won't be too painful for you to hear them?'

'I expect it will be, but you'd better tell me, anyway.'

They sat down together on a fallen tree. After a short silence, Ludovic began to speak. 'Your mother, I take it, has never spoken to you about our marital relationship, Emma? That is to say, our physical relationship, as man and wife?'

'No, never.'

'Well, the long and the short of it is, we never really had one.'

'How can that be, Dad? You had two children, didn't you?'

'We did, and things were reasonably happy between us until the birth of Christian. She had a protracted and difficult labour, and after that she was so terrified of a second pregnancy that sex was out of the question. We had one child, and that was enough, in your mother's book. I don't need to tell you that contraception, for her, was a total no-go area, a sin.'

'Yes, it would be.' She looked at her father and smiled sympathetically. 'That would explain the long gap between Christian and me?'

'Exactly.'

'What made her change her mind, and have another baby?'

'Christian going away to school. She missed him terribly, I think. He was her entire reason for living, particularly as I was away for much of the time. Even when I was at home, she and I lived at arm's length, so to speak, and Chris was far more important to her. When he came home for the holidays for the first time, she realized at once that she had lost him. It often happens, of course. She began to drink rather heavily; it was becoming a problem. Then suddenly, everything changed. She stopped drinking, and invited me to share her bed again. I think, though I don't know, that Gwen was the *éminence grise* behind the whole bizarre business.'

'And after I was born?'

Ludovic laughed. 'What do *you* think? Back to the dog-house, of course!'

'Oh, dear,' said Emma, and laughed too, in spite of herself. 'Poor you.' She took her father's hand and kissed it. 'It's not funny really, it's sad. You don't need to tell me the rest, Dad. I can guess, and I can't really say that I blame you for seeking love elsewhere.'

'But I would like very much to tell you about it, and in any case, you have a right to know.'

'OK.'

'You must have been about two and a half years old when Claudia and I met for the first time. It was at a supper party in Paris, after the opera, and I was placed next to her. She was very serious, composed, and looked like a Pre-Raphaelite painting. She was pale, with big hazel eyes, and the most glorious red hair I had ever seen. She was only twenty-four, a musician, and played the cello for a living. I invited her to lunch with me the next day, and she accepted. That was the beginning.'

'And how old were *you*, Dad?'

'Forty. I should have known better, shouldn't I?' He smiled at her, gently. 'But love isn't like that, is it? There aren't any rules. Either it happens, or it doesn't.'

'I wouldn't know,' said Emma quietly. 'It's never happened to me; I'm sure it never will.'

'You didn't give life much of a chance to prove you wrong, darling, did you?'

'You mean entering the order so soon?'

'Of course that's what I mean. I had hoped that when you were in Italy, you'd meet new people, gain a new perspective on life, broaden your horizons. You know what I mean?'

'Yes, I do. But it didn't happen, I'm afraid. The dear old Petacci did their level best to matchmake for me, but I couldn't bear their young men, and *they* thought *me* very dull indeed. The other people I got to know were either elderly tutors, or eager, earnest young women, just like me, learning their craft. I have to tell you, Dad, that making frescoes is amazingly hard work; you have to have the constitution of a coalminer. At the end of each day, all you want to do is eat and hit the sack. You have no energy at all to go to discos or anything like that, believe me.'

'What a pity, it must have been so dull for you.'

'No, it wasn't, not at all. I loved it, I really did.' Emma hesitated, then went on speaking in her quiet, low voice. 'The problem *now* is, that I haven't been allowed to use my skills at all, so far.' She looked up at her father, who was listening attentively. 'All I do is clean out cowsheds, wash-up endlessly, and hoe turnips. It's very frustrating.'

'It must be.'

'Why are we talking about *me*, all of a sudden? You were telling me about Claudia; and Allegra. Tell me about her.'

'Well, she is tall, like you, and looks just like her mother, except for her eyes. She has grey eyes, exactly like yours and mine, Emma. She often reminds me very much of you.'

'What does she do?'

'She's reading natural history at the university.'

'Does she still live at home?'

'Not exactly. She has a self-contained apartment on the other side of our courtyard, with her own front door to the street. We converted the old storage place for her, as an eighteenth birthday present.'

'Lucky girl. Whose idea was that?'

'Claudia's, of course.'

Emma laughed. 'Why "of course"?'

'Claudia believes in personal freedom. She believes that people should come and go, be together by mutual desire and respect, not because of legal obligations.'

'And do you agree with her, Dad?'

'In theory, I do. But that doesn't mean that I wouldn't find it very difficult to go on living if anything were to happen to her, or if she left me, Emma.'

'You must love her very much?'

'Yes, I do.'

'So, *you* are not free?'

'No, not in that sense.' He put his hand on hers. 'The point is, darling, I don't *want* to be free. Don't you understand? I would marry Claudia tomorrow, if I could.'

Emma sighed. 'And you can't, because of Mother. Is that it?'

'Of course.'

'But after more than twenty years apart, surely you could get a civil divorce automatically?'

'I could, Emma. But I have no wish to undermine your mother completely by doing that, and neither has Claudia. As it is, Flavia's grip on sanity seems to be pretty fragile, not to speak of her dependence on alcohol, poor woman.'

'She's getting worse, isn't she? What can one do?'

'She has her faith, Emma. Don't you think that's enough?'

Emma said nothing, and presently they stood up and began to walk back to the house. At the garden door, she paused. 'When are you leaving, Dad?'

'After lunch. I'd like to get home this evening, if I can. What about you? I could give you a lift to Calais, and put you on the train, if you like. Or will you stay on here with Phoebe for a few days?'

'I'm not sure. Maybe I should spend a bit of time with Mother, in London. Perhaps she needs me.'

'Perhaps she does.'

'Dad,' said Emma, suddenly, urgently. 'Do you think I might come to Paris sometime, and meet Claudia and my sister?'

'I'm sure you could, darling. I would love you to come.'

'It might be wise to ask Claudia first, don't you think?'

'Yes, perhaps. I'll do that, and write to you, OK?'

'OK.' She put her hand on her father's shoulder and kissed his cheek.

'Emma?'

'Yes?'

'If you do go to your mother, don't mention Claudia, will you?'

'Doesn't she know?'

'I have absolutely no idea. But if she does, she has never breathed a single word of it to me. Until she does, I'd rather the subject wasn't raised in her presence.'

'Yes, I see. Don't worry; she won't hear anything from me.'

Ludovic took out his pocketbook, then wrote his Paris address and telephone number on the back of a card, and gave it to Emma. 'I'll talk to Claudia, and write to you at La Falaise.'

Emma looked at the card. Impasse des Cordonniers, she read. 'Sounds lovely, Dad.'

'It is,' he agreed. 'I look forward to seeing you there, soon.'

Gwen had laid the table for breakfast in the dining room. Flavia and her brothers had forgathered there after early Mass, and were drinking coffee and eating toast in silence. Emma felt obliged to join them, although she would have much preferred to have had her breakfast with Gwen and Alexander.

Ludovic, ignoring such scruples, took himself to the kitchen, where he found Alexander seated alone at the table, eating cornflakes. He looked up as his grandfather entered the room.

'Any chance of some coffee?' asked Ludovic, closing the door behind him. 'Where's Gwen?'

'Upstairs, taking a tray to Mum. Coffee's on the stove, Grandpa. I'll get you a cup.'

'Stay where you are, Alex, I'll get it myself.' Ludovic poured himself some coffee, and sat down at the table to drink it.

Alexander pushed the last few rather soggy cornflakes onto his spoon with the aid of his thumb, and swallowed them. 'Emma's a good sort, isn't she, Grandpa? I like her.'

Ludovic smiled. 'I do, too,' he said.

'It was neat, the way she looked after Mum last night, wasn't it?'

'Yes, it was.'

'It was dead tackless of Granny to say all that garbage about Chloe being in a state of grace, wasn't it? Poor Mum, she couldn't handle that, could she?'

'No,' said Ludovic, sadly, 'she couldn't. I can't say I blame her; I find it hard to handle myself, don't you?'

'I keep thinking she's still here, you know.' Alexander looked at his grandfather, his blue eyes distressed. 'I keep forgetting she's dead.'

'I know,' said Ludovic gently, 'one does; it's natural.'

Alexander sighed, and fiddled with his spoon, rattling it against the empty bowl. 'If only we hadn't played that game. It was all my fault, it was me that suggested it. If we hadn't played the game, I wouldn't have been chasing her, and she wouldn't have died. It *was* my fault. I killed her.'

'Alexander, you must try to stop blaming yourself, you really must. Feel sad and sorry by all means; miss poor little Chloe as much as you want to or need to. Grieve for her, and for Mum and Dad, and for yourself, but stop this ridiculous nonsense about it being your fault. It was a tragic accident, nothing more nor less. Blaming yourself won't bring her back, will it, my dear boy?'

'I suppose not.' Alexander wiped his nose with the back of his hand. 'Is that what you really think, Grandpa? About it being an accident?'

'Yes, of course it is. I wouldn't say so, otherwise, would I?'

Gwen came into the kitchen through the garden door, carrying Phoebe's tray. She had chosen to walk round the house rather than go through the dining room, thus avoiding questions regarding Phoebe's state of mind, and need for spiritual counselling.

'Good morning, Gwen,' said Ludovic. 'I helped myself to coffee, I hope you don't mind?'

'Of course not. Shall I make you some toast? Or would you like an egg?'

'No, no, this is fine. You look exhausted, Gwen; do sit down. Alex, get a cup of coffee for Gwen, would you?'

'I *am* a bit whacked, I must say.' Gwen sat down heavily. She looked at Ludovic, and shook her head. 'Poor Phoebe, I'm afraid she'll never come to terms with this.'

'I'm quite sure she won't,' said Ludovic. 'One could never get over the death of a child.' He looked pointedly at Gwen. 'It's fortunate that she still has Alexander, isn't it?'

Her response was swift. 'Yes, of course it is. Thank God.'

Alexander brought the cup of coffee, slopping it into the saucer, and placed it carefully in front of Gwen. 'Thank you, dear,' she said.

'Where's Christian? I imagine he's with Phoebe?'

'No, he's in the library. I think he's phoning his office.'

'I suppose he has to get on with things, poor man. Life goes on, as people are so apt to remark, at times like these.'

'Indeed,' said Gwen, and drank her coffee.

Ludovic stood up. 'Alexander, I must pack my things. Do you want to come and help? Thanks for the coffee, Gwen.'

*   *   *

Christian put down the telephone and looked at his watch: eleven twenty-two. How slowly the time passes when you're having a rotten time, he said to himself. He lit a cigarette, guiltily, from an old stale pack in his desk drawer, then crossed the room and stood at the window, looking across the lawn to the gap in the trees and the pasture beyond, with its decorative little herd of Jersey cows. This is a beautiful place, he thought, as he exhaled acrid smoke from his lungs, but it oppresses me. It always has, I don't really know why. Why is it that I always drive away from here with a sense of relief, as if I were escaping from something?

His mother and his two uncles appeared on the lawn, coming through the arch in the yew hedge. They walked very slowly, their heads bent, and Christian stared at them with something like horror. 'The angels of death,' he said aloud, and drew sharply on his cigarette. Jesus Christ, he asked himself, am I going round the twist, or what? He longed to be back in London, in his safe, normal office, surrounded by safe, normal people, and doing safe, normal work. I must get a grip, get away from here, get back to work. Phoebe will be all right now; she'll have to be. She's got Gwen to take care of her, and Alex. They'll be OK. I'll go tomorrow. Then he realized, with a sinking heart, that tomorrow was Saturday, and the entire weekend loomed ahead of him. He would have to remain here, alternately enduring Phoebe's grief, and his mother and her brothers making the most of every moment they could spend in the oratory. The house was sickly with the odours of incense, snuffed candles, and decomposing flowers. Why the hell didn't I have the poor child's funeral in the church? It was a ghastly mistake having it here, we'll never get rid of the smell of death. Horrified, Christian passed his hand across his eyes. Forgive me, Chloe, he thought; I didn't mean it, darling.

Wearily, he returned to his desk. He stubbed out his

cigarette, and sat down. I'm not up to this sort of emotional tightrope, it's not my scene at all. I can't tolerate much more in the way of hysteria or insensitive blunders, and I don't bloody intend to. Ma will have to leave, today, after lunch. He returned to the window. His mother and her brothers were still there, standing by the fence. Christian drew a deep, resolute breath, opened the window, stepped over the sill and walked swiftly across the lawn. He spoke before he could change his mind. 'It was very good of you all to come down, and I appreciate it; but I think it would be better if everyone left now. Phoebe is extremely stressed; she needs to be alone. If you start immediately after lunch, you will be in London by five o'clock.'

Flavia gazed at him, astonished. 'But don't you think . . . ?' she began, but Christian cut her short. 'No, Mother, I don't.' He turned abruptly on his heel and went quickly back to the house.

Lunch was a silent, awkward business. Phoebe, tense and drawn, sat at her end of the table, eating nothing, clearly anxious for the guests to be gone. Rather to Emma's relief, her offer to spend a few days with her mother had been rejected, and she had decided, after all, to travel to Calais with Ludovic. Christian had made it quite plain that he wished to see the back of them all, so she had not offered to stay on with Phoebe.

Ludovic was the first to rise from the table, and Emma joined him in the ritual farewells. Alexander followed them out to the car. 'I wish you weren't going,' he said, putting his arms round his grandfather. 'I wish I could ring you up, and have a chat sometimes.'

'Nothing simpler,' said Ludovic. He took a card from his pocketbook. 'This is my number in Brussels, after six. This is the code; you dial that first, OK? And this is a number in Paris, where I often am. And this', he said, writing the numbers, 'is the code for France. Ring me there, anytime.'

Alexander took the card, looked at it carefully, and put it in his pocket. 'Brilliant,' he said. 'I will, thanks.'

Ludovic and Emma drove away, and Alexander stood waving, then ran after the car until it disappeared and could be heard no more. Disconsolately, he walked back up the drive. In the courtyard, his grandmother and her two priestly brothers were installing themselves and their luggage in Fr Benedict's Morris Traveller. Christian and Phoebe stood beside the car to see them off. Flavia, smelling of stale vermouth, embraced her son, then turned to her daughter-in-law. 'Poor Alexander,' she said, clutching Phoebe's arm. 'He is so sad and sorry. Why don't you let me take him home with me for a while, darling? I'm sure it would do him good.'

Phoebe stared at her in horror, then wrenched her arm away. 'Get out of here, you drunken old witch!' she screeched. 'Go away! I never want to see you again, and neither does Alexander! He's my son, and I won't have him brainwashed by you and your rotten old priests, do you hear me?'

Alexander, hidden behind the hedge, felt a little comforted by his mother's outburst, and sent up a silent cheer as the Morris Traveller made its slightly erratic departure through the woods. Nevertheless, when his parents had returned to the house and the courtyard was empty, he made his way very quietly across the gravel to the barn, to his usual hiding place, and it was there that he saw Chloe for the first time. As he reached the top of the ladder, he looked towards the window, and saw her sitting there, cross-legged, waiting for him.

Chapter Five

Back at La Falaise, Emma had much to think about. She followed the normal timetable of the religious day, the disciplines of work and prayer, and was in many ways glad to be back, sheltered behind the convent walls, away from the raw emotions and human sorrow to which she had been witness. The violence of Phoebe's grief had shocked and saddened her, as had her own inability to comfort her in any way, other than by offering the platitudes that had seemed appropriate at the time, but had been so abrasively rejected by Phoebe. The death of a child must be terrible, Emma thought, I wonder if one could ever recover from such a blow? Probably not, completely, even with God's help. Into her mind came the painted image of the *Madonna del Parto*, the courageous young peasant, with calm face and protective hand on her ripe, fruitful stomach. I wonder how *she* felt when her son was crucified, Emma asked herself; even if he was thirty-three years old, the anguish, the loss, must have been appalling, unbearable. I wonder what *she* thought about the sacrifice of her child? *God so loved the world, that He gave his only begotten Son, that whosoever believeth in Him should not perish, but have everlasting life.* How could He have done such a thing, in human terms? How could He? And what about Christian, how did *he* feel, poor man? Too late, Emma regretted that she had not tried to talk to her brother, to be some kind of comfort to him. Deep inside her consciousness, she recognized that in his unemotional, conventional way, Christian had merely been going through the religious motions for form's sake, and neither sought, nor needed, counselling from anyone. Their failure to communicate as brother and sister had been as much his doing as hers.

During the afternoon rest periods, Emma did not seek Miriam's company, but sat alone in the cloister, or walked in the orchard if no-one else was there. Miriam, with sensitive understanding and sympathy, did not force her company on her friend, and suppressed the flow of awful jokes that were her particular way of dealing with the irritations and frustrations of life. For several days, Emma thought of very little except Chloe, and the tragedy her death had visited on her family. Her heart bled for them all and she prayed as hard as she could for their salvation. She did not say the prescribed words from her Missal, but her own simple, spontaneous prayers, like those of a child. Please God, take care of them, make them happy again, take away the pain. Knowing that all the sisters would also be praying, Emma tried to believe that the combined weight of their thoughts and prayers might go some way to bringing acceptance and ultimately comfort to the grieving family.

One afternoon, exhausted by her efforts on Chloe's behalf, Emma took a rest. She sat on the grass under an apple tree, and allowed herself to think about her father. What a lot I didn't know about him and Mother, she said to herself. Was I just dim, not noticing that they didn't sleep together, or was there some reason why I closed my mind to it? Maybe I thought it was an impure thought? Holy Mother, keep me from impure thoughts, that's what the nuns always made us say. Suddenly, and quite clearly, she saw herself, aged about eleven, sitting on the foot of Flavia's big white bed, after their usual evening prayers. She had been to tea with Lucy, her special friend, who lived close by. Lucy had taken her upstairs to see her mother, just back from hospital with her newborn son, Lucy's baby brother. Mrs Drabble, comfortably ensconced in bed, and rosy with happiness, was feeding the tiny baby at the breast, and was perfectly happy for the two girls to sit quietly beside her, watching this amazing and rather wonderful spectacle. After his feed, Mrs Drabble had put the baby over her shoulder and rubbed his back until he gave a gentle burp and deposited some of his milk on her nightdress. 'Good boy!' she had said. Then the baby had done a noisy and smelly poo into his nappy, and they had all laughed, as if this was the most adorable action on his part. Clearly, Lucy and her mother had thought so, and Lucy had helped change his nappy in an impressively competent way. Thoughtfully, realizing that there were enormous gaps in her own knowledge of human behaviour, Emma had walked home. She wondered whether to ask Gwen some of the questions that she felt too shy to ask Lucy, but decided that her mother might not like it, if she did.

From the foot of her mother's bed, Emma had fired her opening gambit. 'I saw Lucy's baby brother this afternoon.'

'That was nice, darling.'

'Yes, he's really sweet. He's called Paul.'

'That's a lovely name.'

'Mother?'

'Yes, darling?'

'I know how babies are born, and all that. But how do they get inside their mother in the first place?'

Flavia had hesitated. For some time it had been on her mind that Emma would start asking those sort of questions, and she had vaguely intended to consult the nuns before buying a suitable little booklet of instruction for her. Now, rather wrong-footed, she tried to

103

make light of the subject. 'Well,' she said, 'you know when you see dogs in the park, giving each other piggybacks?'

'Yes.'

'Well, what they're actually doing is making babies.'

'Oh! Really?'

'Yes.' Her mother had laughed, looking embarrassed. 'Human beings are just the same.'

Emma had looked mystified, then rather alarmed.

'Don't worry about it, sweetheart,' said Flavia hastily. 'I'll get you a little book to read, with diagrams.'

'Do people do it backwards, like dogs?' asked Emma, badly needing to know the truth.

'No, they don't. They do it forwards, in bed, at night.'

'Oh, I see.' Emma felt relieved that this curious ritual was not performed in the park, like dogs, but in the dark privacy of the matrimonial bed. Covertly, she looked at her mother, rather appalled at the idea of her parents behaving in such a way. 'Does it hurt?' she asked. 'Is it horrible?'

'Yes,' Flavia had replied, briskly. 'It does hurt; and yes, it is rather nasty. It's just one of those unpleasant sacrifices a married woman has to endure. It's best not to dwell on it.'

'And is that the only way you can have children?'

'Absolutely. You go through all that humiliation and pain, and then your children grow up and leave you.'

'Like Christian?'

'Yes, like Christian.'

'I'll never leave you, I promise.'

'Yes, you will, darling. If my prayers for you are answered, you'll become a nun.' Flavia had looked at Emma, her eyes bright with hope. 'Needless to say, if you entered the religious life, you would not have to endure all the disgusting physical aspects of marriage. But I suppose it's quite probable that you'll fall in love and get married – most women do, poor things.'

Silently, Emma had vowed that such a disaster would never overtake her, if she could avoid it.

The bell rang for the commencement of afternoon work. Emma got up, brushed the bits of twig and grass off her habit, and went to the linen room, where a great pile of sheets, pillowcases and napkins from the guest house waited to be ironed, then folded and hung on racks to air, before being reused. In her present sombre and contemplative mood, she applied herself to the task without her usual rebellious thoughts, finding the hiss of the iron and the warm smell of freshly smoothed linen rather comforting to her soul. Sometimes, she thought, a job well done can be a kind of prayer, though it does rather depend on the task – certainly not mucking out hen houses, for one! As she passed the heavy iron smoothly over the sheets, her thoughts returned to Ludovic, and the account he had given her of his married life, or lack of it. Poor Dad, I suppose he's in a state of mortal sin; has been for years. But how dreadfully sad, if Mother refused his love, not to be allowed to have another chance of happiness when it came his way. He is a good, kind man. He's my father, and I love him. I always have, even when he was so often away. I can't believe in the idea of him being a sinner, though obviously I should. I can't believe that what he is doing is a sin, any more than I can believe that poor Phoebe's lack of faith is sinful. They're human beings, vulnerable and fallible, and their beliefs and actions are perfectly understandable. Who am I to say that they are not?

Three weeks later, Emma received a call from Ludovic. 'Emma?'

'Hello, Dad.'

'I've been telling Claudia about the discussion we had at Abbot's Court, and she would be happy to have a visit from you, any time that suits you.'

'Thank you,' said Emma, feeling slightly unwilling to commit herself, now that the invitation had actually come.

'Don't worry,' said Ludovic. 'There's no great hurry. Just give us a ring when you're ready.'

'Yes, all right. I'll do that.'

'Good. See you soon, then.'

'Yes. Thanks, Dad. Goodbye.'

For a couple of weeks, she thought it over, not at all sure that she really did want to meet her father's other family, and finding herself very nervous at the prospect of being repelled by Ludovic's lifestyle, or worse, conniving at the betrayal of her mother. One morning, she was driving the convent's little tractor, towing trailerloads of well-rotted manure to the vegetable garden, where two other sisters were spreading the fruity-smelling stuff between the rows of crops. It was a job she quite enjoyed, manoeuvring the tractor into the correct position for depositing the load where it was required. As she rattled away to collect another load, the answer came to her. She would go to Paris, but she would not ring up first. I know the address, she thought; I'll just go and take a look. I won't exactly spy on them; I'll just reassure myself. Then I can either go and see them, or go quietly away again, and write to Dad to say I've changed my mind. I don't need to be rude or unkind; just say I understand and wish them well, but my first loyalty has to be to Mother.

After lunch, she requested an appointment with the Mother Abbess, and went to see her that evening. Bending the truth, she explained that her father needed to discuss a family matter with her, and asked for an exeat to Paris.

'Paris? I thought your parents lived in London?'

'My father has a flat in Paris; it's easier to see him there.'

'I see. Very well. You will need some money for the journey.' The Abbess unlocked a drawer in her desk and took out a cash box, from which she took a wad of notes. 'This should be enough, Sister. Will you take a day-return, or will you need to stay a night?'

'I'm not sure, but if I do, I can stay with my father.'

'Your father is a *fonctionnaire* in the European Union, is he not?'

'Yes, he works in the Commission.'

'Very well. You must telephone if you decide to stay.'

'Yes, of course.'

'*Deo gratias*, Sister.'

'*Deo gratias*, Mother.'

At half past three the following afternoon, Claudia saw her pupil to the door, then sat down again and played the first movement of the Haydn cello concerto for her own pleasure. She put her cello on its stand, covered with its silk shawl, and stacked the music books underneath the lid of the piano stool. She went into the courtyard for a moment, revelling in the warmth of the early May sun that filled the tiny garden, its rays piercing the half-unfolded leaves of the mulberry tree. Quickly, she checked that none of her terracotta pots had dried out, then returned to the house, got a basket from the kitchen, and taking her bag and keys from the clutter of books and objects on the table, let herself out into impasse des Cordonniers.

The weather had suddenly become so warm and balmy that Claudia was dressed in the sort of clothes she usually wore in the country, or at the sea. She had chosen a long, Gauloise-blue linen skirt, which fell in soft folds to her ankles, cinched by a snuff-coloured suede belt with a silver buckle. The sleeves of her white shirt were rolled up above the elbow, revealing already lightly tanned arms, and on her bare feet were comfortable, flat leather sandals. Her hair was loosely tied back with a leather bootlace, and her serious, rather beautiful face, still relatively untouched by time, was quite bare, except for moisturizer and a little lip gloss. A sprinkling of freckles, loathed by herself, but loved by Ludo, speckled her nose and cheekbones. She looked exactly as she felt, a confident and happy woman, as she walked down the narrow *impasse* and into rue Mouffetard, where the street-market was crowded with local people, doing their shopping.

Claudia decided to buy food that was simple and easy to prepare, and to have dinner in the garden for the first time that year. Working her way through the stalls, stacked with fresh produce of every kind, meat, fish, vegetables and fruit, she bought a *saucisson sec* for the first course, and some ripe tomatoes and olives to go with it. Then she chose some fresh pasta, a large jar of pesto sauce, some salad leaves and a *banon* cheese. Last of all, she bought a bag of Italian cherries, sweet, black and glossy. She had turned to retrace her steps down the steep and narrow street, intending to buy her bread at the *boulangerie*, when her eye fell on the white veil of a novice nun standing a few metres away from her, half-hidden in the crowd of shoppers. She guessed immediately that it was Emma. She walked quietly up to her and tapped her lightly on the shoulder. Startled, the nun jumped as though she had been stung, and turned towards her.

'Sorry!' said Claudia, smiling. 'I didn't mean to frighten you. It's Emma, isn't it?'

'Yes, it is.' The nun's voice was low and hesitant. 'How did you know?'

'You're the image of your father; don't you know that?'

'Well, yes, I suppose we are alike.'

'I'm Claudia. Hello, Emma. I'm glad you came.' She held out her hand and Emma took it politely. 'I have to get bread, and then we can go home.'

'Let me take the basket,' said Emma, recovering her composure, reassured by Claudia's calm lack of fuss.

'No, no. You're already carrying that grip. This isn't heavy, anyway.'

They crossed the street to the *boulangerie* and Claudia bought two baguettes. 'Is this OK for you, Emma, or would you prefer *quatre-grains*?'

Emma smiled. '*Quatre-grains* is what we eat every day – a baguette is a great treat for me.'

'Right, baguettes it shall be. This is a real village *boulangerie*, and they bake twice a day. We are so lucky that they are still here.'

The assistant wrapped the two long loaves in tissue paper and Emma tucked them carefully under her arm, inhaling their delicious newly baked smell, and taking care not to crack their crisp crust. 'You are right,' she said, as they walked together down the busy street, 'you could easily be in the country.' She looked towards the church at the foot of the hill. 'Even the church is like a village church, isn't it?'

'Yes, it is. This is a really great place to live. It's full of writers and artists, living in the old *ateliers* of artisans, cabinetmakers and suchlike.'

'Is yours one of those?'

'You'll see.' Claudia crossed the street and turned into impasse des Cordonniers.

'What a charming name,' said Emma, glancing at the blue and white enamelled street-sign screwed to the wall on the corner. 'So this was once the cobblers' quarter?'

'Yes, but it hasn't been for a long time, I believe. Our place used to be the workshop of a cabinetmaker, before we took it over. He was such a nice man, but too old to continue working. He had no family to carry on the business, and not even an apprentice. He was glad to sell it to us and move back to his native village in Normandy.'

They walked up the short narrow lane between high, windowless brick walls, and stopped at the cracked panelled door that offered the only clue to the existence of Claudia's home, concealed behind it. The door had once been painted, and was now a soft, faded blue, though a good deal of the paint had flaked off, which was exactly as Claudia liked it. An ornate escutcheon, tarnished to a greenish-black, presented the slot for the key, next to an equally tarnished hexagonal doorknob. A small knocker, of the graceful design called *Fatima's Hand*, completed the door furniture. A little further along the lane was a similar door, but in better condition and fairly recently painted, with a well-polished brass dolphin knocker.

Claudia took the keys from her bag and unlocked her door. 'Come in,' she said, standing aside for Emma to go first. Emma crossed the threshold and entered the light-filled room, its tall glass doors open to the garden. She looked around her, enchanted by the ambience of the place, astonished at the vast number of books and the extraordinary collection of personal treasures that filled the space. In the courtyard, she could see rattan chairs and a green-painted table under the gnarled branches of the tree. No wonder Dad likes it here, she said to herself. Poor Mother, she wouldn't understand this at all; she'd think it was a junk shop. 'What a lovely place this is,' she said, turning to Claudia. 'It's absolutely beautiful.'

'I'm glad you like it,' said Claudia, smiling. She put down her basket and closed the door.

Emma's eye fell on the cello, under its shawl, close to the piano. 'Is this where you give music lessons?'

'Yes, the private ones. I teach at the *conservatoire*, too, and sometimes I'm relief-cellist in an orchestra, though I don't like to do too many concerts nowadays. I like to be here for Ludo, so that we can eat together.'

'How nice for him,' said Emma, shyly.

'And for me, too.' Claudia picked up her basket and made her way to the kitchen. 'I'll put away the food, and make some tea.'

Emma, carrying the bread, followed her and laid the two loaves carefully on the worktop. 'What can I do?'

'Nothing,' said Claudia. 'You must be tired after the

journey. Why don't you go and sit in the garden, while I make the tea? Or would you like a wash? It's so hot, I expect you would. Go up the iron staircase in the garden, and you'll find the guest room and a little bathroom. I think there are towels there, but if there aren't any, do shout, won't you?'

The afternoon was indeed very hot. Emma felt quite uncomfortable in her heavy habit, and wished that the decision had been taken at the abbey to change into their summer things. She took her grip up the rickety stairs and opened the door to the attic room. A narrow iron bed, very like the one in which she normally slept, stood near a small window, and was covered with a plain white quilt. The floor was bare, red-tiled and dusty, and several suitcases, cardboard boxes, and empty plant-pots stood against the far wall. A door in the wall revealed a small bathroom, almost monastic in its spartan simplicity. Emma found herself extremely comfortable there, remembering with a wry shake of her head her confusion when faced with the luxury of Phoebe's guest room. On an old-fashioned towel-horse was one rather threadbare cotton towel, and she felt relieved that she did not have to ask Claudia for one, after all. She unpinned her veil and wimple, took off her habit and shift, poured cold water into the basin and washed with the bar of olive-oil soap that stood in a pierced china soap-dish, decorated with a circle of sepia-printed ivy leaves.

Reluctantly, she dressed again, putting on her wimple but leaving her veil on the hook behind the bathroom door. Then she went down to the courtyard, where Claudia was already seated under the tree, with a tray of tea-things on the green table. 'Better?' she asked.

'Much, thank you,' said Emma, and sat down.

'It's a bit of a hole up there, I'm afraid.'

'No, it's perfect. Just the kind of place I like.'

Claudia poured tea into dark-green cups. Yes, of

course, she thought, it would be. She recollected her own schooldays in a boarding convent, remembering the austerity, the lack of comfort and self-indulgence. She handed a cup of tea to Emma. 'Milk, or lemon?' she asked.

'Lemon, thank you.' Emma sipped her tea, and looked at the pots of flowering plants that stood in groups around the high walls of the courtyard, a fat pink hose snaking over the paving in an untidy manner. 'How nice to have a place where you can leave all the doors and windows open, and feel quite safe. Don't you worry that someone might get over the wall?'

'They'd have to be pretty athletic to do that, wouldn't they? It's at least two metres fifty high, I should think.'

'Yes, it must be.' Emma looked at the narrow, two-storeyed building at the bottom of the courtyard. Its ground-floor windows were shuttered against the light, but a window on the first floor stood open, and a wooden venetian blind clacked gently against the frame, stirred by the small breeze that swirled around the court from time to time.

Claudia followed her gaze. 'That's Allegra's apart-ment,' she said. 'She used to have that room upstairs, where you had your wash. Then we did up the old storeroom for her, when she needed to be more in-dependent. Sometimes we don't see her for days on end; she loves being on her own.'

'My father told me about it. It must be lovely for her to have her own place. I remember how exciting it was to be away from home, when I first went to Italy.' She looked at Claudia. 'Dad says that Allegra looks like me sometimes. Do you think she does?'

'It's the eyes. You both have your father's eyes. But Allegra's hair is red, like mine, and I guess that you are dark, like Ludo used to be?'

'Yes, I am.' Then, to her own surprise, she laughed. 'Not that I've got much of it, now. One's expected to have it cut short, you know.'

'I wonder why?'

'The vanity thing, I suppose. Or maybe it's just a question of one's head getting sweaty and itchy, being covered all the time.' Astonished at her own burst of candour, Emma felt herself blushing, but Claudia did not look at all surprised. She merely agreed that this was the probable, and rather sensible reason behind the custom. She put her empty cup on the tray, crossed her long legs, leaning back in her chair, and gazed at Emma thoughtfully. 'It must have been a shock for you, Emma, when you heard about your father and me?'

'Yes, it was, rather. But I was so preoccupied with poor Phoebe that I postponed thinking about it until later, if that doesn't sound a bit silly.'

'No, it doesn't sound silly, but remarkably sensible and strong-minded of you.'

'The shock was the next day, when I was able to talk to Dad. When Phoebe told me that you and he had a child, I assumed that she was talking about a baby! When Dad told me that Allegra was twenty-one, only four years younger than me, I *was* a bit shattered, I have to admit.' She looked at Claudia, her grey eyes clouded. 'Then, much later, I felt really sad that for all those years I'd actually had a sister and not known about it.'

'Would it have been a good idea if you *had* known about her, and had met her?'

'Yes, I'm sure it would; for me at any rate. I was terribly lonely as a child, all alone with Mother, and Gwen, and the nuns. Christian was away at school, and then university. He's ten years older than me, anyway; we hardly knew each other. We still don't, really. I would have loved to have had a sister.'

'But of course there was a problem, wasn't there, Emma?'

'You mean Mother? Yes, that was a problem, I can see that.' She glanced at Claudia. 'In the circumstances,

I think it was extremely understanding of you not to insist on an annulment.'

Claudia laughed. 'It's kind of you to think that, but I honestly don't mind at all about the marriage thing. It's enough for me to love, and be loved.'

'And Allegra? Doesn't *she* mind?'

'I don't really know; it's difficult to tell how she feels, sometimes. She didn't say very much at the time, and we haven't really discussed it since. I expect she accepted the situation once she got used to the idea. I would be surprised if she hadn't; she adores Ludo, one can tell.'

'That's understandable,' said Emma, softly. 'I rather adore him myself.'

'And how would you feel about him, if it turned out that he and Flavia weren't married?'

A small frown wrinkled Emma's forehead, as she considered this question. Then she looked up and smiled. 'I'd still adore him,' she said.

'Bravo! Of course you would. It's not a problem, is it?'

Emma sipped her tea thoughtfully, and watched a yellow butterfly as it flew erratically from one flower to another. In her mind's eye, she saw Claudia holding the baby Allegra, then playing with the little girl in the park. 'How old was Allegra when you told her that you and my father weren't married?'

Coolly, Claudia looked at Emma. 'We didn't tell her.'

'What do you mean, you didn't tell her?'

'We didn't tell her, because the subject never came up. She has her father's name, McGrath, like you and Christian. I have always used my maiden name, and always would, married or not. For me, it's not just for professional reasons, but a question of keeping my own identity.'

'I see. So she never knew that her father was already married, and had other children?'

Claudia's gaze was composed and direct. 'No, she

didn't, Emma. There didn't seem to be any point in involving her in a situation that had no relevance to her own life.'

Unable to prevent herself from feeling a sense of personal diminishment at this obliteration of herself and her brother from Ludovic's life, Emma stared rather coldly at Claudia, sitting so gracefully in her chair, as though their conversation was the most ordinary and natural of circumstances. 'I see,' she said, quietly. 'So, when *did* you tell her about me?'

'It must be about a month ago, after Ludo came back from the funeral.'

'Oh.'

The telephone rang inside the house, and Claudia rose from her seat and went to answer it. After a few minutes she came back into the garden. 'That was Ludo,' she said. 'It's really annoying, he's going to be late tonight.' She sat down again, and smiled at Emma. 'He's so delighted that you're here. He really wants to see you. You will stay, won't you?'

Emma hesitated for a moment. 'And what about you, Claudia? Do you want me to stay?'

'Yes, I do, very much. I am glad that you have come here.'

'Really?'

'Absolutely.'

'In that case, may I use the telephone? I must phone the convent.'

'But of course. Help yourself.'

It was after midnight when Emma climbed the stairs to the guest room and began to prepare for bed. As she undressed, she thought about the happy evening she had spent with Claudia and her father. Presumably out of consideration for her feelings both as a daughter and as a nun, Ludovic and Claudia had barely touched each other throughout the evening, but in spite of this restraint, the strength of their attachment was obvious,

their mutual affection almost palpable. It was impossible not to feel the warmth of their love, and their
respect for and pride in each other.

Physically exhausted, and suffering from nervous
tension after the events of the day, Emma sat on the
edge of the bed in her shift, and said a silent prayer of
gratitude for her father's happiness. She tried very hard
to stifle a longing that she herself, as well as Allegra,
had been the child of his union with Claudia, and had
grown up in this lovely place.

There had been no sign of life in Allegra's apartment
during the evening, and Claudia had left a message on
her answerphone to say that Emma was in Paris. Now,
she got up, crossed the room to the open window, and
looked across the courtyard. A light was on in Allegra's
upstairs room, and through the slats of the venetian
blind Emma saw two figures lying together on the bed,
a girl with red hair, presumably Allegra, and a dark
young man, their arms round each other, embracing.
Emma stared at them, unable to tear her eyes away, and
before she could collect her wits and step back out of
sight, Allegra got up from the bed and came to the
window, raising the blind. She appeared to be staring
straight towards her, and guiltily, Emma withdrew.
She heard Allegra's shutters being closed with a
strident squawk of their rusty hinges, and when she
looked again, all she could see was a narrow strip of
light.

Profoundly disturbed by the implications of what
she had just witnessed, she got swiftly into bed,
without saying her customary prayers. She lay there,
rigid with unease, bitterly regretting her decision to try
to be a part of her father's life, and realizing the depths
of her own ignorance of the real world. And to think
that I had the temerity to offer poor Phoebe my idiotic
advice in her desperate need, she thought, when my
own experience of life is so pathetically inadequate.
She turned on her side, and stared at the pattern of

leaves, ruffled by the breeze, reflected in the glass of her open window. She closed her eyes and tried to compose herself for sleep, but the image of Allegra in her lover's arms filled her mind, and she found herself tormented by confused emotions, a surprising mixture of disapproval and envy. I am completely out of my depth here, she told herself, I shouldn't have come. I'll leave as soon as I can tomorrow, go back where I belong. At least there they have rules that I can try to relate to, even if I do find it difficult. It was a long time before she was able to sleep.

It was very late when Emma woke; that is to say, late by the conventual standards. Even before she looked at her watch, she knew by the angle of the sun's rays as they streamed through her window, flecked with motes of dust, that it must be nearly nine o'clock. She got quickly out of bed, washed and dressed herself fully, pinning on her veil. She tidied the rumpled bed, and folded her towel. She packed her washing things and nightshift into her grip, and left the room, carefully closing the door behind her. Descending the stairs, she glanced furtively across the courtyard. Allegra's shutters were tightly closed and there was no way of knowing whether or not she was at home.

Claudia was in the kitchen, reading a newspaper and drinking coffee. 'I'm afraid Ludo's gone again,' she said cheerfully. 'He had an early plane to catch. But he'll be back tonight; he hopes you can stay over?'

'I don't think I can.' Emma sat down at the table, and Claudia poured coffee for her. 'I feel quite bad at having asked for an exeat anyway, for what might not seem an absolutely essential reason.'

Claudia laughed. 'That's ridiculous. It was something you really needed to do, wasn't it? After all, this is a family matter, and family is important, no?'

Emma put down her cup. 'That's the whole point, Claudia,' she said seriously. 'It *shouldn't* be important, at all. A true vocation should enable you to unhook yourself from all extraneous ties, and loyalt s. There should be only one supreme loyalty.'

'God, how frightful that must be, I couldn't bear it!' Claudia looked sternly at Emma, her hazel eyes narrowed. 'How can you subscribe to such a repulsive idea, Emma, even for a moment?'

Emma turned her head, avoiding the hostile stare of the other woman. 'I'm sorry,' she murmured. 'It's not easy to understand, I know.'

'It's *crap*! Utter crap!' Claudia banged her clenched fist on the table, and the coffee cups jumped in their saucers.

Emma stood up. 'I must go,' she said. 'It was a mistake to come; I apologize. I didn't intend to upset you, or make you angry.'

'Sit down, Emma, please. It's I who should apologize. It was an unforgivable thing to say; I'm so sorry, my dear.' She smiled at Emma, her anger evaporated. 'I'm afraid I'm far too upfront emotionally; I quite often blurt out things that are much better left unsaid. What do you English say? Fools rush in?'

Emma did her best to respond in a similarly light manner, to diminish the effect of the harsh exchange. 'Don't worry about it,' she said. 'Nuns are quite used to getting a bad press.' She laughed. 'You should hear the things that workmen shout after us in the street. Get yer kit off, darling; things like that.'

Claudia winced. 'Don't tell me, please.' She got up and put her arms round Emma. 'Do stay, Emma. Ludo will be home tonight, and Allegra too, perhaps.'

Uneasily, Emma recalled Allegra's closed windows. It did not seem likely that Allegra was in any hurry to meet her. 'It was nice meeting you, Claudia. I can see how happy you've made my father, and I am happy for you both. But I don't think I should stay another day, I really must get back to the abbey.'

Claudia did not press her. She looked at her watch.

'As a matter of fact, I do have a lesson at ten-thirty. What time is your train? Or do you go by coach?'

'There's a direct train from Montparnasse this afternoon. I'll probably catch that, but don't worry, I can amuse myself in the meantime. I'd like to look at your church, and maybe take a walk in the Jardin des Plantes, since it's so close. I could do with the exercise.'

Claudia went into the studio, and took an envelope from the table. 'This is for you, Emma. Ludo thought that you might not be able to stay, and asked me to give it to you before you leave.'

Emma took the envelope and slid it into the deep pocket of her habit, alongside her wallet.

Claudia, who knew what was in the envelope, did not display any kind of interest or curiosity in its contents, and Emma, secretly gratified to have a small area of privacy between herself and her father, did not offer to open it.

They went to the door together, embraced affectionately, and promised to keep in touch.

Relieved to be alone again, after the stress of so much human contact and long, unaccustomed hours of conversation, Emma sat for a while in the church, then made her way to the Jardin des Plantes, after consulting the map displayed in the window of the tourist information bureau. She did not know Paris at all well, and the botanical gardens turned out to be a pleasant surprise, full of ancient trees bursting into early leaf, and peopled with charming statues, including one of the naturalist Buffon with a bird in his hand. The garden was animated with the shrill cries of children, running under the trees and playing games, and Emma noticed a group of elderly men and women playing cards on a little table set up under a chestnut tree, its pink candles just breaking into bloom. Gardeners on their knees were setting out bedding plants in the formal flower beds overlooking the river, and through the trees Emma could see the glint of sunlight on the tall greenhouses that sheltered the tropical plants. She walked up to the *ménagerie*, a delightfully old-fashioned sort of zoo, small and friendly, and evidently much loved by the mothers and children who appeared entirely at home in the place, as if they came here very often and knew the animals by name.

A clock struck eleven and Emma sat down on a bench and began silently to say Sext to herself, thinking of the sisters back at La Falaise doing exactly the same thing. She gazed at the grass at her feet, listening to the familiar words inside her head. All at once, she became aware that someone was standing directly in front of her, and facing her. She saw a pair of dirty white trainers, with red socks disappearing into the legs of faded blue jeans. Thinking that the feet belonged to a tramp in search of alms, Emma looked up and saw instead the slim figure of a girl, with long red hair cascading from a black baseball cap. Beneath the peak of the cap, a pair of cold grey eyes, Ludovic's eyes, stared at her insolently. Her hands thrust into the pockets of a black-leather biker's jacket, the girl's attitude seemed to Emma to be one of open hostility. Alarmed, she got hastily to her feet. 'Oh!' she stammered. 'You must be Allegra?'

'What makes you think *that*?' replied the girl, rudely. Then, without another word, she sat down on the grass, took out a packet of Marlboros, and lit a cigarette.

Emma, thoroughly put off, but determined not to seem so, sat down on her bench again as calmly as she could. 'I expect it is because you have your mother's hair and your father's eyes,' she said, feeling her way.

'Knock it off, for Christ's sake!' The girl's voice was angry and belligerent. 'Don't give me that bullshit; I don't buy it, understood?'

'I'm sorry,' Emma began, losing confidence rapidly. 'I

don't understand why you are so angry. Have I done something to upset you?'

'You've done plenty to upset me! Just by bloody existing, you upset me! How would *you* feel, if you suddenly found out that your father had a secret family, his *real* family, and more important than you could ever be? What would you feel about *that*?'

'As a matter of fact,' said Emma mildly, 'I've only recently found out about you, Allegra. We're in exactly the same boat, aren't we?'

Allegra scrambled to her feet and thrust her face close to Emma's. 'But you're not fucking *illegitimate*, are you, you complacent cow?' She threw her cigarette on the ground close to the hem of Emma's habit, turned on her heel and ran swiftly away towards the *ménagerie*.

Stunned, Emma stared after her, unable to believe that she had really lived through the last few minutes. After a moment, she stood up and crushed the smouldering cigarette underfoot. Then she squared her shoulders, picked up her grip and began to walk slowly towards the Métro that would take her to Gare Montparnasse. She was extremely early for her train, so she bought a ham sandwich and went to the ladies' restroom to eat it, afterwards settling herself on a bench to wait for her time of departure to be announced. Suddenly, she remembered the letter from her father that Claudia had given her. She took it from her pocket and opened it. It contained a thick sheaf of banknotes, enclosed in a single sheet of writing paper.

Darling Emma, she read, and smiled at the thought of her father addressing her in these terms. *I am often rather worried about you being at the convent, and powerless to make your own decisions, should the need arise. I know that you will probably disagree with me, and consider what I suggest to be a devious act, but I urge you* not *to hand in this money in the usual way, but to keep it in your own possession, please. At the very least, by doing so, you will enable me to feel less concerned about you, my very dear daughter. With love, as always, Dad.*

Deeply touched, Emma counted the money: ten thousand francs. She blinked nervously, mindful that the Rule should oblige her to hand it over when she returned to La Falaise, but already knowing that she intended to obey her father's wish and keep it.

The departure time and platform number of her train flashed up on the information screen. Emma folded the money, returning it to the envelope with the letter, and putting it in her pocket. She got out her return ticket, and made her way to the appropriate gate. As she sped towards Rennes, she gazed at the passing landscape and thought about Allegra, reliving their deeply unpleasant confrontation. Poor girl, she thought, I quite understand how she feels. It's very natural that she should resent and dislike me, and I don't think much of *her*, to be brutally honest. She sighed, realizing that her dream of being a part of Ludo's and Claudia's life had been unrealistic and naive. At the very least, she told herself sadly, I should stay away for Allegra's sake. Her claim on their affections is much more deserving than mine. After all, she is still little more than a child. Then she recalled her first glimpse of Allegra and her boyfriend, through the slats of the venetian blind the previous night, and a bitter little smile compressed her lips. She is much less of a child than I am in *that* respect, she thought, but that's her business, of course.

Chapter Six

After his first encounter with Chloe, Alexander saw her all the time. Sometimes she reappeared in the barn, and would stand beside him until he spoke to her. 'Hi,' he would say, smiling at her, but she did not always respond. She would often turn away as if she didn't know him, and walk towards the ladder, fading from sight before she reached it.

Sometimes it was quite different, and she would sit on the floor beside him, and chat away just as she had always done. At first, Alexander was careful not to mention the fact that she was dead, but on the second or third visit she brought the subject up herself. 'It's awfully cold up there, Alex. I don't think they can have heard of central heating.'

'Can't you run about, to keep warm?'

'Doesn't help, really. They're mostly wrinklies up there; they just sit about listening to the wireless, Classic FM mostly. It's boring; there's no-one to play with.'

'Aren't there any other children?'

'I haven't found any. There are a few really gross teenagers, the sort with rings through their noses, but they don't want to know. It's just like down here, they tell you to bugger off.'

'Shame,' said Alexander. 'What's the food like? Is it OK? Can you have anything you like, like a restaurant?'

She frowned. 'I don't think we're allowed to eat.'

'Would you like a Smartie?' Alexander felt in his jeans pocket, pulled out his rather crumpled tube of sweets, and offered it to her.

She stared at him, her face unsmiling and cold, as though he had sworn at her or said something disgusting. 'I can't, Alexander,' she said, her voice sounding strange, like an old woman's. 'It's not allowed; I *told* you!'

'Oh,' he said. 'Sorry.' He put the Smarties back in his pocket, and when he looked up she had gone, leaving behind the faintest outline of her seated shape on the floor. It was as if someone had drawn a pink line round her image with a pencil torch. Alexander opened his mouth to say, 'Don't go, Chloe. Please stay for a bit,' but he was too late; she had vanished completely.

At other times, she could behave really badly, sitting beside him at school and distracting his attention from the lesson. During one geography period, she had become bored and annoyed with him for failing to respond to her remarks. Miss Henderson, having completed her outline of the map of Australia on the whiteboard, turned towards the class. 'Can anyone tell me where the Great Barrier Reef is?' she asked.

'Up there on the right, stupid woman!' said Chloe loudly.

Horrified, Alexander turned to Chloe. 'Shut up, you daft thing!' he said hoarsely.

'Did you speak, Alexander?' asked Miss Henderson with heavy sarcasm, and the rest of the class tittered.

'No, Miss Henderson,' said Alexander, scarlet with mortification.

'Do you know the position of the Great Barrier Reef?'

'Yes, Miss Henderson.'

'Come up and show us, please.'

As he got up from his seat, Chloe put her cold arms round him and tried to prevent him going, but he pushed his way through her with clenched teeth, and made his way to the whiteboard. Miss Henderson handed him the marker, and he wrote 'Great Barrier Reef' in the correct place. When he regained his seat, Chloe was no longer there.

Presumably he had offended her, for she did not come again for nearly a week, and Alexander began to believe that she had gone for good. He did not know whether to be glad or sorry at this turn of events; on balance, he thought he rather missed her, especially as everyone else was still so sad and miserable at home.

Gwen, though subdued, was her usual kind self. She helped him with his prep, though she was hopeless at modern maths. 'It wasn't like this at all in my day, dear,' she would say, shaking her head. 'I think you'd better ask your mother.'

Alexander, however, felt quite unable to take this advice. Since the funeral Phoebe had seemed to be beginning to be a bit better. She got up in the morning, and drove him to school. She went shopping, and worked in her garden as usual. But she never laughed, or even smiled, and it seemed to Alexander that she was the dead person, rather than Chloe. She lay on the sofa with Winnie the old labrador beside her, and stroked her silky domed head. Watching, Alexander longed for her to stroke his head, and love *him* again. But she spoke to him only when it was necessary; not unkindly, but not kindly either. She still thinks it was my fault, Alexander said to himself; she'll never forgive me.

One night, on his way up to bed, he heard the telephone ringing, down in the hall. No-one seemed to be answering it, so he ran downstairs again and picked up the receiver. 'Hello?'

'Hello, dogbreath. It's me.'

'Oh, good,' he said. 'Where are you?'

'With you, cretin!'

'Oh, yes, I suppose so.' He tried to think of something to say that wouldn't annoy her. 'It's boring without you, Chloe. Come to my room and we'll play a game?'

'Well, I might; on one condition, though.'

'What's that?'

'You're not to walk through me like that again. It's absolutely bloody *agony* when people do that. I won't come unless you promise.'

'All right,' said Alexander. 'I promise.'

'OK,' said Chloe. 'Race you there!'

'Wicked!' He slammed down the phone and rushed up the stairs two at a time. He did not see Gwen standing by the dining-room door, watching him with frightened eyes.

When the weekend came, bringing Christian from London, Gwen decided to have a word with him. 'I am a bit concerned about Alexander,' she said.

'Why? What's up? Is he behaving badly?'

'No, not at all. I rather wish he would. It would be more normal, and better for him.'

'What's the problem, Gwen?'

Gwen looked at him, a worried frown creasing her forehead. 'I think he's hallucinating, Christian.'

'He's *what*?'

'Hallucinating. Several times, I've overheard him talking to some invisible being. I think it must be Chloe. I've actually *seen* him, talking to her on the phone.'

'Really?' Christian looked slightly startled. 'What do you think we should do about it, Gwen? Take him to a shrink?'

'Oh dear, I shouldn't like that at all.' Gwen looked flustered and alarmed. 'I expect it's a passing phase. He misses Chloe badly, I'm sure.'

'We all do, don't we, Gwen?' He patted her arm kindly. 'It's a tough time for us all, but most of all for poor Phoebe.'

'I know that,' said Gwen, then looked him straight in the eye. 'It's time she remembered that Alexander is her child, too. He needs her, Christian, and she seems unable or unwilling to take that on board. It's really not fair on the poor little boy.'

'He's thirteen, Gwen. He's not a baby.'

'He's still only twelve, as a matter of fact.' Gwen's face was flushed, her blue eyes fierce. 'That's not a very great age, in my book, Christian.'

'Well, you may have a point.' He sighed, looking tired. 'I'll see what I can do.'

But Gwen still stood there obstinately, as if she expected more of him.

'What?' he asked impatiently, and then gave in. 'Oh, very well; I'll speak to her. All right?'

'I think you should, my dear.' She picked up his coffee cup and went to the door. 'Thank you, Christian. It's not easy for you, I know.' She left the room, closing the door quietly behind her.

Phoebe sat in her armillary garden, wrapped in her plaid shawl, for the dew was falling and the air felt chilly after the warmth of the day. She gazed at the bright green shoots of the Regale lilies she had planted only a few weeks ago, marvelling at the speed of their growth. The Iceberg roses were already in flower, and their delicate scent hung in the still evening air. Is it really such a little time since it happened? she thought incredulously. It seems like years to me. Sometimes I find it quite hard to remember what she looked like. My lovely Chloe, my poor little baby, is she beginning to decompose? Are the worms already eating her? Phoebe looked at the nodding white faces of the roses, pure against the sombre dark green of the yew hedge, then up at the darkening blue dome of the sky above. Why did this have to happen to me? she asked herself. *Why?* What have I ever done to deserve it? Nothing at all; I'm too boring ever to do anything bad. More's the pity; maybe if I was like that I wouldn't feel so crushed by it all; so despairing; so dead.

The stable clock struck six, and she got reluctantly to her feet and went slowly back to the house. As she crossed the big lawn she noticed Alexander in the paddock. He was riding one of the ponies bareback, and had the other on a leading rein. Round and round the perimeter of the field the ponies cantered, faster and faster, urged on by Alexander, until they finally came to a shuddering halt by the stile. 'There you are!' she heard him exclaim, and he laughed. 'I bet that'll warm you up a bit!'

Phoebe stood for a moment, watching Alexander as he slid to the ground, still chattering to himself, and took the tack off the ponies. How frighteningly quickly children forget, she thought, and continued on her way to the house.

At half past ten, Christian turned off the television, switched off the lights of the sitting room, checked that the garden door was locked and barred, and climbed the spiral staircase of the tower. In the bathroom, he showered, cleaned his teeth and put on his pyjamas. He examined his face in the steamy mirror and was depressed by what he saw. I look a bloody sight older than thirty-five, he thought, observing the bags under his round blue eyes, the silver hair on his temples. He imagined that in view of the fact that his hair was so fair, the signs of ageing were perhaps not particularly obvious, but could not help noticing that there were broken thread veins on his nose and cheeks, and a sagging fold of skin beneath his chin. Shit, he thought, I look more like Ma every day, what a ghastly thought!

Flavia had not telephoned since her return to London, but had sent Phoebe a note of thanks and condolence, enclosing a small coloured card depicting the Blessed Virgin, with a novena printed on the back. Christian did not know what Phoebe had done with this card, and had not thought it prudent to enquire. He took his dressing gown from the peg behind the door and put it on, then climbed the few steps to the bedroom. Phoebe was lying against her pillows, reading. She did not look up as he entered the room. He took off his dressing gown. 'Can I get you anything, darling? Tea, or something?'

'No, thanks,' said Phoebe. 'I'm OK.'

Christian got into bed beside her. He tried to put his arm round her, but she felt stiff and unresponsive, so he withdrew his arm and lay down. 'Phoebe, my love?'

'Mm?'

'Gwen is worried about Alexander.'

'Really? Why should she be? He seems quite happy to me.'

'Gwen doesn't think so, darling. She says she hears him talking to himself, and behaving rather oddly.'

'Well, that's what children do, isn't it?'

'What, talking to people who aren't there?' He hesitated, not wishing to upset her. 'Talking to Chloe?'

'What nonsense! How does Gwen know that? I expect he's just playing games.' She turned her head and looked at him. 'Or perhaps it's his way of saying sorry.'

'What the hell do you mean by that?'

'Well, it *was* his fault, wasn't it? He killed her, if we're truthful about it.' Slowly, tears filled her eyes and rolled down her plump cheeks in two straight lines, then dripped onto her chest.

Christian stared at her incredulously. 'Phoebe, I thought we'd been into all that, many times. It's not true; you know quite well that it was an accident. You really cannot lay the blame for your loss on an innocent child.'

'But I do,' whispered Phoebe, and blew her nose. 'I do blame him; I always will. I can't help it.'

God, thought Christian, I can't handle this. What the hell am I going to do? Perhaps it's Phoebe who needs to see a shrink, or maybe a counsellor. Isn't that the thing nowadays? He lay on his back and waited for the snuffling beside him to subside. I won't say anything just now, he thought. I'll wait until she's less tense. He turned towards her, and her ravaged, blotched face tore at his heart. 'Phoebe, my darling,' he began, and put his hand tentatively on her bare shoulder.

'Just leave me alone, Chris,' she interrupted. 'There's nothing you can do.'

One afternoon, when Phoebe had gone into Gloucester to do some shopping before collecting Alexander from school, Gwen took advantage of her absence to pack away Chloe's clothes. Carefully, she sorted them into separate piles, setting aside those that needed washing. She pulled open the big heavy drawer at the base of the tall mahogany linen-press that stood on the landing beside the attic staircase, and took out the long-forgotten gym shoes and croquet mallets that had languished there for years. Then she hoovered out the drawer, and lined it with some lavender-scented paper obtained from a roll in the linen cupboard. She also found a quantity of pale-blue petersham ribbon, used by Phoebe to divide her sheets, pillowcases and counterpanes into separate bundles, each tied with a neat, flat bow. With a heavy heart, Gwen divided Chloe's clothes in the same way, into piles of sweaters, jeans, skirts, coats and party frocks. She tied them with the blue ribbon and laid each bundle tenderly into the drawer. She supposed that eventually a decision would be reached, and the clothes sent to Oxfam or whatever. In the meantime, she thought it kinder to Phoebe not to draw attention to them. She closed the drawer carefully, then went back to Chloe's room and gathered up all the socks, vests, pants and nightdresses. She put them all into a laundry bag and took it down to the kitchen, intending to wash and iron everything before folding them away with the rest. She decided that she would do this at night, after Phoebe had gone to bed, and hung the bag on the back of the laundry-room door, in readiness.

She closed the door behind her, and went to the kitchen to make herself a cup of tea. While the kettle came slowly to the boil, she allowed herself to remember Chloe, the last of 'her' babies. In the drawer at the end of the table was her bag, and from it she took her travelling folder of photographs, which unfolded in a zigzag pattern to reveal six pictures. She stood it carefully on the table in front of her. The first photo was a formal one of Ludovic and Flavia, looking young and handsome, with the baby Christian. He really was the image of his mother, she thought, and smiled, reliving those far-off, happy days. And *his* children are the image of *him*, so fair-haired and blue-eyed. The second picture was of Emma, aged about three, with her arms clasped tightly round her mother's pearl-encircled neck. Neither mother nor daughter looked particularly happy, and Flavia's smile was rather tense, as if she resented the child's fierce hug. As for Emma, with her dark straight hair and the brooding grey eyes of her father, what a disappointment she must have been to her mother after the angelic-looking Christian. The third photograph was of herself, with Chris and Emma, aged about fourteen and four, on holiday in Gwen's home, on the Isle of Skye. Then came Chris in his cap and gown at Oxford, holding his degree, and Emma, after her Clothing Ceremony in Brittany. Then, last of all, a group including herself, sitting on the lawn at Abbot's Court, with baby Chloe in Phoebe's arms, and Alexander, aged four, trying to break away from the group, while Gwen held fast to the seat of his pants. They were all laughing. She remembered the occasion vividly. Chris had taken the pictures, and Winnie, then little more than a puppy, had kept blundering into the shot, determined to join in.

Gwen looked long at that perfect summer image, finding no comfort in it, unable to believe that the happiness of the house had been so comprehensively destroyed in the space of a few short hours. She folded the frame, snapping it shut, and replaced it in her bag. I must ask Chris if he has any more recent pictures of the children, she thought. I suppose after Alexander goes away to school I won't be needed here any more. She thought of her eighty-year-old mother in her island croft, just above the beach. She thought of the slate-grey sea, the wide sandy shore and the scudding clouds of that far lonely place, and for the first time in thirty-five years, she was gripped with an intense longing to be there.

The kettle sent out a thin plume of steam, and tiredly Gwen got to her feet, put a teabag into a mug and poured boiling water over it.

Ludovic sat in the committee room in Brussels, his earphones switched on, his eyes closed, listening as conscientiously as he could to the biased opinions of his fellow committee members. He had already delivered his own equally biased point of view, and the closed faces of his confrères had left little doubt in his mind that he might as well have saved his breath, for all the success he was likely to achieve on behalf of the country he represented. Why is it always such a bloody uphill struggle? he asked himself. I got into this game presumably with the serious intention that I would be of some use to my fellow men, but it's nothing but a constant battle of wits, a jockeying for position, a trade-off at the end of the day. He opened his eyes and looked across the table at the speaker, whose round, shining, well-fed face, above a too-tight stiff collar, bore witness to the excellent food and wine its owner had consumed at lunchtime. Ludovic looked at his own bottle of chilled Perrier water on the table in front of him, and pursed his lips self-righteously. He switched off the simultaneous translation. He knew exactly what the fat man was saying; he had heard it all before. God, he thought, I can think of better things to be doing on a sunny afternoon than sitting here listening to all this hot air. He stole a look at his watch: ten to five. What's the betting they'll decide to adjourn at five? After all, it *is* Friday, they'll be wanting to get home for the weekend. Thank God, the summer recess won't be long now. Where shall we go this year? The sea, or the mountains?

Ludovic's guess proved to be correct, and by half past six he was on his way to Paris. From the Gard du Nord he took a cab to rue Mouffetard. Normally, he enjoyed using the Métro, but tonight he was feeling his age and sank gratefully into the dark obscurity of the elderly taxi, driven by an equally elderly driver, whose leisurely pace and silent demeanour offered an unusual and welcome relief. He descended from the cab just before impasse des Cordonniers, paid the driver and threaded his way through the still-busy market. He went into a small specialist grocery and bought a jar of caviar, the proper stuff, beluga. Then he stopped at a flower stall and bought a dozen yellow roses. Bearing his gifts, he walked up the *impasse* to his door, and took out his key. At that moment, Allegra's door opened, and she appeared in the lane, slamming her door after her.

'Hello, darling,' said Ludovic. 'Ships that pass in the night, as usual. You're going out, and I'm coming in.'

'Yes.' She stood a little way from him, close to the opposite wall.

'Is Emma still here? Did you get to meet her?'

'No, she's gone; and yes, I met her.'

'Oh, good. I'm glad you two met, at last.'

'Are you really?' Allegra glared at her father, her face grim. 'Well, that must be terrific for you, *Papa*. What makes you think it's so bloody wonderful for me?'

Ludovic frowned, his heart filled with sudden foreboding. 'I'm sorry that you feel that way about it, Allegra,' he said quietly. 'I must have got completely the wrong impression about your reaction, when I told you about my other children. I felt sure that you understood the reasons why your mother and I can't marry; that you didn't condemn us. As a matter of fact, I thought it remarkably mature of you, darling.'

'Oh, did you? And was it so remarkably mature of *you*, as a married man with children, to seduce a woman a hell of a lot younger than yourself, and turn *her* into a whore, and *me* into a bastard? Was it, *Papa*? Or should I call you Ludo now, as she does? You don't feel like my father any more.'

Father and daughter stared at each other coldly. He felt a deep sense of disquiet at the sight of her smooth young face, now distorted with anger and contempt. After a moment, he spoke, his voice barely audible. 'So, what did you say to Emma, Allegra?'

'I told her to fuck off, and leave us alone.'

'I don't believe you!'

'Well, I bloody did! And the same goes for you. Did you really think I'd just roll over and let you get away with this? You may not be aware of it, *Papa*, but I have friends in the media who are *very* interested in your private life, and now I have rather a lot to tell them, haven't I?'

'Allegra, don't you think we should discuss this sensibly, before you do something you may regret?'

'Get real, *Papa*!' She pushed past him and ran down the alley, the sound of her heavy boots echoing against the walls of the narrow passage.

Ludovic put his key in the lock and entered his house. Claudia was not at home. He went to the kitchen and put the caviar in the fridge. Then he chose a tall square glass jar, filled it with water, and put in the yellow roses. He carried them to the studio and placed them carefully on the table, next to the blackamoor's head. He removed the paste tiara normally worn by this handsome creature, and went out into the garden, where he cut a long trailing stem of ivy, speckled green and white. He carried it back to the studio, winding it into a circle and fixing it with a paper-clip, before placing it on the blackamoor's head in place of the tiara. 'That's better,' he said.

He picked up his briefcase and went to the bedroom. He undressed and took a shower, letting the cool water flow over his body until he began to feel slightly cold. He turned off the shower and wound a towel round his waist, then returned to the studio, leaving a trail of wet footprints on the floor. He took off the towel and rubbed his head vigorously, so that his short grey hair stood up in spikes. He dropped the damp towel on the floor and went to the kitchen, where he fixed himself an extremely strong dry martini, ninety-nine per cent gin, the rest Noilly Prat, plus a fistful of ice. Like the perfectionist he was, he carefully cut a thin sliver of lemon zest and added that to the glass. He drank half of this lethal concoction as he stood beside the fridge, naked and still damp. Then he went back to the bedroom and lay down on the bed. He drank the rest of the gin very slowly, and forced himself to confront the situation that Allegra had thrust so painfully upon him. Anaesthetized by the gin, he found it difficult to believe that his skilfully constructed life was about to fall apart. If the story got out, then doubtless all hell would break loose in the UK press, to the hysterical delight of that nation of puritans. Here in France, the whole thing would doubtless be dismissed with a Gallic shrug, and a cynical '*Et alors*?' For himself, it would not matter so very much. After all, he could simply retire into private life and get on with the writing he had always intended to do, and in any case his various pension plans were on the point of maturing, so finance would not be a problem. But what of Christian and Phoebe, and young Alexander? What of Flavia, the classic innocent party in all this? The long-deceived wife, no less? And Emma, his dear Emma, how would she react to seeing her father blasted all over the papers? Poor Emma, how had she responded to Allegra's harsh words? What had happened? Had they met here, in the house, with Claudia present? Or had the confrontation taken place in the street, with Allegra ambushing Emma as she went on her way? He lay on the bed, turning these questions over and over in his mind, until he heard Claudia's key in the lock.

In a few minutes she appeared in the doorway and looked at him, smiling. 'Thank you for the roses, Ludo; they're beautiful,' she said softly, 'but they're not as beautiful as the sight of you.' She sat down on the bed beside him and kissed him, first on his chest, then on his stomach and finally on his mouth.

His arms closed around her and he returned the kiss. Then, gently, he held her away from him. 'Claudia, my love,' he said, 'we have to talk.'

'What about?'

'About Allegra.'

'What about her?'

'She and Emma met, it seems.'

'Oh, good. I hoped they would.'

'I'm afraid it's not good at all, darling.' He took her hand and told her of his clash with Allegra on the doorstep. Leaving nothing out, he even repeated their daughter's choice of abusive words: *whore, bastard, fuck off.* 'She said that if I thought she would roll over and go along with the new situation, I had underestimated her.'

'And then?'

'Then she ran away, down the alley.'

For a few minutes, Claudia sat silently. Then she turned towards Ludovic and their eyes met, serious, troubled. 'Are you angry, Ludo?' she said.

'*Angry*? Why on earth should you think that?'

'I don't know. I just thought you might be.'

'Of course I'm not angry, Claudia. I'm extremely upset; I feel very bad about it. I feel *guilty*, as a matter of fact, that I involved you in a secret liaison, that I cheated you of the possibility of a normal, legal, wife-and-mother life.'

'You've left out one important element.'

'What?'

'Love, Ludo. I love you, and I always will. You love me. We chose this life together, both of us, don't forget.'

'But what about Allegra? Come to that, what about poor Emma, scuttling back behind the convent walls with those repulsive words ringing in her ears?'

Claudia smiled faintly. 'I expect she's heard worse from time to time.' Then she sighed. 'But Allegra, what to do about her? I'm amazed that it took her so long to react in the way that she did. It's more than a month since we discussed it with her. She didn't seem particularly disturbed by the news then, did she? I thought that everything would be OK, that nothing was changed, fundamentally.'

'It's quite possible, I suppose,' said Ludovic thoughtfully, 'that she's talked to her friends, and it's their reaction that has upset her; made her feel vulnerable, deprived of status in some way.'

'How could that be? Allegra is the child of a long-standing and faithful relationship.'

'But the fact remains that in the eyes of some people, she might be regarded as illegitimate.'

'I don't think of my daughter as illegitimate in any way,' said Claudia, her voice cold.

'Neither do I! Of course not! But it's clear that *she* thinks so, isn't it?'

Claudia got up from the bed. 'This is getting us nowhere. Get dressed, Ludo. Let's go out for supper.'

'Must we? I really don't feel like it.'

'If we stay in, we'll just keep going over and over the same ground. Come on, we should try to forget about it, and it'll probably sort itself out by itself.'

Five minutes later they walked together down rue

Mouffetard towards their favourite bistro. Passing a café on their way, Claudia glanced through the window and saw Allegra, her curtain of red hair falling across her face as she leaned towards the dark-haired young man who shared her table.

When they had settled into their seats, ordered their dinner and had an opened bottle of wine on the table, Claudia looked at Ludovic and smiled. 'Did you see her, Ludo?'

'See who?'

'Allegra, of course.'

'No, where was she?'

'In the café, with that young man of hers, Jules Martinez. She looked perfectly happy.'

'Oh,' said Ludovic. 'Good. Perhaps I overreacted.' He did not wish to wreck the evening entirely, so he chose not to mention that the father of young Mr Martinez was the political editor of *Info-Phallo*, a widely read weekly magazine, celebrated for its colourful exposures of corruption and misconduct in high places. It was perfectly clear to him that his worst fears were about to be realized; that it was extremely likely that Allegra was in the process of betraying him at this very moment.

Alexander woke in the middle of the night. He had been dreaming about Chloe and was not at all surprised to see her standing at the foot of his bed. His curtains were closed, so that his room was completely dark, but she was perfectly visible, even alarmingly so. She seemed to be covered in a pearly radiance, and shone like the scales of a pale-grey fish. Her voice, when she spoke, was far from ghostly, and sounded quite normal, if rather impatient. 'I've been here for ages, trying to wake you up, Alex.'

'I was dreaming about you.' Alexander blinked sleepily, wondering if he was still dreaming, and not really awake at all.

'Come on, then! Get up! Come and play!'

'It's the middle of the night, Chloe. I can't play. I have to go to school tomorrow.'

Without replying, she came towards him, took hold of his duvet and ripped it off. Shocked, he sat up abruptly and tried to wrench it out of her hands, but she laughed and pulled it onto the floor, so that he was forced to get out of bed.

'There, you're up now,' she said. 'Let's do something really cool, shall we?'

'Like what?'

'Like go up on the roof?'

'You're mad, Chloe. We're not allowed to do that. It's dangerous and stupid. You're a nutter!'

'What a poncey twit you are, Alex. What's to stop us? Who will know?' She took his hand and dragged him towards the door. To his terror and astonishment, she did not open the door, but walked straight through it, taking him with her. He felt nothing at all; it was as if the door had ceased to exist, but as they walked along the corridor together he looked back over his shoulder and saw that the door looked reassuringly solid and was still closed. They went downstairs to the hall and into the glass court, where the statue of the Virgin rose from a thicket of ferns, illuminated by a shaft of moonlight, her shadow falling intensely black on the tiled floor.

'Where are we going?' asked Alexander, extremely nervously, for he had already guessed what was in Chloe's mind.

'To the top of the tower, prat! Where else?'

'Mum will hear us.'

'No chance. She can't even see me.'

'She'll hear *me* though,' said Alex hopefully.

'No, she won't. You've got bare feet.' She took him by the hand again, and they seemed to skim effortlessly over the worn stone steps of the spiral staircase until they reached the small locked door at the top. 'It's too knackering getting you through, Alex. Unlock the door yourself, lazy thing.'

She waited while he took the heavy key from its hook and unlocked the door. He felt powerless to resist her, and wondered whether he was really in bed after all, and would wake up presently. He turned the iron ring, the door swung open and they stepped over the stone threshold onto the lead-lined parapet that ran right round the top of the tower. Moonlight fell on the mossy stone tiles of the steep roof, and a slight cool breeze stirred the weathercock on its creaking metal post. Chloe led the way right round the inside of the parapet, then sat down on the low stone wall. Alexander sat beside her, rather glad to take his bare feet off the cold lead.

'Look, Alex, you can see the ponies down there. Aren't they small from up here?'

Alex looked down. He felt sick. 'Yes,' he agreed faintly. 'They look like toys.'

'What's the matter? You look a bit green.'

'I'm OK.'

'You're scared!'

'I'm not!'

'You are!'

'No, I'm not!'

Chloe stood up and went to the corner of the tower, and climbed onto the lifesize gargoyle, from whose mouth issued a waterspout in the shape of a long metal pipe. Nimbly, she negotiated the strange creature's spiny back, then sat astride the pipe, her legs dangling, with nothing but clear air between her and the ground far below. She looked at her brother and laughed, the very same excited laughter that he remembered hearing when she had plunged down through the woods to her death. The hair rose on Alexander's neck.

'Don't just sit there, Alex! Climb on that one. It's brilliant; it's just like flying!'

Alexander swallowed nervously, and remained where he was, pretending not to hear.

'Come on, it's easy. Don't be so wet!' Then she said the words he most dreaded. 'I dare you!'

Trembling, he got up and made his way to the corner, and his legs felt as if he were walking through wet cement. Chloe was right, it was quite easy to climb over the gargoyle. It was sitting astride the waterspout, suspended in thin air so high above the ground, that was the problem, but eventually, with fatalistic courage, he managed it. Taking great care not to look down, and clinging tightly to the rusty pipe with both hands, he looked triumphantly along the parapet at his sister, and saw with a tremendous leap of his heart that she had vanished. 'Chloe?' His voice sounded thin and strange. 'Where are you, Chloe?'

'Here! I'm up here!'

'Where?'

'Here, stupid! Look up!'

Very slowly, Alexander raised his eyes and saw her crouched underneath the weathercock. She reached up and spun the golden cockerel so that it whirled giddily round on its spindle, flashing in the cold light of the moon. She looked down at Alexander, her face sad now, and unsmiling. 'I hate it up here without you, Alex. It's dreadfully dull and boring; there's nothing to do, and no-one to talk to. I wish you could be here too, even if you are a bit of a scaredy-cat sometimes. We could do terrific things together, you know.'

'Like what?'

'Lots of things. There's a good game I thought of; it's running in front of cars in the night. It scares the pants off the drivers, they always brake like anything, it's really funny.'

'What if they hit you?'

'Sometimes they do, silly old farts. It's OK, it doesn't hurt.'

'Oh.' Alexander looked up at Chloe, and asked her

something he badly needed to know. 'Did it hurt when you died, Chloe? When you hit the tree?'

'What tree?' She looked at him coldly, frowning. 'I can't remember any tree. What are you talking about?'

'Nothing, it's OK.' He looked away, aware that he had blundered.

'You're an idiot, Alex. I bloody don't need you. You can get lost for all I care.' Her thin little voice was angry and resentful. When he looked up again, she was gone, and the golden cockerel revolved slowly, then came to a halt.

Suddenly, and terrifyingly, Alexander realized the serious implications of his predicament. There was nothing between himself and certain death if he did not keep absolutely calm and work his way back across the pipe to the gargoyle's back and over the parapet. Slowly, inch by inch, one sweating hand in front of the other, he shuffled his way towards the gargoyle until he was able to put one arm round the neck of its beaked head and heave himself onto its rough back. Willing himself not to panic and rush things, he crawled to the comparative safety of the parapet. He sat down heavily on the cold lead lining, his heart pounding, sweat pouring down his chest and back and prickling his scalp. For a long while he remained where he was, recovering his nerve. Then, fearful that Chloe might come back and try to make him do something even more alarming, he crawled towards the door and scrambled through it swiftly, locking it securely behind him.

Shivering with cold and fright, Alexander went down the stairs of the tower. Outside his mother's door he paused, hesitating, longing to go in and tell her what had happened. It's no use, he thought, she'll only be angry. She won't believe me, she'll think I'm making it up. Slowly he continued down the stairs to the glass court, then ran quickly through the hall and up the main staircase to his own room. He put the duvet back on the bed and got into it. He lay down and stared at the ceiling, now faintly visible as the first light of dawn stole through the edges of his curtains. Was I just sleepwalking? he asked himself. Do I really see Chloe, and talk to her all the time, or is it all just a stupid dream? Or p'raps I'm going round the bend, or she's trying to get into my head and make me do what she wants, so that I'll do something really horrible and get killed too. I'm sure that's it. She wants me dead, so that I can be with her, up there, wherever that is. I do wish I could get away from here, get away from Chloe. If this is what being haunted is, I can bloody do without it. His eyelids drooped and he slept, until Gwen came to wake him at seven o'clock, pulling back his curtains so that the sun streamed into the room. He woke, rubbing his eyes, then pushed back his duvet and sat on the edge of the bed.

Gwen turned from the window and saw at once Alexander's dirty face and filthy pyjamas, streaked with sweat and rusty dirt. 'Mercy! What on earth have you been doing, Alex?'

Alexander stared at her. 'Doing? I haven't been doing anything. Why?'

'Look at your pyjamas, dear.'

Alexander looked, and the full horror of his trip to the tower broke over him. The blood rushed to his head as he realized that the events of the night had not, after all, been a bad dream. He wished very badly to tell Gwen about it, and about Chloe's continual invasion of his life, but doubt and confusion robbed him of his usual common sense and he found himself unable to speak of his terrors.

'Tell me what you've been up to, Alex, there's a good boy.'

Alex shook his head. 'There's nothing to tell,' he mumbled. 'I don't think so, anyway. I can't remember.'

Chapter Seven

In the middle of May, Emma received a summons to an interview with the Abbess. She stopped sorting sheets for the guest-house beds, took off her apron and went at once to the Abbess's study. She knocked on the door and entered the room, closing the door quietly behind her. She stood silently, her hands folded, and waited for the senior nun to finish the writing that occupied her. After a few minutes the Abbess put down her pen, blotted the work carefully and covered it with a piece of paper. Then she leaned back in her chair and looked at Emma, her pale-blue eyes bland and expressionless behind rimless spectacles. Her face, framed in the starched white wimple, and shaded by the black veil, was remarkably unlined for a woman who must have been in her fifties at the very least. It was never easy to guess what went on in her mind, for she was not a person given to self-expression of any kind. Her entire life was ordered according to the Rule.

From the first moment of Emma's entry into La Falaise, she had been aware that the older woman had a low opinion of her, and could not help noticing that her lips compressed themselves into a thin straight line whenever their paths crossed, which was sometimes unavoidable. It was, therefore, no great surprise to Emma when her superior informed her, without preamble, that she was to be transferred to their sister house in the Vaucluse.

'May one ask why, Mother?' Emma tried not to sound impertinent, but failed, as she usually did.

'One may not, Sister.'

'Oh, I see,' said Emma, though she was in fact none the wiser. 'Where is the Vaucluse?' she ventured, for she felt she had a right to know.

'It is in the south of France, on the left bank of the river Rhône. Avignon is the departmental capital. You have no doubt heard of it?' This last remark was offered with a hint of sarcasm.

'Yes, of course.' Emma suppressed a smile, for the cheering thought that she would soon escape from the disapproval of this unattractive woman had raised her spirits amazingly and now almost provoked childish laughter in her. She uttered a small embarrassed cough, and asked politely when she would be leaving.

'On Saturday. Sister Beatrice has been unwell. She is going down for a rest and retreat. It will be convenient for you to travel with her.'

'Very well, Mother.' Emma waited for a moment, in case her superior had anything more to say, but the Abbess picked up her pen in a dismissive manner. 'Is that all, Mother?'

'Not quite, Sister.' Once more, she raised her cold eyes to Emma's. 'One has never had the feeling that you were truly committed to the life here, Sister. There is an air of discontent and rebellion about you that you seem unable or unwilling to conquer. I pray that I will be proved wrong, and that you do eventually proceed to your final vows, but at this juncture I feel I should warn you that we do not think it very likely that you will.'

In spite of her negative feelings concerning the Abbess, Emma felt quite shocked at what seemed to her a completely unjustified attack, but found that she had nothing to say in reply, or in her own defence.

'*Deo gratias*, Mother,' she said quietly, with a slight bow.

'*Deo gratias*, Sister,' replied the Abbess, a glint of triumph in her eye.

Emma left the room, and returned to her task. She was not able to talk to Miriam until after supper that night. They walked together under the apple trees in the orchard, as they had so many times before.

'They're chucking me out, Miriam.'

'I know.'

'You *know*? Why didn't you warn me?'

'I was only told about it this morning. I got a right ticking off myself, and a warning from the old bat.'

'What sort of warning?'

'Oh, *you* know, Em. You're not allowed to have special friends, all that stuff.'

'It's idiotic, isn't it? They really do try to deprive you of everything, don't they? Liking one thing or one person better than another, free will of any kind.'

'That's exactly it. Unless you are truthfully able to give up everything – family, friends, possessions, even opinions – the whole thing is a non-starter.' Miriam turned and touched Emma's hand. She smiled sadly, her green eyes bright. 'I'll miss you, Em, but I'm glad you're going, really. You're a distraction, I'm afraid. The old bag is quite right; we're better separated.'

I can't believe I'm hearing this, thought Emma, and she recalled vividly Phoebe's hysterical accusations against the Church, after Chloe's funeral. 'I thought the whole point of Christianity was everyone loving one another,' she said, staring at the grass beneath their feet.

'But we're not "everyone", are we? We're supposed to be the Brides of Christ, aren't we? We can love everyone in a general way, and pray for them, of course. But in the *particular* sense, we can only really love Jesus Christ; you know that, Em.'

The blasphemous and irrelevant thought rose in

Emma's mind that if all the professed nuns are true Brides of Christ, He must have a positive harem up there, but she felt it inappropriate to say such a thing to Miriam, whose distressed expression reproached her. 'I'll miss you, Miriam. I think I'd have left of my own accord, if you hadn't been here to make me laugh.'

'I expect I'll miss you, too, though I shall try very hard not to.'

Emma looked at her and smiled. 'You'll make a terrific nun, I'm sure of that.'

'Whatever makes you think so?'

Emma laughed. 'You're quite prepared to go on banging your head against a brick wall, Miriam, that's why. You've got the right sort of guts for it.'

'I hope so,' said Miriam, and she did not laugh. 'Pray for me, Em, won't you?'

'I will,' said Emma. 'All my life.'

The Abbaye de Villemagne turned out to be as different from La Falaise as the Mediterranean is to the Atlantic Ocean. In place of the bleak granite building, grey and forbidding, battered by cold northern gales and surrounded by windswept muddy fields, Emma found herself in a smiling, benevolent land, bathed in the clear light of Provence, that reminded her of Tuscany.

In view of her frail health, Sister Beatrice had been authorized to take a taxi from Avignon station to the abbey, a distance of some sixty kilometres. Emma enjoyed the drive through a long peaceful valley, the great looming bulk of the north face of the Lubéron mountains blocking the horizon to her right, its dark flanks clothed with forest and scrub, with the occasional white scar of bare limestone. At the foot of its forbidding face lay a neat, cultivated land of vineyards, olive groves and orchards, protected from the *mistral* by windbreaks of tall cypresses and warmed by the golden sun. Set well back from the road, along their own private tracks, were clusters of farm buildings half-hidden under clumps of shady pines and guarded by the dark sentinel shapes of cypresses.

As the car made its way along the valley, Emma observed, perched on the rocky outcrops on the lower slopes of the mountain, several beautiful large villages. One of these in particular followed the crest of the hill on which it stood, its tightly packed limestone buildings seeming to tumble down the precipitous approach from the valley. Crowned by the tall white steeple of its church, the village appeared to be held together by the enormous spreading cedars that grew among the buildings and extended far beyond the village boundaries, their intense green-black colour a vivid contrast to the pale stone houses and the vibrant blue sky above. Circling the foot of the village were cherry orchards, and Emma could easily guess how beautiful their snowy blossom must be in the spring, and imagined, though she could not see them, the glowing red and black of the cherries now ripening among the glossy green leaves.

'Bonnieux,' said the driver, with a jerk of his head in the direction of the village.

'Ah,' said Sister Beatrice.

After another twenty minutes, they turned into a minor road, and drove through an area of gentle wooded hills, lightly clad with evergreen oaks, the ground covered with the aromatic shrubs of the *garrigue*, myrtle, thyme and lavender. The air under the trees felt cool and fresh after the heat of the open valley, and the sharp scents of the undergrowth came strongly through the driver's open window. Slowly, the car made its way along the potholed track, and in ten minutes emerged into a clearing in the woodlands.

As they approached the abbey through the trees, the driver pointed it out to them, jabbing the air with a nicotine-stained finger. '*Vous avez une belle maison, n'est-ce pas?*' The ancient abbey was indeed beautiful, and Emma thought that it looked more like the dwelling of some romantic southern noblewoman, a silver-haired widow perhaps, whose family came down from Paris for the summer, and at Easter and Christmas. The walls of this magnificent group of buildings were of honey-coloured stone, roofed with sunbleached Roman tiles in soft shades of faded apricot. Orchards of fruit trees, and neatly planted rows of lavender, not yet in flower, grew right up to the high walls of the abbey, and as they advanced along the stony drive, Emma noticed a group of three nuns working in a small field, screened by a row of almond trees. They were dressed in blue cotton overalls, wearing their white wimples without their veils, and were energetically scything a crop of hay.

The taxi drew up before the great wooden double doors, high and firmly closed against the world. They got out, Sister Beatrice paying the driver, while Emma retrieved their two small bags from the boot of the car. The cab drove away, and Sister Beatrice pulled the bell rope which hung against the wall. In a few moments the wooden screen behind the cast-iron grille was snapped open and they could see the bespectacled young face of a novice peering at them through the bars.

'*Deo gratias*, Sister,' said Sister Beatrice.

'*Deo gratias*,' replied the novice. 'We are expecting you, Sister.' The screen was briskly shut again, the bolts pushed back and the ancient iron locks turned on the inner side of the door. One heavy leaf swung open, and they entered the house.

At once, Emma was able to see the real quality of the place. The various wings of the abbey were arranged around a large rectangular cloister, its centre open to the sky. This area was a simple gravelled court but had many terracotta pots of different shapes and sizes, filled with roses, oleanders and brilliant, garish geraniums which fell in glorious showers of colour, and scented the still, cool air in the shadow of the cloisters.

149

The newcomers followed the novice nun as she led the way to the Abbess's study. The Abbess seemed to Emma to be a woman of great age, with sunken eyes of a tranquil misty grey in a heavily wrinkled aristocratic face of enormous charm and curious mystery. She gave the impression of having discovered the key to all the perplexities of existence, but having suffered a great deal in the process.

After the brief formalities were completed, the Abbess, to Emma's astonishment, offered them tea. 'You must be tired, after your long journey, and supper is not until seven o'clock. Sister Paul will bring some for us, and I can get to know you a little.' When Sister Paul had departed in search of the tea, the Abbess enquired very sympathetically after Sister Beatrice's health and told her to rest, enjoy the sunshine, and not to feel any great compulsion to return to the normal duties of the house. 'It is a common mistake to believe that it is necessary to be hard at work at all times. Everyone needs rest, and a break, from time to time. You should listen to your body; it may be that the good Lord is telling you to slow down, and devote a little more time to Him.'

The Abbess spoke kindly to Emma, but did not raise the subject of her transfer from La Falaise, or the reasons behind it. Far from feeling grateful for such tact, Emma felt somehow as though she had been condemned without having had the opportunity to defend herself. Standing on a chair, looking through the grille of the small high window in her cell before getting into bed, she smelt the night-scented air, and the sweetness of the newly cut hay in the meadow below, silvery under the star-sprinkled sky, and prayed that somehow in this warm, beautiful, peaceful and sympathetic place, things might be different, that she might at last be permitted to fulfil her long-postponed ambitions.

For two weeks, she said nothing, and applied herself

to the many duties of the house. The guest house was a large one, and the nuns welcomed not only people in need of a retreat, but night-nurses from a local clinic seeking a quiet place to sleep during the day. In addition, they had many summer visitors, tourists in search of inexpensive board and lodging. Emma peeled potatoes by the bucketful, picked beans and early peas, hoed between the long rows of growing vegetables, and washed and ironed dozens of sheets, pillowcases, napkins and tablecloths. The weather was glorious, the nuns bronzed and cheerful, the days passed swiftly and rather happily.

At the end of the two weeks, Emma asked for an interview with the Abbess, and this was granted.

'Sit down, Sister. How can I help you?'

Encouraged by the calm serenity of the old woman, Emma began to explain her difficulty in accepting the continued refusal of her superiors to allow her to undertake the work, the special skill for which she had been trained, and which she so passionately wished to do. 'When I was a postulant I understood that I could not hope to have a special place in the convent straight away, but I really did expect this to change when I took my first vows.'

'What made you think that, Sister?'

'The mother superior in the London convent, where I was at school, told me that it is quite usual for nuns with particular skills to bring these as their particular gift to the religious life.'

The old woman gazed at Emma thoughtfully, and smiled at her kindly. 'I believe that you are a young woman of very strong and sometimes obstinate desires, Sister. I can understand your feelings of frustration, and would like very much to help you, but it is not in my power to do so at present, or in the foreseeable future. You see, in these difficult times, many of our professed nuns are getting too old to carry out the work of the farm and the guest house. Our postulants and novices, as you must be aware, are few, but it is they who have to be responsible for the greater part of the work. You must try to understand that what Our Lord needs from you, Sister, is a pair of strong and willing hands.' The Abbess made a slight gesture with her frail, blue-veined old hand, almost of apology. 'I'm afraid there is little scope in our lives these days for labours of a more intellectual nature. As you know, Sister, our abbey depends entirely for its existence on the revenue from the guest house, the vines and the produce of the farm. Without that, we would be unable to continue the centuries of unbroken prayer that is the chief function of our order.'

Emma's spirits sank like lead, and an uncomfortable mixture of anger and shame filled her heart. Anger at the knowledge that she had been seriously misled, and had so to speak been tricked into doing work that she knew to be a waste of her talents, and deep shame that she should feel this way about it, together with the knowledge that she always would. She raised her eyes to the kindly gaze of the Abbess. 'I understand, Mother. Thank you for seeing me.'

'*Deo gratias*, Sister.'

'*Deo gratias*, Mother.'

The interview was at an end.

Christian, though not a particularly sensitive man, was worried about Phoebe. He was increasingly disturbed by her refusal to try to come to terms with the death of their child. She continued to be very quiet, self-absorbed, unresponsive and often rude in her attitude to those around her, even Gwen. Once or twice he had tentatively suggested that she see someone, a bereavement counsellor perhaps, but had had his head bitten off for his pains. One morning, walking past the window of a travel agent, he noticed a large poster depicting the Trevi Fountain and advertising short breaks in Rome. He went in and asked for a brochure, and when he went down to Abbot's Court at the weekend he showed it to Phoebe. 'What do you think, darling?' he said. 'It might be nice to have a few days away, just us two, by ourselves?'

To his surprise, Phoebe actually smiled, and agreed that it would do them both good. She did not tell him that her depression was beginning to frighten her, and make her doubt her sanity. She clutched at the straw of Christian's offer in the hope that maybe a holiday might help her to recover her spirits, to share her life with him again, and not exclude him from her sorrow, as she knew she had been doing. So, ten days later, they flew to Rome.

It was half-term, and Alexander and Gwen were having rather a cheerful time by themselves, quite enjoying Phoebe's absence, though naturally neither of them chose to mention this. On the Tuesday evening, Gwen was cooking supper, and Alexander was sitting at the kitchen table making a model helicopter from a kit, when the telephone rang in the hall.

'You answer it, Alex. It's probably your mother.'

'OK.' Alexander got to his feet and went to the hall, privately praying that it wasn't Chloe, up to her tricks again. He lifted the receiver. 'Hello?'

'Alexander?'

'Yes.'

'Hello, darling. It's me, Granny. How are you?'

'I'm OK.'

'Good. And Mummy? How is she, darling?'

'I don't know. OK, I think. She's in Rome, with Dad.' As soon as the words were out of his mouth, Alexander realized his mistake.

There was a slight pause, then his grandmother spoke again. 'How nice for her; it must be lovely in Italy just now, such a change from England.' She uttered her little tinkling laugh.

'Er, yes, I suppose so,' said Alexander, wondering whether he could simply say goodbye, and hang up.

'We were just talking about you all, darling, and wondering how you were. Your great-uncle, Fr Anselm, is going back to Africa on Saturday, and we thought it might be pleasant to come down for a couple of days, visit poor little Chloe's grave, and say a few prayers for her.'

'Hang on,' said Alexander firmly. 'I'd better get Gwen to speak to you.'

'No, no! Don't bother, darling. Just tell her we'll arrive tomorrow, after lunch. Goodbye, dear; it was nice talking to you.' There was a click, and the phone went dead. Slowly, Alexander replaced the receiver, and returned to the kitchen.

'Was it Mum?' asked Gwen.

'No, it wasn't. It was bloody Granny.'

'Alex! That is no way to talk about your grand-mother!'

'Well, she's a pain. Guess what? She's coming tomorrow with that gross old Fr Anselm.'

'Coming here? What for?'

'Search me. To say prayers for Chloe, or something.'

'Are they staying the night?'

'Yup. I think she said *two* nights.'

'Hell,' said Gwen, and Alexander laughed.

'What did I tell you?' he said.

'What time are they arriving, did she say?'

'After lunch.'

'Damnation,' said Gwen, looking really annoyed. 'Get that stuff off the table, Alex, please. Supper's nearly ready.'

Flavia and her brother took a taxi from Gloucester station, arriving at Abbot's Court at teatime. Gwen heard the scrunch of gravel in the courtyard as the car arrived. She covered the bread dough she was in the process of kneading with a damp tea towel, wiped her hands on her apron and went to the kitchen door to greet the visitors. At the sight of Flavia, rather bent and

154

frail-looking as she got stiffly out of the car, Gwen forgot her annoyance and hurried forward to help her former employer, whose life, she knew very well, was not a particularly enviable one.

'There you are, Gwen. How nice to see you. What a beautiful day.'

'Yes, it is,' agreed Gwen, and offered her arm, for although perfectly sober, Flavia seemed a little unsteady on her legs. 'It's good to see you,' she added, untruthfully.

'Well, it *is* Fr Anselm's only chance for some years, so we thought it would be appropriate to have a last little visit.' She looked at Gwen and smiled slightly apprehensively. 'Such a pity Christian and Phoebe are away.'

Fr Anselm, having been obliged to part with a sum of money that he considered outrageous, and withholding a tip because the driver had not offered to help him with the bags, sent the car on its way and turned towards his sister and Gwen, rubbing his hands together unctuously as he approached the two women. He gazed around him with admiration and a certain longing. 'What a very beautiful place this is,' he said. 'It must have been a most suitable abode for the abbots of former times.' He looked at Gwen almost accusingly. 'These days, needless to say, such places are the prerogative of the newly rich, and the religious often have to live in depressingly ugly modern buildings.'

Rather annoyed with her brother for casting possible aspersions on her son, Flavia responded tartly. 'Not always, my dear Anselm. Emma's convent in Brittany is a very ancient and noble building, like all the Cistercian abbeys.'

'Oh, well, that's in *France*, Flavia. That's a quite different matter, isn't it?' He managed to imply that the French were in some way less than perfect in that they had succeeded in hanging on to their buildings through the centuries. 'And, of course,' he added, as though the thought had just occurred to him, 'they didn't have Henry VIII to contend with, did they?'

'No, dear, they did not.'

'What about some tea?' offered Gwen. 'I hope you got something to eat on the train?'

'Yes, we did. Thank you, Gwen, some tea would be delightful, wouldn't it, Anselm?'

'Delightful, yes.' The old man beamed at Gwen, his blue eyes tiny behind the thick lenses of his spectacles. Gwen noticed that their metal bridge had dug deeply into his large and fleshy nose, which dominated his equally large and fleshy red face. His sparse grey hair was combed straight back and held in place against his scalp with some kind of dressing. Probably Brylcreem, she thought maliciously; that would have been the thing in his young days. She disengaged her arm from Flavia's and picked up her surprisingly heavy suitcase. 'Come through the kitchen,' she said. 'It's easier than traipsing round to the front door.'

She took them up to their rooms, and dumped Flavia's suitcase on the bench at the foot of the bed. 'What on earth have you got in here?' she asked. 'The crown jewels?'

'Just a few books for Alexander. Where is he, by the way?'

Gwen frowned, guessing at once the nature of the books. Flavia's library of suitable literature for every spiritual need was, she remembered, large and comprehensive. 'I think he's probably seeing to the ponies. Jim doesn't come every day, so Alex has to make sure they're all right. He may even have gone for a ride, I'm not sure.'

'What about poor Chloe's pony?'

'It's still here; Phoebe can't bear to let it go. In any case, it's company for the other one.'

'Does Alex ride them both?'

'He rides his, and takes Chloe's on the leading rein.'

'Is that safe?'

'I think he's quite capable of managing. If he weren't, Phoebe and Christian wouldn't allow it, would they?'

'No, of course not.'

'I'll get the tea.'

'Lovely, Gwen. We'll be down in a minute.'

Alexander stayed out with the ponies as long as he dared without making Gwen uneasy. She heard the clatter of hooves in the yard as he returned from his ride, and smiled indulgently, giving her lump of dough a satisfying whack on the floured board, before cutting it in half and shaping two loaves.

Alex led the ponies into the stable and took off their tack. He put their nuts into the manger, and gave them both a vigorous and prolonged brushing, a thing he rarely bothered to do. When he could not think of any more ways of delaying going in and confronting the unwelcome visitors, he untied the halters of the ponies and led them through the garden to the paddock. Slowly, he returned to the house. He walked quietly through the hall, intending to go to the kitchen, and saw at once that candles had been lit in the oratory, and heard the low murmur of voices, presumably those of his grandmother and her brother. Shit, he said to himself, they're at it already. He stole past the oratory door, which stood slightly open. A whiff of incense reached his nose, and the awful memory of his seriously bad behaviour at Chloe's funeral came vividly back to him. Bastards, he thought, why did they have to come here? I hate them.

He passed quickly through the dining room, observing with horror that the table was already laid for three, and went into the kitchen. 'Why do I have to eat with them, Gwen?' he demanded angrily. 'I don't see why I should.'

'Your grandmother wishes it, dear,' said Gwen, as

though that was the end of the matter. 'I'm sorry,' she added, 'but there it is.'

'Shit!'

'Please, Alex,' said Gwen. 'Language.'

'I can think of a lot worse than shit.'

'I'm sure you can. Please don't.'

The door opened and Flavia came into the kitchen. 'There you are, Alexander, at last. Have you got a kiss for Granny, darling?'

Alexander was extremely tempted to say, 'No, I haven't, you rotten old bag; you've got bad breath.' Instead, he got up from the table with as much grace as he could muster, and planted a brief kiss on her cheek, as far away from her mouth as possible. Flavia clutched his hands with her bony ones and gazed at him with compassion. 'Poor boy,' she said, 'you're so like poor little Chloe, and so like your father, too.'

Alexander pulled away from her, saying nothing. He retreated behind the table to Gwen's side.

'Delicious smell of tuppies, Gwen,' said Flavia, reverting to the parlance of childhood. 'When are we eating? Is there time for a little aperitif before the meal? Is that allowed?'

'Of course,' said Gwen. 'You'll find everything you need in the drawing room. Alexander will bring some ice for you, won't you, dear?'

'How kind,' said Flavia, heading for the door.

'Dinner's at eight,' said Gwen to her departing back.

'How could you be so rotten, Gwen? I don't want to sit in there with them. They'll only start banging on about God and stuff, you know that.'

'Sorry, Alex, you'll just have to cope. I can't do everything.' She stuck a fork into the potatoes. 'It'll be about ten minutes, that's all.'

'Oh, all right. If I must.' He got the ice from the freezer and filled the plastic ice-bucket with cubes.

In the event, no mention was made of the subjects he dreaded, either before or during supper, and he began to relax. At nine o'clock, he rose from his seat, said that it was his bedtime, and asked his grandmother to excuse him.

'Of course, darling. Do sleep well. Tomorrow, if Gwen does not need the car, I thought it would be nice if we could all drive to the cemetery and put some flowers on Chloe's grave.'

'Only Mum does that,' said Alexander, his voice stiff with disapproval.

'Really? Well, she's not here at present, is she? So she'll be all the more glad that we were able to do it for her, won't she?'

Alexander considered this remarkably unlikely, but thought it imprudent to pursue the matter. He said good night and left the room. He went to the kitchen, where he found Gwen cleaning saucepans. 'Bastards,' he said.

'What's the matter now?'

'She's making me go to Chloe's grave tomorrow, and put flowers on it. Mum won't like that, will she?'

'Well, she won't blame *you*, darling, that's for sure. Don't worry, I'll explain it to her.'

'It's not just because of Mum, Gwen. I don't want to go myself. It's creepy, and I hate it, and anyway she's not even there in that horrible white box, I know she's not.'

'No, of course she's not. She's gone to heaven.'

'No, she hasn't,' said Alexander darkly.

'What do you mean, she hasn't?'

He turned away, refusing to meet her eyes. 'Oh, nothing. It was a daft thing to say.'

The following morning, after Fr Anselm had said Mass in the oratory, and he and Flavia had had a late breakfast in the dining room, Flavia came into the kitchen and asked Gwen for a basket and some secateurs. 'I think garden flowers are so much nicer for a child, don't you?' she remarked, and smiled at her old friend with as much affection as her nature would permit, so that Gwen, though deeply suspicious, could detect no hidden agenda.

'Yes, of course.' Gwen dried her wet hands, reached up and took Phoebe's basket from its hook, and got her secateurs from a drawer in the dresser. 'Do you need gloves? There are some here, if you want them.'

'Thank you; that's very thoughtful of you.'

Gwen produced the gloves, and Flavia put them on. 'A bit big for my little hands,' she said, laughing. 'Never mind, they'll be fine, I'm sure. Where is Alexander? I haven't seen him this morning.'

'He's around somewhere. He went out after breakfast. He won't have gone far. He always appears at mealtimes – boys of his age are constantly ravenous, aren't they?'

Flavia frowned. 'I was hoping to take him to the cemetery this morning. That's if it's quite convenient to take Phoebe's car, of course?'

'Oh, well,' said Gwen cheerfully. 'I expect after lunch will do just as well, won't it?'

'If he's not here, I suppose it will have to.' Flavia stared coldly at Gwen, as if she strongly suspected her of conniving at Alexander's absence.

'I have the feeling, Mrs McGrath,' said Gwen, quietly but very clearly, 'that Alex would much prefer *not* to go to the cemetery.'

'Oh? And what makes you think that?'

'At present, Phoebe is very sensitive about the grave. She goes there alone several times a week. She does not wish anyone to go with her.'

'All the more reason for Alexander to accompany me, when she is unavoidably absent.'

Gwen folded the tea towel and hung it on the Aga rail to dry. 'I'm afraid I don't agree,' she said. 'He's a great deal more upset by the tragedy than one would guess from his manner. Poor boy, he misses her terribly, I know. He hates the idea of her being buried.'

'How do you know that, Gwen? Does he talk to you about it? Has he had a chat with the priest at all? He needs spiritual guidance and support at this time. You must realize that, even though you are not a believer yourself, of course.'

Fearing that they were entering dangerous territory, and that she might be rude to Flavia, Gwen refused to be drawn and merely remarked that she felt that these matters were better dealt with by Christian and Phoebe.

'That's your considered opinion, is it, Gwen? So grandmothers have no rights in such matters, is that it?'

'I just don't want him upset, that's all.' Gwen stared at Flavia defiantly, her arms folded, stubbornly determined to protect Alexander as far as she possibly could.

'Don't worry, he won't be upset. He'll feel much better after a little talk, and a few simple prayers.' Flavia picked up the basket and the secateurs and left the kitchen, effectively dismissing Gwen from her confidence.

In the garden, she wandered about, cutting a basketful of pink and yellow roses; she did not know their names, never having had the slightest interest in gardening. She cut some honeysuckle for its powerful fragrance and large yellow and orange flowers. When the basket was full, she went in search of a vase. Although reluctant to have to ask for Gwen's help once more, she could not avoid doing so.

'Phoebe puts her flowers into a bucket of water, and takes them to the cemetery like that,' said Gwen. 'When you get there, you'll find some containers, and a place to throw away the dead flowers from last week.'

'I see,' said Flavia. 'That seems quite sensible. So, where's a bucket?'

'In the stable,' replied Gwen firmly, and continued to cut up carrots.

'Very well, I'll find it.' Flavia sauntered out to the

courtyard with her basket, and Gwen, watching her go, permitted herself a small ironic smile.

At lunch, Alexander was fascinated by the vast amount of Lancashire hotpot that Fr Anselm seemed able to consume, and then do justice to the banana custard that followed. It was Alex's favourite pudding and he silently acknowledged Gwen's kindness to him, as the squashy lumps of banana slid creamily down his throat, even though the thought of the impending visit to Chloe's grave had slightly robbed him of his appetite.

At three o'clock, Gwen backed the Volvo out of the garage, and put Flavia's bucket of flowers into the rear compartment, sloshing the water over her shoes in the process. Flavia and Anselm appeared, Flavia wearing a hat and gloves, followed by Alexander, looking morose. His eye fell on the flowers, and suddenly he rushed away through the arch in the yew hedge and ran across the lawn towards the paddock.

'For goodness' sake, what *now*?' cried Flavia, sounding extremely annoyed. 'Whatever is he doing, wretched child? It's too provoking.'

'Don't worry, he'll be back, I'm sure,' said Gwen, and tried to believe it. She went back into the house.

She was right. In a couple of minutes Alex reappeared, clutching a hastily gathered bunch of buttercups in his left hand.

'Oh, darling!' cried Flavia. '*Wild* flowers! They wilt in just a few minutes, don't you know that?'

'Doesn't matter,' said Alexander, breathing heavily, 'they're Chloe's favourite flowers, and mine too.'

They got into the car, Fr Anselm driving, Alexander in the back. 'As a matter of fact,' he said to no-one in particular, 'buttercups last for quite a long time in water.' So there, you dopey old cow, he added to himself.

When they arrived at the cemetery and had parked

the car, Flavia made a little display of feebleness in the matter of carrying the heavy bucket to the grave. The reason for its weight was its water content, so Alexander quite sensibly tipped the greater part of it into a convenient gutter, and the three of them proceeded to the grave, Alex carrying the bucket as well as his buttercups. Although he had been bracing himself against the ordeal of looking at Chloe's small grave, he had not realized that she already had a headstone of white marble, carved with her name and the dates of her short life, and the words *The Lord giveth, and the Lord taketh away*. Alexander stared at the stone, and a terrible cold sensation crept over him. But it wasn't the Lord, was it? he thought. It was me that took away Chloe's life. He turned away, doing his best to control the wave of panic that threatened to engulf him.

'Where's the rubbish bin?' demanded Flavia, holding out a dripping bunch of Phoebe's flowers. 'And there must be a tap somewhere to fill the vases?'

With an enormous effort Alexander pulled himself together, took his mother's faded flowers from his grandmother, and ran down the path towards the hut near the entrance to the graveyard, where he hoped to find both the bin and the tap. There was an elderly man behind the shed, sweeping the path with a broom. He showed Alexander the bin, and lent him a watering can to carry fresh water to Flavia. It was quite heavy, and as he walked rather erratically back to the grave he saw his grandmother on her knees in the grass, while Fr Anselm, with a little book in his hand, was clearly praying for the repose of Chloe's soul. Alexander put down the watering can and waited until they had finished, then he picked it up again and continued down the path to the graveside. Without speaking, he filled the three green metal vases. As he did so, he observed with sorrow that his buttercups were scattered in the grass, and that Fr Anselm was standing on most of them. 'I'll take the watering can back,' he said quickly. 'I'll wait for you at the gate.' Before Flavia could stop him, he had run swiftly away with the can. Bloody old farts, he said to himself, I hate their guts. He stood on my flowers; I hate him; he's horrible.

That evening, Flavia insisted that Alexander come to the oratory for evening prayers. 'Particularly as you were so insulting to your poor little sister's memory at the grave. It was very unkind of you, my dear.'

Gwen, on her way to the drawing room half an hour later, saw the candlelight flickering through the half-open door of the oratory. She went to the door and looked through it at the ceremony taking place before the altar. Flavia and her grandson knelt on the stone floor, and Fr Anselm gripped Alexander's head tightly between both his hands, while he uttered words from which Gwen inferred that the old man was absolving the boy from his sins. '*Misereatur tui omnipotens Deus, et dimissis peccatis tuis, perducat te ad vitam aeternam,*' he intoned, while Flavia, gazing at her brother with rapturous admiration, crossed herself repeatedly. '*In nomine Patris, et Filii, et Spiritus Sancti, Amen.*'

Angrily, Gwen pushed open the door. 'Dinner is ready,' she said in a loud voice; 'it's getting cold.'

Alexander got up from his knees and, pushing past his grandmother, ran to Gwen's side. They left the oratory together. 'Don't leave me with them again, *please*, Gwen.' He sounded really frightened.

'I won't,' said Gwen. 'I promise.'

'They've guessed,' he said. 'They know I did it.'

'Did what?'

'You know; killed Chloe. They *know*, Gwen. They made me say it was my fault. I had to say I was sorry.'

Furiously, Gwen went to the dining room and removed Alexander's place from the table. Then she brought the serving dishes and left them on the

sideboard, for Flavia and Fr Anselm to help themselves.

In the safety and warmth of the kitchen, Alexander's
agitation diminished and he recovered his nerve
enough to enjoy his supper with Gwen. He told her
about the visit to the cemetery, and about Fr Anselm
treading on his buttercups.

'Old fool,' she said. 'He would.'

'They're both old fools, aren't they?'

'Yes, Alex, I'm afraid they are.' She looked at him
severely across the table. 'Which is one perfectly good
reason for you to get out of your head all this rubbish
about blaming yourself for the accident.'

'Yes,' said Alexander doubtfully, 'I suppose it is.'

'Are you *listening* to me, Alexander? Forget it.'

'OK, Gwen. I'll try.'

Chapter Eight

Returning one rainy evening from the *conservatoire*, Claudia saw that the big flashy Harley-Davidson motorbike was parked yet again beside Allegra's door. This is becoming a daily occurrence, she thought, and frowned. Perhaps young Martinez has moved in? She unlocked her door, went into her house and carefully stood her cello on its stand. Unable to stop herself from spying on her daughter, an activity strictly against her principles, she looked out of her tall rain-streaked windows, and through the dark leafy branches of the mulberry tree towards Allegra's apartment. The ground-floor window was tightly shuttered, but there was a light on in the bedroom upstairs, the window was open and a thin white curtain was half-drawn, revealing nothing.

Ashamed, Claudia turned away from her own window, wishing for the first time since she had lived in that house that she had curtains herself, with which to shut out things better not seen. She took off her raincoat and hung it in the bathroom to dry, then went to the kitchen, ate a piece of cheese and poured herself a glass of wine. She returned to the studio, put her glass on the low table by the sofa, then lit some of her candles, but did not turn on the lamp in the courtyard. She felt as if she were trying to make herself as invisible as possible, something she had never done in her entire life. Skulking, she thought, annoyed by the implication, that's what I'm doing. She sat down on the sofa with her back to the window, and drank her wine slowly, making a real effort to dismiss Allegra from her mind, but finding it impossible.

Claudia was by no means a naive or immature woman, and she had always taken the civilized view that Allegra's private life was her own affair. She knew her daughter to be a well-informed and intelligent girl, able to look after herself within the sexual parameters of normal university life. Claudia would not have countenanced for a single moment the idea that Allegra's developing experience should be any less than or any different from her own at that age. And look at me, she thought; I got pregnant, it has to be admitted. But of course I *was* twenty-four at the time, that's quite a lot older than twenty-one. Or is that just splitting hairs? Am I turning into one of those ghastly middle-aged women who can't bear their daughters to grow up, live their own lives, make their own choices? The thought appalled her and she rejected it at once. So, what's the problem? What is it that I'm so concerned about? Is it the young man himself? Is it that terrifyingly enormous motorbike and the black leather gear that worries me? Or the bottles I can't help seeing when Allegra puts out her bin? And are there only bottles in there? Are there needles, too?

She got up from the sofa and put a CD in the player, glancing out of the window as she did so, in spite of herself. The lights on the other side of the courtyard were all out. Presumably they had gone out, and she felt curiously relieved. She turned up the volume of her music and went to the kitchen, wondering what she would have for supper. Pasta perhaps, and a salad. She took a green pepper and a tomato from the fridge and began to cut them up, to make a sauce for the pasta. I do wish Ludo were here, she thought, and a wave of loneliness swept over her. I'm sure I should try and talk to Allegra, make sure she understands about used needles, things like that. And is it really all right for her to be shacking up with someone like Martinez at her age? At any age? He looks just like a *mafioso*. For the very first time in her deeply satisfying and happy life Claudia felt extremely nervous and quite uncertain of her feelings, as well as her motives concerning her relationship with her daughter. Perhaps I should ring Ludo and discuss it with him, she thought. Then she remembered that Allegra and Ludovic had carefully avoided each other since their confrontation in the *impasse*. Claudia thought it would be rather unlikely that he would feel inclined to discuss Allegra's private life at present. As far as she could guess, his current attitude seemed to be least said, soonest mended. Claudia sighed, and broke some spaghetti into a pan of boiling water. 'Maybe he's right,' she said to the empty kitchen, 'it's best to say nothing; just keep my head down.'

Two days later, her good intentions were blown apart. Coming out of her door on her way to the Mouffetard market, Claudia was forced to flatten herself against the wall to avoid being hit by the huge Harley-Davidson as Martinez, with Allegra riding pillion, roared past her and came to a screeching halt outside Allegra's door. Furiously, Claudia slammed her own door, and walked away as fast as she could down the alleyway. Conscious that she must be presenting the retreating image of the eternal boring parent, Claudia's anger was exacerbated by the derisive laughter that pursued her, and which she could not fail to hear.

That evening there was a knock on the door. It was Allegra, alone.

'Come in,' said Claudia coldly.

'I don't know if I want to, particularly, if you're going to be like that. I only came to say sorry about the bike. We didn't mean to frighten you.' Allegra spoke patronizingly, as though she were reassuring a nervous old woman.

'Come in anyway.'

Allegra advanced into the room, looking around as though she expected to find herself trapped in some way. 'Is my father here?' she asked.

'No. He'll be here on Friday evening, as usual.' It occurred to Claudia that Allegra's visit might actually be intended as an olive branch, so she smiled at her and invited her to sit down and have a drink. Allegra sat on one of the hard chairs beside the crowded table. Claudia poured her a glass of wine, and sat down herself, facing her daughter across the table. The blackamoor's head grinned complacently between them.

Allegra took a sip of her wine, and looked coolly at her mother. 'Did Papa tell you what I said to him?'

'Yes, he did.'

'Did he mind?'

'Yes, he was very upset about it.'

'Good, I meant him to be!'

Claudia sighed. 'I really do understand how you feel, Allegra, believe me. It's natural that you should be confused and angry, and feel that we deliberately deceived you. I realize now that we made a serious mistake, not telling you long ago. You're perfectly justified in feeling that we've betrayed you, even unintentionally. But it doesn't alter the fact that you are our daughter, or that we love you, does it?'

Allegra laughed bitterly. 'And it doesn't alter the fact that I'm illegitimate, either, does it? Anyway, I didn't really come to rake over your sordid past, Mother. I came to tell you that I'm leaving.'

'Leaving?'

'Yes, *leaving*. Getting out; moving house. Is that clear enough for you, or do I have to spell it out? I'm moving in with Jules; he's got a proper apartment of his own, lucky man. He doesn't have to endure his bloody parents spying on him, watching his every move.'

'Is that what you think I do?'

'Yes, of course it is! You're at it all the time, you never stop, do you? You even look in my dustbin, don't you?'

'Of course I don't!'

'Of course you do! I've seen you. You're like an old rag-picker, poking around in the rubbish. What are you looking for? Condoms?'

Claudia put her hands on the table to steady herself and took a deep breath, for she had the uncomfortable feeling that she had stopped breathing. 'Perhaps you are right, Allegra,' she said at last, in a dull, expressionless voice. 'It probably would be easier for us all not to live so closely to each other. I realize that it's normal for you to want to move on, and have greater privacy. I will, of course, continue to pay your allowance into your account every month, as usual.'

'Don't bother.' Allegra got up to leave. 'If you do, I'll only send it back. I've already got myself an evening job in a bar. I don't intend to be a kept woman, like you.'

After Allegra had gone, Claudia turned off all the lights and retired to her bedroom, so that there was no danger of the young people being witnesses to her shock and grief.

Allegra carried out her intentions and by the end of the week her little apartment was shuttered and barred, and the keys had been dropped into Claudia's letter box.

The next evening, coming home with her two shopping bags full of provisions for the weekend, Claudia found two strangers, a man and a woman, waiting on her doorstep. The woman stepped forward politely.

'*Nous sommes bien chez M. McGrath, Madame?*'

'*Oui.*'

'*Et vous-même, Madame? Vous êtes Mlle Claudia Renaud?*'

'*Oui.*'

'*Pardon, Mademoiselle. Un moment, s'il vous plaît.*' The young man produced a camera from behind his back and aimed it at Claudia. Before she could collect her wits, there was a blinding flash, followed almost at once by another. The woman smiled, and shrugged her shoulders apologetically. '*Merci infiniment, Mademoiselle.*' The interlopers walked rapidly away down the *impasse*, leaving Claudia, shattered, on her doorstep.

Two hours later, Ludovic entered the house and found it in darkness. He switched on the lights and saw the two shopping bags dumped on the floor and Claudia's bag on the table. 'Claudia? Are you here?'

'In here.'

Her voice was muffled and barely audible, and Ludovic went quickly to the bedroom expecting to find her unwell. She lay face down on the bed, her red hair half-covering her face. As he sat on the edge of the bed, full of concern, she turned onto her back and he could see that her face was swollen and ravaged with weeping. 'Claudia, my darling, whatever is the matter?'

She sat up and he took her in his arms, while she told him incoherently what had happened, before dissolving once more into tears, soaking the front of his shirt.

'Don't cry, darling. It's all right, I'm here now.' He rocked her like a child, until the weeping stopped.

'It must have been the press, Ludo. I'm so sorry, I should have been more careful; I feel so stupid.'

'Claudia, don't be idiotic. If these vultures think they're on to something, then there's very little one can do to stop them. I'm surprised they didn't hang around to catch me, as a matter of fact.'

Claudia blew her nose. 'Let's have a drink, darling, I'm exhausted. I've had a really awful week. I must tell you about it, now you're here.'

Ludovic poured two cognacs, and they sat together in the garden while she told him about Allegra, and her aggressive boyfriend. 'She's gone, Ludo. She's moved in with him, it seems.'

Ludovic sighed. 'That probably explains everything, my love,' he said, and told Claudia that Martinez *père* was the political editor of *Info-Phallo*. 'We'll soon know, won't we? Watch this space, as they say.'

'So you think Allegra is behind it?'

'I'm very much afraid she may have been, yes.'

'What will happen? Will it mean some sort of scandal; the end of your career? Resignation?'

'I shouldn't think so. This sort of thing is not much of a big deal in France. Just a temporary irritation, with any luck.'

'And if the story is picked up in London?'

'That would be quite another matter.'

Gwen served breakfast in the dining room on Friday morning, immediately after Fr Anselm had said Mass. She brought a dish of bacon and tomatoes, and placed it on a mat before Flavia. 'Which train will you be catching?' she asked bluntly. 'I can give you a lift to the station in time for the next one to Paddington, but I shall be busy doing the weekly shopping this afternoon, I'm afraid.'

Flavia felt extremely annoyed at this ultimatum, for that was how she chose to interpret Gwen's remarks. She thought it highly unlikely that the shopping would occupy the entire afternoon, but could not very well call her old friend a liar. She had rather wished to devote a little more time to her grandson, and try to explain to him the importance of the power of prayer and the reasons for regular confession and absolution. Poor boy, she thought, what chance has he with a mother like Phoebe, and constant interference from Gwen, with her dominant ways? Even Christian does not seem to care very much how his children are brought up, and that was Ludovic's doing; he has much to answer for.

'The morning train will do very well, thank you,' said Fr Anselm impatiently. 'Flavia, are you intending to sit there all day, or are you going to pass me some bacon?'

'Right,' said Gwen briskly. 'I'll be ready to take you in forty-five minutes.'

Feeling thwarted on all fronts, Flavia had little option but to comply, and in fifty minutes the car, driven by Gwen, rolled down the drive towards the lane. Alexander was nowhere to be seen or heard, and they left without saying goodbye.

Crouched aloft in the barn, he watched them go. Quietly, he sat listening to the burbling pigeons on the roof, and watching the nesting swallows as they skimmed in and out of the ventilation holes in the walls of the barn, delivering building materials to their round mud nests high in the roof-space above his head.

Alexander had slept extremely badly, having constant nightmares and waking frequently, soaked with sweat. Wide awake at three in the morning, he had heard the sound of crying, and although she did not come to his bedside, he knew that it was Chloe. It was a dreadfully sad sound, and made him feel like crying himself. He would have much preferred her to appear as she usually did, in person, if that's what you could call it. At least then they could talk to each other, or play a game, but the invisible weeping was something else, and even more frightening. He looked over his shoulder nervously, as if just thinking about Chloe might make her appear. It's no good, he thought, however many times Gwen tells me that it was an accident, that's not what Mum thinks, and neither do I, really. I still think it was all my fault. Mum and Dad will be back on Tuesday, and it'll all start again, I know it will. Quite what it was that would all start again, Alexander was unable to explain to himself, but he was conscious of a compelling need to escape from his present existence, which seemed to him an unbearable mixture of guilt and a nameless terror. The pain he felt at the apparent loss of his mother was scarcely less than that which he was enduring at the death of his sister, and the thought of seeing Phoebe's cold, reproachful eyes avoiding his when she returned from her holiday made him feel already sick with apprehension. He could not decide which was worse: his mother's rejection of him, or the torments he was suffering at the hands of Chloe. Even the house felt hostile now, as if it was waiting for him to make a mistake again, like the business of him sleepwalking on the tower. That is, he said to himself, doubtfully, if it *was* sleepwalking. At the memory of that terrifying episode, his stomach churned violently. He got down from his window, descended the wooden ladder and ran across the yard as quickly as he could, in order to go to the lavatory. Then he went upstairs to his room, and opened the drawer in his chest where he kept his private things. He took his hoard of money, thirty-five pounds in notes, and put it into the back pocket of his jeans. He took the small card on which his grandfather had written down his telephone numbers and put that in his other back pocket. There was some loose change in his drawer as well, and he put that in a front pocket. He shut the drawer carefully. He got his Guernsey sweater from another drawer and put it on. Then he went downstairs to his father's study and wrote a note to Gwen.

> *Dear Gwen,*
> *Robin's mum rang up and invited me for the weekend, so I am going there on my bike. I have taken my clean things for Monday, so I will see you on Monday after school as usual. I hope that's OK.*
> *Love, Alex. X*

Alexander left the note on the kitchen table, and put an empty cup carefully on top of the note. He took his school-bag from the back of the kitchen door, ran upstairs again and put his school clothes into it, and, as an afterthought, a pair of clean pyjamas. He went downstairs again and went out through the kitchen, closing the door carefully behind him, then ran across the yard to the garage to get his bike. He did not really expect to meet Gwen coming back from Gloucester yet, but pedalled as fast as he could towards the main road, just in case. When he got there, he hid his bicycle carefully behind a hedge, then stood on the grass verge, waiting rather nervously for a car to come along. He waited for quite a time, until a young woman in a sporty-looking car drew up beside him, in response to his tentatively held-out thumb.

'Where do you want to go?'

'Bristol, if you're going there, please.'

'You're in luck, I am. Hop in.'

Alexander lost no time in doing so, throwing his bag onto the back seat. The young woman drove fast and well, and soon they were on the motorway. She said very little and Alex sat silently beside her. If she thought that he looked a bit young to be hitch-hiking she did not mention it, and he was encouraged by this, hoping that his height made him look a lot older than his real age. As they drove, he attempted to clarify his thoughts as to the easiest way of getting to Paris, with minimum expense. He decided that his best plan was to find the coach station in Bristol and see what that had to offer.

In the event, this proved unnecessary. A few miles before reaching Bristol, the young woman pulled into a service station. 'I need a pee,' she said. 'How about you?'

'I'm OK, thanks,' said Alexander.

He remained in the car, looking around him at the other parked vehicles. Over to his right he saw that there was a special area for container lorries. He saw one huge white one painted with red, white and blue stripes and the words FRIGOFORT – OBAN – PARIS (RUNGIS) written on the side in large black letters. Alexander made up his mind with impressive speed. He got out of the car, retrieved his bag from the back, and ran across to the lorry park, just as the driver of Frigofort was preparing to climb into his cab.

'Excuse me,' said Alex, 'but are you going to Oban or to Paris?'

The driver of the vehicle was a small man, young and blond, and Alex was very nearly as tall as him. 'Paris,' he said. 'Why? Do you want to go there?'

'I do, as a matter of fact. I'm going to stay with my grandfather. He lives in Paris.'

'Very nice too,' said the driver. 'What's your name?'

'Alex McGrath.'

The driver held out his hand. 'Jock McLean. OK, Alex, get in. I'll be glad of the company.'

Alexander, his heart in his mouth, ran round to the other side of the vehicle and climbed up into the passenger's seat. As the engine of the huge lorry throbbed into life, and they rumbled out of the service station and onto the motorway, he thought he might easily die of excitement. In half an hour they had passed Bristol and were speeding down the M4 towards the M25 and Dover. Jock had the radio on full blast and was concentrating totally on his driving, so they did not have an opportunity to talk very much until they were approaching Dover Harbour.

'Have you got your passport, Alex?'

'Hell, no, I haven't! I forgot!'

'That's OK. Hop over the back, get into my bunk and draw the curtain. They don't usually bother much on the trip out, I expect we'll go straight through. It's coming back that they like to do you over. Drugs, that's what they're after.'

Alexander did as he was told, and after a stuffy

half-hour in Jock's bed, he felt the clank and rattle of the wheels beneath him as Jock drove over the metal ramp, then the sound of heavy chains being moved, and finally the hiss of the airbrakes as Jock brought the huge vehicle to a halt.

'OK, you can come out now.'

They dismounted, both feeling slightly stiff after several hours on the road, and Jock led the way up steep stairways to the Lorry Drivers' Lounge. This was a palatial affair in Alex's opinion and the smell of sausages and baked beans made his mouth water. 'Can I buy you something to eat, Jock? I'm starving, aren't you?'

'Thanks very much, old chap. I don't mind if I do.'

They queued up with the other drivers, picked up their little trays and chose sausages, eggs, bacon, chips and baked beans. It came to ten pounds sixty altogether, and Alex handed over the money.

'I'll get the drinks,' said Jock. 'No alcohol, of course.'

'Of course,' agreed Alex. 'I'll have a Coke, thanks.'

They sat together at a table near a window and the deep throb of the boat's engines thrilled Alexander to the very core of his being. The idea of the green waters of the Channel under him, and the boat pulling him away from England, leaving all his anguish and unhappiness behind, was almost too much to bear, so great was his joy and relief. He tucked into his enormous plate of food with profound enjoyment, and smiled like the Cheshire cat at his new friend, the chief means and organizer of his escape.

It was a fine blustery afternoon, with big white cumulus clouds marching across a blue sky, driven by a following westerly wind as the ferry forged its powerful way towards Calais. Alex had been on holiday to Britanny, twice, with his parents and Chloe, but the voyage had been the long one from Plymouth to Roscoff, so the short crossing to Calais was a new experience for him, and after their excellent late lunch

Jock and Alexander took a walk round the decks, enjoying the stiff breeze and the fresh air. 'Do you do the trip often?' asked Alex, looking at his new friend with admiration, impressed by his being in charge of such an enormous vehicle and its load.

'Twice a week.'

'It must be hard work, all that concentration, and such a long drive, Oban to Paris?'

'Aye, it is. Makes your back ache, too, and no effing mistake.' Jock gave a conspiratorial wink. 'Other parts as well, if you get my meaning.'

If Alexander was somewhat surprised at this confidence, he did not show it. 'Yeah,' he replied. 'I can imagine.' He did not think he would pursue this avenue of conversation, interesting though that might be. 'What's your cargo?' he asked, hoping that that was the correct expression.

'Usually it's live oysters, crayfish, mussels, crabs, stuff like that. Just now, it's farmed Scotch salmon, tons of it, on ice. The Froggies canna get enough of it, so they tell me.'

'Really? How amazing. I always thought they ate snails and frogs' legs, things like that.'

'You're not wrong, Alex, they do. And I've got news for you, laddie, it's excellent nosh.'

'You're kidding!'

'I never am. It's the truth.' Jock pointed a finger. 'Look, there she is! France!'

Alexander looked, and saw a long, flat-looking coastline, green-topped, with shallow sandy cliffs and dunes. It looked disappointingly like England.

Jock looked at his watch. 'We'll be there in fifteen minutes. We've made good time; that'll be yon following wind.'

They made their way down to the car-deck, and Jock insisted on Alexander disappearing into his bunk once more while they went through passport control. Jock held up his own passport and was waved through by a laconic gendarme, who seemed more interested in the mobile-phone conversation in which he was engaged, than checking the credentials of the incoming traffic. Once on the Paris *autoroute*, Alex came forth from his hiding place and buckled himself into his seat again. 'How long does it take to get to Paris?' he asked.

'If the motorway's clear and it's not raining, about four hours. Then I go round the *périph* to Rungis, that's where the wholesale food-market is.'

'What's the prif?'

'It's the ring road that runs right round Paris, bit like the M25. There's a map, in your locker, if you'd like to take a wee look.'

Alex opened the locker and took out the map. He found the *boulevard périphérique*, which, as Jock had told him, ran round the city in a circle, connecting all the ancient sites of the gates of the original walls. This interesting information he gleaned with little difficulty from a small section designated *'un peu d'histoire'*.

'Where does your grandad live?'

'Oh,' said Alexander, who did not actually know, and muttered the first thing that came into his head. 'It's called the Champs-Elysées. But don't worry, I'll phone from your market, and get a taxi, that'll be the best.'

'OK, fine.' Jock had no idea where the Champs-Elysées was, anyway, so he did not think it odd that he should be taking his passenger a good many kilometres beyond his destination. In any case, he was not particularly keen on the idea of making a detour from his usual and familiar route.

They reached the suburbs of Paris at about seven-thirty and joined the slow-moving traffic on the *périphérique*. Keeping to the slow lane, Jock crawled along and, as they reached them, Alex followed on his map the names of the city gates: Porte de Bagnolet, Porte de Montreuil, and on to the Porte d'Italie and the A6 to Rungis.

With the confidence of experience, Jock parked in his usual space. He got down from the vehicle, and proceeded to his check-in point, to make his delivery, and organize the fork-lift truck that would unload the container. Alexander, walking beside his friend, was astonished at the size of the colossal market, and under different circumstances, would have been delighted to have the chance to explore it. Now, anxious to conclude his journey, he looked around for a telephone, and felt in his pocket to check that he still had Ludovic's card. 'Jock,' he said, 'thank you so much for the lift, it was great. Now, I must get on, and find a payphone. There's only one thing; I'll need some French change for the machine, and I've only got English money.'

'No problem,' said Jock. 'How much do you need? I've got loads here.' He took a handful of coins from a pocket, and Alex produced a ten-pound note, and received in exchange a great many francs.

'Are you sure you can spare it, Jock?'

'Aye. I can use your tenner on the boat going back, or change it, whatever. It's no big deal.'

'Brilliant!' said Alexander. 'Thank you very much, Jock. And thanks again for the lift.'

'Anytime. It was nice having you, Alex.'

'Well, goodbye. And thanks again.'

'Bye. Take care.'

Alexander walked purposefully along the avenues of chilled seafood, looking to his right and left in search of a public telephone. At last he saw a line of open booths, with Perspex hoods. Each of them had a queue, and he attached himself to the shortest one, to wait his turn. He examined the French change that Jock had given him, and thought that a selection of one-, five- and ten-franc pieces would probably be appropriate. He carefully extracted the card with Ludovic's numbers written on it, and decided that it would be OK to omit the OO 33 bit of the code, since he was already in

France. Thinking that this piece of reasoning was rather clever of him, he approached the instrument quite confidently, and picked up the receiver. He put a five-franc piece in the slot and dialled the Paris number. Nothing happened. He dialled the number again, and still nothing happened.

'*Il-y-a un problème?*' asked the man behind Alex in the queue. '*Puis-je vous aider?*'

'Yes, please,' said Alexander gratefully. 'Sorry, I don't understand what I'm doing wrong.' He showed Ludovic's card to the helpful man.

'Ah! From 'ere, it is necessary to compose first the code for Paris, and after, your numero.'

'Oh! Thanks!' said Alex. '*Merci.*' The man pressed the button to retrieve the money, and they started the process again. The long mournful note of the ringing tone sounded in Alexander's ear two or three times, then he heard a woman's voice.

'*Oui?*'

'Um, is that Mr McGrath's house?'

'Yes, it is. Who is this, please?'

'It's me, Alexander McGrath. I'm his grandson. As a matter of fact, I'm quite near Paris.'

'*Alexander*! Hold on, I'll call Ludovic right away.' Alex looked anxiously at the meter, and put five more francs in the slot, to be safe.

'Alex, my dear boy! Where are you?'

'I'm at a place called Rungis. It's an enormous market.'

'Yes, I know that. Have you got a pencil? You have? Good. Write this down carefully: rue Mouffetard.' Ludovic spelled it out slowly. 'Have you got that? Good. Now, find a cab and tell the driver to come to impasse des Cordonniers, rue Mouffetard. I will be waiting for you there, OK? If you have any more problems, or can't get a cab, ring again, and Claudia will be here to answer your call. Now, is that all quite clear? Repeat the names of the streets back to me.

Good, that's exactly right. Now, get a move on, Alex. You've interrupted my dinner, you terrible boy!'

'Oh, gosh, really? I'm awfully sorry, I didn't think . . .'

Ludovic laughed. 'Don't be silly, I'm only joking. Go on, hang up now, and get here quickly!'

Alex replaced the phone carefully. 'Everything is OK?' asked his helpful friend.

'*Merci*,' said Alex. 'Yes, everything is OK, thanks.'

He said goodbye and walked towards a sign saying SORTIE, having correctly deduced from his second-year French that this meant way out or exit. It was beginning to get dark, and the high orange lamps outside were illuminated and shone on the rows of container lorries, smaller vans and ordinary cars. He looked carefully around, until he found a parking area with TAXIS painted on the tarmac. There were no taxis waiting, but as he stood there uncertainly, one drove into the parking lot. A young woman got out, and began to look in her bag for money to pay the driver.

Alex touched her arm. '*Excusez-moi, Madame*,' he began.

The woman turned towards him impatiently. '*Oui? Que désirez-vous?*'

'Do you speak English at all?'

'Of course.'

'I wonder if you could very kindly ask the taxi-driver to take me to this address? It is the home of my grandfather, Monsieur Ludovic McGrath.

'*Ah, bon?*' The woman looked at Alexander, and smiled at him quizzically. 'The same Mr McGrath who is working in the European Commission?'

'Yes, that's him.' That's funny, thought Alexander, she seems to know him: how amazing.

The woman paid her fare, then spoke to the cab-driver in rapid French, taking Ludovic's card from Alexander and showing it to the man, who growled something incomprehensible.

'He wish to know who 'ees paying?' asked the woman.

'My grandfather will pay. He will be waiting for me at impasse des Cordonniers.'

The woman relayed this information to the driver, who rubbed his nose doubtfully, then said, *'D'accord, il peut monter.'*

'Get in!' The woman opened the door and gave Alex a push. *'Allez! Vite!'*

'Can I have my card back, please?' Alexander scrambled into the cab, and she thrust the card through the window. 'Thank you very much,' he said breathlessly. *'Merci bien!'*

'Bravo!' she called, as the taxi pulled away. *'Bonne route!'*

The drive into Paris was uneventful, and Alexander sat in the back, clutching his bag, with the events of the long day whirling around in his head. He felt excited, extremely pleased with himself, and enormously relieved and happy that he would soon be safe with his grandfather. Equally, he was beginning to feel very tired indeed and was thankful that he would not have to attempt any more conversations in French that day. It was a strange thing, he said to himself; at school he was supposed to be fairly good at French. It's a different matter when you actually get here, he thought. 'And no effing mistake,' he said aloud.

'Quoi?'

'Rien.'

The church bells of the *quartier* struck ten as the taxi drew up at impasse des Cordonniers, and Ludovic stepped out of the shadows, his silver hair shining in the lamplight. Alexander leapt from the cab and stood close to his grandfather as he paid the driver and thanked him for taking care of his grandson.

'A votre service, Monsieur!' said the man, gratified by the large tip. *'Au revoir, jeune homme,'* he added for good measure, and drove away.

'How weird,' said Alex. 'He's hardly said a word to me all the way here.'

'Well,' said Ludovic, 'you're here now, thank God, and in one piece. Have you had anything to eat?'

'I had sausages and stuff on the ferry, but that was hours and hours ago; about two o'clock, I think.'

'Never mind, we'll soon put that right. Claudia will have been keeping supper hot for us. Come on, it's just up here.'

They turned and walked together up the narrow alleyway. A lamp was lit beside Claudia's door, and shone on the metal hand of her door-knocker. Suddenly, Alexander realized the enormity of what he had done and a wave of reaction and fatigue overwhelmed him. Unable to prevent the inevitable flood of tears, he dropped his bag and turned blindly towards his grandfather. Ludovic grasped the situation at once, put comforting arms round the weeping boy, and held him tightly until the sobs subsided. He felt pretty much like crying himself, so great was his relief at the safe arrival of Alexander.

'I'm OK now.'

Ludovic offered him his handkerchief, and Alex blew his nose and wiped his face, while his grandfather picked up the bag and opened the door. Immediately, Claudia came out of the kitchen to meet them.

'Here you are at last, thank heaven,' she said, and laughed. It was a kind, reassuring, amused sort of laugh, and made Alexander feel that what he had done was not a crime, after all, but might even be something to be quite proud of, for a change.

'Claudia, this is Alexander, my grandson. Alex, this is Claudia. I hope you will be friends.'

Alex held out his hand politely, but she kissed him firmly on both cheeks, and told them to come into the kitchen and have supper straight away. 'You must be starving,' she said.

'Yes, I am, a bit.' Alexander looked around him, dazzled by the beauty and fantasy of the room, lit by the soft shimmer of many candles. 'There's only one thing,' he said shyly. 'I've run away, you see. Gwen thinks I'm spending the weekend with a friend.'

'Where are Christian and Phoebe?' asked Ludovic, looking worried.

'They're in Rome, having a holiday. I suppose I ought to ring Gwen, and tell her where I am, oughtn't I?'

Ludovic looked at his watch. 'It'll be twenty past nine in England. She won't have gone to bed yet, will she?'

'No. She watches telly after supper.'

'Would you rather I phoned her, Alex?'

'Would you?' Alexander looked at his grandfather with gratitude. Though quite prepared to talk to Gwen, he knew that her reproachfulness and dismay in the face of his deception would be his final emotional undoing. 'Give her my love, please, and say I'm sorry, won't you?'

'I will,' said Ludovic. 'You two start supper, and I'll phone Gwen right away.'

Claudia took Alexander into the kitchen, where she had already laid the table for three. She took a round, green-glazed earthenware pot from the oven and put it on a mat in the middle of the table. She took off the lid, and a delicious smell of garlic, herbs and wine filled the air. '*Stifado*,' she said. 'Greek stew; do you like that, Alexander?'

'I don't know, I've never had it,' he answered truthfully. 'But I'm sure I will, it smells terrific.'

Claudia filled a plate with stew and passed it to him. She cut a baguette into large hunks, and offered him a piece. 'Start eating,' she said, serving herself. 'We won't wait for Ludo, he'll be a few minutes, I expect.'

They could hear his voice as he spoke at some length to Gwen. They could not make out the actual words, but he laughed once or twice, and Alexander began to relax, to feel that everything might work out, after all. Ludovic came into the kitchen and sat down at the table. Alexander, his mouth full, looked at him anxiously. 'OK?' he asked.

'OK.'

'Was she cross?'

'No, she wasn't cross. She was pretty surprised though; she hadn't even missed you.' Ludovic shook his head, and tried not to smile. 'She was completely taken in by your note; just as well, in the circumstances, don't you think?'

Alexander had the grace to blush, agreed that it was just as well, and took another mouthful of stew.

After the *stifado*, they had a salad, followed by some cheese and some fresh apricots. Ludovic gave his grandson a very small amount of red wine, with a large amount of water. Alexander thought that it tasted OK, though not especially so, but was flattered to be treated like an adult for once. He drank it slowly, sip by sip.

'I expect you'll be needing your bed, Alexander,' said Claudia, 'so I'll let you off the washing-up tonight. Ludo, you show Alex his room, while I clear away.'

Alexander got to his feet, thanked Claudia for his supper, and followed Ludovic out into the garden and up the iron stairs to the spare room, carrying his bag.

'Did you bring your night things?'

'Yes, I did.' Alexander opened his bag and took out his striped pyjamas. 'And my school gear,' he said, producing his grey trousers and pullover, and clean white shirt.

'My God,' said his grandfather, sitting on the bed while Alex undressed and put on his pyjamas, 'you did a thorough job, old chap. You fooled Gwen completely. It never occurred to her to check with whatsisname's mother.'

'Robin.'

'Yes, Robin, that's it.'

Alexander went to the bathroom, and Ludovic

waited until he came back and got into bed. He looked at his grandson, so gangling and tall, apparently so mature for his age, but in reality still on the right side of childhood, and so infinitely dearer to him than Christian had ever been. 'Why did you do it, Alex?' he asked quietly.

'Why did I run away?'

'Yes.'

'If I tell you, you won't laugh, or be angry?'

'No, of course not.'

'Well, it's because of Chloe. She's trying to get me killed, so that I can be with her. She's lonely, all by herself, poor thing.'

'Start at the beginning, Alexander, and tell me everything that's been happening.'

'Everything? There's rather a lot.'

'Everything. Don't leave anything out.'

So Alexander told him everything, beginning at the very first time he saw Chloe in the barn, after the funeral. He went on to explain how she talked to him on the telephone, and described their terrifying adventure on the roof of the tower, and the most recent and frightening manifestation of his dead sister, the haunting sound of her crying in the night. Then, sadly, he went further and told Ludovic that he knew his mother still considered him to be responsible for Chloe's death, and that he could not help agreeing with her. Finally, he described the visit of his grandmother and Fr Anselm, in all its horrible detail. At last he ran out of words, or very nearly. 'Great-Uncle Anselm said *Deus dismissis peccatis tuis*, or something like that, but it didn't make me feel any better.' He looked at Ludovic, his blue eyes full of anguish. 'In fact, I felt a bloody sight worse, which is why I've come. I hope you don't mind, Grandpa.'

'My dear boy, of course I don't mind. I only wish you'd got in touch with me sooner. Never mind, you're here now, and you can stay as long as you like.'

'Can I really?'

'Yes, you can; really.'

'I won't be a nuisance?'

'You won't be a nuisance.'

'I feel OK here; safe.'

'Good. Go to sleep, now. We can talk again tomorrow.' Ludovic got up and went to the door.

'Grandpa?'

'Mm?'

'I like Claudia; she's cool.'

Ludovic smiled. 'So do I. Good night, Alex. Sleep well.'

'Good night.'

Chapter Nine

One morning in early June, Emma, carrying a pile of clean linen, walked through the grounds of the abbey to the guest house. It was her week for cleaning the bedrooms and changing the sheets of departed visitors. Since her interview with the Abbess, her anger and frustration had grown with each passing day, and it was becoming blindingly obvious to her that from the very beginning of her postulancy she had failed completely to understand the meaning and responsibility of a true religious vocation. With profound shame, she realized that all she had succeeded in doing was having the arrogance to believe that she was in some way special, and could bring a meaningful contribution to the religious life by exercising her particular talents in the peace and tranquillity of a convent. In clinging so tenaciously to this misapprehension, she had cruelly deceived herself, and each night as she lay on her hard, narrow bed and faced the truth of her situation, she forced herself to admit that she had entered the convent primarily as a means of escape, a way of sidestepping the natural progression towards maturity and self-determination. Vaguely, she acknowledged that her mother's malign influence on her childhood and adolescence, particularly in respect of her attitude to sex, had played a major part in this important decision. She remembered her years in Italy, and her knee-jerk responses to the advances of the Petaccis' young men. Was that all Mother's doing? she asked herself. Was I doing exactly what she would have wished me to do? Was she manipulating me all the time, to fulfil her own frustrated desires? Why was I so feeble and pathetic, letting her do that to me? Why didn't I go my own way, live my own life, grow up? I was a fool, she said to herself. It was my life, not hers. I should have taken more time, thought it out more clearly, listened to my father. Perhaps, even now, I should write to him, tell him I've made a serious mistake. After all, I'm only twenty-four; it's not too late to change direction, is it? My life as a nun is over. The whole thing was a waste of time, for them, as well as for me.

The moment of her going was to arrive sooner than she anticipated. As she was vigorously removing the blankets and sheets of a departed guest, a discarded magazine fell onto the tiled floor beside the bed. It had a photograph of a celebrated *couturier* on the cover, under the title in red letters, *Info-Phallo*. Frowning with distaste, Emma picked it up, intending to dump it in the bin with the rest of the rubbish. It fell open in her hands, revealing to her astonishment and horror, a full-page colour photograph of Claudia outside her door in impasse des Cordonniers, carrying two shopping bags and looking extremely startled. On the facing page were two smaller black and white photos, of Ludovic and Allegra, under the headline: LIAISON AMOUREUSE DE LONGUE DATE ENTRE BELLE VIOLONCELLISTE (46 ANS) ET FONCTIONNAIRE BRITANNIQUE (62). LEUR FILLE (21) RACONTE L'HISTOIRE CACHEE.

For a long moment, Emma stood staring with disbelief at the pictures, without reading the accompanying text. The photograph of her father was obviously a library picture, taken some time ago and probably selected because it represented him as an autocratic-looking man, stern and proud, though extremely handsome nonetheless. Allegra looked defiant and unsmiling, the photograph probably taken in a café, for she had a glass of wine on the table in front of her and was smoking a cigarette. As for poor Claudia, she looked beautiful but rather stupid, with her mouth open, her eyes round with alarm, their hazel colour appearing red on account of the camera's flash. She had the look of a trapped animal.

Hardly aware of what she was doing, Emma folded the magazine carefully, and put it into the deep pocket of her habit. She finished removing the sheets from the bed and bundled them into the laundry bag. Then she left the guest house and went to her cell. She took the pocketbook containing her passport, with her father's money concealed within its pages, from its hiding place under the mattress. She slid it into her pocket beside the magazine, and without hurrying, walked out of the convent, down the drive and into the shelter of the woodland beyond. It took her forty minutes to reach the main road, and another twenty to find a bus stop. She rested on a low wall while she waited, more in hope than expectation, for a bus to Avignon to appear. A little anxiously, she considered the question of how to pay for her fare. She was sure that a note for a hundred francs would be accepted with very bad grace, and cause her much embarrassment. After nearly an hour had passed and the question of her fare seemed academic, a very ancient bus hove into view and Emma stood up quickly and stepped into the road, waving her arm as she did so. The bus stopped beside her, wheezing, and she climbed on board. 'Avignon?' she asked, proffering her note.

'*Oui*,' said the driver, taking it without comment, and giving her a ticket and the change. The bus was not very full and she found a seat towards the back and sat down. Watching the sun-drenched countryside unrolling like a beautiful tapestry as she gazed through the window, she wondered whether anyone had noticed her abrupt departure from Villemagne, then realized that in fact she did not care whether they had or not.

Fifty minutes later, the bus arrived in Avignon, and Emma found herself in a wide thoroughfare, clogged with noisy, slow-moving traffic. This turbulent road runs beside the immensely high stone ramparts that encircle the city of the fourteenth-century popes, and still protect the colossal Palais des Papes and the intricate network of streets and little squares surrounding the huge edifice. Emma went through the first great arch she came to, and made her way through narrow, shady streets until she arrived in a tiny, tree-lined square, a comfortable mixture of shops, cafés and private houses. In front of each café, tables and chairs were set out, elegant and inviting under large white canvas parasols. Feeling hot and in need of refreshment, she sat down at an empty table and ordered a carafe of water and a coffee. She took the magazine from her pocket, and spread it carefully on the table in front of her, in order to read it properly. Sadly, she looked at Allegra's stern face and read the text of the interview she had apparently given to the author of the piece. Remembering their unpleasant encounter in the Jardin des Plantes, she was not particularly surprised that her half-sister had decided to punish her parents in such a manner, and in a sense could hardly blame Allegra for her act of vengeance. Nevertheless, Emma felt a deep sense of shock and pain in seeing Claudia and her father pilloried in such a way, and longed to help them if she could. She bitterly regretted her decision to visit them in the first place. If I hadn't gone, she thought, maybe none of this would have happened. She closed the magazine and looked at the date on the cover – 24 May. That's more than two weeks ago, she said to herself, drinking her coffee. I don't suppose there's much point in rushing up there now. In fact, it would probably be the least helpful thing to do. Heaven knows what the press might get up to if they found out that Ludovic had another daughter, and that she was a nun. The very idea of finding a picture of herself in the papers, wearing her nun's habit, and with or without her father, made her feel physically sick.

She ordered another coffee, and slid the offending *Info-Phallo* into her pocket. She looked around her at the people sitting in the sunshine, enjoying the warmth of early summer, chatting to their friends, happy and relaxed. Consciously, she forced herself to unwind, to enjoy the strong, reviving coffee. Slowly calming down, she told herself that very probably the whole disagreeable business was already forgotten, a nine-days' wonder. She studied the occupants of the other tables, as they ate and drank with so much enjoyment, talking and laughing as they did so. They looked cool and comfortable in their thin summer clothes, their bare arms already tanned by the sun, that Emma was seized with an intense longing to be exactly like them; to be comfortable, and above all, to be free.

She asked the waiter for her bill, handed over the money, and left the square, walking along a dingy backstreet that hugged the walls of the Palais. I need some summer clothes she told herself, feeling slightly alarmed at the idea. She followed the little lane, her eyes glancing from side to side as she searched for a suitable shop. Presently, she saw a sign marked *Friperies*. Looking through the window at the display of shabby anoraks and shrunken-looking cardigans, Emma realized that what she had found was a thrift shop. Just what I need, she thought with relief, and went in. The place was much larger than its modest shop-front had suggested, and she went slowly along the depressing lines of other people's cast-off clothing, looking for something suitably nondescript and un-likely to attract attention. It was not difficult. She chose a faded flowered-cotton skirt, two white shirts and a dark-green sunhat. Thinking that her stout brown-leather convent sandals were rather a giveaway, she bought a pair of black gym shoes. Then, after consulting a street-map outside a newsagent's, she found her way to the railway station, and changed in the ladies' lavatory. She folded her habit neatly, and packed it into the empty *friperies* bag. Then she went to the left-luggage office, hired a locker, and stowed the bag in it, locking the door carefully. Carrying her pocketbook and the magazine, she left the station, crossing the busy main road again, and went back inside the shelter of the city walls, feeling extraordinarily naked, but delightfully cool. Catching sight of herself reflected in a shop window, she realized at once that she needed to do something about her strange appearance. Her face and forearms were sunburnt, but her legs and neck were of a startling white pallor. Timidly but resolutely, she went into a pharmacy and bought a tube of instant tanning cream. She found a quiet corner in a dark cul-de-sac, and applied the cream to her neck and legs, hoping that the artificial colour would not look too unlikely compared with her natural tan.

A little further up the street she saw a snack bar, and feeling ravenously hungry, went in and bought a sandwich. The little room was hot and dark. She sat down at one of the three tables, and in order to avoid the unwelcome glances of the barman she picked up a newspaper discarded by a previous client. Turning the pages as she ate her snack, she read accounts of local weddings, football matches, *concours de boules* and an article on the forthcoming attractions of the annual Avignon Festival. There was scarcely a mention of the horrors of world events, and Emma found this deeply soothing to the spirit. In the convent, the only news that the nuns listened to, on the television, was of the horrific variety, death, destruction and famine, in order that they might know where their prayers were most needed. She turned the page and her eye fell on the word TRANSHUMANCE in heavy black type. Under this title was a short announcement informing interested parties that in two days' time the shepherds of Verignan la Roquette would begin their annual journey on foot, transferring two and a half thousand head of sheep from their winter grazing lands around the villages in the Manosque area, to the high alpine summer pastures of the Col d'Allos. The shepherds expressed the hope that anyone interested in maintaining the ancient Provençal traditions would accompany them on the twelve-day walk, camping at night under the stars, and enjoying, for a modest fee, the experience of a lifetime. The article concluded with an address and telephone number for further information, and the advice that strong walking boots would be *obligatoire*.

Emma read the little piece twice, and smiled at the picture it conjured up of the shepherds with their enormous flock, undertaking their long journey to the Alps. What a lovely word, *transhumance*, she thought, and what a lovely thing to do. *Transhumance*, she repeated under her breath; in a way, it's what I'm trying to do, isn't it? Moving from one stage of my life to another. I can't very well rush up to Paris to Dad and Claudia, they've got enough problems already, poor things. In any case, I really do need to prove to myself that I can manage my life on my own. A long walk to the Alps might be the perfect chance to clarify my thoughts, and decide what I really want to do next. She looked at the clock on the wall of the bar: three-twenty. Under normal circumstances, she would have been ironing in the laundry at this hour. Was it really only seven hours since she had walked out of Villemagne? It seemed like a much longer time, an eternity. Suddenly, it occurred to Emma that the Abbess, concerned at her sudden disappearance, might decide to telephone her father, or worse, her mother in London. Quickly, she made her way to the payphone, dialled the Villemagne number, and asked to speak to the Abbess. In a few minutes, she found herself explaining, in a calm controlled voice, that there was a serious crisis in her family, that she needed leave to see whether she could be of assistance to them, and apologized for her abrupt departure. 'It was thoughtless of me not to speak to you, Mother. I'm sorry. I will write to you in a few days, when I see how things go.'

'Very well, my dear. I shall pray for you, and for your family, of course.'

'Thank you, Mother.'

'*Deo gratias*, Sister.'

'*Deo gratias*, Mother.'

Thankful that the Abbess had not probed more deeply, Emma returned to her table and sat down. She unfolded *Info-Phallo* again, and took another brief look at the pictures of her father, Claudia and Allegra, and sighed. I'd better send Dad a postcard, and let him know what I'm doing, she said to herself. She refolded the magazine, then, checking that the barman was not watching her, carefully tore the *transhumance* page from the newspaper. She folded it neatly, and put it in her pocketbook, then left the stuffy little bar.

In the next street she found a bookshop, with a carousel on the pavement outside, displaying picture postcards and maps. She bought a postcard, a ballpoint pen and a book of stamps. Then she looked for a map covering the area from Avignon, through the Lubéron mountains to Manosque, and right up to Digne and beyond, to a height of nearly three thousand metres. It was becoming a matter of urgency to find a bag of some kind to hold all her newly acquired possessions, and a couple of doors further along the street Emma found a shop selling camping equipment and sports gear. The first thing she bought was a stout canvas rucksack. She looked at the rows of Reebok trainers, then asked the young woman in charge whether she stocked real boots for walking – '*Pour randonner?*' The girl climbed up a ladder to a high shelf and brought down a box containing exactly what Emma needed, soft brown-leather boots, lined and padded, incredibly comfort-able, and unbelievably expensive. Feeling slightly lightheaded at the extravagance, she handed over the money, and left. On the other side of the road she saw a *Prisunic* store and finished her shopping there, buying underwear, a towel, a comb, soap, toothbrush and paste, and some socks. She packed everything into her rucksack, then sat down at a table in front of the café next door to have a glass of water, and write her card. She wrote a message to her father and Claudia, hoping that all was well with them, telling them that she had left the convent, was taking a short holiday, would be in touch soon. She did not mention that she had seen the article in *Info-Phallo*.

She stuck a stamp on the card, drank all the water in the carafe, then opened out her map. Following the route from Verignan la Roquette to Col d'Allos with her finger, she felt a sudden rush of excitement at the sight of the apparently endless mountain ranges through which the *transhumance* would have to travel before reaching its destination. This feeling of elation was tinged with alarm at the prospect of being part of a group of complete strangers for twelve days. Carrying her rucksack over her shoulder, she found the nearest post office, dropped her card into the box, and made her way back to the bus station. Making enquiries, she found that she could travel to Manosque that evening, but would have to get a local bus to Verignan la Roquette in the morning.

The journey to Manosque was slow and tiring, with many stops, and it was after nine when Emma found herself in place de l'Hôtel-de-Ville, wondering where she would spend the night. She stood for a moment, admiring a magnificent pair of carved wooden gates, set in a deeply recessed stone arch, and took note of a busy-looking bistro close by. It looked a likely place to get some supper, but she decided that her first priority was finding a room for the night. She looked around the square, and headed for the nearest side street. It was dark and narrow, with tightly packed four-storey houses on either side; quiet, except for a small boy kicking a stone, and a bored-looking, flea-bitten dog, evidently a very distant cousin of a spaniel. Briskly, Emma walked down the street, looking carefully at every window as she passed, until she came upon one displaying a card proclaiming: *Chambre à louer.*

She knocked on the door, and presently it was opened by a tired-looking, grey-haired woman of about forty. Emma explained herself, and the woman, without surprise, said, '*Oui, vous pouvez passer.*' Without further ado, she led the way up three flights of narrow stone stairs to the top floor, where she opened a door and invited Emma to enter. The room was quite large, square, with a red-tiled floor. It was furnished with a rickety table bearing a basin and ewer, a rush-seated chair and a double bed covered in a grey and white check quilt. The single window was open, but the shutters closed, so that the room was dark and rather airless. Emma asked how much it would cost, and they agreed a price for one night. She asked where the lavatory was, and was told that it was on the second floor. The woman, having pocketed her cash, sketched the ghost of a smile at her guest and departed.

Emma put her rucksack on the bed and, crossing to the window, opened the shutters. To her surprise and intense pleasure, she saw spread out before her the anarchic roofscape of the neighbouring houses, built in a seemingly haphazard manner, a jumble of sun-bleached Roman tiles, punctuated by the occasional dark spear of a cypress tree, and watched over by an onion-shaped cupola, an insubstantial affair of lacy wrought iron, that crowned the pale stone bell-tower of a nearby church. In the middle distance, beyond the roofs, Emma could see more cypresses, as well as olive groves and grey-green fields, and beyond them, the looming forested flanks of the mountains. The sky was beginning to darken, but the crest of the mountains and the bell-tower were tinged with pink from the setting sun, and the patchwork of tiles seemed to reflect the warmth of the day, giving off a sweet, scented afterglow. Emma drew a deep breath and looked up into the dark-blue dome above her. A single star hung in the void, brilliant in its isolation. The evening star, she said to herself; how beautiful.

She could quite happily have remained where she was, gazing over the rooftops, breathing the perfumed air, but common sense and the yawning emptiness of her stomach prevailed, and she descended to the street and hurried back to place de l'Hôtel-de-Ville, in search of supper. The bistro near the big wooden gates was still busy with diners, so she entered and asked for steak-*frites* and a small jug of local red wine. The young waiter brought a basket of bread with the wine, and feeling incredibly hungry after her long day, Emma tore off a large piece and ate it, and drank some of the wine. Both the bread and the wine were delicious and as she waited for her steak, she reflected that this was the first proper meal she had chosen and eaten, all by herself, for years. It still felt extremely strange to be out in the world without the protective covering of the nun's habit. Her neck and legs felt conspicuously naked, and although it was quite long and entirely respectable, she found herself involuntarily adjusting her skirt when the waiter approached.

'*Bon appetit!*' He placed the plate of steak with its enormous pile of golden chips in front of her.

'*Merci.*'

When she had eaten all the food, she ordered coffee and drank the rest of her wine slowly, savouring its fruity roundness, holding it in her mouth as Signor Petacci had taught her, so long ago. She took the magazine from her rucksack and turned to the pages

concerning the private life of her family, not so much
to brood on Allegra's cruel and foolish action, but to
look at the picture of her father, Ludovic. How handsome he is, she thought, and smiled. I'm not at all
surprised that Claudia fell in love with him. And what
about Mother? She must have been completely crazy to
turn away from him as she did, after I was born. What
a dreary, sad, dried-up little creature she has become,
poor thing. A bit off her head, too, if one is truthful
about it. Look at her ghastly behaviour after poor
Chloe's funeral; I wonder if Phoebe and Christian will
ever be able to forget the awful things she said, or
forgive her? It's strange how very pious people can
often be the most evil-minded; cruel and insensitive at
the same time. She sighed, folded the paper and put it
away. Then she finished her coffee, paid the bill and
left.

Full of good food, but feeling very tired after her long
adventurous day, Emma went slowly back to her
lodging. She knocked on the kitchen door and said
good night to her hostess, then climbed the long flights
of stairs to her room. Once again, she leaned out of her
high window, entranced by the scene spread out before
her. Soft lamplight now shone in many of the windows, and the great whaleback shape of the Lubéron
was a dense black silhouette against the dark-blue
starry sky. The lithe figure of a skinny black cat crept
over the tiles beneath Emma's window, then leapt with
silent grace onto an adjacent roof. Reluctantly, she left
the window and turned back the cover of her bed. She
crossed the room to the table, poured cold water into
the basin, and washed her face and hands. She undressed, carefully hanging her skirt and shirt over the
back of the chair. She opened her rucksack, took out
her new toothbrush and cleaned her teeth. Suddenly, it
occurred to her that she had forgotten to buy anything
to sleep in. Doesn't matter, she thought, just my pants
will do. Leaving her window wide open so that she

could see the stars, she got into bed, put out the light and lay down. She stretched out her legs and arms in the big bed, enjoying the coolness of the sheets against her bare skin. Presently her eyes closed and she fell into a deep sleep. It had not even crossed her mind to say the usual prayers for the night.

She was woken at six by the church bell, loud and insistent in the clear mountain air. She lay for a moment, blinking, wondering where she was. Of course, she thought, I'm in Manosque, I've run away. She laughed aloud at the idea, and sat up, folding back the sheet. She dressed quickly, combed her short spiky hair, packed everything into the rucksack, and went downstairs.

The landlady was in her kitchen, pouring milk into a saucer for her cat. She looked tired and drawn. Emma thought it very probable that she had not been to bed at all, and wondered whether the bed she had slept in was, in reality, that of this exhausted-looking woman. She offered Emma a bowl of coffee, and they sat together at the long wooden table beside a black iron stove, and drank the hot thick brew, laced with strong-tasting goat's milk.

After breakfast Emma thanked her hostess, shook hands and left. She returned to place de l'Hôtel-de-Ville, and went to the *mairie* in search of information concerning buses to Verignan la Roquette. She found that there was a bus that could drop her about seven kilometres from Verignan, and decided that the walk would be a useful preparation for the long arduous walks to come. The bus did not leave until eleven, so she decided that she had better buy something to wear in bed, for modesty's sake, if she was going to be camping with other people. I suppose I ought to have a sleeping bag, too, she thought, and went in search of these necessities. After a few enquiries she found a general store that sold camping equipment. The proprietor, a helpful and friendly man, on discovering that she was intending to go on the *transhumance*, asked her whether she had equipped herself with trousers and a sweater. 'When you get up high, it is cold at night,' he warned. Taking heed, Emma bought a pair of khaki drill trousers, a thick black sweater and a long flannel shirt to sleep in. All these were packed into the rucksack, and the sleeping bag, tightly rolled, was strapped on the top. The kind man also recommended that she buy a cream to repel insects, and she took his advice. Laden with all this gear, she made her way back to place de l'Hôtel-de-Ville and caught her bus.

It was after four o'clock when Emma walked into Verignan la Roquette. She took off her rucksack, glad to be relieved of its weight, and sat down to rest for a moment on a conveniently low wall, fronting a creeper-clad building. She sat quietly, listening to the afternoon sounds of the dozing, apparently deserted village. House martins screamed overhead as they chased each other down the cool shaded alleyway, lined with shuttered houses. The only sign of life came from inside the café; the staccato clicks of a pinball machine, the sound of a turned-down radio. Bees, their legs yellow with pollen, droned among the blossoms of the creeper, and fat bluebottles buzzed around the dogs sleeping in the dusty road. Gradually, she became aware of another sound, a sort of muffled murmur, and the occasional deep clonk of a bell. Then she noticed a faint, slightly rancid odour, not unpleasant, that reminded her of the smell of boxes of tallow church candles. Of course, she thought, it's the sheep! They must be collecting here, ready for tomorrow. Suddenly, the whole adventure seemed real, as if it were actually going to happen.

She got to her feet with renewed energy, picked up her rucksack and went in search of the shepherds' office, aiming towards the sound of the sheep. After walking along two short streets, and past the square with its dripping fountain, she found herself at the village *boules* park. On the far side of this open space she saw the sheep, hundreds, probably thousands of them, penned together behind makeshift hurdles, a vast field of woolly backs, each ewe or lamb having the initials of its owner clearly painted in large rust-red letters on its flanks. Close to, the smell of the sheep was overpowering, and their nervous bleating filled the air. Around the collecting area, the shepherds' dogs waited and watched, unexcited but alert, their keen eyes bright behind their long fringes of stiff grey hair. The 'office' was in a large barn at one end of the *boules* park, and here Emma signed on and paid her dues, which amounted to a great deal less than she had already spent on clothes and equipment. 'And the food?' she asked the young woman in charge.

'*Compris.*'

'Everything? Wine too?'

'*Si.*'

Emma asked what would be the timetable for the next day, and where she should sleep that night.

'The journey will commence at five o'clock. The shepherds will sleep here in the barn. You can sleep here, too, or if you prefer, there are rooms in the village.'

'I think I would rather be here. I don't want to be left behind in the morning.'

'*D'accord*. You can get a meal in the café, tonight, and we have coffee and bread here, in the morning.'

In the café, she shared a table with a very young couple, also going on the journey to the Alps. They had been the year before, they told her, and, although they had found it hard going, they had both chosen to use two weeks of their annual vacation to go again. 'It's just so perfect,' said the young man. 'There's something extraordinarily primitive about it, but entirely magical.'

'It's true,' agreed the girl. 'Machines will never replace shepherds, that's for sure.'

'All the same, one wonders how long it will last.

Already, quite a lot of the sheep are transported to the high pastures in lorries, crammed together tightly in the heat, without water. It's cruel.' The young man looked worried.

Emma smiled at them, touched by their youthful concern. 'Well, it may be that people like us will help to keep it going?'

'Yes, of course. That's the whole idea.'

She walked back to the *boules* park with her new friends, and they were shown where to set out their sleeping bags in the barn. Before settling down for the night, Emma took a stroll round the park, familiarizing herself with the sheep, long-legged and floppy-eared, and the beautiful *beauceron* sheepdogs with their coarse grey and white shaggy coats, large gentle heads, fat black noses, and watchful eyes half-hidden behind the fronds of white hair that hung like ragged curtains in front of them. The shepherds, about fifteen of them Emma calculated, were gathered in a group around the supply lorry that could drive ahead of the *troupeau*, setting up camp each evening before the arrival of the flock and the walkers. She had been relieved to learn that rucksacks could be stowed in the lorry during each day's march. The older shepherds were wearing a curious assortment of rusty-looking coats, and even waistcoats, black or brown, their trousers tucked into thick leather leggings over heavy boots. On their heads some wore battered peaked hunting caps, and all carried long stout sticks. The younger ones were less encumbered with heavy clothing and wore jeans, checked shirts, the obligatory walking boots and broad-brimmed leather bush hats. They too carried the traditional long sticks.

Emma leaned against a plane tree, fascinated by the atmosphere of controlled excitement that seemed to fill the place. Night was falling, and with it a heavy dew. The sky was already bright with stars; the occasional bleat could be heard from the huge waiting flock, and the answering clonk of a bell. The dogs lay at their posts, tongues lolling, and one of the shepherds walked quietly along the sheepfolds, checking that all was well. This is wonderful, Emma said to herself, I'm so glad I came. She walked slowly back to the barn, quiet now and dark, with a single paraffin lamp burning over the doorway. Her two new acquaintances were already asleep, side by side in their sleeping bags. Glad of their company and grateful for their friendliness, Emma undressed quietly, and wearing her new nightshirt, slid into her sleeping bag.

The sleepers were woken at four o'clock, before the dawn. They dressed quickly, and stowed all their possessions in their rucksacks. At the door a trestle table had been erected, and was set with mugs, jugs of hot coffee and long loaves, *gros pains*, still warm from the village bakery. Shepherds and walkers stood together round the table, and ate their breakfast without ceremony.

At five o'clock sharp, the great journey began. The hurdles were removed and stacked in piles on the ground, while the dogs flew everywhere, taking care that the flock stayed together as one huge unit, any attempts at escape being dealt with by a series of sharp barks, and if necessary an even sharper nip on a sheep's ankle. Then, when all was ready, the leading shepherd, a formidable-looking man of middle years, his dog at his heels and his mule at his side, led the way across the *boules* park, down the narrow rue des Écoles, and right through the sleeping village, followed by the closely packed *troupeau*. Dispersed among the ewes were the *floucas*, the castrated goats, traditional bell-wethers of the flock. Their long horns were decorated with pom-poms of coloured wool, and round their necks they carried big heavy bells, their deep sonorous notes acting as pilots to the ewes. Their heads tossing nervously, the sheep forced their way through the narrow streets of Verignan la Roquette.

The shutters of upstairs windows flew open, and sleepy heads appeared to add loud good wishes for the journey to the prevailing uproar of bleating and barking, and the shouts of the shepherds. In ten minutes, the procession of two and a half thousand animals and their guardians had passed through the village, and were trotting in a sedate manner along the road towards their first stop, ten kilometres distant.

Emma walked by herself, happy to be alone, and gazed around her at the beautiful countryside. On either side of the road stretched fields of lavender, in long, neatly planted lines of compact green-grey bushes, their purple flowers just beginning to open, their pure sharp scent drifting on the moist early-morning air. Dividing the fields were lines of almond trees, and from time to time Emma noticed strange stone cairns with pointed tops, standing alone in the fields, like sentinels. Beyond the fields of lavender, the mountains of the Lubéron to the west were a hazy blue in the pre-dawn light. To the east, above the high peaks of far-distant mountains, the sky began to turn pink, then a luminous pale yellow, and the sun rose, climbing swiftly up into the wide blue void, bringing sudden warmth to the long cavalcade walking peacefully along the road, insignificant in that vast open plain.

Seven o'clock came, announced by the tinny bell of a little chapel half-hidden in a grove of olive trees, then eight o'clock, and the heat of the day began to be felt by the walkers, both animal and human. The distant mountains shimmered in a heat-haze, the powerful smell of the sheep became more intense, and slowly, inexorably, the temperature rose. The sheep reduced their pace and became a little restive, tossing their heads from side to side as though contemplating escape. The dogs trotted beside them alert, watchful, imperturbable, ready to crush any rebellion should the need arise. By nine o'clock it was already seriously hot, the tarmac of the minor road on which they travelled was turning to the consistency of chewing-gum in the heat, and the pungent smell of melting tar mingled with the raw odour given off by the flock.

Emma felt the prickle of sweat in her armpits, and a trickle ran down her back between her shoulder blades. Under her green hat her hair was already drenched with sweat, and she took off the hat from time to time and wiped her face with it. She noticed dark patches of sweat appearing on the checked shirts of the shepherds, and saw that their bush hats, like her own, had dark stains around the hatband. One of the older shepherds came alongside Emma, and asked her if she was all right.

'I'm fine,' she replied, quite truthfully, 'I don't mind the heat at all.'

'That's good.' The elderly man smiled, showing broken discoloured teeth. 'We don't want people passing out. The temperature must be well over thirty already.'

'Really?' said Emma. 'That *is* quite hot.'

'Soon one will rest.'

Ahead of them, about a kilometre further along the road, they could see a village, crowned with the familiar elaborate lacy ironwork cupola of its church bell-tower, nestling among trees on a small hill. 'St Fabrice,' said the shepherd. 'One arrives in thirty minutes.'

He was right, and in half an hour the residents of St Fabrice heard the tinkle of bells and the muffled bleating of many sheep as the long procession approached the village. Housewives stood at their doors, and old men came out of the café to watch as the flock, led by the senior shepherd, attended by Filou his dog and Sarriette his she-mule, forged its way, tightly packed, through the narrow streets to the village square in order to drink from the fountain. The thirsty ewes thrust eager noses into the cool water that filled the great round stone basin. As the thirst of each ewe was satisfied, she made way for another and rejoined the slow-moving river of beige, tallow-smelling wool as it continued its passage through St Fabrice.

On the far side of the village a track led to a wooded valley. The time for the long noonday rest had arrived, and this was an ideal spot in which to spend the hours of greatest heat. Under the trees, the ewes milled about for a few minutes, snatching at the lush grass. Then, one by one, they lay down in the shade, motionless except for the occasional flick of an ear to discourage flies.

Some of the walkers had remained in St Fabrice in order to explore the village and refresh themselves in the café, but Emma remained with the flock and the shepherds, who lay down in the long grass under the trees to sleep. It would be three o'clock, or even four, before the second half of the day's march would begin, and a few of the shepherds walked down to the small canal that irrigated the surrounding fields of barley. They poured water over their sweating bodies and refilled their empty water bottles. On their return, they passed the bottles round, and drinking gratefully, Emma made a mental note to buy herself a water bottle of her own at the first opportunity, and not rely on the generosity of her hosts. She lay under the trees, alternately dozing and watching the pattern of green chestnut leaves against the celestial blue of the sky, and the golden shafts of sunlight piercing the translucent green canopy that afforded such deep cooling shade. Once, she sat up and looked around her at the peacefully resting sheep; at the dogs, watchful but silent; the little groups of shepherds and walkers, half-hidden as they lay in the long grass. The only sounds that broke the silence were the strident percussive music of the cicadas, like mad tree-dwelling violinists, and the small regular tearing noise of Sarriette cropping the grass.

Soon after three o'clock, Emma noticed that the dogs

were standing quietly, their ears pricked, sniffing the air, waiting for their orders. Without prompting from either men or dogs, the ewes had begun to rouse themselves. Silently and without haste they gathered themselves together into a single compact unit in the middle of the field, apparently expressing their willingness to continue the journey. How extraordinary, said Emma to herself, watching them with admiration, I wonder how they know? One by one, the men and dogs resumed their allocated stations and the long slow-moving cavalcade re-formed, and made its way back to the main road, and turned north-east in the direction of the Valensole plateau.

In some respects, the afternoon and evening walk seemed harder than the first leg. Emma found that her legs felt stiff and tired, and it took some time to walk off the soreness of her muscles. The road itself undulated gently up shallow gradients and down again into little valleys, windless and still very warm. From time to time, passing traffic was a problem, when motorists sounded their horns impatiently in their haste to get through the flock. Occasionally such inconsiderate behaviour caused the ewes to panic and flee into the surrounding countryside, and it was during these incidents that the dogs showed themselves to be complete masters of the situation. Taking off with breathtaking grace and speed, the *beaucerons* collected their charges and returned them to the flock, reminding them with a few sharp barks who was boss of the outfit. Watching these wonderful dogs with admiration and affection, Emma wished passionately to have one of her own. It was the first time in several long years that she had actually felt a conscious longing to own something.

The afternoon turned into evening and the heat began to go out of the day. Slowly, the flock wound along the road, following the *floucas*. They crossed a valley, with groves of olives on one side and lavender fields on the other, passed through another village, taking advantage of the fountain once more, then descended the hill on the other side as darkness began to fall. The supply lorry had gone on ahead and they found the campsite already set up, the fire lit, food being prepared and a long trestle table erected on the grass, lit by storm lanterns. On the table were loaves of fresh bread, bottles of wine and dishes of cheese and fruit. Pots bubbling on flat stones round the fire gave off a delicious smell, making Emma realize how incredibly hungry she felt, for she had not eaten anything since her early breakfast, so many long hours ago.

The sheep melted away into the darkness and could be heard cropping the vegetation. The dogs clustered round the supply lorry, ready for their supper, and the walkers sat in groups near the fire, taking off their boots to ease their hot tired feet. Each campsite was carefully chosen to be close to a supply of fresh water, and one of the shepherds took a lantern and led the way to a nearby stream. Following the example of the shepherds, Emma rolled up her trousers and stood in the middle of the stream, so that the icy waters cooled her feet and soothed her tired legs. The water was so cold that it brought tears to her eyes, but the relief from discomfort was so intense that the sensation became a kind of bliss. Bending from the waist, she cupped her hands and washed her face and neck with the spring water. Then, sitting on the bank, she held her wrists under the water for a few minutes.

'Better now?' Looking up, Emma saw in the lamplight one of the younger shepherds, the tall one with long black hair.

'Much better,' she replied politely. 'Thank you.'

The little group, cooled and refreshed by their bathe, made their way back to the campsite and sat down on the benches around the table. Large pots of lamb stew, aromatic with garlic and herbs, and big platters of steaming rice were placed along the table and everyone helped themselves, their appetites sharpened by the freshness of the evening air. The food tasted delicious, the wine flowed like water, and ten long loaves were torn apart and dispatched, first with the lamb, then with the cheese. After the meal, aluminium cans of coffee were placed on the table by the cook, who was also the driver of the lorry. The company, replete and sleepy, chatted quietly to each other for a little longer, watching the dying embers of the fire as it glowed on the ground. Occasionally, the clunk of a bell or a few half-hearted bleats reminded them of the presence of the huge flock, close at hand.

The cook, helped by two of the shepherds, dealt with the dishes, then some of the older men got into the back of the lorry to sleep on the makeshift staging that provided a dormitory for them, and the dogs crawled beneath the lowered tailgate. The walkers and the remaining shepherds unrolled their sleeping bags and arranged them in a circle around the fire. After the long march, and the good food and wine, sleep came quickly. The night would be short. At five o'clock the convoy would move off again.

Chapter Ten

By the sixth day the flock had crossed the wide Valensole plateau, beautiful under the immense blue sky. It was a fertile and productive countryside, the ubiquitous lavender fields interspersed with crops of wheat and barley, and punctuated with olive groves, fruit trees and chestnuts. Poppies, brilliant scarlet against the tender green of the growing wheat, were scattered joyfully along the edges of the fields, and around this shallow basin of intense cultivation the distant mountain peaks formed a blue rim, quivering in the heat.

After nearly a week of exercise, Emma's legs had become strong and supple; the long walks had become a pleasure, and full of interest. As she walked, she took careful note of the wild flowering plants and shrubs of the region, unable to identify them all, and wishing she had thought to bring a small book of reference with her. Herbs, crushed beneath the feet of the travelling flock, filled the air with their powerful scents, and from time to time she would pick a sprig from a shrub in passing, to enjoy its fragrance as she walked. Sometimes they rested at noon under clumps of black pines, resin-scented, with a soft brown carpet of needles beneath. All around grew larch, juniper, rock-roses and flowering broom, dazzling yellow against lichen-blotched rocks.

The climb had now begun in earnest. At Barrême they had already reached a height of thirteen hundred metres, and were at the halfway point of the *transhumance*, among the foothills of the real Alps. As they emerged from the village and continued the slow upward climb, the black-haired shepherd who had spoken to Emma on the first night of the journey detached himself from the flock to walk at her side. 'Did you know that we just crossed the *Route Napoléon*?' he asked.

'Oh? What's that?'

'It's the mountain road that Napoleon took when he escaped from Elba in 1815. He'd got as far as Cannes, but had rather an unfriendly reception there. Normally, he would have continued his journey north by going straight up the Rhône Valley to Lyon, but, to avoid further trouble, he decided to cross the Alps to Grenoble on foot. It was a frightful journey, in winter, along a road that was really only a goat-track. He arrived in Grenoble on the seventh of March, after marching through the mountains by way of Digne, Sisteron and Gap.'

'How long did he take to get to Grenoble?'

'A week.'

'Good heavens!' said Emma. 'He must have been pretty tough!' She laughed.

'I think so.' He laughed too, amused by her reaction. What a strange young woman, he thought, so self-possessed and withdrawn. She looks happy enough, but she doesn't spend much time with people or talk very much. He studied her profile, half-hidden by the green hat, as they walked along the crumbling edge of the road. 'Are you enjoying the trip, may one ask?'

Emma looked up at him, her grey eyes alight with pleasure. 'I am, enormously,' she replied. 'I've never been in such wonderful country in my life, or felt so close to the earth and the sky before.' She turned away, looking down again, as if she regretted revealing so much of herself. They walked on in silence, then, as they approached the campsite, he rejoined the *troupeau*.

That evening they camped in a grove of evergreen oaks, overlooking a wide flat valley, with a river winding through it in a series of oxbows. On the far side of the valley rose the dark humps of rocky, scrub-covered mountains, with cultivated patches of land running down to the river, and a village straggling down the steep hillside. Beyond could be seen more mountain ranges, and behind them, in the distance, were the Alps, their sharp peaks shimmering pure white against the darkening blue of the sky. At this first glimpse of the snow, Emma's heart leapt with excitement and she felt as though she could remain where she was and gaze at their icy perfection for ever.

After supper, she sat beside the fire, disappointed that she could no longer see the snow-covered peaks in the darkness of the night. Then, to her surprise, the man who had spoken to her earlier sat down on the ground beside her and offered her cognac in a plastic mug. She took the mug, and smiled at him rather timidly. 'How kind of you,' she said. 'Thank you.'

'The nights are colder up here; the cognac will keep out the chill.'

'We must be at quite a height already. I saw the Alps earlier, with snow on the peaks; it was beautiful.'

'In half an hour the moon will rise, and you may be able to see them again.'

Emma drank her cognac slowly, as they sat by the fire, enjoying the warmth, saying little. She had noticed him right at the beginning of the trip; it would have been difficult not to, for he was a man of exceptional physical beauty, aged about thirty, she guessed. As well as the untidy black hair, he had brown eyes under thick black brows, and the burnished olive skin, with deep crow's feet around the eyes of those who spend their lives working in strong sunlight. He wore a red and black plaid shirt, and khaki trousers that had seen better days. Emma had already observed, during the long midday rests, his strong, slim body, deeply tanned by the sun. Now, as he sat quietly beside her, she noticed that his hands were not those of a labourer, but long-fingered, clean, with neatly trimmed nails.

'What is your name?' she asked, glancing at him shyly.

'Pascal. What is yours?'

'Emma.'

'Emma. I've never met anyone called Emma; it's a very pretty name.'

'Well, I've never met anyone called Pascal, come to that. That's a pretty name, too.' She laughed, and so did he.

'You make it sound incredibly affected, Emma! *Pretty*, indeed!'

'Sorry,' she said. 'I didn't mean to.'

'Of course you didn't. I know that.'

She looked up at him again, and saw that he was not looking at her but staring out across the valley, his face rosy in the glowing remains of the fire. 'Look, Emma, the moon is rising.'

She followed his gaze, and saw the round white shadowed face of the moon as it appeared behind the distant peaks and slowly crept up the sky, illuminating the snow-capped Alps beneath. She held her breath, awed and thrilled by the crystalline perfection of the scene before her, and knew that she would remember this moment for the rest of her life.

The next day they travelled through increasingly mountainous country, with the distant peaks disappearing from view as they descended into each valley, then reappearing as the trail rose up again in the direction of a high-perched village, and a convenient watering-place for the sheep. Sometimes Pascal walked among the animals, talking to the goats and dogs, checking the wellbeing of the huge flock. Sometimes he walked with Emma.

'Tell me about the goats,' she said. 'Why do you have them in the flock at all?'

'They're a special breed, called Rove, and we use them in the *transhumance* on account of their brown coats. In the autumn, when the snow begins to fall on the summer pastures, it's sometimes difficult to spot the ewes, but the brown goats are easily picked out in the snow, and guide us to the flock.'

'Ah, yes. That makes sense.'

'In the old days, the Rove goats were always used as leaders of the flocks on their *transhumance*. They led the way, and encouraged the ewes to walk on, even on the hottest days. Then, for some reason, they became unfashionable, and by the end of the nineteen-seventies there were only about two hundred left in the whole of Provence. Luckily, a few enthusiasts began to breed them seriously, and now we have around four thousand. All the same, they're still an endangered species and it's lucky that there are some people, like me, willing to carry on with the tradition.'

'So you don't keep sheep?'

'No, I have a herd of goats, and quite a few hectares of lavender, near Manosque.'

'Who looks after the goats, when you're away, like now?'

'My neighbour, François. He has sheep. There they are, they're the ones that have PF marked on their sides. I keep an eye on them for him, on the journey, and he is minding his rams, and my goats, at home.'

'Why don't the rams come up to the Alps?'

'Because they're troublemakers. They fight over the ewes, and fall into ravines and generally make a thorough nuisance of themselves.'

'Oh, poor things,' said Emma. 'What a shame, to have to spend the summer sweltering in the heat down in the plain.'

'Their time comes later,' said Pascal, 'when the ewes come home.'

'Yes, I suppose so.' Emma felt that a change of subject might be prudent, so she asked whether the goats were for milking, or for meat, or what.

'Milking, of course. I make cheese, and sell it all over the area, in the markets, to restaurants and food shops, and to the dealers.'

'Who's doing the milking just now?'

'François and his old mother, Juliette. They make *fromage de brebis* from their own ewes, so they can cope with my goats very well.'

'And what about the lavender? When do you harvest that?'

'We start cutting in the middle of July and the season goes on till mid-September. It's our next big job, but it's not difficult to manage both the cheese and the lavender, because we can hire a mechanical harvester. The machine can cut between three and four hectares in a day, whereas in the old days it would have taken twenty-five people to harvest that amount by hand. In a way, it's rather sad, but it makes economic sense, especially when the women won't accept a very low rate for the job any longer.'

'I don't blame them.'

'Neither do I,' agreed Pascal. 'But if it weren't for mechanization, lavender growing would have ceased long ago.'

'How awful that would be,' said Emma. 'It must be such a marvellous sight when it's in full flower, those incredible sheets of purple, spread over the land; and the lovely smell, so pure and therapeutic.'

'The bees love it, too. I have hives all along the edges of my lavender fields.'

'So, what happens to the lavender after it's been cut?'

'Most of it goes to the distillery at Valensole, it's not far. Then the essential oil is sold to the perfume-makers, soap-makers, trades like that. Some of the flowers are made into lavender bags, for tourists. And then there's the lavender honey, of course; we sell that as well.'

'It must be a busy life, so much to do; looking after the goats, making the cheese and selling it, and seeing to the lavender and the bees?'

'It's good to be busy, to work hard. But I find time for other things, too.'

'What else do you do?'

'Read, cook, listen to music. Sometimes I do a bit of maintenance on the buildings, things like that.'

That night, as they sat by the fire after supper and drank a cognac together, Emma asked Pascal whether his family had always lived in Provence. 'Were you born here?'

'No such luck. My parents live in Paris. My father is a neurosurgeon. My sister is a doctor, too, and she's married to a surgeon herself. I was expected to carry on the tradition, but I failed to do so. I'm the black sheep, the dim one, the drop-out.'

Surprised, Emma looked at him attentively. 'You don't seem dim to me,' she said quietly.

'I'm not, as a matter of fact.' He laughed. 'But I *am* a drop-out, I have to admit.'

'Do you regret that?'

'No, not for a single moment.'

'Will you stay here always?'

'I hope to. That's my intention.'

'What about your family?' asked Emma. 'Do you ever see them?'

'My parents came over for a day last summer. It was nice seeing them, and I think my father enjoyed himself. He seemed interested in everything; he loves the country, one can tell.' He looked at Emma, his dark eyes sombre. 'I'm afraid my mother found it all horribly primitive and uncomfortable though, not her scene at all. Poor thing, she was upset when she got goatshit on her nice Gucci loafers.'

'Oh dear!' Emma tried not to laugh. 'Couldn't you have got her something more suitable, espadrilles for instance?'

'Too downmarket for her; these things seem to matter to Parisians.'

'I suppose they must,' said Emma, and the image of Claudia rose in her mind's eye. 'My father's lover is a Parisian, through and through, but I think she'd fit in very well down here. She's called Claudia, and she plays the cello. You'd like her.'

'Your father's *lover*, Emma? What about your mother?'

Emma hesitated, almost regretting that she had allowed the conversation to drift in the direction of her own family. She drew a deep breath. 'My mother is quite a problem, Pascal. She is an alcoholic religious maniac, not to put too fine a point upon it.' She looked at Pascal, feeling unaccountably anxious.

His eyes met hers, serious, concerned. 'That must make everyone's life very difficult,' he said gently.

'It does, and has for years, mostly for my father.' Then, very quietly, warming her hands at the fire, she related the circumstances of her father's marriage, and his eventual long and happy alliance with Claudia, and their daughter Allegra.

'So you have a half-sister, as well as a brother?'

'Yes, that's right.'

'Well, maybe it's all for the best, isn't it? If your mother wishes not to share her bed with her husband, it's natural he should seek happiness elsewhere, don't you think?'

'Yes, that's exactly what I think. But there's more, Pascal. I haven't told you everything.' She got up, went to the supply lorry and took from her rucksack the copy of *Info-Phallo*. Then she came back to the fire, folded back the pages of the magazine, and without a word, handed it to Pascal. He read the piece dispassionately,

219

looked carefully at the photographs and handed the paper back.

'What can one say? The press are the hyenas of public life, aren't they? Your father is obviously a man of high intelligence; presumably he has always known that he is vulnerable to revelations concerning his private life?'

'I haven't spoken to him since it happened, but I don't imagine that he minds for himself. But he will feel badly for Claudia, and for Allegra, I'm sure.'

'Whatever possessed her to talk to the journalist? Everyone knows how ruthless they can be if they think they're on to something.'

Emma sighed, and explained that Allegra had only recently been told that Ludovic and Claudia weren't married, and had reacted to the news in this devastating manner.

'And what about your mother, Emma? Does *she* know about all this?'

'Not as far as I know, and I hope she never will.'

They sat silently by the dying fire for a long time, then Pascal took her hand in his. 'Is this why you're here with us, Emma? To get away from this trouble?'

'Yes, in a way.' She looked down at their clasped hands, then at his face. 'You see, I have another problem; a more personal one, which ought to prevent me from feeling the deep love and anxiety for my father that in fact I do feel, very much.'

Pascal stared at her, feeling extremely confused. 'Emma, what on earth are you talking about? Why shouldn't you love your father?'

'Because I'm a nun.'

'You're a *what*?'

'A nun. I'm a novice nun. Right now, I should be at the Abbaye de Villemagne, but I walked out.'

Pascal dropped her hand, and carefully stacking the brandy mugs, stood up. 'Good night, Emma. I apologize for intruding on your difficulties. That was not my intention, please believe me.'

Emma opened her mouth to say that he had not intruded on her in any way, that she was grateful for and glad of his company, but he had already gone; where to, she did not know.

The next day, to her great disappointment, Pascal failed to walk part of the way with her, and in the evening he sat as far away from her as possible. Sad and lonely, unable to enjoy the beauty of the night without the sympathetic presence of Pascal to share it with, she sat by the fire on her own, trying to tell herself that it was not important, and failing to convince herself for a moment. Tired and depressed, she crept into her sleeping bag and closed her eyes, trying to sleep.

The following day, the climb got steeper and more difficult, and a good deal of her energy was focused on keeping up with the flock. The sheep seemed to be anticipating the end of the long walk; they sniffed the air eagerly, as if they guessed instinctively the proximity of their goal. With aching muscles Emma plodded on, and when she thought about Pascal, told herself that she was being naïve in feeling hurt by his rejection of her. After all, it was not the first time by any means, that she had encountered the hostility, even fear, that many people experience in the presence of nuns. That night, she sat with the young couple she had met on the first evening, and did her best to be interested in them, and listen to their reactions to the countryside and the history of the great traditional movement of animals in which they were taking part.

'Did you see those huge lorries going by, on the main road below us, just where the river widens?'

'I can't say I did, especially,' said Emma.

'Well,' said the earnest young man. 'It's really rather a scandal. Those lorries contain five hundred ewes, each one of them, you know. Every summer, five hundred thousand sheep are whisked up to the Alps by lorry in the space of a few hours. It's unnatural, and absolutely wrong, in my view.'

'I agree,' said his wife. 'It causes a lot of suffering, even death by suffocation; that's a well-known fact. It's much better for the ewes to travel slowly, on foot, like this, to get acclimatized.'

'Not to mention that it costs five or six times as much to transport them by lorry.' He smiled at Emma. 'That'll probably be the deciding factor, at the end of the day. Quite soon, everyone will return to the old ways.'

'Yes,' said Emma. 'One must hope so.' Her eyes strayed away from her companions, as she looked around the camp, trying to locate Pascal. He was sitting with the rest of the shepherds and did not look in her direction.

By the tenth day, they had reached the lower slopes of the high Alps. The sky was a deep luminous blue, and the snow-capped peaks loomed above them, craggy and beautiful, their dark velvety shadows obscuring the burgeoning green of the summer-flowering herbs and grass already growing on the rocky, lichen-speckled slopes. In the evening, feeling rather enervated by the altitude and the thinness of the air, Emma sat down at the long trestle table with little appetite for the meal. Then, quite unexpectedly, a large plate of couscous was placed in front of her, and Pascal sat down beside her, putting his own plate on the table, and poured wine for her. They ate their supper as though nothing had happened to spoil their friendship, and after the meal they sat by the fire and drank a cognac together.

'This bottle is lasting well,' said Emma.

'It's the second bottle,' said Pascal, and they laughed.

They talked about the small incidents of the day, and did not mention the problems of their respective families. Then, when the fire was beginning to die down, and most of the group had settled themselves for the night, Pascal turned to Emma and looked at her seriously. 'For you to be a nun, Emma, is a cruel waste of life,' he said, and taking her firmly by the shoulders, kissed her.

It was the first proper kiss of her life and, taken completely by surprise, Emma shied away from it awkwardly. Without a word, he released her and prepared to depart. Quickly, she took hold of his sleeve to prevent his going. '*Please*,' she said, 'don't go. Please sit down again, won't you?'

'Are you laughing at me, Emma?'

'No, I am not.'

He sat down beside her, and she laid a hesitant hand on his arm. 'I'm sorry to have been so stupid, Pascal. If you can bear to, would you kiss me again, please?

He turned towards her, and took her face in his hands. 'Do you mean it, Emma? Really?'

'I do. Really.'

The kiss was gentle and undemanding, but all the same she was overwhelmed by the rush of warmth that invaded her entire body, and made her feel at the same moment both tremendously alive and incredibly weak, as though her bones were dissolving. She slid her arms around his hard strong body, resting her cheek against his chest. He held her tightly in his arms and kissed the top of her head. Her short dark hair smelt faintly of woodsmoke. 'Emma?'

'Mm?'

'Is it possible that this is the first time you've kissed anyone? Really kissed anyone, I mean?'

'Yes,' said Emma, sounding surprised, 'it is, the very first time. Do you mind? Is it important?'

'No, it's not important; it's just rather extraordinary, and wonderful. I can't believe it.'

'I'm afraid it's true.' She laughed. 'Do you think you can handle the education of an elderly virgin, Pascal?'

She raised her face to his and he kissed her again. 'Yes,' he said, 'I think I can handle that, Emma, with a

bit of co-operation on the part of the elderly virgin.'
He looked around the campsite at their sleeping companions. 'Though we might have to wait until we can
be a bit more private, wouldn't you say?'

On the evening of the twelfth day the long procession
of animals and men arrived at their destination, the Col
d'Allos. The monumental peaks rose all around them,
some of them bare and craggy, encrusted with golden
lichens, but the gentler lower slopes were like green
velvet, clothed in their new spring growth of short tufty
grasses and the mountain herbs that would nourish the
sheep all summer long. Behind these peaks rose even
higher ones, with the snow still lying on their highest
pinnacles and in the ravines that were too deep for the
sun's rays to penetrate. Over the dramatic alpine scene
the vast blue sky seemed to explode, like a clash of
cymbals. The sheep began to run, scattering joyfully
over the lush pastures, heady with the warm smell of
thyme. The journey was at an end. Pascal and Emma
sat down to rest on a rock, and Bosco, his dog, lay at
their feet, giving the occasional gratified thump with
his tail, as if he were quite aware of his part in the
satisfactory completion of the operation.

'Just look at them,' said Emma, as they watched the
ewes milling around in their version of paradise,
snatching at the sweet, flowering vegetation. 'I would
never have thought that sheep could look happy, but
they look positively ecstatic, don't they?'

'They do, yes.' Pascal took her hand. 'Tomorrow,
Emma, we travel back to Verignan in the lorry.'

'Yes.'

'You haven't changed your mind? You'll come and
stay with me?'

'I haven't changed my mind.'

'You'll come?'

'Yes, I will.'

'Good.'

*　　*　　*

Ludovic, Claudia and Alexander were lunching together in the garden at impasse des Cordonniers. Normally on a Sunday, Ludovic would have taken them to lunch at La Coupole, still his all-time favourite place, but since the unfortunate article in *Info-Phallo*, they had been keeping a discreetly low profile. It was now more than three weeks since the piece had appeared, and as nothing untoward had happened subsequently they had begun to hope that the episode had been, in fact, only a minor irritation, soon forgotten. At the Commission, those colleagues who had seen the magazine merely smiled knowingly. They did not think it a particularly big deal; on the contrary, they thought that Ludovic was a lucky man. Equally, Claudia's fellow-musicians at the *conservatoire* did not consider it a world-shaking circumstance. They, too, chose to ignore it, to her great relief and gratitude.

Christian had telephoned his father on his return from Rome and apologized for Alexander's extraordinary behaviour. 'I'm so sorry he's been such a bloody nuisance, Dad. Wretched boy, what on earth possessed him to pull such a stunt?'

Ludovic laughed, detecting a note of pride in Christian's denigration of his son. 'As a matter of fact, I thought it remarkably enterprising of him, Chris. Not many boys of his age would have the guts to do it, would they?'

'Well, maybe not,' Christian agreed grudgingly. 'How is he, anyway?'

'He's fine; excellent. We're enjoying having him here.' There was a pause. 'How's Phoebe?' enquired Ludovic.

'She's quite a lot better, thank God. She seems much more like her old self.'

'Well, I'm extremely relieved and glad to hear it. It was a good idea of yours, to take her away.'

'I hope so.'

'Was she very upset about Alex coming here?'

'Funnily enough, no, she wasn't. After all, she knew where he was, didn't she?' Christian hesitated, unwilling to tell the whole truth to his father, that Phoebe had not been sorry to find Alex absent on her return to Abbot's Court. 'Actually, Dad, I was wondering if Claudia would mind if he stayed on with you for a few more days?'

'I'm sure she'd be happy to have him. I'll ask her, of course, but I know she enjoys his company, and he likes her, too.'

'Good, that's great. Thanks, Dad, I'll be in touch.'

It was a warm, sunny June day, and after lunch Alexander helped Claudia with the dishes. She made coffee, and they took the tray out to the garden, where Ludovic was lying in a long rattan chair, reading the English Sunday papers. Claudia poured the coffee, then picked up her own cup. 'I have some work to do, so I'll leave you chaps to amuse yourselves for a bit, OK?' She went back into the house, and presently they heard the deep mellow notes of her cello.

'That's lovely,' said Alexander, as he sat cross-legged on the ground beside Ludovic, listening, his senses responsive to the warm scented air of the garden, the aroma of his coffee, and the blue drifting smoke from his grandfather's cigar.

'It is, isn't it? Haydn, I think.' Ludovic smiled at his grandson, so blue-eyed and fair, so different from himself in looks, but so similar in spirit.

Alexander raised his eyes and looked intently at Ludovic. 'I was wondering,' he said. 'Do you think I ought to be going home soon?'

'Do you want to go home, Alex?'

'No, I don't. I love it here. I feel safe.'

'Safe in what respect?'

'Well, Chloe hasn't found me. I don't even *dream* about her here, thank goodness.' He looked at Ludovic seriously. 'Perhaps ghosts can't travel far from where they died? Could that be why?'

'Ghosts are funny things, Alex. It would be quite foolish to deny their apparent existence, but it's my own feeling that they only exist on a very ultrasensitive level that a particular living person is tuned into, probably on a transient basis, while he or she is in a state of heightened awareness.'

'Like me, after Chloe died?'

'Exactly.'

Alexander was not absolutely sure that he had grasped all the implications of the ideas proposed by Ludovic, but he was nonetheless grateful to him for not dismissing his experiences as figments of his imagination, and his fears as rubbish. 'Do you think she will go away, eventually?'

'I expect so.'

'Do you think Mum will ever stop blaming me for the accident?'

'I'm sure she will. Poor woman, she had to blame someone. It's just so sad that she chose to blame you.' Ludovic smiled at Alexander reassuringly. 'No-one else blames you, Alex. You do realize that, don't you? But mothers are extraordinary creatures. If the truth were known, it's very likely that in her heart of hearts your mother blames *herself* for not being there to protect Chloe.'

'But how could she have been?'

'Of course, she couldn't. But she probably feels she *should* have been. Do you understand that?'

'Not really.'

'That's because you can't know what it's like to be a mother, or to lose a child.'

'I suppose not. Poor Mum.'

'Yes, poor Phoebe.'

Alexander stretched himself out on the warm flagstones, resting his head on his clasped hands and gazing up into the leafy interior of the mulberry tree.

The pure sad melody of the concerto floated in the air, and the pages of the *Observer* rustled as his grandfather turned them over, one by one. It's lovely here, said Alex to himself, and no effing mistake. 'So, is it OK if I stay a bit longer?' he asked, after a while.

'Stay as long as you like, old chap. Isn't it a bit boring, though?'

'No, it's not boring,' said Alexander. 'It's utter bliss.'

On Monday morning, Ludovic caught the early train to Brussels as usual, and at ten o'clock Claudia left for the *conservatoire*. 'You'll be all right on your own till lunchtime, Alex?'

'Yes, of course. I'll be fine.'

He was amusing himself, picking out a tune on the piano, when he was startled by a sharp rap on the knocker of the street door. For a moment, the awful thought that it might be Chloe playing tricks crossed his mind. The knock came again. He went to the door and put his ear to it, listening. 'Who is it?' he called loudly.

'Hilary Grant.'

He opened the door. A young blonde woman, wearing a long blue frock and carrying a large black tote-bag, stood on the step. She smiled at Alexander in a friendly manner. 'Hello,' she said, 'is Claudia in?'

'No, I'm afraid she's out. She won't be back till lunchtime.'

'That's a shame; I've got something for her. Can I come in?'

Relieved that she spoke English, Alexander stood aside for her to enter. She came quickly into the house, and Alex closed the door. 'Hilary Grant,' she said again, holding out her hand. 'How do you do?'

'How do you do? I'm Alex McGrath. Won't you sit down?'

'Thanks.' She took a small package from her bag and laid it on the table next to the blackamoor's head. She sat down on the sofa and looked around her at Claudia's beautiful room. 'Nice place,' she remarked. 'You must be the grandson?'

'Ludovic McGrath is my grandfather, yes,' agreed Alexander, thinking that this was a funny conversation.

'You must be very proud of him?'

'Yes, I am.'

'He's quite a big cheese in the Commission, isn't he?'

'Is he? Yes, I suppose he is, if you say so.'

'And what about Claudia? She's not your grandmother, is she?'

'Oh, *no*!' said Alex, sounding shocked at the idea. 'My grandmother is *old*. She lives in London. She doesn't live here.'

'Oh, really? Whereabouts in London does she live?'

'It's a place called Camden Town, but it's not a town, it's in London, really.'

'Yes, I see. And what's your grandmother's name, Alex?'

'Mrs McGrath.'

Stupid boy, thought Hilary Grant impatiently, is he winding me up? She smiled at him, showing pretty white teeth. 'I mean her Christian name? Her first name?'

'Flavia Ernestine McGrath.' Horrible old ratbag she is too, he added silently to himself.

Hilary Grant took out a small black notebook and wrote something in it rapidly, then produced a camera. 'Would you mind if I took your picture, Alexander?'

'No, not at all,' said Alexander, flattered by the suggestion. 'Here, or in the garden?'

'How about here first, and then in the garden?'

'OK,' he agreed, and ran his fingers through his hair rather self-consciously. Wow, he said to himself, this is really cool.

Alexander and Hilary Grant spent an enjoyable half-hour, posing for and taking photographs, in the studio, pretending to play the piano, and in the garden, pretending to water the flowers. She looked at her watch: twelve-twenty. 'Gosh, look at the time, I must dash!' she exclaimed. 'Thank you so much, Alex, you've been great. I'll send you some prints if you like.'

'Thanks, that would be terrific.' He opened the street door for her. 'Goodbye, it was nice meeting you.'

'Goodbye, Alex. Thanks again.' She walked away down the *impasse*, her heels clicking on the pavement.

When Claudia arrived home at one-fifteen, bringing with her slices of *pissaladière* and some salad leaves for their lunch, Alexander told her about Hilary's visit. 'She was awfully nice,' he said reassuringly. 'Very OK.'

'Really? And what did she want?'

'Nothing, really. We just chatted.'

Claudia frowned uneasily. 'What about?'

'Oh, lots of things.' He laughed. 'She wanted to know if you were my *grandmother*! I told her, no way! My grandmother is old.'

'Alex,' said Claudia very quietly. 'What else did you tell her?'

Alexander repeated all that he could recollect of the morning's conversation. 'Then she took some pictures of me,' he finished. 'Lots of them She said she'd send me some prints.'

'Did she really? said Claudia faintly. 'How very kind of her.'

'Oh, by the way. She left a package for you. It's on the table.'

Claudia picked up the package and opened it, knowing before she did so that there would be nothing in it. She was right.

Chapter Eleven

At Col d'Allos, the shepherds who would remain on the mountain with the sheep until the arrival of the first snow in October were installed in their hut, their stores neatly stacked on the shelves, their charges already scattered far and wide over the surrounding green slopes. Flanked by their dogs, they stood waving until the supply lorry was out of sight, then turned and, leaning on their long sticks, surveyed their idyllic world.

The lorry bounced slowly down the rough track, then, reaching a metal road, continued the journey back to base at a rapid pace. In the dark, hot and airless back of the lorry, the shepherds, dogs and walkers were crammed together in considerable discomfort. The farewell supper of the previous evening had been *La Grande Aïoli*, the magnificent celebration dish of Provence, an assortment of pieces of boiled salt cod, hard-boiled eggs, new potatoes, carrots and tomatoes served with liberal amounts of the pungent garlic mayonnaise, the *aïoli*. Not so magnificent the following morning was the overpowering and malodorous stench that emanated from the sweating bodies of the travellers cooped up inside the dark, stifling lorry. Emma sat next to Pascal, with Bosco lying on her feet, and tried to convince herself that this uncomfortable episode was a price worth paying for the great adventure in which she had participated.

After nearly three hours of this disagreeable journey, the lorry arrived in Verignan la Roquette just after noon. Stiff and weary from lack of oxygen, they descended into place de la Mairie. Cheerful, relieved that the boneshaking trip was over, the shepherds exchanged handshakes, promising to meet again in October to bring the sheep back from the mountains. Some of them repaired to the café for a reviving glass or two.

'Would you like a drink, Emma? Are you dying of thirst?'

'I am, but I'd rather have water.' She looked at the fountain. 'Is the water here OK?'

'It's what everyone drinks.'

'Right.' She walked over to the fountain, picked up the metal cup on its chain and filled it from the spout that trickled continuously into the stone basin beneath. She drank about half a litre of water, then looked anxiously at Pascal. 'Oh, sorry,' she said. 'Would you rather go to the café?'

'No, I wouldn't.' He took the cup from her and drank himself. 'We have too much to do. First, we must see whether François has left the van at the *boules* park. Then we need to shop for food.'

They walked up rue des Écoles to the *boules* park, Bosco trotting at their heels, and found the beaten-up old Peugeot waiting in the shade of the plane trees. They dumped their rucksacks in the back of the van, and Bosco, at Pascal's request, leapt in beside them. They installed themselves in the front seats, and Pascal put the key in the ignition, but did not immediately start the engine. He turned to Emma, almost shyly. 'I would very much like to kiss you, Emma, but perhaps you think I am too sweaty and disgusting just now?'

Emma laughed and released her safety belt. She laid a hand on his cheek. 'We are both sweaty and disgusting, my love. If *you* don't mind, neither do I.'

'I don't mind at all. I just thought that perhaps you might be rather fastidious about such a basic thing as sweat.'

'You mean because I was a nun?'

'I suppose I do, yes.'

'What makes you think that nuns don't sweat?' said Emma, and kissed him on the palm of his dirty hand. He took her in his arms and kissed her on the mouth, long and hard. The now familiar warm sensation flowed like an arrow through Emma's body, and her response was total. At last they broke apart, laughing. 'If this is just the beginning,' said Emma, refastening her seat belt, 'what's the main event like, I ask myself?'

Pascal laughed, and started the engine. 'You'll have to tell me, tomorrow morning, won't you? Maybe you'll be disappointed.'

'I don't think so, somehow.'

They shopped in a supermarket in Manosque, then drove slowly along narrow lanes to Mas les Arnauds, a hamlet a few kilometres beyond Valensole, passing fields of ripening wheat, rape and lavender. During the twelve days of the *transhumance* the lavender had come fully into bloom and the surrounding country-side was an amazing sight, field upon field of exquisitely vibrant purple. The air was full of the sound of working bees, and heady with the scent of the flowers, carried on the imperceptible summer breeze.

They drove right into Mas les Arnauds, and Pascal stopped the van beside a wide double gateway in a high stone wall. He got out and opened the gates, then drove into a large courtyard. 'Here we are,' he said. 'This is it.' He jumped down from the cab, and closed the gates.

Emma got down from her seat and stood looking around her. She saw massive stone walls on three sides of the courtyard, which was empty except for a mul-berry tree growing in the middle of the unpaved and

233

uneven dusty ground. The fourth side of the courtyard was occupied by a tall, three-storeyed stone building, with a large central doorway, and many shuttered windows, five to each floor. The only portion of the roof visible from the ground was a double row of semi-circular ends of Roman tiles, overhanging shallow eaves, and providing shelter for a colony of swallows' nests. Evidently, the chicks were already hatched, for the parent birds flew incessantly in and out of the nests, no doubt bringing food to their young.

'Better get the stuff inside; it's so hot,' said Pascal. He handed a box of groceries to Emma, picked up another one himself and led the way into the house. She followed him into a room that occupied the entire ground floor, and put her box down on the long table standing in the centre. The table was old and beautiful, though its wide waxed-elm planks were disfigured with the ring marks of wine glasses, and the black scars left by hot pans. Four country chairs served the table, two on each side. It was cool in the room, on account of the thickness of the walls, and dark, since the windows overlooking the courtyard were shuttered. Emma stood for a moment, allowing her eyes to get used to the gloom, and saw that the floor was paved with old hexagonal tiles of faded pink terracotta, unwaxed and apparently unwashed. Behind the table, on the long wall facing the door was a wide, cavernous fireplace, blackened with soot and containing a large cast-iron stove, with a battered kettle on its cold top, and a rusty flue disappearing up the chimney. At the far end of the room, which must have been at least fourteen metres long, an extremely elegant stone staircase, with a beautiful iron balustrade, rose in a graceful curve to the first floor, vanishing through an arch that formed part of the vaulted ceiling. The stone walls of the room, like the vaulting, were roughly pointed with lime mortar, and drifts of sandy stone-dust lay on the tiles below the skirting.

Pascal had taken his load of shopping to the other end of the room, which was arranged with the minimum requirements for the storage and preparation of food. A stone sink, with a single brass tap, stood under a bull's-eye window, that overlooked a second, very small courtyard. A door beside the sink led to a larder, dark and cool, and lined with thick slate shelves, and it was in here that they unpacked the shopping.

'No fridge, I'm afraid,' said Pascal, more as a statement than an apology.

'You don't need one; it's really cold in here.'

They returned to the van and brought in the rest of the stuff, stowing it in the larder, or in the large carved walnut *armoire* that stood to the right of the sink and housed china and glass, cooking pots and tools, as well as dry groceries.

'Now,' said Pascal, 'a drink, and something to eat. Then we must go and see to the goats.' With the efficiency of one who lives alone, he put bread, cheese, olives and tomatoes on the table, with two green plates, two steel knives, two glasses and a jug of water. Then he went to the larder and came back with a bottle of wine.

'Shall I open a shutter?' said Emma. 'It's a bit dark in here, isn't it?'

'Yes, of course, why not?' Pascal sounded surprised. 'I never bother, usually. I'm out all day, and they keep the place cool in summer, and the heat in when it gets cold.'

'Well, just for a few minutes, perhaps?' Emma went to one of the windows and opened it, then pushed back the heavy shutters. A shaft of golden light poured into the room, turning the limestone walls a soft, pale honey colour, and revealing the dust that filmed the long table. As well as the light, a blast of heat fell on Emma's outstretched arms, and she returned to the table and sat down. She smiled at Pascal, as he poured the wine and cut hunks of bread. 'I see what you mean about keeping the place cool,' she said. 'I'll close it again in a moment.'

Pascal put a glass of wine in front of her. 'Apart from the questions of heat and cold, Emma, there is also the small matter of the inadequacy of my housekeeping,' he said, and wrote 'EMMA' in capital letters in the dust on the table.

Emma laughed and took a sip of her wine. 'Does it worry you?'

'Not at all. I thought perhaps it might rather worry you, though. Women mind about these things.'

'I don't, particularly.'

'I'm glad to hear it, because you may find the rest of the place pretty gruesome.'

'You make it sound like Bluebeard's castle.'

'As a matter of fact, it easily could be.'

Emma piled goat's cheese and tomato onto her bread and ate it hungrily. She ate a handful of black olives, drank some water and sipped her wine, gazing round her at the big bare room. 'This is a marvellous room Pascal. Does it have a history? Why so big? And why the elegant staircase?'

'As far as I know, the place was once a simple *bergerie*, or a fortified farm, probably built in the sixteenth or seventeenth century. The sheep would have been out all day with the shepherds, grazing, and at night would have been brought in to the safety of the yard, and into this ground-floor space in severe weather. The family would have lived on the first floor, with the *grange* under the roof for storing hay and grain, garlic, potatoes and suchlike.'

'So they wouldn't have used this room at all?'

'No, they wouldn't. But in the nineteenth century, when the cholera epidemics were a serious threat, the merchants, doctors, *notaires* and so on, who could afford it, came out with their families from Aix-en-Provence for the summer. They would buy simple farmhouses like this and tart them up to suit their lifestyle, just like the people from Paris, as well as the Swiss and the Germans, even the British, do nowadays. They come down for August, and sometimes for Christmas and Easter, and play at being peasants.'

'Like Marie-Antoinette at Le Hameau?'

'Just like that. They're never here when the countryside is deep in the grip of winter, and the *mistral* blows for ten days without cease.'

'Was the house like this when you bought it?'

'More or less. The place had been abandoned for thirty years or more. It belonged to three very old ladies in Aix, who had inherited it from their father. I made a low offer for it, I couldn't afford much, and eventually they agreed to let me have it.'

'So you just moved in and set up house?'

'No, not at all. The pigeons had got in, and had nested everywhere. The mess was unbelievable. François came and gave me a hand, and it took a fortnight to clean it up. That's how I got to know him. We didn't even attempt to get into the attic space, the *grange*. The joists under the floor are all rotten and disintegrating. We just nailed up the door at the top of the steps and left it.'

'So how do you get to the roof?'

'I don't. It leaks, I must warn you. It leaks into the *grange*, then through the ceiling of the first floor into the bedrooms. I've got buckets everywhere. When we get really heavy rain I expect the ceilings to come down every moment. I'm sure they will, sooner or later.'

'Pascal, are you by any chance having me on?'

'Absolutely not; it's all perfectly true.' He pointed to the *armoire*. 'It wasn't all bad news though. That cupboard was in the house, and this table, and those wooden salt-boxes on the wall, and the *panetière* over there. Upstairs, there's a rather pretty painted Italian bed, as well as some obviously Italian plasterwork and the remains of some frescoes.'

237

'Frescoes?' Emma looked at Pascal, her eyes shining. 'Did you say frescoes?'

'Yes. There must have been a travelling Italian artist, probably from Piedmont, working in the district in the late eighteenth or early nineteenth century. Quite a few of the *maisons de maîtres* or small rustic *châteaux* round here have similar decorations, I believe.'

'How interesting, and how lovely that you have them here.'

'I suppose so, but they're in rotten condition, I'm afraid. It's the damp, of course.' He got up from the table, collecting the dishes and putting them in the sink. 'Come on, we must go and check the goats, and I'll show you the dairy, and everything.'

'OK, fine. But first I need the loo, Pascal. Where do I go?'

'It's outside. Turn left, and it's in the lean-to at the end of the house. I should have warned you, there's no bathroom. Just the sink here, the lavatory and an old-fashioned shower in the yard outside. Will you manage?'

'You forget, I'm quite used to very primitive plumbing arrangements.' She laughed, and went out into the yard.

It was now half past two, and the sun was still beating down relentlessly on the ancient hamlet, a cluster of ragged stone farmhouses, perched on its little hill to catch every passing summer breeze. The streets were narrow and winding, deliberately so, to break the ferocity of the icy *mistral* in winter. Pascal and Emma, with Bosco in attendance, walked past silent, shuttered houses to the other end of the village, where they would find the long, low building that was Pascal's dairy, five minutes' walk from his house. He unlocked a grey metal door and they went in. Inside, everything was immaculately clean, limewashed and fresh-smelling. Along one wall a row of stalls awaited the next milking, gleaming stainless-steel buckets up-ended on scrubbed shelves. On the opposite wall wide shallow pans of milk stood on a long stone slab, and Emma asked why they were there.

'Each day's milk stays there for twenty-four hours to sour, then it's skimmed, and we put the cheese into pierced moulds, to drain off the "little milk". It stays in the moulds for a month, to mature. Then it's wrapped and sold.'

'It sounds like a lot of work.'

'It is. Come and look.' He took her through another door to a cold room lined with deep shelves, where row upon row of cheeses in their small round moulds were ripening, each section marked with the date of the completion of the *affinage*.

'How do you keep it so cold in here?' asked Emma, hugging herself against the chill.

'I have an air-conditioning plant. It's the only non-traditional thing I have, but unfortunately it's necessary for reasons of purity. It also means that I can extend my season for selling the cheese for as long as I like.' He smiled ruefully. 'My old man talked me into it, and he's right.'

Emma laughed. 'So, he *does* take an interest in you, Pascal?'

'Either that, or he's just nosey!'

They left the dairy and went into the adjoining yard. This was surrounded by a palisade of split-chestnut paling, high enough to discourage all but the most acrobatic of goats from trying to escape. 'This is where the kids are kept until they're big enough to go out with the herd every day, and where they all come in at night.' Pascal pointed to a simple lean-to shed that filled one end of the yard. 'They can all get in there in bad weather, though they're quite tough, and really prefer to be outside.'

'How many goats have you got?'

'Fifty-two, counting the kids.'

'And where are they now?'

'Out with François. There's plenty of good rough grazing within a half-kilometre radius of the village, and the owners of orchards and patches of scrub are happy to have their land kept clean by the goats. It's a good system.'

'When do they come in?'

'About five, for the evening milking. We'd better go and find François; tell him that his ewes are OK, and check that Juliette hasn't had any problems with the cheese. After that, we'll take a look at the lavender. It should be ready to start harvesting in a couple of weeks.'

They returned to the house to get the van, then drove down the hill towards the plain, a patchwork of green-gold wheat, yellow rape and purple lavender, shimmering in the hot sun. Beyond the plateau, the dark-green flanks of the Lubéron mountains rose, solid and majestic, and beyond them the far distant pale-blue peaks, heat-hazed, insubstantial.

'Look!' said Pascal suddenly, pointing through the windscreen. 'There they are.'

'Where?' Emma scanned the countryside in front of them, but failed to locate the goats.

'Under those trees. Don't you see them?'

'Oh, yes; there they are.'

The goats were browsing quietly in an almond orchard, and François was sitting in the shade under one of the trees, leaning against the trunk, his dog at his side, perfectly content. Pascal stopped the van, Bosco leapt out of the back and gave a small bark to announce their arrival.

François got slowly to his feet and came towards them, ducking under the branches of the trees. 'You took your time,' he said, looking enquiringly at Emma.

Pascal laughed. 'You reckon?' he replied. They got out of the van, and he introduced François to Emma with proper formality, and they shook hands.

'Your ewes and lambs are in good form,' she said.

'Not one of them is lame, and they're all eating their heads off up there.' She turned and looked in the direction of the Col d'Allos.

François stared at her, astonished. 'Did you go on the *transhumance*?' he asked. 'How did you know which ones were my sheep?'

'They're the ones marked PF, aren't they?'

'Oh.' François looked from one to the other, full of curiosity, but Pascal took his arm and walked towards the goats. 'How's it been? Everything OK? How was the marketing?'

'OK, but I'm glad you're back, Pasc. I don't really like flogging the stuff in Apt, it's too noisy and crowded. I prefer to trade with the dealers, or supply the restaurants; that's enough for me.'

In their detached way, the goats seemed pleased to see Pascal, butting him gently as he stroked their silky brown flanks, or pulled their little grey curved horns. 'Kids have grown,' he said.

'You'll be doing the milking tomorrow morning, then?'

'Yes, of course. Five o'clock, as usual.'

'Good. The old girl will be glad of a rest, after tonight.'

'Haven't you been helping her, François? Twenty goats is a hell of a lot of milking for an elderly lady.'

'Certainly not!' François sounded surprised at such an idea. 'I am out all day with the beasts. The rest is not my affair.' He spat with precision at a spot between his worn canvas boots, then walked away. This extended conversation was beginning to bore him; he was quite ready to resume his silent vigil until the sun was low in the sky and it was time to bring the goats back to Mas les Arnauds.

Emma, waiting at a little distance with Bosco, observed with amusement the exchange between the two friends. François, she knew, was not as old as he liked to appear, with his brown wrinkled face bearing a

241

week's growth of beard, his battered trilby hat and mildewed army greatcoat, held together by a leather belt. What she did not know was that in the pockets of the greatcoat he carried books, his deep and abiding passion. Once a month, the travelling library came out from Aix-en-Provence, bringing with it the books previously requested by François. His tastes were catholic; he read philosophy, mathematics and literature with equal interest and pleasure, and considered himself fortunate to have the time and the silence that made it possible for him to expand his knowledge in such an agreeable way.

Pascal took the hint. '*Allez! Salut!*' he said, and came back to Emma, grinning. They drove away, Bosco's tail thumping on the metal floor in the back of the van. Emma looked back and saw that François had already resumed his tranquil seat under the tree. 'Isn't he terribly hot in that thick coat?' she asked.

'Weird, isn't it? They all do it, especially the older ones. I've seen photographs of his grandparents, cutting lavender in the middle of July, and the old man was wearing a waistcoat as well as a coat, thick trousers and boots, and of course, a hat.' He glanced at Emma and smiled. 'It's almost as if the people in these high places actually fear the sun. They seem to go to great lengths to protect themselves from it. Their houses have thick walls and small shuttered windows. It's to exclude the summer sun as much as keeping out the cold winter winds.'

'Perhaps they're right about the sun? You know; holes in the ozone layer, skin cancer, that sort of thing?'

'Who knows?'

They arrived at the lavender fields and walked between the scented rows, each bush alive with the urgent drone of foraging bees. From time to time Pascal plucked a flower head and rubbed it between his hands, releasing the aroma. 'It's nearly ready,' he said, holding out the crushed flower for Emma to inhale its soothing vapour. 'Can you smell the oil?'

'Yes, I can. It's lovely.' She gazed over the purple haze. 'Look at the bees. They're incredible, aren't they? They seem almost drunk with the scent.'

'I think they are. They make excellent honey, too.' He pointed to the long row of hives bordering the field. 'In a good year, we get between thirty and forty kilos from each hive; it makes a useful addition to the income.'

'I bet.'

The sun was beginning to drop towards the west, and they walked slowly back to the van. Pascal put his arm round Emma's shoulders, and she glanced up at him, smiling, squinting in the low sunlight. He looked down at her and shook his head, as if he couldn't quite believe that she was really there at his side.

'What's the matter?' she said.

'Nothing's the matter. I'm just rather amazed that you're here.'

'Are you happy that I am?'

'Yes. Are you?'

'Yes, I am,' said Emma. 'Very.'

They drove back to the house, and took their rucksacks upstairs to the bedroom. 'Though why we're bothering, I don't know,' she said. 'Everything needs washing; I must see to it, tomorrow.'

The beautiful staircase led to a wide landing with three ornately carved doors. Along the cornice was a frieze of vine leaves, pale green and very faint. Emma studied it with interest, but said nothing. Around the central door was a similar painted embellishment, of intertwined acanthus leaves and scrolls. 'This was probably the boss's room,' said Pascal. He opened the door and went at once to a window, opening it wide and throwing back the external shutters. A flood of bright light revealed a large square room with a high ceiling, parts of which were missing, a fact emphasized by the waiting buckets on the floor beneath.

A square bed stood against one wall, its black metal head- and foot-boards painted in an extremely beautiful eighteenth-century design of the *fête-champêtre* type, its colours as fresh and vivid as the day on which it had been finished. Emma had seen painting exactly like this in Italy, and was astonished to see such a bed in this primitive village backwater. 'Did you say that you thought that a travelling Italian artist had worked here?' she asked, touching the painting gently, marvelling at its perfection.

'That's what the old ladies told me.'

'This is wonderful work, Pascal. It must be at least two hundred and fifty years old. Strictly speaking, it should be in a museum.'

'I'd rather sleep in it, preferably with you.'

Emma laughed, but found herself suddenly unable to respond to this declaration. She felt unaccountably shy, alone in his bedroom with this tall powerful man, whose very presence seemed to have the capacity to stir her deepest feelings so profoundly. 'Where are the frescoes you told me about?' she asked.

'Here.' He crossed the room and pulled aside a shabby cotton curtain on black iron rings that covered the wall facing the bed. Emma stared at the wreckage of a large fresco, its image barely discernible, and extensive areas missing altogether. Suddenly, recognition dawned. 'Good heavens!' she exclaimed. 'It's a Mantegna!'

'It's a what?'

'It's a copy of a fresco by Mantegna, in Mantua. It's Cardinal Gonzaga and his family.'

'Well, how amazing,' said Pascal, much impressed by Emma'a ability in identifying this masterpiece. 'Thanks for telling me; is it a good copy?'

'Hard to tell, there's so little left.'

'How come you know all this stuff, Emma?'

'It's what I do, or rather, what I *want* to do; what I was trained to do.'

'So, what's stopping you?'

Emma looked at Pascal long and seriously, as the incredible realization that here was a house full of bare stone walls slowly filled her mind. 'If you will allow me to work on your walls, Pascal,' she said quietly, 'there is absolutely nothing stopping me.'

'I will make you a present of the walls, from this moment.' He took her hands in his and kissed them. 'I have the feeling that life with you is going to be fun and interesting, Emma. In the meantime, I'm getting pretty hungry, aren't you?'

'Yes, I am, and I badly need a shower, or at least a wash. We both do.'

'Nothing simpler. Why don't you unpack the bags, Emma, and turn down the bed? There are sheets and towels in the *armoire*. I'll go down and light the stove; in half an hour it'll be hot enough to cook.'

'Could I borrow a clean shirt, please, Pascal? All my things are dirty and crumpled.'

'Yes, of course; in the *armoire*, too. Bring one down for me when you come, will you?'

Emma unpacked the bags and threw all the dirty things into a corner of the room. Then she turned down the bed and found that it already had clean sheets on it. Juliette must have been here, she said to herself. She opened the heavy doors of the *armoire* and found rough striped towels, and on a shelf, neatly folded shirts. She chose a denim one for herself, and blue and red checks for Pascal, then went downstairs, half-closing the shutters before she left the room.

In the kitchen the stove was already lit and making a fierce roaring noise in the chimney. Pascal had taken a scrawny-looking yellow chicken from the larder and it now sat on a small grid in a roasting tin, anointed with olive oil and garlic, rosemary sprigs threaded through its thighs and stuffed into its cavity. He ground a good deal of black pepper over the bird and put it in the oven. 'Forty minutes, that's all it will need,' he said.

'In a few minutes, we'll put some carrots in to roast, and some potatoes.'

'Sounds wonderful.'

'I hope.' He poured wine into two glasses and handed one to Emma. 'A quick drink, then a quick shower, OK?'

'As a matter of fact, Pascal, I think I'll have the shower before the drink, if you don't mind. If I sit down now, I'll probably fall asleep, and go off the whole idea of a shower.'

'OK, fine. You know where it is, don't you?' He went to the sink and began to peel potatoes.

Emma picked up her towel and went out into the courtyard. The sun had already set, but it was not yet dark, and a single shimmering star hung in the beautiful deep-blue sky, just visible in the twilight. She stood staring up at the lonely star, and became disturbingly aware that she was beginning to feel incredibly lonely herself, vulnerable and apprehensive. What am I doing here, she asked herself uneasily, with this man that I really don't know very well? Am I running away from something, or trying to find something, or what? And whichever it is, why do I suddenly feel so nervous about being here, with Pascal? Is it the actual physical sex thing that scares me; that I don't feel ready for? Or am I just neurotic, like my mother; an emotional adolescent; running away from life, like I was in Italy? Maybe it would have been better to go on hiding behind the walls of the convent; to keep my head down; not to put myself to the test?

Depressed and uncertain, she made her way to the shower. It stood, aggressively functional, above a square stone trough, set into the ground, with a drainage hole in the middle. The shower-head, green with verdigris and bearing a metal plaque engraved with the words *La Douche Automatique 1904*, was evidently activated by a long chain with a white china handle, marked *Tirez* in black copperplate script. A lump of green soap sat in a recess in the adjacent wall, together with a large bottle of supermarket shampoo. Well, I'd better get on with it, I suppose, she said to herself, though feeling extremely disinclined to do so. She undressed, and standing in the trough, pulled the chain as gently as she could, hoping to release just a small amount of water to start with. Immediately, a huge deluge of ice-cold water fell on her head and poured over her body, causing her to gasp with shock and surprise. Blindly, she reached for the soap and began to lather herself from head to foot. After a moment or two, the water felt marginally less shatteringly cold, and she decided to wash her hair properly, using the shampoo provided. Then, after a final numbing rinse, she pulled the chain again, the flow of water ceased abruptly, and she stepped out of the trough. Wrapping herself in her towel, she picked up her clothes, and, teeth chattering, ran back to the house.

Pascal had just put his vegetables into the roasting tin, and was basting them with the fragrant juices from the chicken. 'You look frozen,' he said. 'Come by the stove and get warm.' He closed the oven door, took his towel and his clean shirt and went out to take his own shower.

Emma stood close to the stove, now radiating a glorious heat, and dried herself vigorously. She put on the clean blue shirt and her crumpled cotton skirt, then hung the damp towel over the back of a chair. She sat down and slowly drank her glass of wine, while the paraffin lamp hissed above the table, shedding its soft wavering light through the room, and a delicious smell began to steal from the stove. How peaceful and calm, and somehow *luxurious* this is, she said to herself, tasting the flavours of berries and cinnamon in her good red wine, and inhaling the rich yet delicate smell of the roasting chicken. How stupid I am, she thought, what can possibly harm me here, what is there to be afraid of? She got up and took two green dinner plates and knives and forks from the *armoire* and set the table for supper. In the cupboard she found a white faïence candlestick with a stump of candle in it, made from a rolled-up honeycomb. Enchanted with the idea of making candles from one's own beeswax, she set it down between the two plates, and lit it with a match from a large box, marked *Lucifer*. She got bread from the wooden *panetière* on the wall, then refilled the glasses from the bottle of wine. She sat down again, and held her glass before the candle flame, so that the wine inside it glowed like fire, with a piercing ruby intensity.

Pascal came back into the kitchen, threw his dirty clothes under the sink, hung up his towel to dry, and took a long swallow of his wine. He broke off a piece of bread and ate it. 'I'm starving,' he said. 'Aren't you?'

'Yes, I am, quite.'

'Won't be long now.' He topped up his glass, then got up and went to the far end of the room. He put a tape into the cassette player, and the urgent sound of two elegantly competing violins filled the room: the Bach double concerto. Pascal came back to the table, sat down and picked up his glass. 'I wouldn't want you to run away with the idea that I am a total philistine, Emma, because of not knowing about the Mantegna,' he said, and smiled at her.

'I'm not in the habit of running away with ideas at all, as a matter of fact.' Emma spoke quite sharply. She looked at him, her eyes slightly unfocused, not very sure that she understood what she had intended to say, or that it made any kind of sense.

'Do you mean that you make a point of being non-judgemental?'

'I suppose I do, yes.'

'How boring,' said Pascal. 'I don't believe you, Emma McGrath.'

Emma flushed, stung by his remark, and frowned.

'How do you know my surname, Pascal? I can't remember telling you what it is.'

'It's the same as your father's, isn't it?'

'Oh, I see. You saw it in *Info-Phallo*, didn't you?'

'I did.'

'OK, so what's *your* full name?'

'Pascal Jean-Luc de Vilmorin.'

'Sounds rather posh,' said Emma, permitting herself a teasing smile.

'Is that a problem for you?'

'No, why should it be?'

'No reason.' He looked at her, suddenly wary. 'Emma, are we by any chance having a quarrel?'

'I hope not. I think I'm very tired and a little drunk, and probably rather terrified of you, Pascal, and doing my best not to be.' She looked at him timidly, trying to smile, and failing.

He reached across the table and took her hands gently in his. 'Don't be terrified, Emma, not even for a second. No-one is going to make you do anything at all that you don't really want to do. Not tonight, not *ever*, is that quite clear?'

'Yes.'

'What we both need now is food.' He got up from the table, took the chicken from the oven, and carved it with the skill and speed that would have gladdened his father's heart. They ate in silence, then washed the dishes under the tap and stacked them in the rack.

'And now,' said Pascal, 'what we both need is sleep. I have to be up at five to do the milking.' He unhooked the lamp, and Emma followed him upstairs. At the door to the bedroom he paused. 'If you would rather sleep alone, I can easily go to another room?'

'No, please don't. I would hate that.'

She took off her clothes and got into bed, exhausted and thankful to be between the cool, faintly lavender-smelling sheets, her head heavy on the soft square pillow. Pascal turned out the lamp, and opened the shutters, so that a slight cool breeze stirred the air. Outside in the courtyard, a golden oriole sang in the mulberry tree, its bell-like notes clear and precise in the darkness. He stood at the window, listening to the familiar sounds of the night, and looking at the stars. Then he, too, undressed and got into bed, and lay down with his back turned towards the already sleeping Emma.

At five o'clock Pascal woke and got carefully out of bed, dressed silently, left the room on bare feet and went out to milk his goats. At eight o'clock, after François had departed with the herd to the grazing, he walked back to the house and made coffee. He took the tray up to the bedroom, and put it on the night-table. He looked tenderly at Emma as she lay sleeping, her long lashes resting like black feathers on her flushed cheek, her slim body only partially covered by the sheet. Then he sat down on the edge of the bed, and waited until she opened her eyes.

For a second, she stared at him blankly, then smiled. 'Hello,' she said, 'you're dressed. What time is it?'

'It's about half past eight.'

'Are you going out?'

'No, I've just come in. I've been doing the milking. I brought you some coffee.'

Emma sat up, put her cool hands on either side of Pascal's unshaven face, and kissed him. 'Come back to bed, my love,' she said.

Chapter Twelve

Flavia sat at her kitchen table, and read Christian's letter for the third or fourth time. On the table in front of her were the uneaten remains of a plate of scrambled eggs, now congealed into a cold lump, together with a piece of toast with one bite out of it. Her half-drunk cup of coffee, slopped into the saucer in her agitation, had formed an unattractive skin on its surface, and when she took an absent-minded sip, tasted cold and bitter. She put down the cup, got up from the table and went to the cupboard where she kept her daytime drinking supply. She took out the gin bottle and poured herself a small glass and drank it, neat. Then she sat down and read the letter again, or rather, those parts of it that most disturbed her.

Imagine my distress and anger, on returning from my much-needed short break with Phoebe, to learn from Gwen that Alexander had run away from home, entirely on account of your insensitive behaviour and that of your meddling brother. You had no business to insist on forcing your beliefs on my son, Mother, and still less to bring your brother and yourself to stay in my house, uninvited. I resent most strongly that intrusion into my home and your interference in the upbringing of my child, and I am both alarmed and deeply angry that you caused Alexander to behave in a way that could so easily have culminated in yet another tragedy. As things are, I have to inform you that it will probably require months of expensive psychiatric treatment to restore the boy's sense of security. I feel, therefore, that I must forbid you to contact us in any way, even by telephone, for the time being, and suggest that you look carefully into your own soul, before vandalizing that of my surviving child.

To say that Flavia was dismayed by this letter from her son would be a massive understatement. It made her feel physically ill; nauseated; faint. Her head felt thick and heavy, and she was having difficulty in seeing the handwritten words on the page in her shaking hand. She folded the letter and put it back in its envelope, then got up and poured herself another drink. She stood at the sink, drinking the gin, staring out of the window at the grimy London garden, long and narrow, tacky and unattractive, even in mid-summer. The yellow brick walls had several climbing roses trained against them, but years of neglect had taken their toll. Lack of feeding and proper pruning had left them straggly, diseased and brown. The very few flowers that had struggled into reluctant life were small and full of canker. Flavia barely noticed their desperate state, so completely obsessed was she with her own perceived injury, unhappiness and fear. It never once occurred to her that a couple of hours' activity in her neglected garden could have done much to alleviate her mental anguish.

After a while, the gin did its work and her chagrin at her son's behaviour turned to anger and belligerence. Bloody little hypocrite, she said to herself, what right has he to criticize me? It's sheer impudence on his part, and I have a perfect right, as well as a sacred *duty* to do whatever I can to make up for the shortcomings of my grandson's parents. I know Anselm would support me in that; Benedict, too. A sudden wave of loneliness made her swallow several times to prevent herself from giving way to tears, for Anselm was no longer staying with her. He had returned to Africa, and she was missing him quite badly. His unshakeable belief in his own authority, and his staunch occupation of the moral high ground in all things had made him a bracing companion. He had swept aside any little neurotic doubts or fears she had occasionally revealed to him, filling the vacuums thus created with his firm didactic utterances, usually of a religious nature. In effect, though she had not been aware of it, Anselm had treated his sister in much the same way as he treated the small boys in his mission school, with autocratic kindness, and she had been happy to respond with the same eager compliance as the children in his care. All the same, she thought, he's not here any more, so I'll have to go and talk to Fr Gordon.

Flavia felt a little guilty about Fr Gordon, particularly as she had for some time neglected attendance at Mass at St Botolph's, in view of the fact that she had her own resident priest in the shape of Anselm, dear good man. She smiled indulgently, remembering his hearty appetite and appreciation of Ludovic's wine cellar. What a good time they had had together; he had even taught her how to make groundnut stew, evidently a regular part of the menu at the Mission, and a great favourite of his. In Flavia's own opinion, unexpressed of course, the dish was an acquired taste.

She put her empty glass in the sink and thought about clearing away the breakfast things. She decided to leave them for the time being, and with sudden resolution, picked up Christian's letter. She went out to the hall, and took her jacket off its hook, with the intention of going up to St Botolph's and seeing Fr Gordon right away, or, failing that, having a quick chat with the Blessed Virgin. The doorbell rang, a loud shrill sound that made Flavia jump, for she rarely had visitors. The milkman always rang on a Friday, to collect his money, but he never came before twelve. Perhaps it was Christian, coming to apologize? Eagerly, with a smile on her face, she opened the door.

'Mrs McGrath?'

'Yes?'

The young man standing on the lower step raised a camera to his face, and before Flavia could take evasive action, he had fired the flash and taken a photograph of her.

'What do you think you are doing, my good man?' she asked, with an attempt at dignity. 'What is the meaning of this intrusion?'

'Excuse me, Mrs McGrath.' A fair-haired woman appeared from behind the photographer, and mounted the steps confidently. She took a large brown envelope from her bag, drew from it a sheaf of photographs, and showed one to Flavia. 'Is this your grandson, Mrs McGrath?'

'Good gracious, that's Alexander!' exclaimed Flavia. 'What is all this about? Are you trying to sell me something? I have plenty of pictures of my grandson already, thank you.'

'No, Mrs McGrath, I'm not here to sell you anything. Look at the picture again. Do you know where it was taken?'

Flavia peered at the photograph, and shook her head, increasingly nervous and confused. 'No, I've no idea. I've never seen that room before.'

'So you don't know about your husband's love nest?'

'My husband's *love nest*? What are you talking about?'

'It's in Paris, in rue Mouffetard.'

'What utter nonsense!' said Flavia, as sternly as she could. 'My husband works in Brussels, or Strasbourg. He is rarely in Paris. *I know*.'

'It's obvious that you *don't* know, Mrs McGrath. May we come in?'

A kind of cold fear crept over Flavia at these words and, not wishing to continue the interview on the doorstep in full view of the neighbours, she stepped coldly aside and allowed the unwelcome visitors to enter her house.

Hilary Grant and her photographer colleague had good reason to be well satisfied with their morning's work. Flavia McGrath had been easily convinced, once she had seen Hilary's copy of *Info-Phallo*, and had finally understood that not only had Ludovic been betraying her for more than twenty years, but had an illegitimate daughter into the bargain. She had stared at the condemning pages, and gently touched the photograph of Ludovic, the man she had once loved. Though she no longer felt very much for him, she was nonetheless proud to be his wife; pleased when people mentioned his name, gratified to refer to him as 'my husband'. Their marriage had given her a kind of status amongst her peers. The shock and humiliation she now experienced was intense, and drove from her mind the first unpleasantness of this horrible day, Christian's unforgiving letter. A single pathetic tear ran down Flavia's nose, as she sat slumped on the hard green sofa in her sitting room. Hilary Grant, who was by nature quite a kind girl, though fast learning not to be in her single-minded pursuit of her journalistic career, produced a small packet of Kleenex from her capacious bag and offered one to Flavia. 'Don't cry,' she said soothingly, 'no man is worth it.'

At these words, Flavia's control completely deserted her and her sobs became violent. Silently, the photographer took out his light meter and then, unobserved by the two women, took a carefully composed shot of Flavia as she glanced towards Hilary, her blue eyes wild and overflowing with tears, the essence of misery. He knew at once that the photograph would sell a million copies. He signalled to Hilary, and they took their leave.

Numbly, feeling very cold in spite of the time of year, Flavia looked at the clock in the hall. It was only twenty past eleven. Finding this hard to believe, she looked at her watch: twenty past eleven. She went into the kitchen, got a fresh bottle of gin from the cupboard, then took the sharp little paring knife from the drawer, and went upstairs to her room.

Christian, on his way to the bank the following morning, went into his local newsagent to pick up his copy of the *Daily Telegraph*, and saw at once the prominently displayed tabloid with the banner headline: DECEIVED WIFE'S IGNORANCE OF POLITICIAN'S FRENCH AFFAIR. Underneath was an enormously enlarged picture of his mother's face, weeping, clearly in some distress. He picked up his usual paper as calmly as he could, and bought a copy of the offending tabloid. Then he took a taxi and drove straight to Flavia's house, reading the article about his father's private life on the way. The cab stopped just outside his mother's front door, and Christian got out and paid the driver. Looking up, he saw the gang of paparazzi advancing towards him, cameras poised, from the opposite side of the road. Horrified, he leapt up the steps and put his latchkey into the lock, but not quickly enough to avoid the avalanche of peremptory orders to look this way and that, the insulting questions, and the repeated flashes of light in his face, that were instantly visited upon him. Angrily, he forced his way into Flavia's house and slammed the door on his tormentors.

Upstairs, he found his mother in bed, barely conscious, her left arm bandaged, attended by a dismayed Fr Gordon. 'I saw the paper quite by chance, on my way back from Mass,' explained the poor man, full of intense concern, his nose pink. 'I came straight round, in case she needed help.'

'How did you get in?'

Fr Gordon looked embarrassed. 'I'd always noticed

that she kept the key on a string, through the letter box. I used to tell her it was a dangerous thing to do. I'm afraid I let myself in, when there was no answer.'

'Quite right. I'm very glad that you did. Why is her arm bandaged?'

'I'm afraid she slashed her wrist with this.' Fr Gordon took the lethal little paring knife from the pocket of his cassock. 'She managed to give herself quite a deep cut; there was an awful lot of blood. I telephoned the doctor at once and he came straight round. He stitched the wound, and gave her an injection. Antibiotics, and a sedative, I think he said.'

'Did the press speak to him?'

'I don't think he said anything to them. He just got into his car and drove away.' Fr Gordon looked at Christian reproachfully, as though the doctor's involvement with the press was of minor importance. 'As you will no doubt appreciate,' he continued, 'this room was in a dreadful state, there was even blood on the walls. I think she must have been trying to take down her crucifix, poor woman. I did try to wash off the bloodstains, but the paper's ruined, I'm afraid. The sheets were soaked in blood, of course, and she had vomited all over the pillows. We did what we could to clean up; changed the linen, made her a cup of tea. The doctor will visit again this afternoon.'

'Thank you,' said Christian, suppressing a powerful inclination to give the little priest a hug. 'You've been wonderful. I'm so grateful to you; you've probably saved her life.'

'One so rarely gets the opportunity to be of real assistance to people,' murmured Fr Gordon. 'I was glad to be able to help, of course.'

'Bloody fucking adulterous whore,' said Flavia, quite clearly, though her eyes were closed.

'Hush, Mother.' Christian looked at Fr Gordon apologetically. 'Sorry about that,' he said.

257

Fr Gordon shook his head. 'I've heard worse in my time, believe me,' he said, with a bleak little smile.

'Could you hold on for a few minutes, while I phone my wife?'

'Surely.'

Christian went downstairs, his heart like lead, telephoned Phoebe and asked her to bring Gwen to London to take care of Flavia. Quietly, without probing, Phoebe agreed to do this. Christian put down the telephone, then picked it up again and dialled his father's number in Brussels.

Emma was in heaven. For the first time in her life she felt really alive, sure of herself and comfortable in her own skin. It was not only the act of loving and being loved that had brought about this euphoric state of well-being, but the simple daily rituals of the house, the village and the surrounding countryside, basking under the long hours of unbroken sunshine. Even in the cool dark kitchen, she could smell the sun, on Pascal's skin as well as her own, in the dust stirred up by Bosco's tail, and in the armfuls of corn, dog-daisies and poppies she brought home from the fields and put hopefully into water. The long table was now a field of glowing colour, with the fallen petals of wilting poppies quivering like scarlet pools of blood on the waxed wooden surface below.

Equally sensuous was Emma's response to the glorious food that Pascal produced each evening with such apparent effortlessness. In view of the limitations of his kitchen equipment, she regarded this as little short of miraculous, and marvelled at the ease with which he used the simple basics of wine and tomatoes, onions and garlic, the pink, brown or black olives and the sumptuous green virgin oil, combining them with the fresh and abundant local vegetables and herbs. Usually, but not inevitably, there was meat in some form, and with the additional luxury of the crisp fresh bread baked twice a day at the village *boulangerie*, Pascal's meals were easily the most consistently delicious that she had ever eaten. It was a far cry from macaroni cheese.

Each morning they got up at five and went to the dairy. While Pascal let the nanny goats into their stalls in groups of six, and did the milking, Emma strained the curd from the previous day's soured milk. Then she took the curd to the cold-room, and ladled it carefully into the freshly scoured moulds, marking each batch with the date. When the milking was complete and all the goats had returned to the yard, ready for François to lead them to the grazing, Pascal and Emma set about the cleaning. They scoured all the utensils, pans and buckets, then hosed down the concrete floor, brushing away the slurry with a heavy yard-broom, until the whole place smelt fresh and clean. Sometimes, as she cheerfully carried out this task with Pascal, Emma smiled to herself, recalling the fierce resentment she had experienced when required to undertake exactly the same function in the convent. After the departure of the goats, and a last check to make sure that everything was clean and orderly, they walked back to the house for breakfast, buying bread at the *boulangerie* on the way.

On Tuesday mornings, Pascal telephoned all his customers for that week's orders. He sold his cheese to the hotels, restaurants and small *alimentations* within a fifty-kilometre radius of Mas les Arnauds, and delivered their orders on most weekdays. On Saturdays, they drove to Apt, a distance of some forty kilometres, where Pascal rented a regular stall at the open-air market. This was the fashionable rendezvous for the rich and famous summer residents of the Lubéron, and any cheeses not already spoken for and delivered were sold out before noon.

'How is it that all these people know you?' Emma

asked, when the eighth or ninth customer, clearly on friendly terms with Pascal, had departed with his or her carefully selected cheeses, wrapped in waxed paper.

'Oh, I've known them all my life.' Pascal looked a little sheepish. 'My people have a *maison secondaire* on the other side of Bonnieux. They come down every summer.'

'Are they there now?'

'No, they come for August and part of September. The old man has to take his vacations when my mother can bear to be away from Paris.'

'I see. She must be a very social person?'

'You could say that.' He laughed. 'My sister may come down earlier with her small children. She'll probably drive over to see us.'

'Don't you ever go there?'

'Very rarely. No time, really, is there?'

'I suppose not.'

By noon all the cheese was sold, and Pascal began to pack up all the boxes and the terracotta crocks in which he transported the very delicate, freshly made soft cheese. They loaded everything into the back of the van, and wiped down the long table under its white canvas awning, ready for Thierry, a local silversmith, who took over the pitch on Saturday afternoons. Then, leaving Bosco on guard in the van, they made their way to a nearby café to have lunch.

Pouring chilled rosé from a jug into thick tumblers, Pascal handed one to Emma. 'So, what do you think of it all?' he said. 'You've been here a week now, and seen how I live. Do you find the way of life bizarre, too difficult? Too rough, perhaps, or maybe even boring?'

'Strangely enough, some of it is quite like my life in the convent. Washing down the goat slurry, for instance. I used to do quite a bit of that, only there it was hen houses and pigsties.' She laughed and took a sip of wine, and ate an olive from the small glass bowl on the table. 'But that's about all I can think of that's at all like anything I've ever done before.' She looked across the table at Pascal, resting her chin on her hand, her small, serious, sunburned face framed in her spiky, badly cut dark hair. 'I love the goats, and the dairy, and funny old François. I think your house is beautiful, and it's heaven not to be forever fretting about dusting and stuff like that. It's a real pleasure that you let the place speak for itself; that you allow the stones to breathe, if you like. I think this is the loveliest countryside I've ever seen, and I still can't get over the lavender fields, and the rivers and mountains all around, and the air, and the extraordinary clarity of the light. Most of all, I absolutely can't wait to get started on restoring the Gonzaga family.'

The food arrived, a salad of grilled goat's cheese, fried *croûtons* and bits of bacon and olives, drizzled with green olive oil. They ate hungrily, enjoying the crunch of the *croûtons* with the soft hot cheese, and the pungent taste of the olives.

'Talking of the Gonzagas, how about going to Aix next week to buy the stuff you need?'

'That would be great, but aren't we too busy? Will there be time?'

'Certainly there's time. We'll make time; it's important.'

Emma looked at him, with gratitude and love. 'Thank you, Pascal. You're the very first person who's ever thought that it's important. Mostly, it's always been a question of higher priorities, and the fresco-making has finished up on the backburner.'

'How stupid.'

'Yes.' She broke off a piece of bread and mopped up the oily residue on her plate. 'I must sit down this evening and make a list of the pigments I'll need, and all the other paraphernalia. I must try and calculate the cost. I have about eight and a half thousand francs of

261

my father's money left, so I must be careful not to be too extravagant.'

'Don't worry about the money. We have enough. You must get whatever you need.'

'I don't want to use your money, Pascal.'

'Why not? Are you too proud?'

'No.'

'Don't you trust me?'

'Yes, I trust you, Pascal.'

'Well, then.' He picked up her hand and held it in his. 'If we're really going to be together,' he said seriously, 'that's how it should be. We share everything; money, work, everything, OK?'

'OK.' She smiled at him, her eyes soft. 'You forgot to mention the most important thing of all.'

'What's that?'

'The education of the elderly virgin.'

Pascal laughed. 'You've been an exceptionally fast learner in that department, I have to tell you.'

'In any case, I suppose I couldn't really describe myself as a virgin any longer, could I?'

'No, darling, you couldn't. Do you mind?'

'Do I *mind*? Are you crazy? It's the most tremendous thing that ever happened to me.'

'Me, too,' said Pascal quietly, and kissed her hand.

Since it was Saturday and fresh fish was on sale in the market, Pascal bought a large bag of live langoustines for supper, rather to Emma's surprise. 'Isn't it the closed season for shellfish?' she asked. 'Doesn't there have to be an R in the month?'

'Does there?' said Pascal. 'Probably; I don't really know. I wouldn't be prepared to swear to it, but I don't think there's *ever* a time that you can't get some kind of shellfish here.'

'How very French,' said Emma, smiling.

'Would you rather not eat the langoustines?'

'I'd love to eat the langoustines.'

They drove home to Mas les Arnauds, through the beautiful countryside, with the northern flank of the Grand Lubéron to their right and the distant peaks of the Lure away to their left.

'This is such a magical place, and so unspoilt,' said Emma. 'I can't understand why it isn't crawling with modern developments.'

'The whole area is a National Park. It's the biggest in France, around three thousand hectares, and every centimetre of it is protected, thank God.'

'Indeed.'

Back at Mas les Arnauds, they unloaded the van at the dairy and Emma washed the crocks carefully, stacking them on their shelf in the cold-room. François had already brought the goats home, and Pascal let in the nannies and began the milking.

'It's nice that you don't have to kill your animals for meat, isn't it?' Emma took the full bucket of milk and poured it carefully into the wide pan on the stone slab.

'Sorry to have to disappoint you, but we do.'

'Oh, dear! Why?'

'We couldn't rear all the male kids. The most promising-looking ones we keep for breeding, but it's the chop for most of them.'

'What a shame. Poor little billies.' She looked at Pascal and smiled. 'If you're going to be born a goat, it's clearly an advantage to be a female.'

'And if you're not a goat, is it such a disadvantage to be a female?'

'It can be. I think it very often is.'

'In what way?'

'I think girls are frequently brainwashed into a submissive attitude to life; a desire to please, to do the things expected of them by parents or teachers.'

'Is that what happened to you, my Emma?'

'Yes, it was; I realize that now. I was stupid and scared of life, and I took what I thought was the easy way out, by trying to be a nun. I had this vision of myself, sitting in a cell painting pictures, just like Fra Angelico.' She laughed ruefully. 'As things turned out, nothing could have been further from the truth, in real life. It was idiotic of me even to think of it.'

'Didn't anyone try to stop you?'

'Yes, my father did.'

'But you chose to ignore his advice?'

'Yes, I suppose I did. I had this woolly idea that by entering the religious life one can become absolutely free. I thought it would allow me to escape from familial obligations, like the possibility of having to live with my mother, and from the hassles of trying to make a career for myself. I thought I could avoid the conventional pressures to get married, and take on the drudgery of childcare and housekeeping. All I really wanted to do was paint frescoes. I thought that in a convent I could do that. I was wrong.' Emma thought for a moment, then she raised her eyes to Pascal's, as he sat milking his goat, but nevertheless looking at her intently. 'I think that my real motive was to protect myself, mentally as well as physically. I wanted to belong only to myself.'

'You didn't consider the possibility of love?'

'No.'

'So, what made you change your mind?'

'That piece in the paper about Dad and Claudia. If I had really had a true vocation, I could have remained completely undisturbed by the whole thing and dismissed it from my mind as irrelevant to my life in Christ. But I couldn't do that. It upset me deeply, and I felt real distress for them, as well as an ultimate sense of failure for myself. I realized at once that I would never be anything but a disaster as a nun. I couldn't bear to go through all the rigmarole of telling my superiors that their reservations about me were correct, and enduring the humiliation of being "released from my vows", as they call it. My instinct was to run, so I did.'

'Perhaps it was time, anyway?'

'Perhaps it was.'

'I'm glad you did, Emma.'

'Yes, so am I.'

When the work was completed they locked up the dairy and drove home. While Pascal prepared his langoustines by throwing them live into a pan of boiling water, Emma, to avoid being a witness to this massacre, went upstairs to look again at the fresco in their bedroom, and make a list of the materials she would need to buy in Aix-en-Provence. First she made a note of the pigments she would use: yellow ochre; green oxide of chromium; burnt umber; cobalt blue; raw sienna; cadmium red; black; titanium white; terre verte and last of all her favourite colour, Pozzuoli red. As she wrote down the names, her heart lifted in anticipation of the pleasures to come, when she would have repaired the damaged and missing sections of lime mortar, and would be ready to redraw the image. She tried to remember the brushes she would need for the work: very fine ones for drawing, others as fat and round as golf balls, and some flat ones with splayed edges for making subtle gradations of colour. Then, of course, she would need several bags of lime mortar, specially mixed for the job, as well as fine sand and plasterer's trowels. Looking at the damaged fresco, with so much of it missing, she realized that she would have to buy a book containing a reproduction of the original Mantegna, in order to make a series of enlarged paper cartoons of the design, enabling her to transfer it accurately onto the wall.

In her mind's eye, Emma could see the travelling Italian artist at work, and wondered about his life. If he had decorated so many houses in the area, perhaps he had settled there, married, maybe had children?

She looked at the two little dark-haired boys in the foreground of the fresco, so delicately drawn, with such serious expressions; elegant in their loose short doublets and vertically striped hose, one leg blue and white, the other rose-pink. Fine golden fillets bound their smooth foreheads, holding their shoulder-length hair in place. Emma smiled, and for the first time in her life, did not feel alarm or revulsion at the possibility of the advent of children into her own life. Just as well, she said to herself. We're not doing anything to stop it happening, are we?

Down in the kitchen, Pascal was putting the finishing touches to a spectacular-looking salad, composed of his langoustines, now cooked and vibrantly coral-pink, with yellow new potatoes and purple baby artichokes, on a bed of lettuce and rocket, arranged around a white bowl of tarragon-flavoured mayonnaise.

'Pascal! That is *so beautiful*! How is it that you know how to do all this lovely food? Who taught you?'

'My old ladies did. Or rather their cook, I imagine.' He took a box from the shelf over the chimney, and putting it on the table, lifted the lid. 'Come and look,' he said. Inside the box were frayed and yellowing pages that had evidently fallen from an ancient exercise book. The pages were spotted and foxed, and some were torn, but Emma found it quite easy to read the faded brown copperplate handwriting of the author of this Victorian cookbook. Gently, she examined the pages. There were receipts for meat, fish, game and poultry, with sauces to complement the dishes. Soups and vegetable dishes, cakes and confitures, everything was there. 'How wonderful,' she said at last. 'Did you really learn everything from these pages?'

'Every last thing.'

'It's amazing; and do you really like cooking?'

'Yes, I do, but that's not so surprising. My father likes cooking, too.'

'Your father sounds like a nice man, Pascal. I hope to meet him, one day.'

'Come to that, I'd like to meet your father, too. I bet there aren't many men of his calibre, with such a romantic love life as his.'

'Awful when you get found out, though?'

Pascal laughed. He poured wine into their glasses, and they sat down to their supper. 'I don't imagine he regrets it, do you?'

To Emma's surprise, the drive to Aix-en-Provence was comparatively short, a distance of less than fifty kilometres, and almost all of it on the *autoroute*, that followed the valley of the Durance river, then headed south to the outskirts of the old city. Pascal had found the address of an artists' colourman in the *pages jaunes* of the telephone book, and they parked the van in a side street and found the little square in which his shop was located. The tiny establishment was concealed behind a narrow glazed door, painted olive-green, with a small bronze bell on a spring which gave a discreet tinkle as they entered. In the gloom, they could see a high counter, in front of a wall completely covered in small square drawers, each one marked with the name of a colour, painted in gold letters. The air was heavy with the smell of turpentine. From behind a rust-coloured chenille curtain appeared a very old man, white-haired, with faded rheumy eyes behind wire-framed half-moon spectacles. He wore a long dusty black smock and a Moroccan embroidered skullcap. Emma almost laughed, so precisely did his appearance fit the received image of his occupation. His manner, however, was far from flamboyant. He took a long time finding the reference book on Mantegna that she asked for, and seemed almost reluctant to sell her the tools and pigments, the brushes and layout paper she needed, and very disinclined to fetch the sacks of lime mortar and fine sand from the storeroom behind the shop.

'Can I help, perhaps?' offered Pascal.

'*Non, ce n'est pas grave,*' muttered the old man, retreating through his curtain, twitching it shut with a rattle of metal rings. Emma and Pascal looked at each other, eyebrows raised, but said nothing. In a few minutes the old man returned, with the heavy sacks on a small rubber-wheeled trolley.

'I'd better bring the van to the door, then load them quickly, before we get a parking ticket,' said Pascal. 'You stay here, Emma, and settle up, OK?'

'OK.'

The old man, with many sniffs and grunts, made parcels of the little glass jars of pigments, and put the pad of paper and the book into a bag. He packed the brushes into a long black metal cylinder, then laboriously totted up the bill, which came to more than a thousand francs. Emma took her pocketbook from her bag and was handing over the cash, when Pascal reappeared and pushed the trolley out to the waiting van. Emma picked up her parcels and followed him, and the agitated proprietor, obviously terrified that he was about to have his trolley stolen, came quickly to the door to safeguard his property.

Pascal locked the purchases safely into the back of the van, and they drove back to their former parking place. 'Did you get everything you needed?' he asked.

'Yes, everything. It's a wonderful shop.'

'It's a pity he's such a ghastly old fart, though.'

Emma laughed. 'Doesn't matter. He's one of a dying breed, isn't he? I wonder if anyone will carry on, after he goes.'

'I wonder.'

The parking space was still fortunately free, so he reversed the van into it, and checked the time still remaining on the meter. 'There's just time for a coffee at Les Deux Garçons.'

'What's that?'

'You'll see.'

They walked up the narrow street and turned into the cours Mirabeau. This sensationally beautiful street, five hundred metres long, divided along its length by four enormous fountains, was shaded by a double avenue of immensely tall and luxuriant plane trees, whose upper branches leaned towards each other, forming a cool green tunnel. On the sunny side of the wide street, tables and chairs sprawled over the pavements in front of the many cafés, and Pascal took Emma's arm and propelled her towards one of these, which had 'Les Deux Garçons' emblazoned over its doors in large gold letters.

'What a stunning place,' said Emma, as Pascal pulled out a chair for her. She looked about her, shading her eyes, taking in the colourful scene, watching the traffic driving slowly along under the canopy of the trees, the gypsy woman pushing a bright-blue cart loaded with brilliantly coloured flowers, the university students trawling along on big motorbikes, even more of them sprawled around café tables, drinking coffee, reading, and endlessly talking. The atmosphere was electric, vital, alive, and Emma laughed. 'How amazing,' she said, 'it's exactly like Tuscany!'

A waiter, a black waistcoat over his white shirt, and a very long white apron covering black trousers, took their order and vanished through the elegant Edwardian gilded glass doors of the café.

'Do you know Italy well?'

'I know Tuscany and Umbria quite well. I was a student in Florence for four years.'

'Studying painting?'

'Well, restoration of frescoes; the painting techniques of the Italian Renaissance.'

'Aha! Now everything is clear to me.'

Emma smiled. 'So, now you understand how frustrating and difficult it's been for me?'

'Indeed.' The coffee arrived, real Italian *espresso* in small white cups, ferociously strong. 'It's strange,' Pascal said thoughtfully. 'There *you* were, in Florence, doing what you wanted to do, qualifying, and then being deflected from your course. And there was I, in Paris, reading medicine and hating it, deliberately *not* qualifying, in order to do what *I* really wanted to do: rear goats, make cheese, and grow lavender.'

'Was there a big fuss when you did that?'

'My mother minded a lot. I'm afraid she has a low opinion of me. She admires successful people; achievers, you know the sort of thing. She expected me to be a clone of my father, just like my sister.'

'And your father? Did he mind so much?'

'No, he was great. He lent me the money to buy the house and the land. I'm still paying him back.'

'And the goats?'

'I bought them after the first lavender crop, and rented the building for the dairy.'

'And you don't regret leaving Paris? The life? Your friends? Your family?'

He shook his head. 'Not at all. I'm happy to see them when they come, especially my father, but I don't miss their way of life. His is too stressed, in my view, and hers seems utterly pointless to me.'

'How strange,' said Emma, and the image of Flavia, neurotic, destroyed by alcohol, and destructively meddling by nature, came vividly to her mind. 'That's pretty much how I see my mother's life, too, poor thing.'

I must write to Dad and Claudia soon, she thought guiltily. I haven't really spared them a thought since I left the convent, and it's three weeks now. I hope everything's all right. I really must send a card and give them my phone number, at least.

'What are you thinking about, Emma? You look sad.'

'No, I'm not sad. I was just thinking about my father and Claudia, and wondering if they're OK.'

'I expect they are,' said Pascal. 'They're old enough to look after themselves, Emma. You have your own life to lead now, haven't you?'

'Do you really think so?'

'Yes, I do.'

Chapter Thirteen

Ludovic took a taxi from Waterloo to Camden. He had cancelled his meetings for the rest of the week and caught the last train from Brussels, hoping that in view of the lateness of his arrival in London, he would avoid a confrontation with the press. The cab turned into the familiar tree-lined street, and he peered through the windows a little warily. It had been raining, and the streetlamps cast wavering reflections on the puddles under the dripping trees. Thank God, he said to himself, they'll have gone home. The taxi drew up at the foot of Flavia's steps, and, after thrusting a note through the glass partition and telling the driver to keep the change, Ludovic pushed open the door and got out. He glanced over the roof of the cab and saw to his horror the TV cameramen and newspaper photographers, waiting under the trees on the other side of the road. The taxi did a U-turn and drove away, leaving him alone and exposed on the pavement, fumbling in his pocket for his keys. The powerful blinding lights of the TV cameras were switched on and the crowd of cameramen flowed over the street like a black and silver tide, flashbulbs popping. Ludovic, with as much dignity as he could muster, decided not to run like a criminal, but stood his ground and submitted to their impertinent questions and peremptory orders.

'Mr McGrath! Look this way, sir!'

'This way, please, Mr McGrath!'

'Come on, Ludo, give us a break!'

'Tell us about the love-nest, Ludo!'

'Been two-timing the old woman, then?'

'Tell us about the redhead!'

'Still fancy a bit of the old leg-over, Ludo? She must be a hot little number, eh?'

A small, bespectacled, sandy-haired man, wearing a greasy raincoat, thrust his way to the front of the crowd and waved a finger under Ludovic's nose. 'This is a resigning matter, isn't it, Mr McGrath?'

With a sinking heart, Ludovic recognized the acne-scarred features of a well-known and self-appointed guardian of public morals. 'That's your considered opinion, no doubt.' Ludovic spoke politely, without rancour.

'It's a question of *honour*, isn't it? The public will *demand* it!' The small man glared at Ludovic, the malevolence in his large bloodhound's eyes unmistakable. The hectoring tone of his voice rose to a lugubrious whine. 'I expect you'll try to wriggle out of it, like all you sleazy politicians. You all think you can do as you bloody like, and get away with it, don't you?'

A dark-haired woman, with a jaw like a hatchet, elbowed her way in front of her fellow-journalist, and Ludovic hastily ran up the steps to the door. The woman leapt after him and stood close to him as he thrust his key into the lock. 'It must be quite a neat trick, keeping two women and their kids for twenty years.' She gave a coarse laugh, and clutched his arm. 'How'd you manage it, Ludo? Fingers in the till?'

'Excuse me,' said Ludovic. He wrenched his arm from her grasp and she lost her balance, stumbling down the steps and crashing into her colleagues. Ludovic hesitated for a split second, then hurled himself through the door, slamming it behind him and shooting the bolts. There was a moment's silence, then he heard angry voices, followed by a prolonged peal on the bell and a thunderous knocking on the door. Breathing heavily, he leaned against it, and groaned, furious with himself for playing into their hands so foolishly. He could imagine only too vividly tomorrow's tabloid headlines, plus the probable coverage of the incident by the TV news, claiming violent assault on his part of a defenceless female journalist, the story backed by the evidence of a cleverly edited clip.

The knocking grew less insistent, the doorbell ceased to ring, but the ugly, hostile voices could still be heard on the steps outside. Satisfied that it was fairly unlikely that they would go to the lengths of actually breaking into the house, Ludovic put his briefcase on the hall table, and went slowly upstairs. Outside Flavia's room, he paused for a moment, straightening his tie and trying to compose himself, then tapped on the door and went in. Flavia was lying in her big white bed in the dimly lit room. Her eyes were closed and her hands lay quietly outside the coverlet. Her left arm was bandaged, and at the sight of it Ludovic experienced a sharp pang of genuine remorse and bitter regret that he had been the unwitting cause of her attempted suicide. Although he had been an unbeliever for a very long time, he was painfully aware that his wife must have been in a desperate state of mind even to consider taking her own life. For a Roman Catholic, that would count as a mortal sin, under any circumstances at all.

Gwen stood by the window, peering through a crack in the curtains at the mob in the street below. She turned her head as Ludovic entered, and he saw that her expression was far from friendly. Her lips were pursed, and tight with disapproval.

'How is she, Gwen?'

'She is as well as can be expected.' Gwen's voice was as unbending as her demeanour. 'In the circumstances,' she added coldly.

Hearing Ludovic's voice, Flavia opened her eyes and made a feeble attempt to raise herself, but fell back against the pillows. He advanced to the side of the bed and Flavia held out her hand towards him imploringly, gazing up at him, her sad blue eyes blurred with tears. He sat on the edge of the bed, took her cold and scrawny little hand in his, and stroked it rather hopelessly. He felt nothing for her, but was nonetheless filled with a terrible guilt, as though he had killed a sparrow, not even accidentally, but carelessly, at the very least. Gwen, saying nothing, picked up Flavia's supper tray, and left the room.

'Darling Ludovic,' said Flavia faintly. 'I knew you'd come back to me.' A tear rolled down her wrinkled cheek. 'Gwen said I shouldn't count on it, but I knew you wouldn't let me down.' She tried to smile, but it was more like a grimace of pain.

Utterly at a loss, desperate not to inflict any more unnecessary suffering on her, Ludovic lifted her hand to his lips and kissed it gently. To his consternation and huge surprise, she leapt up in the bed, winding her wasted arms round his neck in a vice-like grip, her cheek against his ear, trapping his chin against her bare shoulder. The smell of baby powder filled his nostrils and his gorge rose in revulsion. 'Darling Ludovic,' she whispered, 'don't leave me again, will you? I love you, darling, you know I do.'

She began to weep in earnest, and he sat there, transfixed with horror, patting her back as though she were a sick animal, unable to say the words she longed to hear; knowing that sooner or later he would be forced to. In anguish, he thought of Claudia, the woman he loved and who had loved him for so long, and of Allegra, the catalyst of this present disaster, but still very dear to him in spite of that, and his heart bled. It bled for Claudia, for Allegra, for himself, and even for Flavia. It was blindingly clear to him that of all the women in his life, Flavia, by the very nature of her weakness and vulnerability, had the greatest claim on his presence, if not of his heart. Knowing that to promise to stay with her would be to condemn both himself and Claudia to a lifetime of misery and regret, he nevertheless did so. 'I won't leave you, my dear,' he said quietly.

Flavia loosened her grip from his neck and began to kiss him eagerly, on his cheeks, on his eyes, and finally, with a frantic attempt at passion, on his reluctant mouth. 'Come to bed, darling, please. I'll make it up to you, I really will, I promise.'

Appalled, he took her hands in his and pushed her gently back onto her pillows, covering her flimsily clad body with the quilt. 'You need to rest, Flavia. Please try and sleep. I won't leave you, I promise.'

She looked up at him, her eyes bright with hope. 'We'll have good times again, won't we, Ludovic?'

'Yes, of course we will.' He stood up, preparing to go. 'It's been a long day, Flavia. I must go to bed. Good night, my dear. I hope you'll feel better soon.'

'Good night, darling.'

He crossed the room to the door, and she called to him softly. 'Ludovic?'

'Yes?'

'God bless you, darling.'

Tiredly, he smiled at her, and left the room, closing the door quietly behind him. He felt defeated, exhausted, badly in need of a drink, and extremely hungry. He had not eaten since his lunchtime sandwich, but the thought of Gwen's Protestant rectitude was too much to take on board, so he decided against going to the kitchen in search of food. He went silently downstairs to retrieve his briefcase, took a bottle of whisky from the dining-room cupboard, then went equally silently upstairs again, to the bleak privacy of his old room.

There, he took his mobile phone from the briefcase, lay down on the hard narrow bed, and dialled Claudia's number.

'*Oui?*'

'Claudia.'

'Ludo! Where are you?'

'I'm in London, darling.'

'Is everything all right, Ludo?'

'No, everything's bloody all wrong. It's a ghastly mess. The media people are crawling all over the place. They're staked out in the street here. I walked right into them, sod it.'

'Oh, God, poor you! How awful.'

'Claudia?'

'Yes?'

'It looks as though I'll have to stick it out here for a bit. I can't explain on the phone. I can't say when I'll be back.'

'You don't have to, Ludo. I understand.'

'Do you? Do you really?' His voice sounded strained, close to breaking point. 'Claudia, could you hang on to Alexander until Christian is able to come and pick him up?'

'Of course I will. Don't worry about it, darling; I'll look after him.'

'Thanks, I knew you would.'

'Ludo?'

'Yes?'

'I love you, darling. Never forget that, whatever happens, will you?'

'I won't,' said Ludo, and his voice broke. 'I don't think I can bear this,' he said. 'I need to be with you, my darling.'

'Try not to worry. Everything will work out, you'll see.' Claudia sounded a good deal more confident than she felt.

'Please God,' said Ludovic sadly, and they said good night and hung up.

In Paris, the hot July days passed slowly. Rather than run the risk of exposing Alexander to the press again, Claudia took him with her to the *conservatoire* and to the rehearsals of the orchestra. For his part, Alexander found these new experiences enthralling and saw for the first time in his life the point of education, work, achievement as an end in itself, and all kinds of ideas began to surface in his mind. He examined the clarinet on the table in the studio at impasse des Cordonniers and asked Claudia to teach him how to play it.

'Better still,' she said, opening a drawer in the china cabinet, 'we'll start with a recorder.' There were several to choose from, ranging from a tiny sopranino to a hefty bass instrument. Alexander picked this one and blew a mournful note on it. Claudia laughed and took it from him. 'First things first,' she said, and selected a rather dull-looking middle-sized one. 'This is what we all start on, OK?'

'OK.'

Alexander proved an apt pupil, practised conscientiously and made rapid progress. His cheerful presence made life a good deal less depressing for Claudia, as she waited for better news. As the days passed, she found herself beginning to weaken in her optimistic belief that all would eventually be well. Ludovic telephoned every day, late at night, sounding terribly depressed. After a week, he was able to report that the press had suddenly departed, in order to cover a much more dramatic story. Two terrorist bombs had exploded in a store in central London, leaving many dead and hundreds injured, some of them horribly mutilated. How appallingly ironic, and how cruel, thought Ludovic, as he let himself out of the house into the mercifully empty street; it takes a ghastly thing like a bomb attack to let me off the hook. What kind of a rotten world do we live in, that justifies the crude and cynical attitude of media journalism, merely to sell more newspapers and clog the airwaves with scandal or disaster? He felt a humiliating sense of shame that his own initial reaction to the bombing should have been profound relief for himself, rather than horror at the appalling outrage itself. Somewhere deep inside himself, Ludovic recognized the basic injustice of his deliverance, and when his Minister at the Department informed him drily that his conduct from henceforth should be impeccable, his own guilt forced him to agree. It was not the safeguarding of his career that informed his feelings, but rather a compelling desire to expiate the wrong he had visited on Flavia, that drove him remorselessly to the inevitable conclusion. From now on, he told himself numbly, it is my first duty to prevent any further damage to her, whatever it takes. But what of my duty to Claudia, he asked himself. What of that?

All day long, as he attended a meeting, lunched at his club, then walked unmolested in St James's Park, these questions of conscience filled his anguished mind. He found himself incapable of finding an honourable solution, that would be acceptable to everyone. A terrible sense of loneliness engulfed him, and he stared at the ducks on the lake, wishing himself dead. In his heart, he felt increasingly convinced that his life with Claudia was over, their happiness at an end, that this was the price he must pay for the damage he had inflicted on his wife's well-being, and for her future peace of mind. He became aware of a bitter taste in his mouth, and a burning pain in his chest, and knew that the cause of it was not indigestion, but his heart breaking.

That night, he telephoned Claudia, and told her that she must consider herself free to remake her life; that she should not wait for him, since the probability of his ever being able to be with her again was remote.

'Have you stopped loving me, Ludo? Is that what you're trying to say?' Claudia's voice was rather cold, and very quiet.

'How can you ask me such a thing?'

'If you loved me, you wouldn't give a damn about the gutter press, or anything or anyone else at all, would you? Now, suddenly, your reputation seems more important to you than our life together, doesn't it?'

'Claudia, please try to understand. It's not a question of reputation, it's a question of Flavia.'

'Flavia?'

'Yes. What I'm trying to tell you is that I cannot bring myself to inflict any more humiliation and suffering on her than I already have. It's a question of right and wrong.'

'I see. So, from now on you will be living with Flavia as man and wife, is that it, Ludo?'

Ludovic sighed. 'It's in name only, Claudia. How can you doubt it?'

'Oh, darling, I'm sorry,' said Claudia, dissolving into tears. 'Of course I don't doubt it. God, I wish you were with me, Ludo. Here, in bed.'

'I wish,' said Ludovic. He hung up, went to the bathroom and was violently sick.

In her own room, Flavia lay in her soft bed, rosy with her new-found happiness.

August arrived, and with it the Parliamentary recess and the summer vacations. Christian had not yet come to fetch Alexander, and Claudia felt increasingly confused and dismayed, wondering what the future held for her. It was hot in impasse des Cordonniers, in spite of the shade of the mulberry tree, and the air felt dry and dusty, heavy with pollen. Claudia was now at home all day, and she tried to think of things to do that would amuse Alexander, but he seemed perfectly content to practise his recorder, or lie under the tree, reading. I suppose he's beginning to be an adolescent, she said to herself; he probably enjoys being alone, daydreaming. Doing her best to convince herself that her life was not totally ruined, she gave her little house a very thorough cleaning, dusted and tidied all her books and manuscripts, and polished her mirrors and candlesticks. She cut branches of white rugosa roses from her garden, arranged them in a tall glass jar and stood it on the table in the studio, between the clarinet and the smiling blackamoor's head. When she could find no other domestic jobs with which to occupy herself, she got out a fresh packet of manuscript paper, and sat resolutely down at the piano to work.

Allegra was bored, and at a loose end. Jules was out at work all day, leaving her to her own devices. Her friends had all gone to their families in the country, were on holiday at the sea, or backpacking round India. Her evening job in the student bar had ceased at the end of term, and she had therefore plenty of time for introspection. The longer she reflected on the recent past, the more she began to regret the damage she had inflicted on her parents, and the more she realized that she was actually missing them quite badly. I still don't want to *live* with them, she told herself firmly; but maybe it was a bit stupid to cut the knot so drastically. I suppose I was a bit unfair on them really – they didn't intend to hurt me, and in any case, I don't really give a toss about them not being married. Who cares, these days, anyway?

She went down to the street level in the modish steel elevator of the high-tech apartment block in which Jules lived, and headed for the Métro and rue Mouffetard, seized with a sudden longing to be sitting under the mulberry tree in Claudia's garden, listening to the bees and imagining herself to be in the country. She arrived in the *impasse* without seeing anyone she knew and let herself into her own empty house, glad that she had retained one spare key when she had thrown the rest through her mother's letter box. She went to the casement window of her studio-kitchen and opened it, then gently pushed the shutters slightly apart, so that she could see into the garden. The familiar summer scents of the leafy courtyard drifted into the room. Suddenly, to her surprise, Allegra heard the sound of a recorder, and she saw a strange, fair-haired boy, sitting on the ground under the mulberry tree. He was playing a Bach partita, one of a set of easy transcriptions Claudia had made for Allegra, when she was a beginner herself. She hesitated for a moment, torn between curiosity and resentment at the boy's presence, then climbed over the sill and advanced quietly towards him. At first he did not see her, and continued to play the short piece until he reached the end, which he did with a flourish and a slightly sharp note.

'Bravo!' Allegra said, and clapped her hands.

The boy looked up, startled, his blue eyes round. 'Hello,' he said. 'Who are you?'

'Allegra. Who are you?' She sat down on the warm paving stones beside him.

'I'm Alexander.'

'Alexander who?'

'Alexander McGrath. I expect you know my grandfather, Ludovic McGrath?'

'You could say that,' said Allegra. 'He's my father.'

'*Really?*' exclaimed Alexander. 'How *weird*!' He looked into her face, frowning, as if trying to make sense of this astonishing assertion. 'So you must be *my* father's sister, is that right?'

'Half-sister. Same father; different mother.'

'Oh.'

'Is that a problem, Alexander?'

'Not at all. Is it for you?'

'No,' said Allegra. 'It isn't.' She took the recorder from him and rattled off the partita at the correct speed and with joyful precision.

'That was lovely,' said Alexander. 'Play something else.' So she did.

Presently Claudia appeared, carrying a tray of lemonade. Alexander got to his feet and took the tray from her. She turned towards Allegra, slightly guardedly. 'Hello,' she said. 'How nice to have a visit from you.'

Allegra, her cheeks flushed, got up and embraced her mother awkwardly. 'It's not just a visit. I came to say sorry.'

Claudia smiled and hugged her. 'There's no need. It was as much my fault as yours. It was wrong of me not to tell you about everything, years ago. I'm as sorry as you are, darling.'

They sat down together under the tree, and Claudia dispensed the lemonade, ice-cubes clinking in the frosted glass jug. Alexander looked at them both, so *French*, he thought, so beautiful with their wonderful red hair, so *foreign*. He smiled at them, delighted to be a member of their enchanted world, albeit on a temporary basis. When I grow up, he told himself, I'll live in Paris and marry someone just like Allegra, but a bit younger perhaps. He sipped his lemonade, making it last, prolonging the moment.

'And Papa?' asked Allegra. 'How is he?'

Claudia stared at her daughter, her eyes full of pain. 'Haven't you heard about the English papers?' Her voice was low, discreet.

'No, what about them?'

'They really crucified him, Allegra. He's with his wife now, and likely to remain so.'

'Oh, no! How awful! God, I'm so *sorry*!'

Allegra spent the rest of the day with them, and telephoned Jules to say that she needed to spend time with her mother. Late that night, after Alexander had taken himself to bed, they discussed the entire sad business together, Allegra comforting her mother as best she could, bitterly regretting her part in the collapse of her parents' life together.

'It's not your fault,' said Claudia forlornly. 'How do we know that some other disaster would not have taken him back to her?'

'Like what?'

'Like illness, or something. Terminal cancer, for instance.'

'At least that *would* be terminal, wouldn't it?' said Allegra. 'As things are now, the vile old cow might have her horrible hooks into him for years and years.' In spite of herself, Claudia laughed, but Allegra shook her head. 'It's not funny really, it's sad. You should have got things on a proper formal footing, when I was born.'

'Too late to tell me that now, darling.'

'I hate her,' said Allegra fiercely. '*And* him.'

'No, you don't.'

'You're right, of course I don't. I love him; I love you both. How could I not?'

They went very late to bed, Allegra sharing her parents' big bed with her mother. She had made plans to go to Corsica with Jules's family, but in the morning she changed her mind and decided to move back into her apartment for the time being, in order to give moral support to Claudia. 'At the very least, I can amuse Alexander for you; take him around, let you get on with your work. Just till we see what's happening, OK?'

At Mas les Arnauds, the lavender harvest was in full swing, and the air for miles around was full of the intoxicating scent released as the little mechanical harvester cut and tied each bush into a compact round bundle with great precision. As each perfect bunch was disgorged from the back of the slowly advancing machine, a man armed with a pitchfork picked it up and stacked it with its neighbours, leaning against the previously cut row, to dry for a few days in the hot sun, before collection and delivery to the distillery, and the final extraction of the essential oil.

Emma, hard at work on her Mantegna, did not take part in the lavender harvest, but remained alone in the cool of the house. She had made a drawing of the fresco, using her reference book as a guide, then squared it up and transferred it to several large pieces of paper, cut to fit the working area of her wall, the pencil lines tallying exactly with those remaining on the damaged original work. Next, she repaired the areas where the mortar had fallen off the walls, using a trowel to apply fresh mortar to the dampened surface, smoothing it on in layers until she was within three millimetres of the final layer, the *intonaco*, which would be a mixture of fine sand and lime. When the new mortar was dry enough, she set about transferring her cartoon to the wall. This was an operation she had always enormously enjoyed as a student. Once the paper had been fixed in position, she took a darning needle and punched holes close together along the lines of the cartoon, then, using a small muslin bag tightly packed with dry red pigment, she dabbed the surface of the paper, so that the drawing appeared as a series of red dots on the wall beneath. Then, having carefully taken down the cartoon, she joined up the dots left on the wall with a fine brush loaded with wet pigment, so that the outline of the design reappeared like magic, in its intended position.

Emma had spent the best part of three weeks doing this preliminary work, and as each day passed she grew increasingly confident as all her old skills came back to her. Working in the silence of the cool old house, she sometimes felt as though she could hear her own heart beating, so complete was her happiness and sense of fulfilment. Early every morning she went with Pascal to the dairy, and was becoming as swift and efficient as him at making the cheese, and quick to notice any problems with the goats themselves; things like injuries, thorns in their hooves or torn ears. She learned how to look after such things, and how to administer an appropriate remedy if the need arose.

Each day after breakfast, Pascal departed on his daily deliveries and Emma went upstairs to her work, first removing the large wet sheet hanging in front of the fresco to prevent it drying out until the entire painting was finished. Each day she mixed together enough fine sand and lime to make the *intonaco*, and applied it carefully to the small area which she must paint completely in one day. It was dry enough to work on in minutes, and she pinned her cartoon back in place, and once more dabbed dry pigment through the holes, restoring the image. Patiently, lovingly, she joined up the dots, then, with exactly the same sensation of being in the right place and doing the right thing she had experienced so long ago in Florence, she dipped her brush into her pigments and began to paint.

Pascal did not always return to the house at lunch-time, and on these days Emma worked on until she had finished her quota for the day. She would sit for a moment, examining every tiny detail, rarely finding flaws, then she would clean her brushes and palette. Lastly, she would take the sheet from its bucket of water and rehang it carefully in front of the fresco, to maintain it in perfect condition for the next day's work.

Tired, but deeply contented, she would go down-stairs to the kitchen, make some tea, then sit at the table turning over the fragile pages of Pascal's cook-book, making up her mind how to cook the chicken, or the rabbit, or the leg of young lamb waiting in the larder for their supper.

One afternoon, she had just decided to walk down to the *alimentation* and buy some bell peppers to make a garnish for a rabbit, stuffed with thyme and roasted, which she thought sounded rather delicious, when there was a soft knock on the open door. Emma looked up and saw a strange, grey-haired man, tall, though slightly stooped. He had dark eyes under strongly marked black eyebrows, Pascal's eyes, and she guessed his identity at once. 'Hello,' she said, getting up from the table and going to the door. 'You must be Pascal's father?' Calmly, surprising herself, she held out her hand. 'I'm Emma McGrath, how do you do? Come in.'

'How do you do? Yes, you're quite right, I am Pascal's

father; is it so obvious?' He laughed, shook her hand and came into the kitchen.

'Pascal won't be back till about seven, when he's finished the milking. I was just going to go down to the shop and get some stuff for supper. Would you like to come with me?'

'I would, Emma. But first, could I possibly have a cup of your delicious-smelling tea?'

'Of course! I'm so sorry, how rude of me!'

They sat comfortably at the table, drinking tea and chatting as if they'd known each other for years. Paul de Vilmorin did not ask Emma about herself, or her relationship to Pascal. He did not give a reason for coming alone to see his son, and Emma did not raise the question herself. After tea, they walked together to the shop and Emma bought her peppers and a pot of basil. Paul bought a basket of peaches and a bottle of white wine from the chill cabinet. On their return to the house, they saw Pascal's battered van parked next to the elegant dark-blue Mercedes coupé of his father. In the courtyard they found Pascal, bronzed and naked, standing under *La Douche Automatique*. He turned off the water, towelled his head, then wrapped the towel around his waist. 'Lovely to see you, *Père*,' he said, giving his father a damp hug. 'I see you've brought your icon of international success with you.'

Paul laughed. 'To be human, my son, it's necessary to have one or two little weaknesses,' he said. He turned to Emma, smiling. 'Don't you agree, my dear?'

'I do,' said Emma solemnly. 'Absolutely.'

Chapter Fourteen

At the beginning of September, Ludovic returned to his work in Brussels. True to his promise, he did not once go to Paris, in spite of his intense longing to see Claudia, but returned each weekend to London, like a lamb to the slaughter. For him, the month of August had been a nightmare of loneliness, boredom and pain. Oppressed by a masochistic belief in his own culpability, and a vaguely formulated search for atonement, Ludovic had done his best to behave kindly and courteously towards his wife, and she had responded with a fragile gaiety. Mercifully, she did not offer herself again to her husband, as she had in her first desperate attempt to rekindle their long-dead spark of passion, and for this he was deeply thankful. Each evening, after the unexceptional meal cooked by the sullen Gwen and eaten in the cold dining room, they had adjourned to the sitting room and played Scrabble. It was a game that Ludovic utterly detested. Flavia, on the other hand, adored it, and her poor grasp of the basics of spelling in no way diminished her enjoyment of this pastime. Ludovic, his spirits depressed beyond belief, could not be bothered to challenge her frequent errors, with the consequence that she won every game, which at least had the virtue of making her extremely cheerful. Even allowing for the agreeable visits of Anselm and Benedict, Flavia had not enjoyed herself so much for years, and as the days passed she allowed herself to feel pretty confident that she had seen off the challenge of Claudia and her illegitimate child; that Ludovic had given up this adulterous affair and was now once more her exclusive property.

Gwen, however, was unrelenting in her disapproval of Ludovic. She did nothing to conceal her feelings, and blamed him for her unwelcome return to London. From time to time, as she passed his bedroom door late at night, she heard him talking quietly on his telephone and was unable to prevent herself from eavesdropping. She was not able to hear very much of what he said, but it was quite enough to convince her that Flavia was mistaken in her assumption that the battle was over and that the victory was hers. Feeling that she was being used as an unwilling pawn in an elaborate deception, Gwen was far from happy to be back with Flavia. She missed Phoebe and was homesick for Abbot's Court, with its nice big warm kitchen and her large, comfortable bedroom with all her own things, including her private television and video recorder. Equally, Gwen worried about Alexander, and thought it an extremely bizarre circumstance that the boy should be staying in Paris with his grandfather's mistress – 'whore' was the word she actually chose to describe Claudia in her mind – and when Christian came to visit his mother, Gwen took it upon herself to tell him her views on the subject.

'I would be grateful if you'd try to mind your own business, please, Gwen,' he replied bluntly. 'Alexander seems to be having a very enjoyable break, and the change will have done him a great deal of good.' He observed Gwen's pursed lips and downcast eyes. 'As a matter of fact I have spoken to Mlle Renaud on the telephone several times; she seems an exceptionally nice woman. I don't wish to hear you referring to her as my father's mistress again. Is that understood?'

Gwen drew herself up, looking mutinous. 'Very well,

Christian, if you say so. Nevertheless, I would like to know when I will be going back to Phoebe. I am not prepared to stay with your mother for ever.'

'Don't worry, we'll sort something out. In the meantime, you won't let us down, will you, Gwen?'

'Do I have a choice?' She glared at him, her blue eyes belligerent, and left the room.

Christian sighed, realizing that he could not count on Gwen's co-operation for much longer. In any case, he was becoming quite worried about Phoebe being alone for so much of the time, without Gwen, and even more concerned about what her attitude would be towards Alexander, on his return home. He went back to King's Bench Walk, telephoned Claudia, and arranged to collect his son the following week.

Phoebe drove her old Volvo into the courtyard at Abbot's Court, slammed on the brakes, switched off the engine, unfastened her safety belt and got crossly out of the car. She lifted the tailgate, took out the bags of shopping and carried them to the kitchen, kicking open the door with her foot. She dumped the heavy bags on the table and went out again to fetch the rest of the stuff. She was feeling angry, neglected and increasingly irritated at Gwen's continued absence in London. In the beginning, Phoebe had thought it quite reasonable that Christian should require Gwen to help out in his miserable old mother's hour of need, but fairly soon her compliance had turned to anger and resentment, particularly in view of the fact that her mother-in-law had been the cause of a good deal of anguish for all of them in the course of the last few months. Phoebe had not succeeded in extracting from Gwen the full horror of Flavia's behaviour to poor Alexander, not to speak of that of her foul old brother, but she had had little difficulty in filling in the gaps for herself. She was both furious and incredulous that one evil old woman could wield such power over the lives of others, and rather despised both Ludovic and Chris for allowing her to continue to do so.

Rather to her surprise, Phoebe had found herself remarkably unmoved by the press coverage of her father-in-law's private life, and, unlike Christian, thought the whole affair rather romantic. In fact, on seeing the photographs of both Claudia and Allegra in the Sunday papers, she had felt totally in sympathy with Ludovic, and extremely impressed by the beauty of the women he loved. Good on you, Ludo, she said to herself; though what possessed you to marry bloody old Flavia in the first place, I'll never know, detestable woman. The sight of the ravaged features of her mother-in-law, spread across the front page of a tabloid newspaper, had initially given Phoebe a slight shock, but this had rapidly turned to a secret and pleasurable feeling of delighted revenge, and she felt no pity for Flavia at all. In a curious way Phoebe began to realize that the damage to Christian's mother was catastrophic and permanent, and that it was probable that she no longer had the power to dominate the lives of others, unless, like Ludovic, they chose to allow it.

Phoebe unpacked the shopping and put it all away, still quietly cursing Christian for depriving her of Gwen's help and support. In fact, though she was not yet aware of it herself, Christian had unwittingly done her a good turn in this respect, for in Gwen's absence she had been forced to do a great many boring daily tasks. The bad temper that this provoked did a great deal to deaden the pain and grief in which she had seemed to be permanently trapped. Phoebe looked at the kitchen clock: one-fifteen. She sighed, keenly aware that the day was slipping away, with little accomplished. She yanked open the door of the dishwasher, forgetting that the spring was broken, so that it fell heavily against her bare shin, causing her to yelp with pain. 'Bloody sodding thing, I hate you!' she shouted, and snivelling, began to empty the dishwasher, putting away the clean dishes in a hap-hazard manner, making no attempt to do the job in her usual scrupulously neat fashion. Then, equally untidily, she threw in the previous night's dishes and pans, as well as her breakfast things, and slammed the offending door on them thankfully. Anxious not to make yet more mess to have to clear up, she looked in the fridge for something for lunch, and found a bowl of cold pasta and a tomato. She ate these not very appealing items standing by the fridge, then put the bowl and spoon into the dishwasher, taking care not to drop the door on herself again. Then, feeling thirsty, she got a pint of milk from the fridge door and took a long swig straight from the bottle. She replaced the milk, looked aggressively round the kitchen, ready to pounce on anything else waiting to get up her nose, but could find nothing. Thanks be to God, she said to herself, unconsciously echoing her mother-in-law.

Picking up the basket that held her gardening gloves and tools, secateurs and twine, together with a cardboard box full of snowdrop bulbs, Phoebe went out into the garden. A fine misty rain was falling, but she chose not to let it worry her, so great was her pleasure and relief at being out of the house, and in her beloved garden at last. It was a time of year she loved, the dying of the summer flowering and the return of the garden to an ordered green calmness, its shrubs and hedges neatly clipped, the withered plants cut back, and all the stone paths weeded. The entire place smelt moist and green, like a bunch of watercress. Ignoring the silent appeals from the shaggy lawn beneath her feet, Phoebe walked straight across the grass and under the branches of the beech trees that grew along the fence, forming a barrier between the garden and the paddock beyond. She put down her basket, and taking handfuls of snowdrop bulbs from their box, she scattered them thickly in the grass. Then, kneeling, she took her special bulb-planting tool from her basket and set to work, planting each tiny bulb exactly where it had fallen. In her mind's eye, she could see the fragile white nodding heads that would appear in early February, and the ever-increasing sheets of snowdrops in subsequent years. All afternoon she worked, crawling over the damp grass, already speckled with a few dry brown beech leaves, until the entire boxful, five hundred bulbs, had been planted. She sat back on her heels, wiped the mud off her planter and took off her gloves. I'll have to buy some more, she thought. Five hundred is nowhere near enough; I'll need at least a couple of thousand.

In the paddock, she could hear Denis from the neighbouring farm calling the cows, and watched as the little herd followed him through the far gate to the milking sheds beyond. She got to her feet, picking up her basket and the empty box. She began to stroll slowly towards the house, pleased with her afternoon's work, but bored with the idea of having to think about cooking a meal for herself. The stable clock struck six, and the resident fantail pigeons took off with a startled clapping of wings from the roof of the tower. Phoebe looked up at them, a flurry of white wings against a cloudy sky, and it was then that she saw Chloe, sitting on the edge of the parapet, her thin legs dangling, her fair hair blowing in the wind. For a heart-stopping second, Phoebe remained rooted to the spot, then Chloe waved to her and called out something, but the wind snatched the words away, and Phoebe could not hear what she had said. 'Hello, darling,' she called back. 'What are you doing up there, naughty thing?' She was amazed at her own self-possession. 'Come down at once, for goodness' sake!'

'OK.' Chloe swung her legs over the parapet and disappeared behind the battlements. Phoebe dropped her basket and ran as fast as she could across the lawn, into the house to the foot of the steps to the tower. She could hear Chloe talking to herself as she came down the stairs, a curious childish chattering sound, then she came round the last spiral bend and jumped off the bottom step into her mother's waiting arms. Overjoyed that her dead child had come back to her, Phoebe was nevertheless horrified at how terribly cold and insubstantial the little girl's body felt, as Chloe flung her thin arms round her mother's neck and hugged her tightly.

'You've been away!' It was an accusation.

'Yes, Daddy took me to Rome for a few days. But I've been back for ages, haven't I?'

'You're not going away again?'

'No, I'm not planning to.'

'Well, good. I don't like it when nobody's here.'

Chloe slid through Phoebe's arms, and went out of the glass court into the hall. Phoebe followed her. At the door to the oratory, Chloe paused. Phoebe stood still and waited.

'They frightened him away, didn't they?' said the child in a vague, disinterested voice and before Phoebe's disbelieving gaze, she seemed to glide effortlessly through the heavy closed door. Stunned, her heart hammering, Phoebe pushed open the door and followed her daughter into the place that held such horrible memories for her. Chloe was sitting hunched on the altar steps, her arms clasped around her knees. Without hurrying, Phoebe walked quietly towards her and sat down on the front bench, close to her. 'Who frightened who away, Chloe?' she asked gently.

'Granny did, and horrible old Great-Uncle Anselm. They both kept telling Alex how wicked he was, and made him kneel down and do confession. They really spooked him, so he ran away, stupid thing. I'd have told them to get lost.'

'How do you know all this, Chloe?'

'I was there.' She came and stood in front of Phoebe, putting her cold hand on her knee. 'It's a pain he's gone away,' she said in the whining tone that Phoebe remembered very well. 'There's no-one to play with now, is there?'

'Did you play with him, darling?'

'Yes, all the time. But he's still a bit of a wally, Mum. He wouldn't jump off the tower.'

'Jump off the tower, Chloe?' Phoebe felt her scalp crawl with fear. 'Did you try to make him do that, darling?'

'Yes, I did. It's really cool; it's like flying. But he didn't want to do it, he was too chicken. He's always been a bit of a wimp, always saying boring things like "Don't do this, don't do that, Chloe, it's *dangerous*." Stuff like that.'

'Stuff like what?'

'Like when I ran down the bank into the lane. You know, that time when the bike hit me. He kept yelling at me to stop, but I couldn't anyway, I was going too fast.'

'Alexander told you to stop, darling?'

'Yes, he was always bossing me around like that.' Chloe leaned against Phoebe's knee and sighed, a faint chilled whisper of breath. 'He's rather gross, but he's the only brother I've got, and I do miss him quite a lot. It's so *boring* on my own, Mum. But you know *boys*, don't you? They don't want to know, do they?'

'No,' said Phoebe gently, stroking her dead child's hair. 'I don't think they do, really.'

Then, imperceptibly, almost without Phoebe noticing, Chloe was no longer there. Sadly, but rather comforted by this encounter, Phoebe continued to sit quietly in the oratory, watching the flickering red lamp, as the flame guttered in a draught. For a very long time she remained where she was, trying to recall everything that Chloe had said and beginning to realize how unjustly she herself had treated Alexander, and what an appalling time he must have been having since Chloe's death. Poor boy, she thought, what a stupid, insensitive, selfish cow I've been to him. How could I have done that to him? How could I?

Alexander's face, with his blue eyes and fair hair, so like Chloe's, and his worried expression, so like Christian's sometimes, rose before her eyes and smote her heart. For two pins, she would have knelt down and asked God's forgiveness for her unkindness. Instead, she got to her feet and left the oratory. She walked through the rooms of the house, turning on the lights as she went. She went out into the garden to retrieve her gardening things, glancing up at the tower in case Chloe might still be there, but could see nothing on the roof except the pigeons, settling themselves for the night.

After supper, she sat at the kitchen table, idly turning the pages of a magazine, and thinking about everything that had happened since the death of Chloe. She still felt sad, but not unbearably so. Nothing will ever be the same again, she told herself, but then nothing can ever be quite so bad, either. Who knows, she thought, perhaps Chloe hasn't really gone. Maybe the whole life and death thing is just an illusion? No-one can really know, that's for sure. How can they? One thing I *am* quite sure about, she's not lying under that bloody stone in the cemetery. She's here, with me, in the house and in the garden. She'll never grow up, never leave me, and I'll be here for her as long as I live. After that, it won't matter, will it?

When Christian telephoned, as he did every night, Phoebe told him that she had been planting snow-drops, but, anticipating his probable negative response, she did not tell him about her encounter with Chloe.

'By the way,' he said. 'I've arranged to go to Paris on Saturday to collect Alexander. I hope that's OK with you, darling?'

'Yes, of course it is,' said Phoebe. 'Why wouldn't it be?'

'Great. Well, good night, sweetheart. Talk to you tomorrow.'

'OK; fine. Good night, darling. Sleep well, won't you?' Phoebe put the phone down and smiled, comfortable in the knowledge that she had wisely kept her secret to herself.

On the following Saturday morning Christian took the early train to Paris. It was a beautiful early-autumn day, the sky was blue and the leaves on the chestnut trees golden and crisp underfoot where some of them had already fallen. On such a day it was impossible not to feel rather cheerful, and Christian, in spite of his many preoccupations, could not help being glad to be alive, and happy to be in Paris, that most beautiful and romantic of cities. I really must come here with Phoebe sometime, he said to himself; I don't think she's ever been. She'd love it, I'm sure. He made his way through the crowded rue Mouffetard, enjoying the market stalls, the people, and the smells of delicious cooking stealing through the doors of restaurants as he passed. So busy was he, taking in the sights and sounds of the lively street, that he missed the narrow entrance to impasse des Cordonniers, but found it without difficulty as he retraced his steps. He walked slowly up the alleyway and located Claudia's door. He stood for a few minutes, leaning against the opposite wall. He looked at the beautiful old door, elegantly carved and panelled, its graceful door-knocker blue-grey against the weathered peeling paint. His eye strayed towards the honeysuckle that cascaded over the high, crumbling brick wall that appeared to connect Claudia's house to its neighbour. Christian's upbringing and education had not included much in the way of aesthetic appreciation of architecture or even simple beauty, and his interest in such matters was largely rooted in their potential monetary value. Nonetheless, he saw at once that this place was as different from, and as infinitely preferable to, his mother's house as it was possible to imagine. He found it quite easy to understand what an irresistible temptation it must have represented to his father, trapped in an unsatisfactory marriage. Be that as it may, he reminded himself sternly, marriage is marriage, for better or worse, there's no getting away from it. Christian braced himself, intending to be polite and friendly, but firm and non-committal on the subject of Ludovic and Flavia.

He knocked on the door, which was answered almost immediately by Claudia herself, calm and composed, wearing baggy blue jeans and an oversized Guernsey sweater belonging to Ludovic. Her long wavy red hair was loose, and framed her unmade-up face, emphasizing her pale ivory skin and luminous hazel eyes. Christian recognized her at once from the press photographs, but was unprepared for her beauty and youthful appearance. He found it difficult to believe that she had a daughter only a few years younger than his own sister, and for a moment he felt rather awkward and unaccountably shy.

'Come in, Christian,' she said, smiling at him. 'Alexander and Allegra have gone out to see an exhibition at Beaubourg and have lunch. I hope you don't mind? I thought it would be easier for us to talk, if we were alone.'

'Of course, quite right,' he agreed. 'What a sensible idea.'

'Do take off your coat.'

Christian hung his coat on the bentwood stand that stood beside the street door.

'I made us some lunch, just a snack really,' said Claudia. 'I thought it would be pleasant to sit in the garden. It's still quite warm, isn't it?'

'How kind. I do hope I'm not being a nuisance?' Christian's eyes flew round the room, astonished at its originality, enchanted by its airy brilliance and

298

romantic atmosphere. 'What a beautiful room,' he said, feeling that some sort of comment was expected of him. 'Have you lived here long?'

'For twenty-two years, since I met your father, Christian. We made this place together.'

Christian blushed hotly, appalled at what he thought of as his gaucheness and lack of savoir-faire. 'I beg your pardon,' he stammered. 'I didn't intend to pry into your private life.'

Claudia laughed, and fleetingly touched his burning face with a cool finger. 'It's not very private any longer, is it, my dear?'

'I suppose not.' Christian looked miserably at Claudia, and for the first time it dawned on him that she too must be suffering as deeply as his parents, her life equally in ruins. He could not think of anything at all to say to her.

'Go and sit in the garden, and I'll bring the lunch. You must be hungry, and probably rather longing for a drink, I expect? Which would you prefer, vodka or wine?'

'I'd love a glass of wine,' said Christian. 'Thank you.'

He went out to the garden and sat down on a long rattan chair under the mulberry tree. He tried hard to relax, to stop feeling defensive and unsure of himself. He lay back against the cushions and stared at the dark pattern of leaves above his head. He thought about Ludovic, realizing that he had never really known his father at all well. For as long as he could remember, he had considered him to be a quiet, reserved man, good at his job, distinguished, responsible, a good provider. Now, on reflection, he saw that there had always been a distance, a lack of communication, between himself and Ludovic. In Christian's mind, he had regarded his father as rather lacking in warmth, remote, a man of few emotions. You could ask him for his money, but never for his love, would have been Christian's analysis of Ludovic's character, had his opinion on the subject been sought. Looking around him, he realized the triteness and improbability of this diagnosis. Clearly, it was unlikely that a man so cold and unresponsive would have lived for more than twenty years with a stunningly beautiful woman like Claudia, in such a romantic setting as this. Equally, he must have been pretty special himself, to have kept the love of such a woman for so long. Lucky old them, he said to himself wryly, thinking of the long hypocrisy of most marriages, including his own sometimes.

Claudia came out into the garden, carrying a tray, and Christian sat up.

'Don't move. Stay where you are.' She put the tray on the table, seated herself on the chair beside it, and handed Christian a tall glass of chilled white wine. As she had promised, the lunch was extremely simple. In a dark-green bowl were thick slices of ham, garnished with parsley-speckled savoury jelly. Claudia handed him a plate of this delicious stuff, together with a knife and a piece of *pain Poilâne*, the heavy sour-dough bread currently fashionable in Paris. She offered him white unsalted butter and a little glass pot of coarse pink sea-salt.

Christian sipped his cool wine, and ate his ham sandwich, and thought it the most exquisite food he had ever tasted. 'That was delicious; thank you so much,' he said, replacing his plate on the tray. 'And talking of thanks, I must tell you how much Phoebe and I appreciate your kindness to Alexander. I feel we have abused your hospitality disgracefully, leaving him with you for so long.'

'Not at all. I've enjoyed his company, and so has Allegra.' She smiled. 'They seem to get on very well together. She's been giving him lessons on the recorder.'

'Really? I hope he hasn't been noisy, or a nuisance?'

'No, of course he hasn't. He's a very nice boy, and remarkably mature for his age.' She looked deliberately into Christian's eyes. 'He's very like Ludovic, isn't he?'

'Oh? He's supposed to look like me.'

Claudia laughed. 'I'm not talking about his *appearance*, Christian. I mean that he's very like Ludovic in character.'

'Do you really think so? In what way?'

'They're both blessed with the same keen intelligence, and a sensitive uncritical respect towards the attitudes of other people. Equally they are both cursed with a tremendous propensity for feeling guilty, and this makes them very vulnerable. I think your sister Emma is the same.'

Christian stared at her, completely taken by surprise. He frowned. 'I'm afraid I can't agree with you, Claudia. My mother, yes; you could describe *her* in that way, poor old thing. *Frailty, thy name is woman*, just about sums her up, actually.'

'You haven't understood what I mean.'

'Haven't I?'

'I don't mean that they are *frail*, as you put it. I mean that both Ludo and Alexander have a tendency to blame themselves for the tragedies or inadequacies of others.'

'That's rubbish! My father certainly *should* blame himself for humiliating my mother as he did, and it's right and proper that he should do his utmost to restore her confidence and put things right between them, isn't it?'

'Christian, have you any idea at all why your parents' marriage failed?'

'I wasn't particularly aware that it *had* failed.' He looked at Claudia coldly. 'Presumably he met you, found you fifty times more attractive, a great deal younger and much more interesting and fun than my mother, and that was that. He dumped her; the usual story.'

'No, that wasn't how it was, at all.'

'Oh?'

'Why do you suppose that there is a ten-year gap between yourself and Emma?'

'I don't know. These things happen.'

'In their case, it was the result of an enforced celibacy.'

'Enforced *what*?'

'Celibacy. They did not sleep together. It was entirely her decision, Christian. Think about it. For eight long celibate years he remained faithful to her. Then she decided to have a second child, with the same ruthless rejection of your father once her desire for the child had been gratified. After that, it was another three miserable years before he met me, Christian. Can you imagine what those years must have been like for him?'

Christian shook his head, bereft of speech. He stared at Claudia, red-faced, squirming with embarrassment. His initial reaction was one of extreme distaste in the face of her crude revelations in respect of his father's sex life, or lack of it, but this knee-jerk response was followed almost at once by a sudden rush of sympathy for Ludovic, as a man. He did not have to ask Claudia whether she was really telling the whole truth; remembering the separate bedrooms in the Camden house, he knew that she was. He cleared his throat. 'What I *can* imagine', he said at last, 'is what a glorious thing it must have been for him, poor man, to find someone like you.'

'It was a glorious thing for me too, and still is. As far as I am concerned, nothing is changed. Can you understand that?'

'Yes, of course I can. I'm quite sure it's the same for him, Claudia. God, it's a mess, isn't it?'

'Yes, it is.'

There was the sound of a door banging, then footsteps, and Alexander, followed by Allegra, came into the garden.

'Hello, Dad.' Alexander looked at his father with bright, slightly anxious eyes.

'Hello, old chap. Had a good time in Paris?'

'Terrific. It's a really cool place, Dad. I'd like to come and live here one day, if you and Mum wouldn't mind.'

Christian laughed, and stood up. He stared at Allegra, so tall and thin, with her mother's hair and Ludovic's grey eyes.

Allegra gazed steadily back at him. 'Christian?' she queried doubtfully, unable to see anything of her father in this man.

'The same,' he replied. 'And you are Allegra, my half-sister, aren't you? Is it permitted to give you a hug, Allegra?'

'Of *course* it is, *volontiers*!' She flung her arms round Christian's neck and kissed him.

Alexander observed this exchange with a mixture of relief and satisfaction. He turned to Claudia. 'Allegra and I were thinking, wouldn't it be great if she could come to Abbot's Court for a visit before she goes back to college? What do you think?'

'I think, fine, but you'll have to ask your mother, darling, won't you?'

Chapter Fifteen

For Pascal and Emma, life in Mas les Arnauds seemed pretty nearly perfect. The fresco was at last finished, and the stern figure of Count Gonzago could now be seen raising his right hand in formal greeting to his son, Cardinal Francesco. The young cardinal holds the hand of his younger brother, who in turn holds that of his little nephew Sigismondo, himself a future dignitary of the Church. Behind Sigismondo stands another small boy, his brother. Surrounded by courtiers, these people pose proudly before an imaginary landscape, a city on a hill beneath a cloud-filled blue sky, a tall exotic tree emphasizing the perpendicular composition of this portrait of the noble family of Mantua. At first sight, the colours seem sombre and restrained, a blend of subtle greens and browns, ochres and russets, offset by the icy blue of the sky. Then, slowly, one becomes aware of the warm flesh tones, the rose-pink of the cardinal's shawl, the little boys' gaily striped tights, and realizes that the entire fresco is flooded with glowing colour and light.

'That dog behind Gonzago's legs could easily be Bosco,' said Pascal, as they lay in bed together. 'It just goes to show how long the *beauceron* has been around, doesn't it?'

'He's adorable, isn't he? He's even holding up his

paw, just like Bosco does when he thinks you've forgotten his supper.'

'I don't care what you say, Emma, I still think the cardinal's brother looks like a girl.'

'That's exactly what I always thought he was.' Emma rested her cheek in the crook of Pascal's shoulder, sleepily, her eyelids drooping. 'I thought that she was the mother of the two little boys, but when I was researching Mantegna's work, I found out that I was wrong. In fact, he's a chap.'

'Weird,' said Pascal. He turned his head and kissed her forehead. 'How would you feel about it, if those two little boys were yours, my Emma?'

She opened her eyes and looked at him. 'I'd love it. Would you?'

'More than anything.'

'Girls, too?'

'Naturally.'

'Where would they all sleep?'

Pascal laughed. 'I'll have to make time and money, and repair the house properly, won't I?'

'Can we afford it?'

'Emma?'

'Mm?'

'Let's stop worrying about the house, darling, and do something about the babies, OK?'

'OK.'

It was now mid-September and the lavender harvest was almost over. The extravagantly scented purple fields had become neatly clipped green ones, no less beautiful in their winter mode. Deprived of their lavender flowers, the foraging bees were forced to fly further afield, seeking out their nectar in woodlands and on drystone walls, now clad in late-flowering ivy. The heat of the sun was becoming less ferocious and a period of soft, still weather had set in.

'It's incredible,' said Pascal, as they sat in the warm,

305

balmy courtyard after supper, 'in less than a month the first snow will arrive at Col d'Allos, and it'll be time to bring the sheep down again. Then the rams will run with the flocks, and the whole cycle will start again.'

'And what about the goats?'

'The milking nannies are beginning to dry up now, and soon we'll let them run with the billies. In February their kids will be born, and their milking season will start again. In a week or two, our currently pregnant nannies will drop their kids and our second milking season will take over. That way, we can make cheese all year round.'

Emma took a sip of wine. 'It doesn't sound as though we'll get much time for repairing the roof, does it?'

'Don't worry; I'll make time.'

'I could help, couldn't I?'

'No, too dangerous. You might fall.'

'All right, be like that. I'll start making a garden, then. I can't fall off that, can I? We could have a useful little *potager* here, couldn't we? Salad and herbs, things like that?'

'What about your work? Aren't you going to start a new fresco?'

'Yes, when the cold weather comes. Just now, it's so beautiful outside, it seems a crime to be indoors.'

On Saturday they drove to the market at Apt, and set out their stall as usual. The August visitors had nearly all departed, particularly the families with school-children, so the market was much less crowded and frenetic and people were more inclined to chat, to taste things, taking their time over their shopping. Pascal was in the process of giving advice to a client about the best wine to drink with a dessert of fresh figs and goat's cheese, when an extremely elegant woman appeared through the shoppers and stopped at the stall. She was small, with the kind of simple ash-blond haircut that costs a great deal to buy. She was wearing dark glasses, and a white linen frock with a gold mesh belt.

'*Bonjour, Madame,*' said Emma politely. '*Puis-je vous aider?*'

The elegant woman smiled at Emma and held out her hand. A shower of fine gold bracelets jangled on her wrist, as she introduced herself. '*Bonjour, Mademoiselle.* I am Madame de Vilmorin, Blanche.'

'Oh, goodness!' exclaimed Emma, taken by surprise. 'Hello! How do you do?'

Pascal said goodbye to his customer and turned towards his mother. He smiled, a little warily it seemed to Emma. 'Hello, Mother. What brings you here? I thought you shopped in Cavaillon? I see you've met Emma?'

'I've had that pleasure, yes. I came to see you for two reasons, my dear Pascal. One, to buy some of your delicious cheese, and two, to invite you both to luncheon tomorrow. We have friends staying, the Saint-Denis, you remember them, of course? They would love to see you again, and hear all about your little farm. Olivier is such a *dear* man, so environmentally concerned, so *green*, and so very left-wing, needless to say. It seems he admires your way of life down here, Pascal.'

Pascal forbore to say that it didn't sound very much as if his mother shared Olivier's views on the subject, and looked at Emma, his eyebrows raised, silently asking her to decide whether or not she wanted to go. Quickly, not wishing to offend his mother, Emma accepted the invitation. 'Thank you. We haven't planned anything for tomorrow; we'd love to come.'

'One o'clock, then?' Mme de Vilmorin bought several cheeses, paid, smiled at them both with an inclusive sweep of her very white teeth, and went on her way. She had not once taken off her dark glasses.

Pascal and Emma looked at each other. 'I'd never have guessed that she was your mother, Pascal,' she said, and smiled. 'What colour are her eyes?'

'I don't know; I've forgotten. Blue? Grey? Does it

307

matter?' He sounded irritated, put out.

Emma laughed. 'No, of course it doesn't.' She stood on tiptoe and kissed his cheek. 'Just idle curiosity, nothing more nor less.'

The next morning, determined not to be intimidated by Pascal's mother or her expensive clothes, Emma decided to wear her khaki trousers and one of Pascal's newer denim shirts. I can't compete with her, she thought, and in any case I don't want to. She looked at her reflection in the blotched silvery mirror hanging on the bedroom wall. It had a very beautiful but badly damaged baroque frame, which she had already promised herself to restore, when they could afford the costly books of precious gold leaf. Her face, burnt by the sun, was now a smooth deep golden colour, her grey eyes looked large and luminous, her lips seemed redder and fuller than she remembered. It must be happiness, she said to herself. She combed her hair, then frowned, observing how peculiar it looked, shaggy and uneven. She went downstairs to the kitchen, where Pascal was plucking a pair of young pigeons in readiness for their supper. 'Pascal, where are the scissors?'

'In the drawer, where you put them, darling.'

She took the scissors from the drawer. 'Have you nearly finished the poor little pigeons?'

'Yes, I have, you sentimental creature. Why?'

'I want you to cut my hair, please.'

'Are you sure? Shouldn't you go to a shop for that?'

'Who cuts your hair?' Emma persisted.

'I do. It's an annual shearing.'

'Right. Do mine, please. It's a mess like this.'

'OK.' He took the plucked pigeons to the larder, then gathered up the newspaper covered in their bloody feathers and stuffed it into the stove. He washed his hands under the tap. 'Now,' he said. 'Sit on the table, and keep still.'

She got onto the table, and he took the comb from

her. Wetting her hair from a jug of water, he combed it straight down from a centre parting, and then over her eyes. He picked up the scissors. 'Shut your eyes and don't move.' Emma did as she was told, and listened nervously as the blades of the scissors went snip-snip, steadily, first across her eyebrows and then right round her neck, just below the level of her earlobes. 'Shake your head.' She shook her head. 'OK. You can open your eyes and get down.' She got down from the table and picked the bits of wet hair off her shirt. Pascal looked at her critically, then smiled. 'That's better,' he said. 'You look quite beautiful, or have I told you that before?'

'You have, but I still like hearing you say it.' She put her arms round his neck and kissed him. 'Come to that, you look pretty beautiful yourself.'

The kitchen clock struck twelve, and Bosco thumped his tail on the floor. 'Come on,' said Pascal reluctantly, 'I suppose we'd better get going.' They went out to the van, Bosco leapt into the back, and they drove towards the road that would take them to Bonnieux.

The de Vilmorins' place was an hour's drive from Mas les Arnauds, and a few kilometres beyond Bonnieux. As they approached the *domaine* up a long narrow lane, Emma realized that she must have passed the entrance on her journeys to and from Villemagne. It seemed like an eternity since she had walked out of the convent, though in fact it was barely three months. Guiltily, she thought about her nun's habit, stuffed into the locker in the left-luggage place in Avignon, then forgot about it as they drew near the entrance. The house was a large converted farmhouse with the usual attendant cluster of outbuildings, hidden behind high stone walls and surrounded by ancient cedars. The traditional solid wooden double gates had been re-placed with electronically operated metal ones, which gave the place the appearance of a prison. Not being in possession of a remote control with which to induce the gates to open, Pascal had to get out of the van and operate the entryphone installed in the wall. A short crackling conversation ensued, and the gates opened slowly. Pascal jumped back into the driving seat and drove in. 'I should probably have left this old heap outside,' he said, as he negotiated the short tarmac drive to the parking area. 'Take a look at the competition.'

Emma laughed, trying not to feel too impressed by the big BMW estate car and the superbly polished green Range Rover parked next to Paul de Vilmorin's sleek Mercedes. 'It doesn't matter, does it? It's only money.'

'You're absolutely right,' said Pascal, 'but one is only human, especially me. My problem here is trying not to get aggressive in the face of my mother's patronizing attitude.'

'You should have told me. We needn't have come.'

'Too late now,' said Pascal. 'Here's the old man.'

They got out of the van as his father came to greet them. Paul kissed Emma's hand, and embraced his son.

'Is it OK to let Bosco in, Dad?'

'Perhaps better not. We have a visiting dachshund, that seems to be of an abnormally sensitive nature. It suffers from a slipped disc, would you believe?'

'*Merde!*' said Pascal. 'How did that happen?'

'Apparently it was being taken for a walk in the Tuileries Gardens when it rather rashly attacked another dog, a large black labrador. The owner of the labrador aimed a kick at poor defenceless little Tonton, causing the lamentable, and evidently incurable, condition of the slipped disc.'

'It sounds to me as though Tonton was asking for it,' said Emma.

'Between ourselves, I've rarely had the misfortune to meet a more repulsive animal,' said Paul quietly, and they all laughed guiltily.

'Poor old Bosco, you'll have to stay out here,' said Pascal.

'Won't he be too hot in the van?'

'Yes, he will. I'll let him out for a pee, and then he'll lie here in the shade.'

'Will he stay there?' asked Paul.

'Of course; what else?'

Bosco had his pee, then lay down as instructed, and the three of them went through an archway and into a shady courtyard. Paved with stone tiles, sheltered by a large acacia tree, enclosed by the apricot-washed stone walls of the house, this outdoor room was furnished with a white marble table on a wrought-iron base, and matching iron chairs with pristine white linen-covered cushions. The surrounding walls of the house were lined with massive green-glazed Anduze pots, in which grew large shrubs of laurustinus, clipped into identical round balls. The whole effect was extremely chic, civilized and elegant, exactly like the little party already seated at the table.

Blanche de Vilmorin, wearing narrow trousers and a halter top in her favourite white, rose from her seat as they entered and floated gracefully towards them, a smile on her immaculately made-up face. After greeting Emma briefly, she put her delicately tanned and scented arm through Pascal's and led him to the table. 'Here he is, Olivier!' she said gaily. 'One has lured him from his lair at last!'

Olivier Saint-Denis got to his feet and clasped Pascal's hand, expressing his pleasure at meeting him again. He was a man of between fifty and sixty years of age, grey-haired, overweight, and of a kindly disposition. He smelt of Givenchy's Monsieur.

'Hello, again, Pascal. You are more than ever handsome.' Mme Saint-Denis, or Catherine, as she preferred to be called by the young, took off her blond tortoise-shell spectacles and offered her cheek for Pascal to kiss. This he did, observing as he did so the three

311

millimetres of white at the roots of her glossy black hair, worn in a chignon. She, too, was wearing white, with gold sandals and a lot of heavy gold jewellery.

'Catherine,' said Paul. 'I'd like you to meet Emma McGrath. Emma, Catherine Saint-Denis.'

Emma shook hands with Catherine, then with Olivier, and sat down in an unoccupied chair. At once, there was a furious commotion under the chair, and a shriek of agony. Horrified, Emma leapt to her feet.

'Oh, really, Catherine!' exclaimed Paul crossly. 'It's your bloody little dog again. Get him out of there, for goodness' sake, before he bites someone.' He turned to Emma, a humorous glint in his eye. 'Are you all right, my dear?'

'Perfectly, thank you.' She laughed. The dog was hauled out from under the seat, and was installed on Catherine's lap, whimpering. Emma sat down again.

'Goodness me, what a drama!' said Blanche. 'Pimm's, Emma? Or would you prefer white wine? We have quite an amusing little *vin de pays*. One tries to support the local producers, you understand.'

'Wine would be very nice, thank you. If I could have water in it, please?'

'Because it's undrinkable?'

'Not at all.' Emma felt her cheeks grow hot. 'Because I find wine too alcoholic in the middle of the day.'

'Wise girl,' said Paul, and his wife gave him a quelling look. He poured the wine, put ice and water in it, and handed the enormous antique glass to Emma, who thanked him gravely, not daring to smile.

'What about you, Pascal?'

'The same please.' He sat down in the seat next to Emma, and looked challengingly at his mother, who said nothing.

The conversation was predictably dull. Olivier Saint-Denis enquired after the goats, and the lavender, and Pascal gave accurate, brief replies. Then they discussed the weather for ten minutes, and after that moved irresistibly to the subject of crime, a topic close to the hearts of most owners of summer residences in the Lubéron. They exchanged opinions on burglar alarms, and security in general. They repeated several well-known horror stories concerning the disappearance during the owner's absence of the entire contents of houses, including complete bathroom suites and fully fitted kitchens. In general, they seemed to mind more about the difficulties of obtaining insurance after such calamities, than the actual loss of their treasured possessions.

'I never lock my house,' said Pascal. 'I've never had the slightest need to.'

'Nothing worth stealing, that's why!' said his mother, laughing merrily.

'That's not true, as a matter of fact.' Five pairs of eyes turned towards Emma, and she hesitated shyly, but refused to be intimidated. 'Pascal has some really lovely old things, especially his beautiful painted bed. It's eighteenth-century Italian, in wonderful condition. I keep telling him it should be in a museum.'

'Really?' Blanche looked at Pascal, a malicious gleam in her eye. 'So, what do you intend to do with it, Pascal? Sell it?'

'Certainly not,' said Pascal coolly. 'It's the only decent bed in the place. We sleep in it, of course.' A little bell tinkled within the house.

'Of course,' agreed Paul smoothly, and stood up. 'Lunch, I think.' He offered his arm to Emma and they entered the house.

They passed through the sitting room, a large and beautiful space, painted palest ivory, with long sofas covered in natural linen-union on either side of a monumental stone-hooded fireplace. The floor was covered in beige sea-grass, and the walls were hung with a great many paintings, which Emma recognized, with a sense of shock, as the work of early Impressionists. Golly, she said to herself. From the beamed ceiling hung a large chandelier, dripping with lead crystal. The remaining sources of artificial light took the form of chrome table lamps in various sizes, with glossy black shades. After dark, these lamps were designed to throw pools of light over the occasional tables, which held carefully composed arrangements of honey-coloured marble ashtrays, antique leather-bound books and ornate wrought-iron *cache-pots* containing miniature pine trees, in the Japanese style.

Lunch was served in the kitchen, though this seemed to Emma an inappropriate description of the room. A rectangular marble table stood in the middle of the tiled floor, and was laid as if for a banquet, with much glittering silver and crystal, and beautiful linen napkins. Over the table hung a similar chandelier to the one in the sitting room, and at each place was an antique faïence dinner plate from Moustiers, in the delicate pink and green pattern *Venezia*.

'It's just a simple meal,' said Blanche. 'I don't like making too much work for the *bonne* on Sundays.'

The lunch, served by a young girl wearing a black dress and a frilly white apron, began with a delicious chilled vichyssoise. This was followed by a whole poached salmon, covered in a thin film of aspic and elaborately decorated with slices of cucumber and tomato, embellished with chives and blue borage flowers. Curiously, the menu reminded Emma of the sort of food her own mother had once been accustomed to offer guests, when she wished to impress.

Rather to her relief, Emma had been placed on Paul's right, with Catherine Saint-Denis opposite her, on his left. She chatted to Paul for a few minutes, then, remembering the rules of the game, turned to Olivier, on her right. 'Do you live down here?' she asked. 'Or do you come just for the summer?'

'I'd love to live here all the time,' he replied. 'But Paris still has its grip, and in any case I have quite a few years yet, before I can retire.'

'Oh, I see. What do you do?'

'I'm in Overseas Aid, in the European Commission.'

'What a coincidence,' said Emma, smiling. 'My father works in the Commission.'

'Really? How interesting. What did you say your name was?'

'McGrath.'

'McGrath? He looked at her. 'Is your father by any chance Ludovic McGrath?'

Too late, Emma realized her indiscretion, and her worst fears were immediately confirmed.

'Ludovic? Are you talking about Ludovic, poor man?' Catherine leaned across the table confidentially. 'Isn't it sad? He had to go back to his wife after all that ridiculous fuss. What a charming man he is, so culti-vated. Do you know him, Emma?'

'Yes, I do. He's my father.'

Catherine, momentarily at a loss, hesitated in the embarrassed silence that followed, then smiled at Emma apologetically. 'Well, how *very* nice. He is an excellent man, and a good friend. One wishes him well, my dear.'

Emma could not detect any malice in Catherine's attempt at making good her blunder, so she smiled at her and took a forkful of salmon. Paul refilled the glasses and normal conversation was resumed.

After lunch, coffee was served in the garden, then Pascal looked at his watch and said that it was getting late. 'We have to get back for the evening milking, Mother.'

'What a shame,' she said. 'A farm is just as much of a tie as small children, isn't it? I thought you might like to stay for a swim?'

Pascal shook his head, smiling, and got to his feet. Emma stood up. 'Another time, perhaps?' She shook hands with everyone and said goodbye.

Paul accompanied them to the van, where Bosco lay waiting under his tree. 'I'm sorry about Catherine,

Emma,' he said. 'She is a kind-hearted woman, but foolish at times.'

'Not at all,' said Emma. 'How was she to know, poor thing? It was my own fault, entirely; I walked right into it.' She turned to face him. 'Can you tell me, please, what is happening? What has happened?'

'As far as I know, there was a quite vicious attack on your father in the English papers.'

'Worse than the article in *Info-Phallo*?'

'Much worse, I'm sorry to tell you. Most unpleasant.'

'Oh, dear, how awful. Poor Claudia, is she OK?'

'I don't know them at all well, Emma, so I can't tell you, I'm afraid. I expect it will sort itself out; these things often do, don't they?'

'You're very kind,' said Emma quietly. 'Thank you, Paul. Goodbye.' She kissed his cheek and got into the van beside Pascal, and they pulled away, both of them glad to be going home. For a few miles they drove in silence, while Emma thought about her father and Claudia, saddened that their life together seemed to have ended so disastrously. Recalling vividly the time she had spent with them in impasse des Cordonniers, she remembered clearly their undisguised love for each other, the happiness manifest in her father's demeanour, and the grace with which the beautiful Claudia wove her joyful spell in that enchanted place. She tried to imagine Ludovic reunited with Flavia, and spending all his free time in the Camden house, but could not. Having found her own fulfilment and happiness, it broke Emma's heart to think that her father's should be shattered. 'What can one do, Pascal?' she asked. 'There must be some way of helping them?'

'Like what?'

'I don't know. It's so difficult. It would be only too easy to rush in and make matters worse, wouldn't it?'

'Why don't you just write to Claudia, a normal sort of letter. Tell her about your fresco, things like that, and see how she responds.'

'Tell her about you, Pascal?'

'Why not?'

So Emma wrote to Claudia that night, and every morning she opened the mailbox half-expecting a letter from Paris, but none came.

A week after Alexander's return home, Phoebe telephoned Allegra and invited her to stay at Abbot's Court.

'It's very kind of you,' said Allegra, 'but wouldn't I be in the way? You must be very busy, and Alex will soon be back at school, won't he?'

'That's one very good reason why I'd be glad of your company. Can you drive?'

'Yes, of course.'

'Good, that's great.' Phoebe paused, then explained herself candidly. 'The thing is, Allegra, my housekeeper is in London at present, and I would be very glad of an extra pair of hands, as well as your company, if that doesn't sound rather rude?'

Allegra laughed. 'It doesn't sound rude at all; it sounds honest. Thank you for the invitation, I'd love to come. When do you want me?'

'As soon as possible. What about Friday, then you can travel down from London with Christian?'

'Friday it is, Phoebe. What's his number, so that I can liaise with him about train times and stuff?'

'Brilliant! Have you got a pencil?'

Phoebe put down the phone, feeling rather happy, as well as more confident and in control than she had for weeks. Determined to avoid inflicting any further emotional damage on Alexander, she had decided to refrain from mentioning Chloe, or her continued haunting presence at Abbot's Court. She was no longer finding it difficult to behave towards her son in her old affectionate way and for this he seemed hugely thankful. As for his clandestine trip to Paris, she said very little about it, but made it plain that she blamed his grandmother and old Fr Anselm for upsetting him in the first place. She found, to her profound joy, that she could almost summon Chloe at will, merely by thinking about her, particularly if she happened to be alone in one of her secret places, like the armillary garden. Of course, she thought, that's where I was when she was killed, poor little girl. Chloe almost always seemed to manifest herself immediately behind Phoebe, putting her cold little hand on her mother's neck as she knelt beside a flower bed, or sat on a garden bench. She would stay with her for a while, chatting, then gradually her voice would fade like a bad telephone line and she was no longer there. One afternoon, Phoebe and Alex were walking back from feeding the ponies, when Chloe called her from the top of the tower. She looked up and saw her dead child standing beside the weathercock, waving, her hair blowing in the wind. Phoebe glanced anxiously at Alexander, but it was obvious that he had not seen or heard anything.

On Friday evening, Alex came with her to the station to meet the train bringing Christian and Allegra from London. On the drive back to Abbot's Court, Alexander sat in the back with Allegra, the pair of them chattering away in a bizarre mixture of French and English, punctuated with bursts of laughter. Phoebe and Christian exchanged amused smiles. Clearly, the advent of Allegra was good news for them all.

Chapter Sixteen

Almost six weeks had passed since Ludovic had gone back to his wife, and Claudia was missing him cruelly. After the departure of Allegra to England, her mood had swung between a tense, self-torturing anxiety and violent fury and resentment. On the whole, it was less painful and humiliating for her to feel angry with Ludovic for dumping her, and increasingly this was how she forced herself to interpret his behaviour towards her.

Life had not been quite so depressing when she had had the company of Alexander and Allegra. Their cheerful presence had helped her a great deal in maintaining an unruffled calm and confidence. Now, on her own, with a great deal of time on her hands to reflect on everything that had happened, she was beginning to see very clearly what the probable outcome would be. Ludovic called her almost every night, but the calls were getting shorter and shorter, and he sounded increasingly depressed and resigned to what he evidently considered to be his just deserts. He seemed unable to think of very much to say to her, and it was this lack of communication that finally got to Claudia, causing her to weep bitter tears into her pillow after practically every call. Every morning, in the cold light of day, she would tell herself to get a grip, to recognize him for a vacillating, easily manipulated man who had betrayed her at the first sign of trouble. She told herself repeatedly that if she had a shred of pride she would tell him to go to hell and leave her alone to get on with her life without him.

Resolutely, she attended rehearsals of the orchestra and gave her usual private lessons, but each evening found her at home alone, restlessly pacing round the house, waiting for Ludovic to call her. She could not eat, or play her cello for pleasure, or even listen to music. She felt sick with anxiety, and by nine o'clock each evening she was also fairly drunk, which at least had the merit of turning her despair into rage. That bloody evil woman, she thought bitterly, why *should* she have the right to claw him back after all these years? Why? Why? And why should I go on feebly saying that I understand, when I bloody don't? And why should that miserable old cow be allowed to get away with pulling that suicide stunt, and take him from me, just like that? Why? The answer stared her in the face. It's because he believes it's a question of ethics, and he thinks he's doing the right thing. 'But he *isn't*!' she shouted to the empty room. 'He's a two-timing, double-dealing bastard, and I hate him, and his fucking wife!'

She snatched her glass from the table but when she raised it to her lips found that it was empty. Impatiently, she went to the kitchen to refill her glass, and in her haste her sleeve caught the mouthpiece of the clarinet, jutting over the edge of the table. There was a tremendous crash and she cried out in alarm. Turning, she saw her precious blackamoor's head lying on the floor in smithereens, drenched in the spreading pool of water from the glass containing a single red rose that had stood beside it on the table. That, too, had been smashed to pieces and sharp splinters of glass had exploded everywhere. The red rose lay in quivering ruins, its petals like dark blobs of blood on the floor.

The telephone rang, and stepping clumsily over the broken fragments, she went to answer it. '*Oui?*'

'Hello, darling. How are you?'

'Go to hell, Ludovic!' she screamed, her fright and distress turning to violence. 'Leave me alone! I hate you! Do you hear me?' She slammed the phone down and burst into hysterical tears.

For a long time, Claudia lay on the sofa and wept uncontrollably, her heart breaking, all her courage gone. Then, abruptly, her tears ceased. He can't even be bothered to ring back, she told herself coldly. She blew her swollen nose, and getting up, went to the kitchen for a dustpan and brush. Sadly, she swept up the shattered blackamoor's head, and every tiny needle of glass she could locate. Then she got a roll of kitchen paper and mopped up the water on the floor. Turning her attention to the mess on the table, she saw Emma's letter lying in a puddle of water and quickly separated the pages, to prevent them sticking together. I suppose that's something to be thankful for, she thought. At least, *she* seems to be happy; I really must write to her soon.

Three days later, she sat down and wrote a long letter to Emma, telling her everything that had happened. *And now, Allegra has gone to England, Emma, and Phoebe appears to have taken her over completely, and they are all great friends. It seems that I am to have everything taken from me, at the end of the day.*

She went out to post the letter, and when she got back she found Ludovic, waiting at her door. Stiffly, refusing to touch him or even look at him, she unlocked her door and he followed her inside.

'Why didn't you let yourself in?' Her voice sounded remote, icy.

'I don't feel that I have that right, as things are, Claudia.'

'Oh? This is no longer your home, I suppose?' She turned away and retreated to the far side of the table.

'Have you come to give me notice to quit, Ludovic? Is that the purpose of this visit? Does your wife know you're here?' Her voice sounded shrill, brittle, not at all like herself. Horrified at her own capacity for vindictiveness, she felt nonetheless powerless to stop herself from destroying everything that had been so precious to them both. Shaking with tension and anger, she glared at him, her arms crossed. 'You should have instructed your lawyers to write to me, and saved yourself the embarrassment of a meeting. Who knows, maybe you've already been spotted by a snooping journalist, sneaking in here?'

Ludovic listened to her angry words, and watched her miserably, with a deep sense of shock and guilt at the horrifying change his absence had wrought in the woman he loved. He had never before experienced the smallest misunderstanding between himself and Claudia, much less this implacable hostility. He could think of nothing to say that might ameliorate her present attitude. 'Perhaps I'd better go,' he said, his voice barely audible. 'It was probably a mistake to come.'

'Why *did* you come?'

'I came because I love you, Claudia.'

'Oh? I find that increasingly hard to believe.'

'I've been worried sick about you, since we spoke the other night.'

'Really? You didn't ring back, did you?'

'No.'

'I might have done something stupid, like your crazy wife, mightn't I?'

'Yes, you might.' He sighed, and looked away, unable to meet her angry, accusing eyes.

'I suppose you didn't really care. It took you three fucking days to find out, didn't it?'

'Oh, Claudia, please stop it, darling. What are we doing to each other?'

Suddenly, the anger went out of Claudia and she

322

slumped against the table, supporting herself on her hands. 'I don't know,' she whispered; 'and frankly, I don't much care any more.'

Facing her across the table, Ludovic noticed for the first time that something important was missing. 'What happened to the blackamoor?' he asked.

'I broke him.' Claudia's head drooped, and tears poured from her eyes. Ludovic moved quickly to her side and held her close to him. Presently she lifted her tear-stained face to his, and he kissed her. It was as though he had never been away.

In the early morning, Claudia woke to find herself alone in their bed. Ludovic came out of the bathroom, already showered and shaved, and almost dresssed. 'Are you leaving already?' she asked sleepily.

'I have to go to Brussels, darling.'

'Will you be back tonight?'

'No, I'm afraid I can't. I have a late meeting.'

'On Friday, then?'

'I don't think that will be possible.'

She got out of bed without another word, put on her bathrobe and went to the kitchen to make coffee. Ludovic drank his coffee, then kissed her on the cheek, and picked up his briefcase and umbrella. He was mentally already in Brussels. She followed him to the door, pulling her bathrobe tightly around her. 'Ludo?'

'Claudia?'

'We can't do this again, darling. You do realize that, don't you?'

'Why not?'

'Because now, for the first time, I really do feel like a whore.'

He frowned with disbelief. 'How can you say that? You know it's not true.'

'But it's how you've made me *feel*, Ludo.'

'I'm terribly sorry.'

'So am I, more than I can say.'

He took her hand. 'I must go, I'll miss the train. I'll ring you tonight.'

'No, don't do that, Ludo, please. It's better not. Either you're with Flavia, or you're with me. You'll have to choose.'

They looked at each other in silence, and she saw that his eyes were full of pain. Touching his face briefly, she opened the door. After a moment's hesitation, he left.

At Abbot's Court, Phoebe's life had become more than merely bearable, it sometimes hovered on the edge of happiness. No longer isolated in her grief, she found that the lively youthful presence of Allegra seemed to have brought the house to life again, and driven out the evil elements that had threatened to crush her spirit.

Allegra appeared positively to like housework, and when Phoebe got back from delivering Alexander to school each morning, she found the washing-up done, the kitchen floor swept, the beds made and a fresh pot of coffee keeping warm on the hob.

Allegra knew nothing at all about gardening, but was eager to learn, and Phoebe explained to her the principles of pruning. 'It's too early to cut the roses back, or they'll make new growth and the frost will damage them. What we *can* do now is cut out all the dead wood and weak, twiggy bits, and rake out all the rubbish under the bushes.'

'So when do you do the major pruning?'

'In the dead of winter, when the roses are dormant.'

'Fascinating – what a lot you know, Phoebe.'

'Not really,' said Phoebe, modestly. 'I just pick it up as I go along, you know. I read books, too.'

'Isn't it odd?' Allegra carefully removed a thorny brown branch from *Parkdirektor Riggers*, taking care not to get it caught in her long red hair. 'I'm the one studying natural history, but I know next to nothing in the practical, gardening sense.'

Phoebe laughed. 'And I know nothing at all in the academic sense; maybe that makes us a good team.'

'I hope so, Phoebe.'

Phoebe smiled. 'It's so lovely having you here, Allegra. You've made a huge difference to Alex, I can't tell you.'

'He's a terrific boy; it was great having him in Paris. He's awfully like my father, don't you think?'

'Do you really think so? I always think of Ludovic as rather remote, not much in the business of being involved with people, if you know what I mean?'

'I know what you mean, but he's not really like that at all. At least, not to the people he loves.'

'Like Claudia?'

'Claudia, yes; and me.' Allegra looked at Phoebe, trying to judge exactly how far it was wise to go, in discussing her parents' private life with her. 'He loves Emma, too, and Alexander. One can tell.'

'Emma? But he rarely sees her, surely?'

'That's true, of course. But she came once to Paris, and stayed with them.'

'Really? And did you meet her, too?'

Allegra laughed. 'Yes, I did. I was frightfully rude to her, I'm afraid.' She looked at Phoebe shyly. 'I was sorry afterwards, because she's quite harmless, really.'

It was Phoebe's turn to laugh. 'I don't blame you! Nuns are hard to handle, aren't they? They're so unquestioning in their faith, so utterly convinced that their values are the only ones worth having. So incredibly smug; is that what I really mean?' She cut through a dead branch and pulled it out of the thicket. 'Are you a Catholic, Allegra? Like the rest of them?'

'No, I'm nothing so far. I haven't even been baptized, it seems.'

'Good heavens! Why not?'

'They think I should decide for myself, in my own good time, and I agree with them.'

'In that case,' said Phoebe, 'why on earth has Ludovic

sacrificed himself to Flavia in this abject way, if he has no great religious belief himself?'

'I don't know.' Allegra sighed, looking serious. 'I really don't know, Phoebe. I wish I did. I can tell you this, though. It will destroy my mother, if it's to be permanent.'

'It will wreck more lives than just hers,' said Phoebe robustly. 'Mine, for one. I'm absolutely furious with Chris for hijacking Gwen to look after his rotten old mother, if you want to know. Flavia ought to be in a home, really, but Chris will never agree to that, even though I keep telling him he'd better come up with some answers pretty swiftly. I really can't cope here without Gwen for much longer. I never realized how much I depended on her.' She grinned at Allegra. 'Thank goodness you came to help out, just in time, before I threw a mega-wobbly.'

Allegra smiled, amused at the idea of the placid Phoebe doing such a thing. 'You don't seem to be that type, Phoebe.'

'Hah!' said Phoebe darkly. 'I have hidden depths, my dear.'

Allegra's presence was a source of joy to Alexander, too. After his return to Abbot's Court, and before the arrival of Allegra, he had been very worried that Chloe might come back to torment him, but to his intense relief she had not done so. The house had begun to feel friendly and normal again, the inhabitants no longer creeping silently about the place, submerged under the weight of their sorrow, and in Alexander's case, his guilt. His mother, too, had become a different person, and was kind and affectionate towards him. She had ceased to mention the accident, and slowly his feelings of fear and guilt receded as he allowed himself to hope that Phoebe no longer blamed him for Chloe's death. Equally, the absence of Gwen seemed to draw his mother closer to him, and this made it easier for him to distance himself from the grim episodes with his grandmother and Fr Anselm.

Allegra had brought with her laughter, jokes and fun. She usually collected Alexander from school in the afternoon, and after tea they would ride out with the ponies. Allegra rode the larger of the two on account of her long legs, and Alexander would ride Chloe's pony, his own legs trailing.

'Those ponies are too small for any of you now,' said Phoebe. 'We'll have to start looking out for something bigger for you, Alex.'

'A proper hunter?'

'Why not?'

Allegra had brought the recorders with her from Paris, and after supper she and Alex would sit by the fire in the drawing room, and Phoebe would work at her needlepoint and listen, entranced, as they played duets together. 'Carols must sound lovely on the recorder,' she remarked. 'Will you come back for Christmas, Allegra, so that you and Alex can play for me?'

'I'd love to,' said Allegra. 'That is, if Claudia doesn't need me.'

On her return from the Saturday market at Apt, Emma found Claudia's letter in the mailbox. Pascal had dropped her at the house and gone on to the dairy, to do the evening milking and shut up for the night. She carried the bags of shopping into the kitchen and put everything away, before sitting down at the table to read the letter. She read the three pages twice, then put them back into the envelope and sat staring into space, deeply disturbed and saddened by what Claudia had told her. Horrified by the news of Flavia's attempted suicide, Emma's immediate reaction was that her mother must have been in a state of absolute despair even to have contemplated such an action, in the certain knowledge that such a mortal sin would gravely endanger her chances of everlasting life. Poor unhappy old woman, she thought, tears filling her eyes; what a ghastly mess she has made of her own life, as well as doing her best to undermine the lives of practically everyone around her, including mine. I wonder if she really did mean to kill herself, or whether it was actually just a dramatic way of drawing attention to herself, a means of dragging Dad away from Claudia. That must have been it; I'm sure she'd never risk her immortal soul by killing herself, however desperate she felt. Still, whatever her motives, it was still a cry of anguish, poor thing, one can't get away from that. She felt terribly sorry for her mother, but beneath her genuine concern for Flavia lay a deeper, and more urgent question, the destruction of the happiness of her father and Claudia. Their deep love for each other had clearly demonstrated to Emma the beauty and fulfilment of two lives joined in an intensely committed relationship. It was their example, she was sure, that had given her the courage to take her own personal leap in the dark with Pascal.

When Pascal came in, she showed him the letter, and he read it carefully. 'How terrible,' he said quietly. 'Your poor mother, what a dreadful thing to do.'

'Indeed,' said Emma sadly, and a tear slid down her cheek.

Pascal sat down, and took her hand in his. 'Do you think she really meant to do away with herself, Emma?'

Emma shook her head, then blew her nose. 'No, I don't think she did. It would have been an entirely unbelievable thing for her to do. If only for the sake of the good opinion of her brothers and her sister, she wouldn't have done it on purpose.' She sighed. 'All the same, it *was* a cry for help, wasn't it?'

'Yes, obviously. What a mess, for everyone concerned.'

'Catherine Saint-Denis was quite right when she said

that Dad had gone back to my mother, wasn't she? Claudia seems to think it's for ever.'

'Poor woman,' he said. 'She sounds pretty desolate, doesn't she?'

'It's all wrong,' said Emma. 'It shouldn't happen. I can't believe there's nothing to be done.' She looked at Pascal, her face full of concern and dismay. 'Can't we do something, Pascal?'

'Well, I'm absolutely in favour of love, Emma, but I'm not at all in favour of sticking one's nose into other people's lives.'

'What do you mean?'

'I mean, it's better to let them sort out their troubles for themselves.'

'Pascal?'

'What?'

'Have you forgotten *everything* I told you about my mother, and how it was between her and Dad?'

'No, I haven't forgotten,' said Pascal, 'but nevertheless I imagine that your father must have his own reasons for deciding to toe the received line, both religious and political.'

'You're not serious?'

'I am, absolutely. His career was very probably in jeopardy.'

'Pascal! How can you say that? He wouldn't consider that *at all* important, any more than Claudia would!'

'OK. It's the religious thing, then. It has to be one or the other, doesn't it?'

'God, I hope not,' said Emma. 'That really would be the ultimate hypocrisy. I can't believe he'd do such a thing.'

'Don't you think he feels he's got to be there to prevent your mother harming herself again? Perhaps he's doing it for your sake, and your brother's, too. No-one would much like to have a suicide for a parent, would they?'

'If that's the case, I think he's making a terrible mistake.'

'Do you really?'

'Yes, Pascal, I do. No-one should have to be his brother's keeper. And what about poor Claudia? And Allegra? Don't they count at all?'

That evening, before they went to bed, Emma decided to talk to her brother in London. The telephone was answered almost immediately, with its owner's customary lack of grace. 'Yes?'

'Christian?'

'Is that you, Emma? Are you in Britanny?'

'No, I'm in Provence.'

'Oh, really? Have you been transferred?'

'No, I haven't, Chris. Well, yes, I suppose I have, in a way. It's too difficult to explain. Listen, we need to talk.'

'Do we, Emma? What about?'

'About Dad, of course.'

'What about him?'

'Christian, stop being so obtuse, please, and listen to me.'

'OK.'

'I think it's quite appalling that Dad should be the victim of Mother's emotional blackmail, and even worse that Claudia should be destroyed in the process.'

There was a long silence. When Christian spoke, his voice was cold. 'I can see that you have considered only the rather attractive romantic aspects of the situation, Emma. Does it not occur to you that the moral and religious implications are much more important?'

'What on earth are you trying to say, Chris? Are you implying that Mother is blameless, and has a moral right to reclaim Dad as her husband, in every sense of the word? You must know that that's a

330

complete non-starter, and really rather obscene in the circumstances.'

'I don't know anything of the sort, Emma. It's quite sad about Claudia, I agree. She's a nice woman, and I like her. Nonetheless, she's been involved in an adulterous relationship for years, and she shouldn't complain if Dad repents and goes back to his lawful wife. I'm talking about the well-being of *our mother* here, Emma.'

'I know you are, more's the pity.'

'Look, old girl, you don't really understand these things, being a nun. How can you, with so little experience of real life?'

'For your information, Christian,' said Emma crisply, 'there are quite a lot of things you don't actually know about me. My life is no longer the open book you so patronizingly assume it to be, and I have a great deal more experience than you realize.'

'Oh, really? Since when? You do surprise me.'

'Well, stop being surprised and let's discuss this business properly, and see what we can do to *help* sort things out, shall we?'

Christian sighed. 'Look, Em, don't rock the boat, for Christ's sake. Ma is so sweet and happy now, it's rather touching to see her, and she's got Gwen looking after her, so she's never left alone.'

'What about Phoebe? She can't run that huge place without Gwen, surely?'

'Phoebe's fine. You may find this hard to believe, Em, but she's got Allegra staying with her just now. They get on like a house on fire.'

'Yes, I know,' said Emma quietly. 'Claudia told me.'

'So why don't we just keep our heads down, and be thankful, OK?'

'All right, Chris. I can see that it's pointless trying to convince you otherwise.'

'You got it, Em. Goodbye.' He rang off, before Emma

could reply. She looked at the dead phone in her hand, frowning, then hung it on its hook.

Pascal looked at her sympathetically, then poured wine into a glass and handed it to her. 'If this means such a lot to you, my love, perhaps you *should* go to London and see if there's anything you can do?'

'Would you mind, if I did?'

'No, of course not, if you really think it will do any good.'

'I'll think about it; see how I feel tomorrow.'

At the end of each working day, Ludovic returned to his impersonal and ugly service flat in Brussels. He drank two very strong whiskies, then lay down on his narrow single bed, closed his eyes and waited for the hours to pass. He was finding it difficult to believe that it was possible to endure such anguish on a daily basis and not die of it. Physically he felt extremely unwell, and sometimes so weak that he could barely stand, but much worse were the tormented thoughts that perpetually filled his mind. Over and over again, like an endlessly replayed videotape, he relived the events of his last night with Claudia. He could see her quite clearly, leaning on the table, her beautiful hair falling on either side of her bent head, her tears splashing onto her outspread hands, as she said, 'I broke him,' in response to his query about the blackamoor's head. Just as I have broken her, he thought. Dear God, what have I done to her? 'For the first time', she had said, 'I feel like a whore.' And what does that make me, Claudia? A cheat and an adulterer? He recalled vividly how passionately and tenderly they had loved each other that night, after the weeks of separation and loneliness, and his body responded fiercely to the memory. He turned his aching head from side to side, trying without success to deny the rush of feeling that flowed through him, then, with a groan of despair, he turned over and waited for the agonizing moment to pass.

At three in the morning he woke, cold and stiff, still wearing his shirt and trousers. He switched on the light, and went to the kitchen to make some coffee. Barefoot, he took the mug to the bleak little study, with the intention of looking through some papers. Instead, he sat on the hard leather chair with the warm mug in his hands, staring at his naked feet. Did I really think that I could find a way to go on seeing her, he thought; sleeping with her from time to time, under the rose? Is that what I really planned to do? Was I slowly evolving a way of life in which I was publicly reconciled with Flavia, but taking advantage of Claudia when the opportunity presented itself? What kind of a criminal does that make me? he asked himself. He remembered her last, cruel words to him. 'Either you're with Flavia, or you're with me,' she had said. 'You'll have to choose.' He felt the fleeting touch of Claudia's cool hand against his face, and then the intrusive image of Flavia came back to haunt him, as it always did. He saw her in her bed, fragile, distraught, smelling of stale gin, slumped against her pillows, her wrist in the heavy bloodstained bandage. With a sickening, leaden certainty, he knew where his duty lay, and what his choice would have to be.

For a few days, Emma tried to convince herself that Christian was probably right and that it was best to let sleeping dogs lie. Pascal, too, seemed to be on the side of non-interference, and she could understand both these points of view, without necessarily agreeing with either of them. Finally, she decided that it would do no harm to telephone Claudia, and see how she was. She waited until the hour of the cheap rate, then dialled Claudia's number.

'*Oui?*' Claudia's voice sounded guarded, subdued.

'Claudia, it's me, Emma.'

'Oh, hello. How are you, Emma?'

'I'm fine, what about you? I got your letter, Claudia.

I don't have to tell you how sorry I am about all this trouble.'

'Thank you, Emma, it's kind of you. Things are even worse now, as a matter of fact.'

'Why? What happened?'

'Ludo came to see me last week. I behaved like a hysterical idiot, Emma. I really wrecked everything, once and for all. I told him not to contact me again. I said that he would have to choose between me and Flavia.'

'What did he say?' asked Emma gently.

'Nothing. He left.'

'Did you mean it, Claudia?'

'No, of course I didn't. You know how it is with me, don't you, Emma? I'll never love anyone else.'

'*You* could always contact *him*, couldn't you?'

'No, I don't think I could do that.' There was a slight pause, then Claudia spoke again. 'Don't worry about me, Emma. I'll just have to get over it, won't I? It's all my own stupid fault. It was always me who insisted that proper legal arrangements weren't necessary. I've brought it all on myself, haven't I?'

'No, of course you haven't,' said Emma firmly. 'It'll be all right, you'll see, Claudia.' She said goodbye, promising to call again soon. She crossed the room and put her arms round Pascal's waist, as he stood at the stove softening onions and garlic in a frying pan.

'OK, I get the message,' he said, and laughed. 'When you make up your mind to do something, Emma, there's no stopping you, is there?'

'Like getting into bed with you, my darling?'

'That, too.'

Later that night, as Pascal and Emma were having their supper, his father telephoned and asked to speak to Emma. Greatly to her surprise, and delight, he had been asked to approach her on behalf of a friend, with the offer of a commission.

'It's rather a nice place, Emma; a *château*, eighteenth century. I should imagine there's enough restoration work to keep you busy for several years. Would you be interested?'

'Yes, of course I would. Thank you, Paul, how kind of you to mention my name to them.'

'Good, that's excellent. Shall I give them your number, so that they can contact you direct?'

'The thing is, Paul, I have to go to London, and I don't quite know how long I'll be away. But they could speak to Pascal in the meantime, and maybe come over and see my work here? Then I could get in touch with them when I get back. How would that be?'

'No problem, I'm sure. I'll speak to them. Have a good trip, my dear.'

Emma thanked him and replaced the phone. She sat down at the table. 'What a marvellous man your father is; I really do love him. I hope you'll grow to be just like him.'

'You'll have a long time to wait.'

'I don't mind waiting.'

'You can't go to London in those clothes, Emma. You look like a tramp. We'll have to go to Aix, and get you some more suitable things.'

'Whatever for? I'm perfectly happy wearing trousers and a sweater, so why should anyone else object?'

'Well, I do, for one. I wouldn't want your father to think you were living in some scruffy New Age set-up.'

Emma laughed. 'Isn't that rather what we are doing?'

'No, not at all. *They* live on social security; *we* work jolly hard.'

'OK, but won't new clothes cost an awful lot?'

'Probably. We can set it against your future earnings, if you feel so strongly about it.'

'That's a very good idea; I'd forgotten about that.'

In the event, they had a most enjoyable day in Aix, shopping in the smart boutiques in the narrow streets off the cours Mirabeau. To Emma's amusement, Pascal took a typical Parisian's interest in all the purchases, and had strong ideas about what suited her best. They bought a rather chic light wool suit, the colour of mulberries, with a fitted jacket, a narrow skirt just above the knee, and matching opaque tights. To complement this outfit, Emma chose flat-heeled, knee-length oxblood leather boots, and a tote-bag in the same colour. To go under the jacket, Pascal chose a pale-grey ribbed-wool sweater, and a black silk shirt.

'We must have spent a fortune,' said Emma, as they carried the smart bags to the van.

'We haven't finished yet.' Pascal looked at her, and grinned. 'Your underwear leaves much to be desired, my love, don't you agree?'

'Pig!' retorted Emma. 'Yours is no big deal!'

'Very true, but mine is not going to be scrutinized by prying eyes, and yours probably is.'

'OK, point taken.'

They bought underwear, some extra tights, and a nightdress, in a chain store for the sake of economy, then they took themselves to lunch in the cours Mirabeau. The lunch was delicious, protracted and extremely expensive by their standards. They began with a salad of warm duck livers, then had sea bass, stuffed with fennel and grilled over charcoal. With it, they drank a chilled Pouilly Fuissé. They lingered over the goat's cheese and the ripe purple figs, and drank their coffee slowly, enjoying the rare luxury of the pursuit of pleasure while the rest of the world hurried about its business. Four o'clock chimed from several nearby bells. They finished their coffee, and Pascal asked for the bill.

'We'll get a parking ticket,' said Emma. 'I think we're already over the time.'

'Emma, there's something I want to give you, if you'll have it.' He took something from his pocket and offered it to her. It was a small, delicate ring, with two linked

336

silver hearts on a narrow band. 'It's not worth anything at all. I think it came out of a cracker, but I'd like you to have it, if you don't think that's idiotic.'

Emma took the ring. 'It's lovely,' she said, and slid it onto her middle finger. 'I don't think it's idiotic at all.'

'Wrong finger.' Carefully, Pascal removed the ring and slipped it onto the third finger of her left hand. 'There,' he said. 'It fits perfectly.'

Emma held up her hand and looked at the ring. 'Pascal,' she said, smiling at him tenderly, 'I am really quite surprised at you. First, you take me out and make me dress up in a thoroughly conventional manner, spending a bomb in the process, and now you have given me what I take to be an engagement ring. I hope that doesn't mean that we're going to dwindle into clones of our parents, does it?'

'No chance,' said Pascal, and laughed, a little self-consciously. 'I'm just looking after my interests.'

'What do you mean by that?'

'I'll tell you when you get back, Emma.'

Chapter Seventeen

Emma arrived at Heathrow on the following Friday afternoon and took the Piccadilly line into London. It was nearly six o'clock by the time she reached her mother's house. For a moment she stood on the pavement looking up at it, wondering a little nervously what she might find on the other side of the door, then she went up the steps and rang the bell.

After a short pause, the door was opened by Gwen, who peered at Emma suspiciously, before realizing who she was. 'Mercy! It's you, Emma! Come in, child!'

'Hello, Gwen.' Emma entered the house. Gwen closed the door, and the two women stood, eyeing each other cautiously, while a dozen questions hung in the air.

Gwen spoke first. 'Well, Emma, what a surprise. What happened? Did the Mother Superior throw you out?'

Emma laughed. 'Not exactly. I threw myself out, as a matter of fact, and not a moment too soon.'

'Oh, well, fancy.' Gwen gave an embarrassed little cough. 'Would you like a cup of tea? Your mother's out at present. She's away down to St Botolph's.'

'Thanks, Gwen. Tea would be lovely.'

They went to the kitchen and Emma sat down at the plastic-topped table, while Gwen put the kettle on to boil, and took cups from the cupboard.

'You'd better tell me everything that's been happening, Gwen, before Mother gets back.'

'Yes, you're right, I had better.' Gwen made the tea, put the pot on the table, and sat down. She filled the cups and handed one to Emma. 'It was all that unpleasantness in the papers that did it,' she said. 'This brash young woman pushed her way into the house with a photographer, and they took these pictures of your poor mother looking terrible, hysterical really. They told her what your father had been up to all these years, with that friend of his, in *Paris*.' She managed to make the city of light sound like a place of ill repute.

Emma drank her tea thoughtfully. 'Surely, Gwen,' she said at last, 'Mother must have had some idea that Dad had a life of his own, outside the confines of their marriage?'

Gwen looked at Emma, severely. 'No, I don't think she was ever aware of anything of the sort. And if she did suspect anything, she was able to close her mind to it. It was having the truth rammed down her throat that tipped her over the edge. You know how she's always been, Emma, about the Blessed Sacraments, the sanctity of marriage and all that, don't you?'

'But what if it wasn't a marriage at all, Gwen, in the full sense of the word?'

Gwen looked prim. 'I wouldn't know about that, Emma. Never having been married myself, I'm not qualified to have an opinion on the subject, am I? All I know is that it was a dreadful shock to the poor wee thing. I suppose you know that she tried to do away with herself, don't you?'

Emma sighed, and put down her cup. 'Yes, I heard about it. Did she really mean it, Gwen, or was it just done to give everyone a good fright, and bring them running?'

'Emma! What a cynical attitude to take! I'm surprised at you, I really am.'

'Are you, Gwen? *Honestly?*'

'Well, she *is* your mother, dear, when all's said and done.'

'That's true, of course, and I'm very sorry that she's had to suffer this humiliation. But there's another side to it, Gwen, you know that.'

'Oh? And what might that be?'

'Poor old Dad. His life is in ruins, too, isn't it?'

Gwen gave a derisive snort. 'If it is, it's no more than he deserves, playing fast and loose all these years. At his age, too.'

'Gwen,' said Emma, smiling. 'You've been reading the papers, haven't you?'

Gwen flushed darkly, and turned angry blue eyes on Emma. 'It's no laughing matter, my girl.' She lowered her voice. 'Your mother could quite easily have killed herself. She cut herself very badly. It was a mercy that Father Gordon found her, and got the doctor. He was only just in time, in my opinion. There was blood all over the sheets. It took me days to bleach out the stains.'

'I'm sorry, Gwen. I'm not laughing, really. You must have been having a horrible time.'

'Yes, well, I have. I'm glad you've come to help at last. It's high time I got back to Abbot's Court. I'm really needed there. Everyone seems to have forgotten about poor Phoebe, don't they?'

Before Emma could reply, they heard the front door bang. There was the sound of light, quick footsteps and Flavia came into the kitchen. Emma got to her feet. 'Hello, Mother,' she said. 'How are you?'

Flavia stood in the doorway, speechless with surprise and shock at the sight of her daughter. She stared at Emma's bare head and short dark hair, then at her smart new clothes. Slowly her horrified gaze travelled downwards and came to rest accusingly on Emma's knees, clearly exposed below the hem of her skirt. 'What is the meaning of this?' she quavered, her voice shaking, her face taut with disapproval. 'What are you doing here, dressed like a whore?'

'I've come to see you, Mother.'

'Don't be impertinent, Emma. You know perfectly well what I mean.' Flavia's temper rose, as did her voice. 'You've bloody well been expelled from La Falaise, is that it? Is that it? After all I've done for you, after all our prayers and intercessions for you, is *this* to be my reward? How could you do this to me, Emma? After all I've suffered at the hands of your father, why have you come to torment me, and bring even more shame and disgrace on me? How could you do it, how *could* you?' Her voice cracked, and she raised a hand to her forehead, closing her eyes melodramatically.

'Oh, do shut up, Mother, and stop jumping to conclusions, for heaven's sake. Sit down and have some tea.'

Flavia's eyes snapped open suspiciously. 'What do you mean, "jumping to conclusions"? What are you trying to tell me? If you haven't been expelled, why are you dressed in that immodest fashion? You look exactly like a low-class tart.'

Refusing to be goaded by her mother's insulting words, Emma waited until she had sat down, and Gwen had poured her some tea. 'I left the abbey some time ago, Mother, of my own volition.'

'Oh? And what possessed you to do such a wicked thing? I suppose you were involved in a dirty lesbian relationship, were you? Everyone knows what nuns get up to in the privacy of their cells, don't they? What happened, did someone come in and find you at it?'

Emma looked at her mother with a mixture of pity and contempt, and shook her head incredulously. 'I left for the right reasons, Mother. I no longer had a vocation. In fact, I doubt very much that I ever had one, not in the true sense of the word. It was as simple as that.'

Flavia banged down her cup in its saucer, spilling

341

her tea as she did so. Her fury, disappointment and chagrin were expressed in a long, hysterical tirade on the subject of failed nuns, their deviousness, dishonour and sexual proclivities, that was alarming to witness and degrading to hear. Emma and Gwen sat grimly in their seats, stunned, powerless to stop the flow of bile that poured from the murky depths of Flavia's bitter heart. At last, exhausted, her eloquence failed her, and she began to sob noisily, covering her face with her hands.

Hastily, Gwen got to her feet and put an arm round Flavia's shaking shoulders. 'Come along now, Mrs McGrath, you'll be making yourself ill again, and we don't want that, do we? Let's get you to bed, shall we? Then I'll bring you up a hot-water bottle and some warm milk.'

Flavia allowed herself to be persuaded by Gwen, but at the door she paused and looked back at Emma, red-eyed and unforgiving. 'You're exactly like your father,' she said coldly. 'He is an unbeliever, a lapsed Catholic, an adulterous womanizer and an offender against God's holy laws. One can only assume that you are cast in the same sinful mould, in spite of all my love and care of you, Emma.' She took Gwen's arm, and made what she imagined to be a dignified exit.

The door closed behind them, and Emma stared at it with disbelief. You evil old cow, she said to herself, why the hell have I gone to the trouble and expense of coming here at all? What am I trying to do here, anyway? She gazed at her hands, lying on the table before her, twisting Pascal's ring on her finger, finding it difficult to believe that they had been separated for only a few short hours. She looked at the kitchen clock: seven-twenty. It'll be eight-twenty at home, she thought; he'll have finished the milking now, and be preparing supper. She sighed, and got up from the table. She left the kitchen and went out through the glazed door at the rear of the hall that led into the small back garden. She paced aimlessly round the walls of this sad neglected place, trying to sort out her thoughts and decide what, if anything, she could do to help in the present situation, or whether her presence would merely serve to make matters worse. I should have realized that Mother didn't know I'd left the abbey, she said to herself. I suppose no-one knows, except Dad and Claudia. Poor old thing, it was obviously an awful shock for her, and she's had her fair share of those lately, God knows. Remembering her mother's pronouncements on the state of the spiritual health of herself and her father, Emma smiled wryly. Isn't it strange, she asked herself, how frequently very pious people use offensive words like 'adulterous womanizer' or 'whore' in their condemnation of quite ordinary fallible mortals? I wonder whether they are themselves so very blameless, when such harsh epithets spring so readily to their repellent little minds?

At the end of the garden, she turned and looked back towards the house. A light sprang on in the landing window, then Gwen appeared and half-drew the curtains. Emma gazed up at her, hoping for some sort of reassuring signal, but none came. Sadly, she returned to the house, picked up her grip from the hall and went upstairs to her old bedroom on the top floor.

Flavia, comfortably ensconced in her bed and leaning against her soft pile of snowy pillows, smoothed the white sheet with her blue-veined hand, immaculately manicured and blazing with diamonds. Since Ludovic's re-entry into her life, she had begun to take her appearance rather seriously, visiting the hairdresser on a weekly basis, and paying greater attention to her wardrobe. Quite what her motives were in this respect was not at all clear to her. Vaguely, she supposed that it was meant to reassure Ludovic that she was still an attractive woman, content to be his wife, and stand by him in spite of the vicious public revelations of his adulterous liaison and bastard child.

Gwen hung Flavia's clothes in the wardrobe, then came quietly to the foot of the bed. 'If you're feeling a bit stronger now, perhaps I ought to go down and start the supper?'

Flavia ignored the suggestion. 'Why did she come, Gwen?' she asked.

'I suppose Christian must have told her you weren't well. She came to help, I expect.'

'Why didn't Christian tell me that she'd broken her vows?'

'Perhaps he didn't know himself. It was a complete surprise to *me*, you know.'

Flavia glanced suspiciously at Gwen, as if she doubted the truth of this. 'But surely, *someone* must have known?' she said. 'Ludovic must know; they've always been very thick, haven't they?'

'I can't say I've noticed that, particularly.'

Flavia shook her head, dismissively. 'He must have known. Why didn't he tell me?'

'Perhaps he thought it might upset you, and decided not to.'

'Upset me?' Flavia's voice rose slightly, and Gwen raised a placating hand. '*Upset* me?' She glared at Gwen, her face flushed with righteous anger. 'It will very likely *destroy* me, Gwen. She's done it on purpose, to spite me. Why else would she do such a terrible thing?'

'Well,' said Gwen, as soothingly as she could, 'people do change their minds, don't they? It's not the end of the world, I dare say.'

Staring Flavia in the face was the appalling prospect of her personal humiliation when both her brothers, not to mention Fr Gordon and the nuns at the convent, found out about Emma's disgrace. 'It may not be the end of *her* wicked, fornicating and immoral world,' she said bitterly, 'but it may bloody well be the end of mine.'

'I must go and get started on the cooking,' said Gwen flatly, unmoved by Flavia's capacity for self-torture. 'Mr McGrath will be here in time for dinner, I expect.'

'Oh, will he?' Flavia sounded quite astonished. 'Is it Friday? It must be Friday? Yes, of course; I went to confession.'

And you'll doubtless go again pretty soon, if you can't stop thinking such filthy thoughts, said Gwen to herself. 'Yes, it's Friday. Will you be coming down? Or shall I bring your meal up for you?'

Flavia shrank into her pillows, and closed her eyes. 'I'll stay here, Gwen, if you don't mind. I don't want to have to talk to my daughter just now. I've had about all I can endure for one day.'

'Very well,' said Gwen. 'I'll tell them you have a headache, shall I?' At the door, she turned back. 'Try not to be too hard on Emma, Mrs McGrath. I'm sure she means well, and is trying to help. She's still the same person, isn't she, even if she is no longer a nun?'

'Thank you, Gwen.' Flavia nodded dismissively, and Gwen left the room. Flavia turned her head and gazed at the picture of Emma, so serious and beautiful in her habit at the Clothing Ceremony. She stretched out a hand and turned the photograph face down on the night-table, then sank back against her pillows and let the bitter disappointed tears fall.

Ludovic arrived at the house just before eight-thirty. He let himself in, took off his waterproof and hung it up. He could hear voices through the half-open kitchen door, and assuming that Flavia was in there with Gwen, he went quietly into the dining room to fix himself a drink. The table was laid for two, as usual, and he poured himself a whisky and carried it to the sitting room. A small coal fire smouldered sulkily in the grate, sending a column of dense white acrid-smelling smoke up the chimney. He considered giving it a poke, decided not to interfere, and sat down in one of the armchairs. Staring at the sullen fire, he slowly drank his whisky and tormented himself by thinking about Claudia, and visualizing what she would probably be doing at this very moment. Warmed by the whisky, but feeling no less miserable, he took the evening paper from his pocket, unfolded it and scanned the creased pages in a desultory manner.

The door opened, and he looked up, expecting to see Flavia. For a few seconds, he did not recognize the young woman who came into the room, and half-rose from his seat politely, wondering who she might be.

'Hello, Dad.'

'Emma! It's *you*, darling! What a surprise; when did you get here?' Swiftly, he crossed the room and they hugged each other, laughing, though in fact Ludovic felt deeply moved, so great was his pleasure at seeing her.

'I got here this afternoon. I didn't realize you'd be here; it's wonderful.' She kissed his cheek, and hugged him again.

'Let me look at you, darling.' He held her away from him, the better to take in her new appearance. 'My God, Emma, what a transformation; my little ugly duckling has turned into a swan. You look absolutely lovely, my dearest child.'

Emma laughed. 'Was I really such an ugly duckling, Dad?'

'Yes, you were, to my mind, in those killjoy medieval clothes.' He looked at her seriously, his eyes dark. 'It nearly broke my heart to see you disappearing behind those prison walls, my love.'

'And now I'm breaking Mother's heart. It seems that no-one told her that I'd left the abbey. She was pretty upset when she realized what I'd done. In fact, she was so angry with me that she had to go to bed. She won't be coming down for supper.' Emma looked at her father, and smiled ironically. 'Needless to say, she is quite convinced that I got the chuck for some evil misdemeanour.'

'Yes,' said Ludovic sympathetically, 'that would be par for the course. It's how her mind works, I'm afraid.'

'She said that I look like a whore, Dad. Do you think I do?'

'No, of course I don't, darling. And neither do you, do you?'

'No, I don't. But it hurts, just the same, doesn't it?'

'Don't let it get to you. It's the only way to handle it, Emma. I should know.'

'Yes, of course.'

They stared despondently at each other, not wishing to be too disloyal to Flavia, but at the same time aligning themselves against her malevolence towards them both.

Ludovic picked up his empty glass. 'I'm going to get myself another drink, Emma. What about you? Can I get you anything?'

'Thanks, Dad, I'll have some wine with dinner. I'd better go and give Gwen a hand. She's going to take Mother's supper up on a tray.'

'Sounds like a good idea,' said Ludovic. 'I must go up and see her, I suppose.' He put a hand on Emma's cheek and smiled at her. 'It's a great comfort that you're here, darling. I'm so glad you came.'

'So am I,' said Emma; 'even if it's only to see *you*.'

Ludovic got himself a fresh drink, and went upstairs to Flavia's room. He knocked on the door, and went in. She was lying against her lacy pile of pillows, looking quite pretty in the soft, flattering light of the bedside lamp. 'Good evening, my dear,' he said. 'I hope you had a pleasant week?' He sat down in the small Victorian armchair by the window, and took a sip of his drink.

Flavia looked at his glass. 'Didn't you bring me a drink, Ludovic?'

'Oh, sorry! I thought you kept a supply up here?'

'Well, I do.' Flavia sounded peevish, defensive. 'It would have been civilized if you had offered me a drink, that's all.'

'I beg your pardon, my dear. Can I get you one, now?'

Flavia shook her head pettishly, and Ludovic observed that she already had a half-full glass on her night-table. He cleared his throat. 'It's a very nice surprise, having a visit from Emma, isn't it?'

'Do you really think so, Ludovic?'

'Yes, I do.'

'Why didn't you tell me that she had been expelled from the abbey?'

'She wasn't expelled, Flavia.' Ludovic's voice remained quiet, but firm. 'She left of her own accord.'

'How do you know that? Have you proof? Did the Mother Abbess tell you so?'

'Flavia, I hope you're not suggesting that our daughter is a liar?'

'That is exactly what I *am* suggesting. She was always secretive and devious, even as a child.' She looked at Ludovic, her blue eyes gleaming with malicious triumph. 'She's just like you've always been, a cheat and a liar, and incapable of keeping her vows.'

'Flavia,' said Ludovic patiently, 'please try not to prejudge Emma. I believe that there were many reasons why she felt unable to live according to the Rule any longer. At least you should give her the opportunity to explain her decision to you, in her own good time, don't you think?'

'Vows are vows, Ludovic. That's something you've been able to forget quite easily when it suited you, isn't it?'

'And mercy and compassion, understanding and forgiveness are equally important, aren't they?'

'That's true, Ludovic, but first it's essential that the sinner repents, and experiences genuine remorse, just like you did, darling.' Suddenly, the facile tears slid down her cheeks, and he saw, with a mixture of revulsion and pity, that a trail of mucus ran from her nose. Silently, he took his handkerchief from his pocket and handed it to her.

There was a tap on the door, and Gwen came in, carrying Flavia's supper on a tray. Flavia blew her nose and peered at Gwen, red-eyed, waif-like, pathetic, and Gwen shot a look of vexation in Ludovic's direction. He got to his feet and left the room, without another word.

'Sit up, there's a good girl, and have your nice supper.'

'I'm sorry, Gwen, I couldn't possibly. I'm too upset.' Flavia dabbed at her eyes.

'Just try a little. You must keep up your strength.' Gwen put the tray down, and lifted the cover from the dish. A tantalizing smell of prawn curry filled the air.

For a moment Flavia was severely tempted. 'Really, Gwen. It should be cod on a Friday, shouldn't it?'

'Prawns make a nice change, and they're quite cheap these days,' replied Gwen persuasively.

'No, no, I couldn't possibly. Please take it away.'

'All right, if you say so. Would you like some pudding?'

'Well, perhaps a little.'

Gwen picked up the rejected tray and left the room.

Flavia closed her eyes, feeling martyred but nonetheless virtuous, and her stomach rumbled in protest. She leaned over the side of the bed, opened the door to the cupboard beneath her night-table and, taking out the brandy bottle, topped up her glass. She replaced the bottle, reached for the reserve supply of her favourite ginger nuts, and munched her way through the remains of the pack.

After supper, Emma cleared the table and helped Gwen with the washing-up. There was a feeling of constraint between them. Gwen seemed ill at ease and faintly disapproving, as if she were heartily sick of them all, and losing patience. I can't say I blame her, thought

Emma, she's pig-in-the-middle, poor woman. She picked up the coffee tray, said good night to Gwen and went in search of her father. She found him in the sitting room watching the TV news. The small coal fire had managed to struggle into life and now gave off quite a cheerful glow, if not a blaze. Emma put the tray on the low table, and poured the coffee. She handed a cup to Ludovic, and sat down on the sofa, tucking her legs beneath her. 'Now,' she said, 'we ought to talk, Dad.'

'Oh, dear. Must we?' Ludovic sighed, and switched off the TV.

Watching him, Emma saw how drawn he appeared, old, and somehow diminished. 'Are you OK, Dad? You don't look at all well.'

'I don't *feel* particularly well, Emma. In fact, I feel pretty ghastly, most of the time.'

'You're not ill?'

He shook his head, and smiled. 'No, I'm not ill. Not in the physical sense, anyway.'

'That's what I thought. It's Claudia, isn't it?'

Ludovic raised anguished eyes to hers, then turned away towards the fire, saying nothing. Emma put down her cup, and got up from the sofa. She knelt at her father's knee, forcing him to look at her. 'This has got to stop, Dad. It's killing Claudia, and I can see that it's killing you, too.'

'What do you mean, it's killing Claudia? How do you know that, Emma?'

'She wrote to me, and we spoke on the phone.'

'Did she tell you about our last meeting?'

'Yes, she did.'

'Did she tell you that she told me that she wanted me out of her life?'

'Not exactly, Dad. She told me that she had been stupid and hysterical, and had said that you would have to make a choice, between herself and Mother.'

'That's exactly right, yes.'

350

'She didn't mean it, Dad.'

'Did she tell you that, Emma?'

'Yes, she did. She also told me that she'd never love anyone but you, darling, and I believe her. She was terribly sad.'

There was a long silence. Emma leaned against Ludovic's knees, and gazed into the fire, waiting for him to speak.

'Marriage can be an appallingly difficult business, Emma. I can't regret marrying your mother, because if I hadn't done so I wouldn't have had you for a daughter, or Alexander for a grandson. Equally, I can never regret for a second my life with Claudia, or the birth of Allegra.'

'Exactly,' said Emma quickly; 'and now, your first loyalty has to be to Claudia, of course. You love her, and she loves you. It's utterly wrong that you should be parted like this. It's cruel and obscene, and totally unnecessary, in my opinion.'

Ludovic smiled and put a gentle hand on her head. 'How is it that you know so much about the ethics of love, Emma?'

'Because I'm in love myself. I know exactly how it feels, Dad, and I can't bear the idea that you and Claudia should be torn apart for the wrong reasons. God knows, people who really do love each other are pretty thin on the ground, aren't they?'

'You've noticed?'

'How can one not?'

'I agree with almost everything you say, Emma, and if you were in my shoes I'd probably say exactly the same to you.'

'So, what's the problem? Surely, you can find a way to be with Claudia again, at least for most of the time?'

'The huge and insurmountable problem is your mother. There's no getting away from the fact that I have betrayed her, ruined her life, deprived her of her self-respect and reduced her to a hysterical wreck. I can't leave her again, now, you must see that?'

'As far as I can remember, she's always been pretty much of a hysterical wreck, so what's new? I don't agree that you can't go back to Claudia. You *must* go, Dad. Can't you see that it's the right thing to do? If it comes to the crunch with Gwen, I could always stay here with Mother for a bit, until things calm down, couldn't I?'

Ludovic shook his head. 'No, that's out of the question. I couldn't allow you to do that.'

'Why not? She'd soon settle down, and then I could go home.'

'Emma, are we going to sit here all night, arguing, while you arrange my life for me?'

Emma laughed. 'Probably. Why not? We haven't had a proper talk for years, have we?'

'In that case,' said Ludovic, 'why don't you put some more of that feeble coal on the fire, while I get a drink. How about you?'

'Thanks, a brandy would be lovely.'

Emma did her best to encourage the fire, Ludovic came back with the drinks, and they settled down again, Emma sitting on the floor at her father's feet. 'Tell me what's been happening to you, Emma. I must say that for a former nun you seem to hold some pretty radical views.'

'It's quite a long story – it might take all night. Are you sure you want to hear it?'

'Try me.'

'Well,' said Emma, taking a sip of her brandy, 'after I left the abbey, I did rather a wonderful thing. I went on the *transhumance*.'

'What's that?'

'It's a long, slow walk through Provence, taking thousands of sheep from their lowland winter pastures up to their summer grazing on the high alpine slopes.'

'How interesting. Did you enjoy it?'

'Yes, I did. It was exactly what I needed, to help me to see my life for what it was, and get rid of all the confused mental baggage I'd been carrying around for so long. The whole thing was an absolute revelation to me, Dad; the stunning landscapes, the enormous blue sky, the shepherds and their brilliant dogs, everything. Every night we camped out under the stars; it was magical. I saw the snowy peaks of the highest alps in the moonlight, and it made me realize how narrow and blinkered my existence had been until that moment, how much of life I had been missing. I knew then that my decision to leave had been the right thing for me.'

Emma held out her hands to the fire, while she considered how much more she felt ready to reveal to her father. After a moment, she turned towards him, and smiled shyly. 'I met a man, Dad. He's called Pascal. He keeps goats and makes cheese, and we are lovers.'

Ludovic looked at his daughter, his eyes soft, then, leaning forward, kissed her. 'Dearest Emma, I am so glad to hear it. You've become a real woman at last, and I thank God for it, always assuming that He exists. If you think that I will allow you to make a living sacrifice of yourself, in the way you suggest, you are very much mistaken. You must go home to your Pascal, of course.'

'But what about you and Claudia? Don't you think that's important, too?'

'Yes, of course I do.'

'So,' said Emma. 'What can we do?'

'We could always try praying, I suppose?'

Alexander wheeled his last barrowload of logs from the stableblock, under the arch in the yew hedge and across the lawn to the main entrance to the house. He gave the heavy door a push with his booted foot and propelled the barrow across the stone flags of the hall and into the glass court. Carefully, choosing his logs according to their shape and size, he arranged them in a double layer on the stack he had already built against the wall, next to the spiral staircase. It was a satisfying job, with the added bonus of looking beautiful as well as neat, if one did it with proper skill and attention to detail, and Alexander took a professional pride in doing it better than Jim. He stacked the last log, stood back and surveyed his handiwork with some complacency, then rattled away with the empty barrow, enjoying the echoing metallic clangs it made as it bounced over the stone floor of the hall. At the garden door, he very nearly collided with his father, coming in with Winnie from their gentle stroll round the lawn.

'Watch it, you clumsy oaf!' said Christian loudly. 'You nearly hit me with that bloody barrow. What's it doing in the house, anyway?'

'Sorry, Dad! Logs, Dad!'

'So?'

'Mum says it's OK to bring in the barrow; the floor cleans itself, she says.' Alexander grinned at his father, sure of his ground.

'Oh, very well, if she says so. But don't *run*, you stupid boy!'

'Yes, Dad. No, Dad. Sorry, Dad.'

'Bugger off, Alex, you cheeky sod!'

Alexander laughed, and departed with his barrow. As soon as he was out of sight, he ran, bouncing his barrow with a spurt of exuberant joy. He parked it in the stable, then made his way across the yard to the kitchen door, intending to find something to eat. At the door, he met his mother on the way out, carrying a basket. 'Done the logs, Mum.'

'Good. Here, take the basket and come and give me a hand. We need potatoes for lunch.'

'OK. Can I get an apple first?'

'Yes, of course, but *hurry*.'

They walked round the house to the vegetable garden, and Alexander dug carefully along the line of potatoes, while Phoebe picked them up, wiped them on her apron, and put them into her basket, moist and white, ready for the pot.

'Where's Ally?'

'Gone down to the village for eggs,' said Phoebe.

'P'raps we ought to have our own hens? What do you think Mum?'

'I think, forget it. I'm run off my feet as it is, without a lot of smelly chickens to look after.' She looked at Alex and smiled. 'Unless, of course, you fancy doing it yourself? Feeding, mucking out, putting them to bed, letting them out in the morning, washing the eggs? How about it?'

'No, thanks, I've got plenty of jobs already, and all my prep as well.' He ran the fork carefully over the empty row of potatoes, levelling the ground. 'That's the trouble with living in the country, Mum, isn't it? Unless you're very rich, and have loads of help, it's non-stop unpaid labour, isn't it?'

Phoebe laughed. 'Do you think we should pay you for your chores, Alex?'

'I wouldn't say no, if you offered.'

'I'll have to ask your father, darling. See what he says.'

Privately, Alexander thought this a rotten idea. He could guess what Christian's opinion on the subject would be, and dismissed from his mind the alluring prospect of gainful employment. They walked slowly through the rows of beans, lettuces, cabbages and artichokes to the greenhouse, where a rampant crop of tomatoes had produced more fruit than they could possibly consume.

'It was bliss in Paris, Mum,' said Alexander suddenly, pulling off a tomato and inhaling its delicious pungent smell. 'Everything was so *easy*. There was a lovely street-market, just two minutes' walk away. I used to go with Claudia, nearly every day, sometimes *twice*, if she thought there was something we needed. It was really good fun, and much nicer than a supermarket.' He bit into his tomato. 'You could get anything at all you wanted, and in the *boulangerie* they baked the bread twice a day. That doesn't happen here, does it?'

'No, worse luck,' said Phoebe, carefully selecting the ripest tomatoes. 'And what about the chores, Alex? Didn't you give Claudia a hand?'

'Not really. There never seemed to be very much to do. It's not an enormous place, like this. There's just one nice big room with tall windows, and you can walk straight out into the garden, and that's really small, no grass to cut. There's a shady tree, and chairs and stuff and a few flowers in pots. It's not a big deal, like here.'

'You surprise me, darling. I always thought you loved it here, in the country. The ponies, fishing, all that?'

'I do. But I loved it there, too. Actually, in a funny way, you could easily think you *were* in the country there; it's very quiet, it doesn't feel at all like being in a town, and there always seems to be plenty of time to sit and enjoy it, instead of slaving away all the time, like you do here.' He glanced at his mother slightly anxiously, in case she should think he was comparing Abbot's Court unfavourably with impasse des Cordonniers, but she looked perfectly composed and relaxed. 'What's really nice', he went on, 'is being able to go to concerts, and museums and things, without it being a mega upheaval, and having to drive for miles, and park, and all that. Everything seems to be just round the corner in Paris.'

Phoebe was not particularly interested in the cultural activities on offer in Paris, but she was extremely curious to know what it was that both Ludovic and Alexander, and, she suspected, Christian, found so attractive about Claudia and her lifestyle. She sat down on the brick wall that bordered the raised bed in the greenhouse. 'Tell me about Claudia,' she said. 'She was really nice to you, wasn't she?'

'Yes, she was. I like her a lot.'

'What does she look like? Is she pretty?'

'Not *pretty*, no. I think she's more what you call beautiful. She looks like Ally, only old, of course, and she has sort of greenish-brown eyes, not grey, like Ally and Grandpa.'

'What about her hair? Is it grey?'

'No, it's not. It's the same as Ally's.' He looked at Phoebe, and his eyes were grave, almost sad. 'I do miss Grandpa. I really love him. I love them both, Mum.'

'More than me, darling?'

'No, Mum, you'll always be the best.'

'Even after me being so foul to you?'

'You couldn't help that. Grandpa told me. It's the nature of things with mothers, he said, so then I understood.'

'Did you, darling?'

'Yes. If it'd been me that got killed, I expect you'd have blamed Chloe.'

Phoebe doubted this, but she put an arm round her son's bony shoulders and hugged him. 'You're very like Ludovic, and he's a very nice man. Do you miss Chloe, Alex?'

'Not much,' he replied, honestly. 'I try not to think about her. Do you miss her?'

'Yes, I do, a lot. But not as much as I used to. I don't go to the cemetery very often now. It's strange, but since you and Allegra came, I can feel Chloe here, around the place.' Alexander gave her a worried look. 'It's not something tangible, just rather a happy feeling.'

Alexander looked relieved. 'You don't *see* her, then? I mean, like ghosts, or anything?'

'No,' said Phoebe untruthfully. 'Nothing like that.'

'Oh. Good.'

That night, lying beside her sleeping husband, Phoebe pondered her conversation with Alexander in the greenhouse, and for the first time it occurred to her that it was a real disaster that the long attachment between Ludovic and Claudia should have been so brutally terminated. It's not just tragic for them, she thought, it's an awful cross for poor Allegra to have on her conscience. It's sad for Alex, too. I can tell how much it meant to him, being with them. In her mind's eye, she saw Alexander as he might have been in a few years' time, going frequently to Paris, a valued member of Ludovic's family, a close friend of Claudia and Allegra. Lucky boy, she thought a little wistfully, I wish I'd had that sort of chance when I was his age. Perhaps then I mightn't have been quite so eager to marry dull old Chris. She turned towards him, slid an arm round his deeply sleeping body, and kissed his warm back. Count your blessings, Phoebe, she told herself.

Chapter Eighteen

Emma sat at the little desk in her poky schoolgirl's bedroom, writing a letter to Pascal.

It is only five days since I got here, she wrote, *but it feels much more like five years. Everything I do or say seems to get on my mother's nerves, it really is terribly difficult. She is extremely angry with me, and anxious that the priest at our church or the nuns at the convent don't find out that I've broken my vows. Sometimes I feel it's quite pointless my being here, but I am still desperately trying to find a way of persuading her to let poor Dad off the hook, or at any rate discuss it.*

Darling Pascal, I miss you so much. At night I lie in the narrow little bed of my childhood, with lumpy mattress and antediluvian squeaky springs, and think of our beautiful painted bed at home. I think of us lying there together, happy, and my heart aches with loving you, and needing you.

It was the first love letter that Emma had ever written. She signed it, sealed the envelope and addressed it. She put on her jacket and ran downstairs, intending to go out, buy some stamps and post the letter. As she went through the hall the telephone rang, and she hesitated, though she knew that it was very unlikely that the call would be for her.

Gwen came out of the kitchen, gave Emma an impersonal glance and picked up the telephone. 'Hullo . . . yes . . . yes, she is . . . what name shall I say, please? . . . one moment.' She covered the mouthpiece with her hand. 'It's for you, Emma. A Mr de Vilmorin, or something like that?'

Emma's heart leapt, and she took the phone, incredulous that Pascal should telephone during the day. 'Pascal?'

'It's not Pascal, my dear. It's me, Paul.'

'Paul! Is anything the matter?'

'No, absolutely not. I am in London for a few days. I wonder, are you free to have lunch with me, tomorrow?'

'I'd love to, Paul. Thank you very much.'

'I have a car, Emma. I thought it might be nice to drive to Oxford for lunch. It's years since I was there; I'd love to see the place again, if you would?'

'Sounds great.'

'Would ten-thirty be too early to pick you up?'

'No, not at all. That would be fine. Have you got this address?'

'I have. See you tomorrow, Emma.'

'I'll look forward to it. Goodbye, Paul.'

She put down the phone, pleased that Paul had invited her out, and rather comforted by his presence in London. In a strange way, it made Pascal himself seem less far away.

'Emma?'

Emma turned towards the kitchen door. 'Yes, Gwen?'

'Could I have a word, please?'

With a sinking heart, Emma slipped her letter into her bag, and followed Gwen into the kitchen. Gwen came straight to the point. 'Are you intending to stay here permanently? Will you be taking on the care of your mother?' She looked at Emma, her manner cold and unbending. 'I need to be kept informed, you know. I think you should know that I have no intention of remaining here. Phoebe needs me at Abbot's Court; she relies on me, and I wish to go back to her.'

Emma sighed. 'I'm sorry, Gwen. I know it's hard for you, but you must know how difficult it is to discuss anything with Mother just now, without offending her. I'm doing my best, but nothing's decided yet.'

'Very well, Emma. I hear you, but I mean what I say. Will you be in for lunch?'

'Yes, I will, today; but I'll be out all day tomorrow.'

'As long as I know.'

'I'm just popping out to post a letter. I'll be back in good time for lunch.'

Gwen did not reply, and Emma left the room, feeling like a reprimanded schoolgirl. On her way to the main road and the post office, she ran into Flavia, presumably on her way home from St Botolph's.

'You're not intending to go to church, Emma?'

'I wasn't, no.'

Flavia gave her a hard look. 'Well, if you *should* feel the need to confess, it might be better if you looked for a priest in another parish.'

'Don't worry, Mother. I don't think the need will arise, somehow.'

Flavia raised her eyebrows. 'You do surprise me. You consider yourself to be without sin, is that it?'

Emma laughed. 'None of us is perfect, Mother. Excuse me, I'm in rather a hurry. I must catch the post.' She went swiftly on her way, not allowing her mother time to argue.

After lunch was over and the washing-up done, Emma went into the sitting room and looked through the books in Flavia's glass-fronted bookcase. She decided that this was as good a time as any to read *Middlemarch*, a book that had been for many years on her list of essential reading, but yet to be undertaken. Gwen had laid the firelighter, sticks and coal in the grate, ready for the evening, and for a moment Emma felt inclined to put a match to it, for the afternoon was dull, and a thin rain was falling. On second thoughts, she decided that such an action on her part might cause ructions, either with Gwen or with Flavia, so she abandoned the idea and settled down in a chair to read.

After forty minutes or so, her mother came into the room. 'Good heavens, it's awfully chilly in here. Why on earth didn't you light the fire, Emma?'

'Sorry, Mother. I'll do it right away.' Emma lit the fire, sat down again, and opened her book.

Flavia ensconced herself on the sofa, still muttering about the cold. She picked up the *Telegraph*, and turned the pages, scanning them impatiently, then folded the paper and put it back on the sofa table. She stared at her recalcitrant daughter, apparently engrossed in some pointless book, unaware of the deafening silence that filled the room, and which she, Flavia, felt an overwhelming compulsion to break. At last she could endure it no longer. 'Is that book so much more interesting than talking to me, Emma?'

'No, Mother, of course not.' Emma closed her book, and waited for Flavia to speak.

'Why have you come home, Emma? Is it simply to torment me, and add to my burdens, or are you in some sort of trouble?'

'What sort of trouble had you in mind, Mother?'

'There's no need to adopt that insolent attitude, Emma. You know perfectly well what I mean.'

'I take it that you suspect that I might be pregnant?'

Flavia's eyes were hard and accusing. 'Well, *are* you?'

'Not as far as I know, Mother. I could be, it's quite possible.' Put that in your pipe and smoke it, you evil-minded old woman, she added silently to herself, and almost laughed.

Flavia turned an alarmingly dark shade of red, and Emma began to regret her provocative words. She need not have worried, for her mother recovered swiftly.

'That letter you went out to post? Presumably it was written to your lover?'

'Since you're so keen to know, Mother, yes, it was.'

'I see. I trust he intends to stand by you, my girl, if you *are* pregnant?'

'Really, Mother, what on earth are you getting at?'

'All I'm saying is, don't expect to come running back here with an illegitimate child, if the man doesn't come up to scratch. You've brought enough shame on us, without that.'

'Who do you mean, when you say "us", Mother?'

'Your family. Your father and me, of course.'

It's now or never, said Emma to herself and drew a deep breath. 'You're not still pretending that you and Dad are a real married couple, are you, Mother? Don't you think it's time you grew up, and faced the truth?'

Flavia, wrong-footed, but remaining in control, managed a harsh little laugh. 'What do *you* know about marriage, may I ask Emma? You don't have the least idea what you're talking about, and I doubt you ever will.'

'I'm not stupid, Mother, and neither is Christian. We both know why Dad left you, to all intents and purposes. You brought it on yourself, didn't you?'

'What do you mean?'

'Sex, Mother. Or lack of it, to be precise.'

'Don't be disgusting, Emma. If you read the Nuptial Mass, you will see that it states quite clearly that sex in marriage is for the procreation of children, and nothing more.'

'Rubbish!' said Emma. 'Are you seriously trying to tell me that you shouldn't sleep with the man you love, unless it's for the express purpose of fertilizing an egg?'

'That's precisely my view on the subject, though I can think of less repulsive ways of putting it.' Flavia looked at Emma with an air of triumph. 'In any case, your opinions on the subject are entirely academic. Ludovic has given up his sordid affair, as you're doubtless aware. He is back where he belongs. Every-thing is forgotten and forgiven.'

'It most certainly is not, Mother! He *doesn't* belong here, in this loveless house! He belongs in Paris, with Claudia, the woman he loves and who loves him, and has done for more than twenty years.' Emma rose from her chair, knelt beside Flavia, and tried to take her hand. 'Why can't you do the right thing, Mother, and let him go? Wouldn't that be the forgiving, under-standing thing to do?'

Flavia drew back her clenched fist and punched Emma in the face as hard as she could. Shattered, Emma staggered to her feet and backed away, her hand to her cheek. Flavia, livid with righteous anger, stood up and left the room without another word. Shaking, Emma stood with her back to the fire, and listened to her mother's footsteps as she mounted the stairs to the sanctuary of her bedroom.

At ten-thirty the next morning Paul de Vilmorin's car drew up at the kerb, and before he could switch off the engine, Emma had run down the steps and jumped into the seat beside him. 'Drive on, for heaven's sake,' she said, 'or my mother will insist on grilling you!'

'*Merde!*' said Paul, laughing, and drove away. 'What's going on, Emma?'

'God, don't ask! It's a nightmare, it really is. I'm so glad you're here, Paul. I need a break from her.'

'Family problems?'

'You remember what Catherine told us, at your house?'

'Yes, I do.'

'Well, it's true, all of it. I'm afraid I've probably made matters worse, now. I came with the rather unwise idea of trying to persuade my mother to release my father from his marriage vows, but all I got for my pains was a sock on the jaw!'

'Oh, poor you! Did it hurt?'

Emma laughed. 'Yes, it did, like hell!'

'So, what's the situation now?'

'She's sulking in her room. She was spying on us through the curtains, I know. She probably thinks I'm up to no good with you, right now. Oh dear, what a mess! Let's not talk about it.'

They drove out of London and took the M40 to Oxford. The day was warm and sunny after the rain, and as they drove slowly down the Banbury road into the ancient city, the scent of bonfires drifted over the red-brick walls of dons' houses. Golden leaves detached themselves gently from the soot-blackened branches of trees, and floated softly to the ground.

'Do you know Oxford well?' asked Emma.

'Pretty well. I spent two years here, at the Radcliffe, as a postgraduate.'

'Really? That explains your excellent English, I suppose?'

'Not really. I already spoke it when I arrived. My mother was English. She married my father in the Thirties, between the wars.'

'I see. So Pascal would have spoken English, too, from a baby?'

'Yes, he did; both he and his sister, Nina. They were very close to their grandmother. She was a kind woman, very original, a serious botanist. She made exquisite drawings of plants. It was a passion with her, and she filled dozens of folios with them; I have them still. I think it was probably her example that prompted Pascal's change of direction, and his decision to live in Mas les Arnauds.'

'Yes, I'm sure it would have been.' Emma glanced at Paul as he cruised slowly down Little Clarendon Street, and turned into Walton Street, looking for a parking space. 'Did you mind about him giving up medicine?'

'No, not at all. I always suspected that his heart wasn't really in it. I was thankful that he got out before it was too late, and he felt committed.'

'But your daughter? She's a successful doctor, isn't she?'

'Yes, she is. Nina is a calm and sensible woman. She seems able to combine marriage and a career quite effortlessly, lucky girl. Here we are.' Paul reversed the car into a two-hour parking space, and they walked the short distance to Le Petit Blanc, where he had reserved a table.

The restaurant was a sympathetic place, light and airy, overlooking a leafy courtyard, with plenty of room between the tables, and young, attentive waiters. They began with oysters, and then chose *crêpes* filled with Gruyère, spinach and pine nuts. They drank the house white, with a bottle of Badoit. For Emma, it was the first really delicious meal that she had eaten since arriving in England, and she savoured it slowly, with pleasure, thinking of the lovely food at Mas les Arnauds.

The coffee arrived, *espresso*, strong and black in tiny cups. 'Tell me something, Paul,' said Emma, crumbling a lump of brown sugar with her spoon. 'Or don't tell me if you feel it's none of my business – I won't mind, I promise.'

'Fire away.'

'Why is Pascal on such difficult terms with his mother? Is it because he disappointed her, when he decided to drop out of medicine?'

'More or less.' Paul took a sip of his coffee, and frowned. 'Blanche is a very determined woman, Emma, and she assumed that Pascal would follow me into surgery. She only married me because she considered me a good investment. She was right about that; wrong about Pascal. Apart from material considerations, I, too, have failed her. My affections and interests are no longer centred on my marriage, and never really were.'

'How sad,' said Emma.

'Yes, it is, and in a sense it's largely my fault. You

366

see, although I never had the good fortune to meet the right woman, as your father did, I do have the enormous satisfaction of my work, on a daily basis. Each morning brings a new excitement and challenge, and I am totally committed to the hospital, and the patients. So you see, I have neither the time nor the inclination for the social life that is Blanche's *raison d'être*. In every respect except that of financial success, I know I have been a disappointment to her. We are complete strangers to each other, and lead virtually separate lives.' Paul drank the rest of his wine, and smiled at Emma. 'Poor Blanche, she has to comfort herself with little flirtations. She has a special closeness to Olivier Saint-Denis, has had for years. He adores her. The sad thing is that I don't mind at all; in fact I'm only too thankful that she enjoys his attentions, to tell you the truth.'

'What about Catherine? Does she mind?'

'I think she does, though we've never discussed it.'

'Why are you telling me all this, Paul?'

'I don't really know why, Emma, except that I feel that we have rather a lot in common, the same core values, perhaps. I suppose I thought that you would be able to understand how guilty I sometimes feel about the failure of my marriage, and how much I dread retirement. The thought of not going to work every day fills me with a terrible boredom.'

'I felt exactly like that once, myself,' said Emma, sympathetically. 'I thought that all I ever wanted to do was make frescoes all day long, and not allow myself to have distractions of any kind, especially things like marriage or children.' She raised her eyes to his, shyly. 'Then I went on the *transhumance*, and met Pascal, and everything changed completely.'

'I think that your advent into his life is crucial for him, too. One can tell, one only has to see you together.' Paul reached across the table and picked up her hand. 'Am I being a matchmaking father, Emma?

Or is the match already made? He gave you this ring, didn't he?'

'Yes, he did.'

'I'm glad. It belonged to my mother's family.'

'Really? He told me he got it out of a cracker!'

Paul laughed. 'He would say that, wouldn't he? How typical of him.'

'It's nice that it's a family thing.' Emma looked at Paul, smiling. 'But in a way, I loved the idea of it coming out of a cracker.'

'That's the whole point about you, my dear Emma – you would, wouldn't you?'

After lunch they drove back to the city centre and parked in St Giles. They walked together through the gardens of Balliol, then strolled down the Broad and spent a happy half-hour in Blackwell's bookshop. Paul bought several books, including one on Italian frescoes. 'I'd better inform myself on your subject, Emma. I wouldn't want you to think of me as a philistine.'

'That's exactly what Pascal said, how very strange.'

'Not really. Pascal and I are very alike; I feel very close to him.' He looked at Emma gravely, and smiled. 'I hope to be close to you, too.'

'I think you already are, Paul.'

Flavia watched Emma's departure through her window, then finished dressing. She took her Missal from her night-table, went downstairs to the hall, put on her coat and called to Gwen that she was going out for a while. She walked quickly up the road and round the corner to St Botolph's. She went into the empty church, genuflected and sat down close to the statue of Our Lady. Tired and depressed after a sleepless night, she had no wish to speak to anyone, not even Fr Gordon. She merely hoped that the benevolent presence of the Blessed Virgin would soothe her wounded spirit, and bring peace to her tormented soul. For a long time, she gazed devotedly at the plaster face of her old friend, silently repeating the Hail Mary, endeavouring to empty her mind of the anger and resentment that Emma's unwanted interference had provoked, and allow tranquillity to take its place.

The door of the church opened with a dull clatter of its heavy iron latch, that echoed through the empty building. Flavia did not look round to see who had come in, but opened her Missal at random and kept her eyes firmly fixed on its pages. Soft footsteps approached, and stopped at the other end of the pew. Unable to ignore the presence of the newcomer any longer, she looked up, and saw Fr Gordon standing there, smiling kindly at her.

'Good morning, Mrs McGrath,' he said. 'How nice to see you. I hope I'm not disturbing you?'

'No,' said Flavia, slightly flustered; 'not at all.'

'May I sit down?'

'Of course.'

He sat down, and turned towards her. 'I've been waiting for an opportunity to have a word with you.' He paused for a moment, looking serious. 'It's a rather delicate matter, Mrs McGrath. It concerns the honest admission of your sins, in the confessional.'

'What do you mean?'

'You haven't really levelled with me, have you?'

Flavia frowned, offended by his words. 'I am always very thorough in my confession,' she said. 'I never leave things out, you must be aware of that. Sometimes I have quite a lot of difficulty in remembering any sins at all, if you want to know.'

'None at all, just now?'

'No, I can't think of any.'

'How about attempting to take your own life, my dear?'

'What nonsense!' Flavia retorted hotly. 'Whoever told you that?'

'No-one told me, Mrs McGrath. I broke into the house and found you, don't you remember? I saw the newspaper and I went round at once. I found you drunk and unconscious, with your wrist slashed, and bleeding badly. It was me that called the doctor.'

Aghast, Flavia stared at the pale young priest, at his soft red hair and freckled face. Horrified, utterly dismayed, she could find nothing to say to him. Her brain seemed frozen, paralysed.

After a long silence, Fr Gordon spoke. 'Would it help to talk about it?'

'What is there to talk about?' asked Flavia curtly, finding her tongue.

'The difficulties of your marriage, perhaps? It's what we're here for, you know.'

'My marriage is not in difficulties, thank you.'

'Mrs McGrath, I'm afraid that I *did* read the article in the paper, and I felt very sorry for you.'

Flavia said nothing.

'Can you tell me why it was that your husband left you in the first place?'

'He didn't leave me!' said Flavia angrily. 'I threw him out!'

'Why was that?'

Suddenly, Flavia's composure deserted her completely, and her voice rose sharply. 'It was *sex*!' she snapped, her cheeks flaming. 'Ludovic was like a wild beast, totally without control. I was forced to forbid him to touch me, and remind him that the sex act is primarily intended for the procreation of children, not for drunken personal gratification.'

'Ah.' Fr Gordon spoke very quietly. 'Now I understand.' He looked at Flavia, and shook his head. 'Poor man,' he murmured.

At this implied criticism of herself, Flavia flew into a rage and let loose a volley of abuse and filth that astonished Fr Gordon and caused him many subsequent sleepless nights, as he came to realize how narrow and inadequate was his knowledge of the nature of women.

Having rid herself of every disgusting epithet that she could call to mind, Flavia got to her feet and walked out of St Botolph's for ever, slamming the door behind her. She went home and, still fuming, gave Gwen a piece of her mind. At last, exhausted, she retired to bed.

Gwen went immediately to the telephone and rang Phoebe. 'I'm sorry,' she said, 'but I will not take another week of this. I want to come back to Abbot's Court, Phoebe, at once. Otherwise, I shall retire and go home to Skye.'

Phoebe drove Allegra up to London, and saw her off on the train to Paris. Feeling cheerful and confident, and stimulated by the rush of adrenalin generated by driving in the London traffic, she drove to Christian's bank, and parked in the car park. She waited for a few minutes in the reception area, until the doors of a lift slid open and Christian appeared, ready to take her out to lunch.

'That was delicious,' said Phoebe, an hour later, touching her napkin to her lips. 'Potted shrimps, what a treat.'

'We should do this more often, darling.'

'Yes, I think we should.'

The waiter removed their plates, and Phoebe put her elbows on the table and leaned closer to her husband. 'Christian, I've been thinking about things. I think it's quite dreadful about Ludo and Claudia. She's utterly devastated, poor thing. Ally says so; she's awfully worried about her.'

Christian sighed, uneasily. 'I rather agree, but you know very well that Ma can't just be dumped in a home, Phoebe; she'd never agree to it, would she? But someone has got to cope with her, that's quite obvious. What if she played the suicide card again – how would we all feel?'

Phoebe very nearly said, 'Relieved,' but stopped

herself just in time. 'Well, she can't go on monopolizing Gwen like this,' she said firmly. 'I had a call from her the other day, and she's not prepared to stay with your mother any longer. She even threatened to retire to Skye. In any case, I'm absolutely fed up with it, too. I must have Gwen back at Abbot's Court, Chris, especially now that Allegra's gone back to Paris.'

The main course arrived: superb little pink lamb cutlets, in a pool of sorrel sauce, with a *mousseline* of celeriac. Christian watched the wine being poured, tasted it and pronounced it satisfactory, then looked at his wife. 'Why did you have to bring up this dreary subject, darling Phoebe, just when we're having one of our extremely rare treats?'

Phoebe laughed. 'It's not spoiling *my* appetite, I can assure you.' She bit into a morsel of cutlet. 'Come on, Chris, get a grip. It's time we thought of something, isn't it?'

'Oh, God,' he said. 'You're probably right. I suppose we could try twisting Emma's arm, couldn't we? She might agree to stay with Ma for a few months. She might even be quite glad to do so, actually.' He shook his head in disbelief. 'I did suggest it to her tentatively, but incredibly, she seems to have got involved with a farmer, somewhere up in the French Alps. A bloke who makes goat's cheese, I think she said. What sort of a return could one expect from that kind of product, I ask myself? If it comes to the financial crunch, I expect she might be quite glad of the excuse to come home, don't you?'

Phoebe gazed at Christian with a mixture of exasperation and affection. 'You really don't understand anything at all about people, or love, do you, Chris? Sometimes, you're an absolute nerd.' She laughed.

Christian flushed, stung by her low opinion of him. 'OK,' he said crossly, 'what do you suggest, if you're so incredibly clever?'

'I suggest we bring your mother to Abbot's Court.'

'You can't be serious, Phoebe.'

'I am, perfectly. The old bakery in the village is for sale. Flavia would get a packet for the Camden house, and she could do the bakery up properly; make it really nice. I wouldn't mind Gwen popping down every day to check on her, drive her to church, all that.'

'Darling Phoebe, that is the most terrible idea. She'll drive you mad in no time.'

'Probably,' said Phoebe calmly. 'I've thought of that, and I expect we'll have quite a few rows, until she learns that she has to keep to her own territory, and stick to the rules.'

'What about Alex? What if she tries her nonsense with him again?'

'She won't dare. I won't allow it, and I shall tell her so, in no uncertain terms. It will be the *strictest* of the rules, Chris, right from the start.'

'You must be nuts, Phoebe. I can't believe I'm hearing this.'

Phoebe smiled and took a sip of her wine. 'You know, darling, much as I love Abbot's Court, it *is* sometimes rather lonely down there, on my own all week. Soon Alex will be going away to school, and even if Gwen would agree to stay with Flavia, I don't want her to; I really do need her with me. I'd rather put up with your mother living in the village, than not have Gwen.' She touched her husband's hand. 'When Flavia starts getting on my nerves, I could always come up to London with you for a few days, couldn't I? Go shopping; see a play?'

'Yes, of course you could, darling.' Christian, that most unromantic of men, covered his wife's hand with his. 'Phoebe, are you by any chance developing into an excellent woman?'

'I shouldn't think so. Certainly not a pious one, anyway.'

'Thank God for that.'

*   *   *

373

Phoebe drove to Camden Town and parked outside the house. She rang the bell, and Gwen answered the door. 'Phoebe! What a lovely surprise! Come away in, at once.'

Delighted to see each other, the two women embraced, then Gwen took Phoebe into the sitting room, where she found Flavia and Emma sitting as far as possible from each other, in an uneasy silence.

'Phoebe! How nice!' Emma's face lit up and she came to her sister-in-law and gave her a hug.

'Goodness, Emma, what a transformation! You look terrific.'

'Thank you, Phoebe, so do you. Are you well?'

'Yes, I am, Emma.' She smiled, acknowledging the unspoken concern in Emma's question. 'I'm fine.'

Phoebe turned her attention to Flavia, who sat feeling ignored, wrapped in her own silent cocoon of self-pity. Phoebe was slightly shocked to see her mother-in-law looking so frail and shrunken, as if her clothes were too big for her. Consequently, she over-compensated in her determination to be cheerful and matter-of-fact. 'Come on, old thing,' she said loudly. 'I've come to take you home.'

Slowly, Flavia raised her eyes and looked at Phoebe, disbelievingly. 'Are you talking to me?'

'Of course I am. I've come to take you and Gwen back to Abbot's Court.' She sat down beside Flavia, on the sofa. 'Don't you want to come?'

Flavia began to resist, to reiterate that her place was beside Ludovic. Then, recollecting her terrible humiliation at the hands of Fr Gordon, she turned to Phoebe and clutched her arm anxiously. 'You're not playing games with me, Phoebe, are you? You really do mean it?'

'I really mean it.'

'Oh, darling, how kind you are, I always knew you had a heart of gold.' Flavia shot an accusing look at Emma, then turned the full force of a grovelling smile on her saviour, the once-despised Phoebe. Before she could change her mind and withdraw her invitation, Phoebe asked Gwen to pack for Flavia and herself.

At six-twenty the front door opened, and Gwen and Emma came down the steps carrying the suitcases. Gwen opened the tailgate of the Volvo and they stowed the luggage in the car. 'Wait there, Gwen,' said Emma, 'and I'll bring the rest of the stuff.' She ran back into the house, got the two remaining suitcases, and brought them to the car. 'That's the lot, thank heaven,' she said. She turned to Gwen. 'I hope this won't prove to be yet another disaster, Gwen. I'm really very sorry you've had such a hard time.'

'Well,' said Gwen grudgingly, 'it's been a difficult time for us all, I dare say. I'll be perfectly all right once I'm back with Phoebe. She really appreciates me, Emma. I'd do anything for her.'

'Yes, of course.'

Flavia and Phoebe came down the steps, and Emma embraced them both. They installed themselves in the car, Flavia in the back, and Phoebe drove away. Emma watched them out of sight, then went back into the house, with her mother's overwrought, crumpled face etched into her memory. Confused and suspicious, Flavia had at first found it difficult to believe that someone – especially the unworthy Protestant Phoebe – actually wished her to live near them, but as the suitcases were brought down one by one, her confidence began to grow. As the afternoon turned into evening, she recovered sufficient spirit to make it clearly understood that she regarded the loss of the sinner Emma and that of the adulterous Ludovic as crosses she would gladly bear.

Emma closed the front door, then sat down on the stairs, resting her head against the banisters, listening to the intense silence that filled the empty house. Emotionally exhausted by the tensions of the long afternoon, she closed her eyes, and watched the images that rose before her inner eye, and listened to the voices of the past; the ghosts of her parents' marriage, and of her own lonely childhood.

The horn of a car sounded in the street outside, breaking the spell, and, opening her eyes, Emma got to her feet, wondering how long it would be before Flavia succumbed to the temptation of wrecking Phoebe's life. She went to the telephone and dialled her father's number in Brussels. She got his answering machine, and after the tone, began to dictate a message: 'Dad, it's Emma. Can you call me when you get in?'

Suddenly, he broke in. 'Emma? Is anything wrong, darling?'

'No, everything's right, Dad. You can go home.'

'Go *home*, Emma? What do you mean?'

'Phoebe has taken Mother and Gwen to Abbot's Court. I hope it's for ever, Dad. In any case, it's for the time being. You can go home to Claudia, right away.'

'I can't believe it!'

'It's true. And I can go home to Pascal.'

'My dearest girl, this is wonderful, unbelievable.'

'Yes,' said Emma softly, 'that's exactly what it is. Hang up now, Dad, and ring Claudia straight away.'

'I will. Emma?'

'Yes?'

'Be happy, darling.'

'You too, Dad. Love to Claudia.'

She put down the phone, then picked it up again, and dialled Pascal's number. The long ringing tone sounded hollow, very far away.

'*Oui?*'

'Pascal?'

'Emma! Where are you?'

'In London; I'm coming home.'

'That's good. The snow is on the Alps; it's time to bring down the sheep. We go up on Sunday; can you be here by then?'

'Meet me at Marseille, tomorrow. I think the plane gets in at one something. You'll have to check.'

'Don't worry, I'll be there.'

'Pascal?'

'Emma?'

'You remember you said you'd tell me something when I got back?'

'I remember.'

'What was it?'

'You're not quite back, yet, are you?'

'Oh, yes, I am, at least in spirit. So tell me.'

'You know what it is, Emma, don't you?'

'Tell me. I want to hear you say it.'

'I love you, Emma. Now and for ever.'

Emma smiled, filled with a huge warmth and happiness. 'I thought that might be it,' she said.

'Did you doubt it?'

'No, darling, I didn't. Not for a moment.'

Postlude

Notwithstanding the deep reservations of both Christian and Emma, their mother's move to the West Country proved to be far from the disaster they had anticipated.

From the moment she clapped eyes on the old bakery, a humble little building of a few linked medieval rooms, Flavia knew that her heart's desire was within her grasp. After making enquiries, she hired a local architect of a conservationist persuasion, and instructed him to transform the bakery into a miniature convent. The young architect was greatly amused, not to say intrigued, both by his client and by the commission, and within a year the work was completed.

Flavia designed for herself, and had made by a dressmaker, a couple of simple but dignified outfits in pale grey worsted; a floor-length, long-sleeved gown, with a matching grey silk veil. Clothed in these garments, she entered on the most rewarding period of her life. Ministered to from a domestic point of view by Jill from the village, and visited once a month by her brother Benedict, to hear her confession and attend to her spiritual needs, Flavia, to all intents and purposes, lived the life of an enclosed nun.

Twelve years later, having just said Compline, she suffered a massive stroke and died, as likely as not in a state of grace.

THE END

THE GOLDEN YEAR
Elizabeth Falconer

One enchanted summer in Provence and its aftermath.

Summers, to Anna, had always meant the Presbytery, the mellow old stone house in Provence where her mother, the formidable Domenica, lived. Now that Anna's marriage to Jeffrey was all but over, she thought that she had herself well organized, dividing her time between her riverside home in London, her two teenage children and her career as a gilder and restorer of antiques. And then there were her summers in France – a chance to eat and drink magnificently, to sit in the sun and to recharge the batteries. She hardly realized how narrow and lonely her life had really become.

But one summer her brother Giò, an antiques dealer in Paris, brought down a new friend to the Presbytery. Patrick, a handsome television director, suddenly opened up Anna's life in a new and wonderful way, offering her a wholly unexpected chance of happiness. But she did not immediately see that others might not share her joy, and that her beloved brother Giò could have quite different ideas about Patrick and the future.

'A DELIGHTFUL EVOCATION OF THE SIGHTS, SOUNDS AND FLAVOURS OF LIFE IN PROVENCE'
Family Circle

0 552 99622 X

BLACK SWAN

THE LOVE OF WOMEN
Elizabeth Falconer

Nelly and Hugo lived a seemingly enviable life, with
their three adorable little girls, their holidays at the
beautiful family home in the Channel Islands, and
their large, if disorganised, London house. Why,
then,did Hugo feel increasingly inadequate? He began
to wonder why Nelly had married him instead of
Basil, their close ally from Cambridge days. Basil had
instead become an indispensable family friend, and
Nelly's demanding job as a hospital doctor seemed to
overshadow Hugo's own successful but
unremunerative career as a writer – Hugo felt as
though his only function in Nelly's life nowadays was
to babysit the children and keep an eye on the erratic
au pair. One day, in a fit of rebellion, he packed his
bags and went to stay with Basil's mother in her
peaceful Paris flat on the lovely Ile St-Louis.

Basil, meanwhile, was facing an uncertain future.
Tied by loyalty to Nelly and Hugo, and with a
muddled and ambivalent series of past relationships,
he was at first reluctant to commit himself when he
met Olivia, the self-confident young English art
student living in Paris who was interested in the
work of Basil's late father, a much-admired Russian
painter. While Hugo discovered how hard it was to
escape from family ties, Basil was to find that
friendship and love do not easily mingle.

'AN UNHURRIED, LUXURIOUS STORY OF
RESOLUTION AND DISCOVERY . . . THE NOVEL'S
CHARM LIES IN ITS UNPRETENTIOUSNESS AND
THE AUTHOR'S AFFECTION FOR CHARACTERS'
Elizabeth Buchan, *Mail on Sunday*

0 552 99623 8

BLACK SWAN

THE COUNTER-TENOR'S DAUGHTER
Elizabeth Falconer

Dido Partridge's life as a daughter of an exotic operatic soprano and her counter-tenor lover, Signor Pernice, has been a strange one. A childhood spent mainly in the dressing rooms of the great European opera houses had led naturally to her present bohemian existence in a grand old houseboat, once her mother's, moored on the Thames. This unusual home she shares with Jacob, a film director and her erratic but long-term partner, until her friends' hints of Jacob's frequent infidelities are proved true by her discovery that he had been entertaining another woman on the houseboat. Disposing of his belongings overboard and booking the first flight out of Heathrow that she could find, she ends up in Corfu, in a beautiful, unspoilt bay where she reads, swims and eats the lovely but simple food prepared for her by the local taverna keeper.

Gradually, as the pace and tranquillity of Corfu begin to work their magic on her, Dido becomes aware of Guy, an attractive lawyer who left London for the solitude of the island when his disability – the result of a childhood accident – became too much for him to bear. Guy's resentful sister Lavinia, who may know more about Guy's accident than either of them is prepared to admit, can never forgive Guy for inheriting the great family mansion in Ireland where, by coincidence, Jacob is now directing a film. As Dido and Guy start to heal the wounds which each of them has acquired through the years, they both begin to see how their lives can change.

0 552 99624 6

BLACK SWAN

WATERWINGS
Joan Marysmith

Brigid, recently widowed and alone in the world apart from her erratic daughter Perdita, escapes from the predictability of Wimbledon to the wilds of Northumberland, where she is to housesit for some friends at their remote home on the edge of the Cheviot Hills. But her hope of tranquillity is shattered by the unexpected arrival of Simon, her friends' prodigal son. Si has a newborn belief in his supernatural powers and a messianic vision of the New Age; deeply into paganism, healing and sacred energy, he tries to persuade the local vicar to take part in celebrating the Earth festivals while he prepares the house for his disciples to appear. Meanwhile, Brigid frets over the intrusion into her privacy and the lack of sophisticated foodstuffs in the local supermarket.

But as the seasons pass and both Simon and the neighbours manifest themselves in various unexpected ways. Brigid is drawn into an alien Celtic landscape in which she discovers a side of herself she never knew.

0 552 99689 0

BLACK SWAN

A SELECTED LIST OF FINE WRITING
AVAILABLE FROM BLACK SWAN

99630	0	**MUDDY WATERS**	*Judy Astley*	£6.99
99619	X	**HUMAN CROQUET**	*Kate Atkinson*	£6.99
99722	6	**THE PULL OF THE MOON**	*Elizabeth Berg*	£6.99
99687	4	**THE PURVEYOR OF ENCHANTMENT**	*Marika Cobbold*	£6.99
99715	3	**BEACHCOMBING FOR A SHPWRECKED GOD**		
			Joe Coomer	£6.99
99670	X	**THE MISTRESS OF SPICES** *Chitra Banerjee Divakaruni*		£6.99
99587	8	**LIKE WATER FOR CHOCOLATE**	*Laura Esquivel*	£6.99
99622	X	**THE GOLDEN YEAR**	*Elizabeth Falconer*	£6.99
99623	8	**THE LOVE OF WOMEN**	*Elizabeth Falconer*	£6.99
99624	6	**THE COUNTER-TENOR'S DAUGHTER**		
			Elizabeth Falconer	£6.99
99657	2	**PERFECT MERINGUES**	*Laurie Graham*	£5.99
99611	4	**THE COURTYARD IN AUGUST**	*Janette Griffiths*	£6.99
99774	9	**THE CUCKOO'S PARTING CRY**	*Anthea Halliwell*	£5.99
99754	4	**CLOUD MUSIC**	*Karen Hayes*	£6.99
99771	4	**MALLINGFORD**	*Alison Love*	£6.99
99689	0	**WATERWINGS**	*Joan Marysmith*	£6.99
99696	3	**THE VISITATION**	*Sue Reidy*	£5.99
99732	3	**A PRIZE FOR SISTER CATHERINE**	*Kathleen Rowntree*	£6.99
99749	8	**PORTOFINO**	*Frank Schaeffer*	£6.99
99763	3	**GARGOYLES AND PORT**	*Mary Selby*	£6.99
99753	6	**AN ACCIDENTAL LIFE**	*Titia Sutherland*	£6.99
99700	5	**NEXT OF KIN**	*Joanna Trollope*	£6.99
99720	X	**THE SERPENTINE CAVE**	*Jill Paton Walsh*	£6.99
99723	4	**PART OF THE FURNITURE**	*Mary Wesley*	£6.99
99642	4	**SWIMMING POOL SUNDAY**	*Madeleine Wickham*	£6.99
99591	6	**A MISLAID MAGIC**	*Joyce Windsor*	£4.99